Radical Peel

By Susan Hunter

Hudson Run Press
New York

Hudson Run Press
Publishers since 1999
Lake Luzerne, New York 12846

Cover Design by Sooki

Library of Congress Cataloging-in-Publication Data
Hunter, Susan S.
Radical Peel / Susan Hunter

ISBN 978-0-9702932-7-5

1. Body Parts and Witchcraft
2. Albinos in Africa
3. Female Detective
4. Zambia

About the
Malinga Mutende Crime Series

Radical Peel is Volume 4
in the Malinga Mutende Crime Series.

Volume 1 in the series is
Bill Kills: A Wild Game in Botswana,
to be released in 2021

Volume 2
Elephant Murders | Starbuck (May 2015)
Volume 3
Elephant Murders | Justice (June 2015)
Volume 5
Elephant Murders | Memories (June 2015).

Crosses of the Poor: Wilson and the Mailonis, the first volume of
the companion series featuring Malinga's albino DI colleague
Wilson Mwiinga, will be published in 2021.

Beauty is but skin deep, ugly lies in the bone;
Beauty dies and fades away, but ugly holds its own.

Albert Einstein

Albinism is caused by genetic mutations that affect the
production of the pigment melanin. Albinos around the
world face day-to-day health issues, including ocular
sensitivity, severe sunburn and cancer, but in Africa they
have a bigger problem: being hacked to death for their body
parts. The superstitious believe that albinos are ghosts or
spirits with magical powers that can be transferred by
wearing or eating their body parts.

This book is dedicated to finding
justice for humans and animals everywhere

The killings are on-going, brutal, and must be stopped.
They are as ugly in reality as they are on the written page.

1 | A National Laughingstock

Killing them was easy. Flaying them was not.

Weighing nine pounds, a human's skin was easily the body's largest organ – and its most delicate. Separated from their fleshy base, the skin's epidermal, dermal, and subcutaneous layers collapse into a shapeless mass. Keeping them intact was tedious and exhausting work, even for a practiced surgeon. There was no hurrying the job. Patience paid handsomely in this line of work.

As Stewart slid the girl's skin into the chemical bath that would keep it fresh until tomorrow's shipment, he exhaled fully for the first time in three hours and a smile of satisfaction slid across his lips. The results were perfect, and the rewards would be high. If he could sustain this level of production, he would be finished in a few months and retire to England where he belonged. Once he fulfilled Victor's dreams – and his own – he could go home.

But first he had to settle the score with Deputy Police Inspector Malinga Mutende. Stewart scowled as he scrubbed his knuckles and brushed his fingernails clean. She would get everything she deserved. Thanks to her, he was running out of time sooner than he liked. The public's demand to find the killer was becoming insatiable.

There was no bargaining with her. Before she'd come on the scene, policemen happily forgot everything they saw for a little baksheesh. But not Malinga, who insisted on being a lightning rod in a storm of public hysteria, condemning the skin killings as *muti* murders and promising to bring the witch doctors who were responsible to justice. Her histrionics kept women vigilant and communities alert.

And they would be the source of her own demise. His smile broadened. The storm she'd created would make it easy to publicly humiliate her. And Malinga trusted him. As the CID's principal forensics consultant, he'd worked side by side with her on a number of cases, including this one.

Stewart dried his hands and lifted them over his head to stretch his shoulder and back muscles. Lowering his lanky frame into a chair near the fireplace, he thought about Victor's call. The man might be a genius, but it would be difficult to give him what he wanted.

In a country where thousands of children lost their lives to malnutrition and disease every year, the loss of an elephant should bother no one. But since Malinga cared, everyone else did, too. Since she'd caught the poachers last year in a high-profile chase across Asia, public outrage remained high and the guards on Zambia's free-roaming herds had been doubled. There were millions of humans, but the death of even one elephant brought a perilously endangered species that much closer to extinction.

Victor knew that, but he was still demanding an elephant. Since most of Stewart's potential accomplices in the Zambian Wildlife Authority were in jail, in hiding, or in exile, he'd have to find someone new on the inside who could help. It wouldn't be difficult, but he'd have to tread carefully. He shook his head, lips drawn in a tight smile.

Zambia. Corruption was unavoidable, even his own. Where else could you collaborate with serial killers to create a successful international business? His partners – two of Zambia's most powerful witch doctors, or *sangomas* – were beyond the law, revered at the highest levels of power. They gave Stewart all the bodies he needed as long as they got the parts they wanted when he was done, although he had to keep his boundaries firm.

He absolutely refused to skin the girls alive, although the *sangomas* insisted it would strengthen their magic – and the dollar value – of the remains. Their brutality disgusted him, but he would soon make them pay. He was laying the trail of evidence right to their door. It wasn't hard. Even the police believed that the girls had been murdered by witch doctors flying through the night on broomsticks fueled with baby's blood.

In a country with more than forty thousand witch doctors and only one thousand orthodox physicians, honest *sangomas* were a comfort to the poor, providing herbal treatments, bone setting, and midwifery. Most were pillars of society, advising villagers on everything from marital harmony to crop failure, providing spiritual guidance and counseling, countering wicked *juju* and exacting revenge, if necessary, on their enemies.

Their wickedness was all a question of degree. Well-known *sangomas*, corrupted by wealth and power, had the run of a country still governed by superstition and unfettered greed. The President would murder his own sister if a *sangoma* told him it would bring him good luck – or sexual prowess.

Stewart sighed. His *sangomas'* endless demands were draining him, but he was ready to endure the few months it would take to harvest a few more bodies. But that would be all he could endure. He had to return to England while he still had control. Some of his victims had been so young and lovely, he'd been tempted to defile them. Imagine! A renowned surgeon, a paragon in his field, having such urges.

Sometimes he thought he was losing his mind. When his wife was alive, he'd tolerated – even enjoyed – the casual serendipity and contradictions of African life. But when she died, charity and mercy flew from his heart. He'd changed so much he was virtually unrecognizable, even to himself. He loathed the very Africans he'd loved with a hostility so deep it nauseated him. If his younger self, the earnest young doctor who came to Zambia three decades ago to help the poor, had met the Stewart Bleming he'd become today, he'd kill him.

Fortunately, his exit strategy was working. Since he'd learned to plastinate human flesh, substituting polymer for tissue, at one of Victor's conferences several years ago, his sales had been brisk. The organ trade had fattened his retirement fund, thin after thirty years of doctoring Africa's poor. Demand for human skin had grown relentlessly, the price for transplant organs was spiraling, and profit margins were high.

To the Chinese, who paid top dollar for animal trophies and ivory, humans were just another novelty specimen for their collections. Although they were Stewart's best customers, the fact that they were virtually tax-free thanks to deals with the Zambian government galled Stewart mightily. Their profits on Zambia's copper, gold, and platinum mines were enormous.

The British had civilized Zambia and developed its infrastructure, only to see their President give it away to the Chinese. But he couldn't complain too loudly. Because he was consulting physician with the Chinese coal mine in Sinazongwe, the manager shipped Sewart's specimens along with the coal, no questions asked. He knew his Chinese customers would pay handsomely for this girl's skin.

Gazing at her body, gleaming in the fire's light, his spirits rose. She would have thanked him for immortalizing her youthful beauty. Bleaching aged the skin badly, and beautiful girls like her suffered terribly. Stewart was excited that this specimen had turned out so well. In less than twenty-four hours, Victor, the genius who'd taught him the trade that restored him after his wife's death brought him to the edge of despair would be here.

Stewart checked the petrol supply for his generator, cranked the sound on his telly so he could hear it over the torrential rain, and poured himself a glass of brandy. Not only would his plan yield enough to retire, it would humiliate Malinga and put the *sangomas* behind bars where they belonged. It was perfect. He cranked the sound on his telly a few more notches – the rain was deafening at the height of the rainy season – and set his brandy on the side table.

He was lowering himself into his overstuffed wingback to watch the Cup Game when the outside door burst open and banged against the wall. He jerked himself up and went to shut it, but Kivuli shoved him back against the wall so his father could enter. The *sangomas* swept past him, their costumes dripping on the floor, and rushed to the laboratory to inspect the girl's corpse.

"She's a fine one," the old man muttered, fingering his necklace with one hand, reaching out with the other to touch the girl's body.

Stewart glowered at him. "Yes, she is. I've finished with her. Take what you want and dump the rest near the stadium." The *sangomas'* eyes widened. "Don't worry. No one will see you. Everyone is watching the game."

The son sniggered and started to nod, but when the old man shook his head, he shook his head, too. "Too risky. Pay us more."

Stewart started to object but thought better of it. Since Kivuli had returned from South Africa, he bristled with an aura of barely contained violence that frightened Stewart, especially after what he'd done to Bertha's baby. Besides, he was right. Stewart welcomed the risk because he enjoyed the look of frustration on Malinga's face, but he couldn't expect Redbone and Kivuli to feel the same way. He handed each of them a large-denomination *kwacha* note. They tugged the girl's body off the table and disappeared into the night, banging the door against the wall as they departed.

Stewart slammed the door shut and locked it behind them. He took another sip of brandy to calm his nerves and congratulated himself on the cleverness of his scheme. Malinga's public humiliation would be delicious. Another body found in the most public of places. An even more frightened public. Outraged demands for justice and retribution, and for a new Deputy Inspector. If he were lucky, she'd be replaced by a DI who would work with him instead of against him.

Malinga was the first woman to achieve such a high rank in the Zambian police force, and she'd be the last if Stewart had anything to do with it. Promoted Deputy Inspector after cracking a major cross-border international fraud operation in Chobe National Park, Malinga's reputation grew when she collared the elephant poachers in Asia last year. Her sole weakness? Trusting people like him too much.

He chuckled. She couldn't last much longer. She was becoming a national laughingstock as the bodies piled up. At the very least, she'd be demoted, maybe even fired. How lovely it would be to hasten Malinga's demise, to bring her distinguished career to a quick and less than-perfect end. Stewart laughed. Recommending Bertha to Malinga when her nanny quit had been a stroke of genius. Bertha, his very own Trojan Horse.

He settled into his chair, relaxing as the Cup Game preliminaries got underway. Victor's impending visit was already changing his life. After Bertha freshened the guest wing for Victor's arrival that morning, Stewart saw the house in a whole new light. What had become a musty prison when his wife died three years ago had been transformed into a haven where he and Victor could work in secret to realize their wildest ambitions.

Stewart's skills were improving daily. This girl hadn't suffered much, but while her skin was saleable, the rest of her was not because electric power had failed during her plastination. He hoped Victor could suggest solutions to the power problem before they took on his final project.

The Crown of His Career.

Stewart smiled. Victor always spoke in capitals. He was German, after all. A genius, true, but a man of incredibly bad taste nonetheless.

Stewart nestled deeper into the cushions of his chair, feeling more content than he had in a long time. His plan to bring Malinga to her knees was almost complete, his plan to frame the witch doctors was rapidly taking shape, and he was confident that he'd find a way to satisfy Victor's dream.

He drifted off to sleep, lulled into a sense of security by the drum of the rain on his rooftop, completely unaware of the danger wending its way toward him through the darkened night skies.

2 | Shiny Corpses Are a Bit Okay

Malinga jerked awake. The girl's corpse called to her again, beckoning frantically with its skinless arms.

Come closer! You must save the others! Hurry!

She's remarkably persistent for a dead person, Malinga thought, rubbing her eyes. Her remains had been shiny, red, and muscular. It – she – was the fifth young women stripped clean of skin in a month of nightmares since the murders began. Malinga closed her eyes, ground her teeth, and cursed herself. The girls were calling to her. She'd missed something obvious.

But what could it be?

She massaged her temples to forestall the vicious migraine she knew was coming on. Corpses were routine in her business, but they usually didn't look like this and they usually didn't talk. She groaned. She was getting little enough sleep as it was.

I heard you the first time! I'm doing the best I can!

Do it faster, the corpse insisted, her voice tearing at Malinga's brain. It was uncanny, eerie, and annoying. Shivering, Malinga pulled the covers tight under her chin. The latest corpses were so far from routine they . . . well, they gave her nightmares. Not just partially skinned or missing a few essential pieces, but completely, elegantly flayed. Forensics said the killer's skills were improving with each body he dumped.

Who's doing this? What kind of animal is he?

Before this string of murders, she thought she'd seen it all. Corpses swollen from snake bite, hung from trees by vengeful elephants, chewed by crocodiles. Corpses that had been stabbed, shot, cut, dismembered. She'd never given them a second thought until this group came along. These girls made her skin crawl. Worse, they left her with very few clues. The investigation was going nowhere.

Malinga stared at the ceiling fan revolving slowly above her head. Serial killers were rare in Lusaka, Zambia's bustling capital of two million, and rare in the country as a whole. Combing through thirty years of police files had yielded only three. Now, in just under a month, she was handling two new sets of *muti* murders.

The first involved a pair of taxi drivers, driven to Vic Falls in the boots of their own vehicles and sold to a former member of Zimbabwe's secret police. The murderers were caught red-handed with their victims' heads in a sack. Classic *muti*. An open and shut case.

But the girls' killer was different, an absolute professional, no witch doctor run amok. He harvested what he needed, dumped the bodies on the roadside, and left no clues. An invisible and completely cold-blooded ghost.

Malinga hugged herself. She'd never seen anything as grisly as last night's corpse, bloodless and gleaming in the light rain. The girl's exposed muscles and tendons, gritty with bits of dirt from the roadside, glistened cleanly, like they'd been polished. The tissues were hard, filled with plastic like the other corpses.

"A shiny corpse is a bit okay," her deputy, Davison, had volunteered as the girl's corpse was loaded into the police van. "It's not bloody. It doesn't look human. Not even African." Malinga looked away, frowning.

"Am I not right?" he insisted. When her frown deepened, he shrugged his shoulders. "As for me, there is only one thing I don't like about these corpses. It is the way the fat stands out from the muscle like an overfed Chinese chicken."

When Davison laughed, Malinga felt her throat tighten. "Okay, Davison. Enough."

Asedi, her other deputy, raised her head from the paperwork on her desk and joined in. "These girls are missing more than their skin. The killers take their eyes, tongues, and hearts for magic charms. Someone is profiting from selling their parts. Mark my words. These girls are suffering so a rich man can send his kids to private schools in their own Benzes."

Malinga stared at her, startled by her unexpected perceptiveness. "You're right, Asedi. Someone's making big money from these deaths. Profit's at the bottom of every *muti* killing. Outrageously high profit."

Asedi nodded. "Last year, South Africa reported three hundred *muti* killings, but I reckon they had at least twice that number. In Zambia, I'm sure there were twice that many again. We don't know how many there really are because people are afraid to tell us."

"Zambia had three times. Even four. I am sure," Davison said.

"Maybe even five or six!" Asedi declared, refusing to be bested. "Zambia's not like South Africa. We have more witch doctors than real doctors, and we don't have as many policemen."

"With no birth registration, it could be seven or eight," Davison countered, his voice rising. "An unregistered child who disappears in the bush never existed."

"We will never know the total," Asedi concluded triumphantly. She turned back to Malinga, suddenly indignant. "The last report said that we police are to blame, that we hide information about ritual murders and take bribes to keep them secret."

"Imagine!" Davison said. "Do they think we are the crazy ones?"

Asedi put her hands on her hips. "We women are always hunted. They kill us because they think we have special powers. Why do they think we are the weakest, too weak to defend ourselves?" She pointed an accusing index finger at Davison. "The husband is anxious for children. The witch doctor says 'bring me the parts of a young woman and your wife will bear fruit.' A *sangoma* speaks and another woman loses her life."

"Just look at Mongu," Davison said. Police in Zambia's westernmost city, on the border of Angola, had found a mutilated body on the dry plains of the Zambezi River. Ambushed early in the morning, the woman was returning home alone after walking her children to primary school. At least they hadn't witnessed the murder, Malinga thought. They would grieve, but their needs would be met by doting grannies and aunties, and their sleep would never be disturbed by images of their mother being butchered.

"The Chipata case was worse," Asedi declared.

Davison glared. "I think Mongu . . . '

Malinga, hands raised like an umpire, stepped between them. "Let's get back to work. We have a lot to do."

Hours later, their voices still rang in her head. The naiveté of her good-natured deputies never failed to astound her, but they were all she had. She sighed and closed her eyes. Lack of resources made police work in Zambia challenging. Few criminals were brought to justice, especially ones as savvy as the killer they hunted now.

Casting the duvet aside, Malinga pulled herself up and leaned back on her pillows. She might not have much to work with, but this was one killer who was not going to get away. She'd promised the girls who came to her in the night that she'd get him.

And she knew they'd never let her rest until she did.

3 | A New Mengele

"If I can't help you plastinate a body, no one can," the little man exclaimed. "I not only invented the technique, I built an empire on it! Look at how rich I've become! So can you, Stewart! Your problems are purely mechanical, just like mine.

"Only yours can be fixed. Mine are permanent. Look! I became an old man overnight!" Victor raised his shaking hands and guffawed. His wife rolled her eyes and Stewart laughed uneasily, wondering about the sanity of a man who made corpses his life's work, a man married to a woman half his age who smelled like an accident in a perfume factory.

The Von Sorges had come straight from the airport to his home and Victor had been laughing like a bloody hyena ever since. Wakened from his fireside doze by the sound of their taxi, Stewart had flung back the door and opened his arms in welcome but froze when he saw what stood there.

It was Victor, all right, but not him at all. He'd become an open-mouthed, wide-eyed manikin, his face pasty under his trademark black fedora, a mask glazed with a thin layer of sweat. His signature Van Dyke had softened into a straggly goat's beard, and his look of surprise wasn't the inquiring stare of a slightly mad inventor, but a permanent expression of pain.

Stewart had guided him along the entry hall to show him the specimen cases he'd crammed with his work. Von Sorge nodded his approval of each one as he passed. When they reached the library, Stewart led him close to the fire and helped steady him as he sunk into the waiting chair.

"Welcome to my home, Doctor. If you'd like to rest for a few hours, your rooms are ready. We can talk when you're refreshed."

"Nonsense!" Von Sorge snorted, raising his hands in shaky protest. "I am fully awake. And I insist you call me Victor from now on. Everyone else does." Drool ran from his open mouth, but he batted Anita's hand away when she tried to mop up the dribbles.

Anita persisted. "Now, Victor. I told you . . ."

To be sure, Stewart thought, that the god who invented Parkinson's was an Old Testament deity. In Anita, he'd given Von Sorge an Old Testament woman, with hypnotizing breasts, elevated to their limits and barely concealed behind a very tight cashmere sweater the color of bone.

It intrigued Stewart all the more because bone had also been his late wife's favorite color. But that's where the resemblance ended. This blousy, overdrawn female was a travesty of womanhood next to his feminine, ladylike Mary. Her stiffly coiffed, bleached blonde hair looked like a wig. Mary would never have been caught dead in one. But now she is, Stewart thought sadly. Dead, that is.

My Mary's dead and nothing matters any more. Everything that was beautiful in my life has gone with her.

Victor's imperious voice pulled him back to the present. "Be a good girl, Anita, and try to find us some tea."

"My maid will help you," Stewart said gallantly, embarrassed by the man's rudeness. Bertha, summoned by the gateman, had already glided silently into the library. She motioned to Anita, who followed her into the kitchen.

"Thank you for coming to Zambia," Stewart said, turning back to Victor. Von Sorge's half-closed eyes flew open and he jerked his smile into a grin, shifting stiffly in his chair. He began to speak deliberately, with a slight German accent. Stewart pulled his chair closer so he could make out the man's rapid-fire stutter.

"The pleasure is all mine, Stewart. I am glad to be here and very impressed with your specimens. You should be proud of what you've accomplished at such an early stage in our craft."

Stewart smiled modestly. Plastination, as Victor called the process he'd invented for preserving corpses by replacing body fluids with plastic resin, was actually quite simple, but required a realiable power supply. "I'm afraid that Zambia's frequent power outages play havoc with my results. They make it almost impossible to maintain the vacuum needed to perfect the technique."

"But you've persisted, Stewart! Look what you've accomplished! I'm so glad you've embraced my noble cause." Victor's eyes shone. "If more students could learn from my corpses . . ." Seeing Stewart's frown, he laughed. "That is what they are Doctor, so that is what I call them. I am not shy about it."

Stewart shrugged. "You're right. People are entirely too fastidious about these things," he said. "You've broken the mold."

"I certainly have. One of my neighbors calls me the New Doctor Mengele. Imagine! He compares me to that Nazi bastard who was Hitler's darling and his foremost torturer! He did medical experiments on living human beings! Imagine!" Stewart flinched, thinking of his witch doctor partners.

"I am no Mengele," Victor continued. He jerked his head from side to side in a stiff gesture of denial. "I would never experiment on living humans. All of my models are volunteers, and they are perfectly dead from other causes before they arrive in my lab." Victor tried to spit, but nothing came out.

"I'm not even German! My parents fled from Poland to escape the Russian occupation when I was five days old. They put me in a laundry basket and threw it on a horse-drawn wagon for the trek to Berlin. Life was very hard for us, and for me more than anyone. As a child, I had a rare bleeding disorder. I was confined to bed and had no friends. I almost died when I was six," Von Sorge droned on, "but the doctors struggled to keep me alive. Do you have any idea what that's like?" Von Sorge's eyes seemed to glow, and fever spots stood out on his cheekbones. "Do you have any idea, Stewart?"

Stewart pulled himself up in his chair and shook himself awake. He found plastination fascinating, but Victor's life story decidedly not. Especially so early in the morning. "I can only guess."

"My doctors were like gods! So I decided to become a physician, too." Von Sorge lifted a shaking fist and struck his knee. "But I was rejected because I was a freethinker. Those bloody bastards said I was willful and undisciplined, but I had more vision than they could have if they lived a thousand lifetimes.

"When I finished my training, I worked in the lab, embedding anatomical specimens in transparent plastic blocks. Day after day, the same thing. Block after block after block. One day, I woke up! I realized I could push acrylic into the cells rather than pour it around them. I got a patent, but it took me six years to perfect the method. You see, while the idea is simple, doing it is very complex!"

Stewart nodded. He knew just how simple the procedure was if you had reliable electricity, but in the interest of courtesy, he resigned himself to listening to Victor's explanation. "I embalm the body and remove the muscles or organ groups I want. After I vacuum out the fluids and soluble fats, I replace them with silicone rubber and epoxy. Then I pose them and cure them with light, heat, and gasses. Ah, but Stewart! I forget! You know all this already! I am boring you!"

Stewart shook his head, stifling a yawn, and poured Victor a cup of tea from the pot Bertha set before them. The cup rattled so badly in Victor's grasp, Stewart was afraid he would spill the steaming liquid on himself. Much to his relief, Victor managed to get the cup to his mouth. He slurped nosily and set the cup back on the tray.

"Perfecting the technique was one thing. Winning social approval for the idea was another kettle of fish. The German Archbishop, who is a completely slimy bastard, I assure you, said I was creating a spectacle! He shut up when I plastinated St. Hildegard of Bingen's heel bone for him. I offered to plastinate Pope John Paul II, but the discussions went nowhere. Bloody churchmen! Utterly plagued by superstition!"

Victor shook his head and smiled. "They tried to stop me time after time, calling my work blasphemy. Can you imagine? What a primitive word! They couldn't stop me, especially after I married Anita. She is English, my second wife. She is a genius! I made her my business manager, and she helped me found my Institute for Plastination in 1993. Our grand expositions, Body Works, premiered in Japan in 1995. Forty million people in over one hundred countries have seen the show since. They are no longer shocked by the bodies. To the contrary! They are fascinated by them!"

Von Sorge smiled fondly at his wife, who returned his tender glance with a kiss blown from her collagened lips. They're perfectly matched, Stewart thought. Her money, his fame. At one time, Victor probably exuded wolfish sex appeal, a good match for Anita's exaggerated but still sinuous beauty. When Victor began the long process of reaching for his teacup again, Stewart lifted it and put it in his shaking hands.

"Thank you, Doctor. Few people understand what I am trying to accomplish as well as you do. I have been followed by controversy all my life, but all I ever wanted to do was bring anatomical knowledge to as many people as possible. Look at what those idiots did in Prague a few months ago! Legally, they claimed that any dead body found in their streets must be buried, including the ones in my exhibit!"

Victor tried to smile. "You see why I need your help, Stewart. I will never be thrown out of another country again. Especially by some bloody black African bastard. The white and yellow ones were bad enough." He looked sideways at his wife.

"Of course, once the skin is off . . ."

"They all look alike!" Anita said. They started to giggle, and soon they were laughing like hyenas. Stewart had to look away.

4 | Short Resources, Short Skirts

Malinga sat up straighter and squared her shoulders. No more flayed bodies, no more *muti* killings. She'd outwit this killer just as she had the elephant poachers in Africa and Asia. They'd been as ruthless as these witch doctors, but Malinga knew she was smarter. Sure, she'd have to summon all her reserves, both mental and physical. But first, she'd have to deal once and for all with her ex-husband, who was still threatening to take her children away despite the injunction she'd placed on him last year. Herbert had never made her life easy, so why should he start now?

She hugged her knees to her chest, unsure she could deliver what she'd promised in the press. Zambia's Criminal Investigation Division was woefully short-handed. While Malinga struggled to keep Asedi and Davison on track, her boss was on an 'educational' jaunt in Europe, and Wilson, the CID's other DI, had taken a long holiday on Zanzibar. To add insult to injury, their new President had wasted so much of the police budget on special guards for his election rallies that there was very little money left, even for petrol. Police couldn't reach a crime scene unless the victim's family fetched them. Officers often stalled their investigations so they could milk the victims for cash.

Witch doctors could melt into the bush or slip across the border in the blink of an eye. How did she hope to catch them if she couldn't even chase them? Short of resources, with bodies piling up, she was shouldering the department's entire workload with little prospect of relief – or reward. After she'd solved the poaching case, her boss, Inspector Crispin Chikanda, took over the international coordination work she'd started. By rights, it should have been hers. Just yesterday, he'd extended his European trip for another two weeks to study international animal trafficking – and French wines – with Interpol in Marseilles.

Now that Wilson was back, he was Acting Inspector, and Malinga had little doubt Chikanda would put him in charge of her investigation. Wilson would claim all the credit and get the pay increase that went with it. Malinga frowned. There was no way she'd let that happen. She needed a pay increase herself. Her house was so small, her new maid, Bertha, couldn't live in.

Recommended by the doctor, Bertha was cheap – the new ones from the country always were – but Malinga wasn't sure she could trust her. Young and susceptible, rural girls were targeted by ruthless criminals, who enlisted them in their schemes. Time would tell if Bertha could resist the temptations of city life.

When Malinga stretched, her yawn turned into a grimace. The wave of new *muti* murders was an obvious strike against young women. Death was the ultimate retaliation for unacceptable behavior. As women broke new ground in Zambia, violence against them was increasing.

Just last week, she had to dress down a senior police officer in Kitwe who thought that his city's taxi drivers, who were attacking young women in short skirts, were in the right. The drivers stripped the girls of their skirts and forced them to parade through town in their underwear. The chief and his headmen agreed: the girls got just what they asked for and just what they deserved.

"This is a Christian nation," her officer retorted when Malinga expressed her annoyance. "Those young women are not only breaking local law, but they are violating the laws of God."

"Since when," she asked him, "did God have anything to say about hemlines, Robert? Since when do you have his direct line? As far as I'm aware, Kitwe hasn't passed a referendum against short skirts, but we do have a law against theft. The taxi drivers broke the law, not the girls. I don't care about your personal feelings. Get out there and enforce the law as it's written. It's not yours to make!"

He'd mumbled something about what God would do to women with too much ambition and hung up the phone. Malinga had considered disciplinary action, but by the next morning, a few of the younger taxi drivers behind the 'Short Skirt War' had been arrested and fined. Their female victims looked more frightened than victorious in the press interviews. Society was working against them and the drivers knew where they lived.

Malinga stretched again, her long frame extending nearly the whole length of the bed. Village girls coming into Lusaka for work were younger and more innocent these days. The more help they needed, the less they could count on from the police, who were not only short staffed, but unsympathetic. Would Bertha be reliable once the city crept into her bones? Would she be tempted by the discos and the clothing stalls?

I have to keep an eye on her, Malinga thought. But thank heavens I've got a maid! And thank heavens I have parents who are willing to help me with the kids. This afternoon, Katanga would go to her grandmother's for a few days so Malinga could work the long holiday weekend in peace. With the help of nannies and relatives, women could gain their independence from worthless husbands, a critical advantage in Zambia where a woman's biggest risk factor for HIV infection was a permanent relationship with a man.

Malinga slipped a bathrobe over her slim frame and slid her feet into her slippers. It was useless to try to go back to sleep. The scene behind the national stadium last night was still too vivid. It would look terrible in the newspapers. This new body brought the total to five victims, including the student from the Pharmacy Institute. Seven if you counted the victims in Mongu and Chipata.

I hope this isn't a national trend.

Malinga glanced around her bedroom. Bertha had done a first-class job with the laundry. The sheets were so crisp and fresh, they looked new. She'd dusted, washed the windows, and reorganized Malinga's desk.

My desk.

Malinga drew in her breath.

Where's my case file?

5 | The Long Road from Kyrgyzstan

"I've been exiled too many times!" Victor said. "And for no good reason! I was a professor in China and director of the Plastination Research Center in Kyrgyzstan when those countries threw me out! China even accused me of using prisoners' bodies without their families' permission and demanded that I return my specimens. All lies, but the paperwork was so skimpy I had no choice. I had to protect my reputation."

"Your reputation is unparalleled," Stewart said. "Hundreds have attended your conferences, me among them."

"That's the reason I came to Zambia to see you, Stewart. You were such an ardent student! When I saw how eager you were to learn, I thought 'there's a man who is truly like me.' It was then I decided to make you an offer." Victor cleared his throat. Try as he could to arrange his face into a smile, the best he could do was a sneer.

"I want to found a laboratory in Zambia at the university. Not a body factory like China and Kazakhstan, but a proper research and teaching laboratory."

Stewart nodded. "It would be my privilege to help you in any way I can."

Victor's eyes opened even wider and he laughed. "You will do more than help, Stewart. You will oversee my operations!"

Stewart shook his head. "I appreciate your confidence, Victor, but I couldn't possibly do that. I was planning to . . ."

"But you must, Stewart! There's no one else who can do it. I certainly can't! The Parkinson's is closing in on me." He looked down at his hands with disgust. When he looked back up at Stewart, his face jerked into a smile. "But more importantly, this will be a very good deal for you. You must consider it carefully. The demand for bodies far exceeds my ability to provide them. The faster we can plastinate corpses, the more medical students we can teach, especially in poor countries like this" he said, pounding softly on his knee for emphasis, his face ghoulish but oddly charismatic.

Stewart averted his eyes, embarrassed that he was motivated by profit, a longing for retirement, and revenge. Victor's dream was larger, selfless, and unwavering: to improve medical education and lower its cost so the poor had more care.

"You can help me, Stewart. You've accomplished so much already. You're nearly there."

Stewart was dumbfounded. And happier than he'd been in a very long time, happier than he'd been since his wife had died. But he still shook his head. "I appreciate your confidence in me, Victor, and I'd like to help, but I plan to return to England by the end of this year."

Victor scoffed. "You can always return to England! Postpone your plans! What can England possibly offer you besides bloody cold and bloody rain? I am offering you riches beyond your wildest imagination!"

Stewart laughed. "It's a tempting proposition, Victor. I would consider staying on, but . . . "

Von Sorge's grin widened. "No buts, Stewart. You've accomplished too much to give up so soon. The climate is perfect here, and you have all the volunteers you need! You could make endless piles of money!" He chortled, spilling his tea onto the table.

Victor's callousness made Stewart uneasy, but he had to admit that the anatomist was right. The possibilities for wealth were unlimited. Zambia was just a start. If he controlled Victor's southern Africa labs, he'd be in line to take over global operations when Victor died. With a little effort, he could secure a much brighter future for himself than he'd dared imagine. Why run and hide in England now?

"I'm seventy years old," Victor said. "The Parkinson's is killing me. It can't happen soon enough as far as I'm concerned, but I can't die until I finish my final show. Once they see it, my bloody critics will have nothing to say." Victor giggled maniacally and started to choke, but waved away the water Stewart offered him. "Body Works fans have seen corpses doing everything, even having sex, but my last exhibit will be truly spectacular!" He turned imploring eyes on Stewart. "I can't do it without you. Only you can make my dreams come true."

Anita yawned noisily. Her lipstick, drawn wide on her pouty lips, was slightly smeared. Stewart could hardly take his eyes off her mouth. Victor's eyes flicked to his wife, following Stewart's gaze.

"My darling, can you bring us another cup of tea?" he asked. "We'll go to our room soon, but first Stewart and I must strike a bargain."

Although the doctor's choice of words caught his attention, Stewart found it hard to concentrate. Anita's buttocks shifted from side to side beneath her tight skirt as she followed Bertha back to the kitchen. Victor was saying something to him, but he couldn't focus enough to understand what it was.

6 | A Ripe Peach

Relief surged through Malinga when she spotted her case file on the desk, lying on top of the other files she'd brought home from the office yesterday. They were neatly lined up, papers tucked in, pens and cell phone ranged alongside them. Flipping quickly through the file, she saw that everything was exactly as she'd left it. Bertha had just tidied up.

Malinga exhaled hard. She had to learn to trust Bertha. The kids liked her. She was quiet, modest, and a very good cook. "You can trust her," Stewart had said when he recommended her.

It's a shame she's a bleacher, Malinga thought, but so many Zambian women were. Rich and poor, they did it for status and to make men fall in love with them – so hopelessly they wouldn't notice when the punishing toxins in the bleaching potions destroyed their skins as they grew older.

Malinga walked to the bathroom mirror and pushed the wild tendrils of her natural into a soft crown around her head. No makeup or hair extensions. They were tiresome and matronly. She inspected her triangular face and touched her high cheekbones.

The bags under my eyes are becoming permanent. I've got to get some sleep.

She rubbed some color into her cheeks and brushed her teeth, crisp white against her coffee-colored skin. In uniform or street clothes, Malinga had a tall, rangy, honest attractiveness that drew people to her.

Especially men who are no good for me.

She sighed, her thoughts drifting. The only man who had been good for her, Eitone Mazoka, had disappeared into thin air along with the elephant tusks from Kafue. It had been months, but she still had no news of the tall, amber-eyed park ranger with whom she'd fallen hopelessly in love. She'd never been so heartbroken, but in some ways, she was glad he was gone.

I can focus on my family and my work again.

This afternoon her team would comb through the evidence on the serial killings to find fresh leads. The lab reports on the latest body would be ready by the time she reached the office. Over the four-day holiday weekend that was coming up, her team planned to review all the evidence they'd assembled. Scant as it was, she hoped they'd find something to move them forward.

Her old school mate, University of Zambia criminal psychologist Danise Hatchitapika, would provide preliminary psychological profiles of the victims. Wilson was back from his vacation and the French pathologist who'd arrived from Interpol a few days ago – Jacques? Pierre? Jean? – was already hard at work. Malinga doubted he'd be very effective in Zambia, but any extra pair of hands were welcome.

Malinga knew she had a bias against Europeans – British, French, German, Portuguese – because they'd left Africa in ruins. But they weren't the only culprits. If Zambia's own politicians weren't so greedy, the country would have emerged from poverty a long time ago. European colonialists started the process of impoverishment and degradation, and now Chinese, South African – even Canadian – corporations were draining the country of billions of dollars of resources, money that could have been used to end Zambia's poverty. Their strategy? Cultivate chaos and reap the rewards.

Enough politics, she thought, forcing herself to chase the troubling thoughts from her mind. It's time for Katanga and I to have some fun.

Malinga was looking forward to their morning appointment at the salon. She showered, dressed, slid her files into her briefcase, and padded down to the kitchen. It was a brilliant, sunny Saturday, her first break in more than a month. Bertha had set up the coffee maker, and Malinga's cup sat on the tea tray beside some freshly baked scones.

I'm going to miss this pampering tomorrow, Malinga thought, but she'd agreed to share Bertha with the doctor until he left for England. She'd drop her at his compound on her way to the mall. After the salon and lunch, Malinga would drop Katanga off at her grandparents and head downtown to the station.

But first, the sweet kind of adventure that kept her close to her daughter as she approached the rocky shoals of adolescence. At eight, her son was a year younger, but couldn't wait to be a man. Shiko was with his father, gone since yesterday afternoon, so the kitchen was considerably quieter than usual.

Malinga relaxed and flipped on the radio. When she heard the first of the news, her stomach tightened and her mood darkened again.

"Another young woman, completely stripped of her skin and vital organs, was found late last night on the outskirts of Lusaka," the reporter said with entirely too much relish. "Police refused to comment, leading to speculation that they still know very little about these killings. Deputy Inspector Malinga Mutende, who's leading the CID investigation, said they expect an arrest shortly."

He laughed. "If you recall, that's exactly what she said after the last body was found. Guess you weren't fast enough to save this poor girl, eh, Miss Mutende?" the announcer sneered. Malinga cringed. "Police were embarrassed when another girl's body was found in a ditch by the national stadium last night. This is the fifth such body they've found, but as far as we know, they have no suspects. Despite the fact that there's a brutal killer lurking out there, police are urging the public to remain calm and go about their business . . ."

Malinga snapped the radio off. Her shame was intense, but her growing sense of guilt was stronger. More women would die unless she found the killers fast. Everything she'd worked for was at stake. As she stirred her coffee, she considered cancelling her date with Katanga but decided against it. None of her team would be in until the afternoon, and there'd be no lab results until later in the day. Girlfriend time with Katanga was exactly what she needed right now.

Sipping her coffee, she remembered that the latest victim had been a bleacher like the other girls. It might mean something, but since bleaching was such a popular practice, she doubted it was much of a clue. Even Katanga wanted to try it.

Malinga made a mental note to remind Katanga not to mention bleaching to her parents. It would upset them terribly. They'd fought in the independence struggle against the Brits and were fiercely proud of their color. In their estimation, the practice of skin whitening was akin to treason.

Malinga realized that if she didn't intervene, Katanga stood to learn a lot from her grandparents' reaction. Her father was a very persuasive man, key in Malinga's own decision to join the police force. With his encouragement, she went straight from college to the academy, one of the first females to attend, and she'd excelled at everything. But the glass ceiling was very low. Wilson had been on the force for five years when he made Deputy Inspector. It had taken her seven.

Malinga poured herself another cup of coffee and stepped out on her patio to enjoy the morning sun. Not very Zambian, drinking coffee instead of tea, but she'd picked up the habit when she went for training in San Francisco several years ago. She was glad she'd gone.

Zambians who stayed home forgot that they were only eighteen million souls in a world of seven billion. Not that size made much difference in the world of crime. Zambia might be small, but Lusaka was growing fast and police work was becoming as schizophrenic as the city. The influx of South African and Chinese investors brought a whole new range of crimes, including the skin trade and body snatching.

But it was still Africa. Just last week, she'd arranged a special detail to escort a truck carrying giraffes from the Zambezi National Park to the President's State House garden in Lusaka's center, backing traffic up for hours. The President spoke out against bleaching and for women's rights, but cultivated the appetites of an old rajah. She shrugged. The contradictions of development. The growing pains.

Her hands circled her coffee cup, drawing on its warmth as she stood in the strengthening sun. When the light hit the new roses her gardener was tending, he looked up and waved to her. The air smelled fresh. It had rained for a long time last night, soaking her team while they recovered the girl's body from the stadium. The long rains, almost a month late, would arrive any day now. Malinga sighed. The rains made police work so difficult. Any clues they might have gathered were erased by the downpour.

She walked toward the roses. Now that it was clearing, she and Katanga could scout the Arcades Mall flea market after they finished at the salon. Katanga loved the tie-dyed t-shirts almost as much as her mother had when she was a teenager. Malinga reached out to caress a new rose, colored like a ripe peach.

Girls flush with the beauty of youth are being harvested like beef cattle. They are as vulnerable as this new rose. If she were a little older, Katanga might be one of them.

Malinga's blood quickened and before she knew what she was doing, she'd squeezed the rose so hard, it fell apart in her hand. She released the flower in horror and brushed the thought away with its petals. It was time to redouble her efforts before another girl fell victim to the killer.

7 | God's Chosen One

"Business will be good in Zambia, Stewart, I can assure you. A lab here will ensure a constant flow of bodies to my exhibitions, besides adding black skin to all the white and yellow."

"Not that there's very much of it. Skin, that is," Anita said.

Victor began to laugh, but Parkinson's had reduced his laughter to a few short barks. "We'll sort out the details after I've had a nap. For now, I just want to know if you're interested."

"Of course I am, Victor. It's the opportunity of a lifetime!"

"I'm so happy to hear you say that, Stewart! You understand me so well. I know we'll partner seamlessly. I'll make you wealthy beyond your fondest dreams."

"I see the possibilities, but . . ."

"But nothing! My internet sales are mushrooming just as I predicted." Von Sorge snorted derisively. "When I started online sales, the public was outraged. Now I can't keep up with the orders. Once my anatomy curriculum goes on-line in the U.S., demand will skyrocket. It's the first course to use plastinated specimens."

Victor strained forward in his chair and pointed a shaking finger at Stewart. "You must help me. I need more bodies! I can't meet the demand I've got right now. I need a fresh source of volunteers, or my web business will collapse. If you help me, I guarantee our profits will be huge. Bodies go for more than one hundred thousand dollars each, torsos for close to that, and human heads for more than thirty grand."

Stewart almost choked on his tea. He'd been giving his work away!

Victor sat back and tried to smile, but his face contorted involuntarily. "If we offer other species, we can grow the market astronomically. But if we don't have a steady supply of human and animal specimens, it won't work."

"Will it work on such a large scale?"

"Oh, yes! Dear God, yes! Before they shut me down, my factories in China and Kyrgyzstan processed hundreds of bodies! I have a small factory in Germany, but they banned our internet sales. That's why we need a factory here." He stopped to sip his tea. His red-rimmed eyes looked swollen and unnaturally large. Unearthly, Stewart thought. And not a little crazy.

"We are running out of raw material, Stewart. We have only three thousand donors . . ."

"Three thousand? That's a huge number!"

"Yes, but it's not enough. They have to die first, remember? Some of them are quite young." Von Sorge smiled crookedly and jerked his hands up. "With partners like you, the business will grow quickly. Our exhibits will be places of enlightenment and contemplation, of philosophical and religious self-recognition."

Stewart lifted his chin. As odd as Victor was, the little man's dreams inspired him. If he collaborated, he'd make a fortune. "Your dreams are as big as life itself, Victor!"

"Bigger," Von Sorge said. "I am marked by destiny." He dropped his shaking hands to his lap and was silent. The room grew still. When he started to speak again, his voice was so low Stewart had to pull his chair closer to hear him.

"In spite of what I've contributed, my critics continue their attacks." Von Sorge turned his head stiffly toward Stewart and shrugged. "No matter. It's the burden I bear as an anatomist." He chuckled to himself. "Do you know the meaning of *Sorge* in German, Stewart?"

Stewart had no idea. He shook his head. Von Sorge frowned "It means worry, care, anxiety, fear." Stewart nodded sympathetically. "I rejected my fears a long time ago. My exhibits bring old taboos to the fore so the audience can confront their preconceived beliefs about death like I did."

Confront? Stewart almost laughed at von Sorge's choice of words. Flogged was more like it. He'd felt absolutely flagellated by the endless display of skinless bodies in gymnastic poses, grimacing at him from beyond death. If it brought anything to the fore, it was his gag reflex. How ironic, he thought, that Von Sorge now resembled his manikins more than a living man.

"I have suffered much, but it's the price of doing glorious work," Von Sorge said. "God gave me this gift and guided me every step of the way with little signs. One day, when I saw a woman slicing ham in a butcher shop, I knew God was telling me to use a meat slicer on my bodies. When bubbles rose from the kidney slices I embedded in liquid Plexiglas, he showed me how to use a vacuum to remove them." He chuckled. "Of course my first efforts were spectacular failures. I extracted plenty of bubbles, but the kidney turned pitch black and shriveled."

"At that point, most people would have given up, Victor. Why didn't you?"

"I despaired for a week when God gave me another sign. He told me that I was in too much of a hurry. I slowed the process down and cured the specimen in a laboratory kiln. That was January 10, 1977, the day I decided to make plastination my life work."

Stewart smiled to himself. No wonder they called this man Mengele. "Would you like a glass of brandy, Victor?"

"I rarely indulge. It interferes with my medications." He paused, looking hopeful. "But I enjoy it so much. Since Anita is resting" – he nodded toward the couch – "I will take a glass."

Victor's hand shook noticeably when Stewart handed him the glass, but he managed to swallow most of it on the first toss.

"More?" Stewart asked.

"No, no. Really. I can't," Victor said, but held his glass up for a refill. "Sometimes I feel like God's protégé, Stewart. He gave me so many things. But then he gave me Parkinson's, so I know he's a jealous bastard. Why else would he punish me like this?"

Von Sorge tried to raise his shaking hands toward heaven, but could get them no higher than the arms of his chair. He rubbed his right hand nervously. "I am so happy God told me to come to Zambia. I feel like I've known you all my life, Stewart, and now you will be one of my key disciples."

Stewart smiled apprehensively. "Disciple?"

"In a manner of speaking. Don't worry. I'll make you'll rich. Von Sorge Productions supplies four hundred institutions in forty countries, but we have no reliable African distributor. You will have a monopoly across the continent."

"How would I do that?" Stewart asked.

"Once you've established your laboratory at the University of Zambia, you can expand across the continent. You'll make hundreds of thousands of dollars each year on the franchises alone. But that's small potatoes! Just the beginning! Imagine the foreign development money we could attract to improve African medical education! Of course, you'll have to find a steady source of raw material, but you're well on your way already."

Stewart's eyes glowed. He'd be famous and he'd be rich. But it wouldn't be simple. Unless he discredited Malinga, he'd never be able to take advantage of the riches his new partnership with Victor promised. He'd have to get rid of the witch doctors, too. Not only were they venal and rapacious, they knew too much.

Stewart smiled. Perhaps he would plastinate them. It would certainly be poetic justice, and no one would recognize them once he was done. He grinned at the thought but shook his head. Let the police take care of them. If nothing else worked to put them behind bars, he had irrefutable evidence of the baby killing.

They'd given him the video.

8 | *Muti* Murders

"It just is, Mom," Katanga said, buttering her scone. "It's nicer to be white. Everyone at school wants to be lighter. Look at the fashion magazines. Look at Giselle."

"Not now, Katanga. Scoot up to your room and change. Celestin expects us at ten." Malinga watched her daughter skip up the stairs, dog at her heels, and shook her head. Half of Katanga's schoolmates were bleachers. Mothers began bleaching their children's skin when they were infants. Katanga's friend Margaret and her mom Patricia supplemented home treatments with regular trips to South Africa for injections.

Katanga argued that bleaching only had horrible side effects if you used the stuff they sold in local markets. She didn't realize that bleaching victimized poor and rich alike, emptying their pockets and stealing their youth. The Zambian government had threatened to ban bleaching products late last year, but nothing came of it. Politicians willing to sell their ethical commitment to the highest bidder were bribed. Public sentiment was on their side. All the big stars were bleaching.

Giselle, the Cape Town music sensation whose skin was two shades lighter than it had been only a few months ago, said the 'improvement' made her feel more confident. "I wanted to see what it would be like to be white. I'm happy I did it. I feel so beautiful! But don't worry! I'm still black inside," she'd cooed, anticipating the reporters' objections. One-third of all South African women bleached. In Nigeria, almost all women lightened their skins. The craze had spread to India, South America, and the U.S.

Malinga frowned. The last victim's facial skin had been removed, but there was still enough left to see that she'd been a liberal user of the cheapest kind of products. Her knuckles were much darker than rest of her fingers. She'd even used bleach on her breasts and genitalia, what was left of them.

Katanga may be right about the number of women who were bleaching, Malinga thought, but if I have anything to say about it, she'll never be one of them. Beside the health risks, maintenance was costly. One treatment was never enough.

They couldn't afford many luxuries at the moment, Malinga thought. Not until I get the support money Herbert owes me. If your father weren't a lawyer, I'd put him in jail in an instant. It might kill the Golden Goose, but he rarely contributes to the children's upkeep by turning over any of his golden eggs, so it wouldn't make much difference.

"Get dressed right now, young lady!" she shouted up the stairs. She heard a muffled shout in response, followed by the sound of feet pounding down the stairs. Malinga knew her daughter's striking height and supple strength would be great for police work, but she also knew better than to propose it. Katanga had her heart set on the arts.

The girl's head emerged around the doorway. "Mom," she said, "let's go to the Mint for lunch! I love it and lots of kids from school will be there." Before Malinga could answer, Katanga disappeared again and she heard the car door slam. Malinga smiled. Katanga's biggest asset was her speed. Cheerfulness ran a close second, followed by strength of mind, lack of fear, a willingness to take people at face value, and kindness.

Shiko could be rambunctious, but he was also a decent, thoughtful child. If I've done anything right in my life, my kids are it, Malinga thought as she locked the house and headed for the car. Their Jack Russell greeted her, jumping so high Malinga was afraid he'd scratch the car's bonnet.

"Hold Benny while I back out!" she called to John. Her gardener scooped Benny up and laughed when the terrier licked his face.

"Ready? Seatbelt fastened?" she asked her daughter, and was just putting the ancient Land Cruiser in reverse when Bertha stuck her head out the back door.

"Mum!" the maid called. "Wait! You promised to drop me in Kalingalinga!" She ran to the car, threw her bundled clothing on the back seat, and climbed in after it.

"Sorry, Bertha!" Malinga said, feeling slightly guilty. She could breathe easier now that Bertha was helping her, but the maid still needed her time off. Her three children, ages three to six, were cared for by their grandmother. The fourth had died last year under circumstances so tragic, Malinga's heart ached when she heard what the woman had endured.

Katanga had coaxed the story out of Bertha when she'd chatted with the maid one afternoon shortly after she started working for them. Bertha's baby, a boy less than two years old, had been the victim of a *muti* murder. He'd bled to death after the killers chopped his genitals off and tossed him on a rubbish heap.

"Mummy, it was awful. I cried so hard, but Bertha never did." Malinga explained that Bertha was probably too numb to grieve, but Katanga woke up with nightmares every night for the next week. When Malinga reached over and gave her daughter's knee a squeeze, Katanga grinned at her. "I'm so happy we're together, Mummy!" she exclaimed.

Malinga turned left on Bishops Road, right at the intersection, and took the next left onto Alex Nkata Road along Kalingalinga's western edge. Stewart lived on the backside of Kalingalinga where it bordered the forest, but Bertha wanted to be dropped at her own house first.

Malinga navigated carefully. Children darted across the streets, dense with construction traffic and scurrying shoppers. Kalingalinga's fifty thousand residents burst with energy and entrepreneurial perseverance. Ironworkers welded scrap steel into large garden gates for the well-to-do. Everything from wedding gowns to brassieres waved cheerfully at passersby from the tailoring shops. Like Bertha and Malinga, the lives of this compound's poor were intimately entwined with the lives of the rich in adjacent neighborhoods.

Although security was always a risk and housebreaking was common, Kalingalinga was so well located, rich investors were eyeing it for development. Christopher, Malinga's office assistant, had bought a small piece of property here many years ago with the shillings he'd saved from renting one of his rooms. The value of his property was taking off, but he had no proof of ownership and was now being threatened by eager developers.

Malinga was following his case closely, providing what help she could.

She glanced at her daughter when Katanga coughed. "The air's so hazy," Malinga said. "Lusaka needs to ban open fires, or we'll all die of emphysema. Isn't your place near here, Bertha?"

Her maid pointed to the next right, and Malinga turned into a rutted alley barely large enough for the car, lined by neat houses with tiny gardens framed by hedges and flowers planted near the doorways. The largest had two rooms with an outhouse in the back. Fetched from common taps, city water was expensive and inevitably spread cholera during November and December's heavy rains, when Kalingalinga, like other poor compounds in Lusaka, floated in its own sewerage.

"Our children are dying like rats because they are drinking that dirty water," Bertha complained, her face bitter. "Boys with bad tummies relieve themselves in plastic bags and throw them into our gardens. When boys grow up like that, our girls will not marry well. It is a curse from God."

"I heard that two children died last year, washed away by the floods," Katanga said. "And some of the houses collapsed."

"More than one hundred. God is angry, that is what I am saying. Women must obey their husbands, stop wearing trousers, playing football, boxing, going to bars."

"But Esther Phiri is an international star," Katanga objected. "When she wins boxing matches, she shows us how much girls can do. And Mom wears trous . . ." She stopped when Malinga squeezed her thigh.

"We have sinned against God," Bertha intoned. "The Bible warns us, but we take no heed. We must listen to our ancestors and change our ways before it is too late." Malinga bit her tongue. She was annoyed, but not a little relieved that her new maid was so conservative. Most of the 'charms' of city life would be too sinful to appeal to her.

Malinga skirted one last muddy rut and drew the Land Cruiser up near Bertha's tiny yard. When she looked over her shoulder to back up, something slapped her windscreen so hard she jumped.

"Mommy!" Katanga whispered, eyes wide. "That man just hit us with a chicken!"

9 | Grant Me Three Wishes

"I'm not perfect," Victor said, "but make no mistake. I am the world's best. I wanted to become even better, but then this happened!" He jerked his hands up in shaky rage. "My Parkinson's is progressing so quickly I can barely speak. I've tried everything to stop it, even this!" He lifted his hat to show Stewart the electrodes protruding from his scalp, and smiled at the shock on Stewart's face. "Shake your head all you like," Von Sorge said, "but it's slowed my disease. With God's help, of course. Do you believe in God, Stewart?"

Stewart nodded but looked away. The man was experimenting on himself. Von Sorge at a distance was an undeniable genius, but in the flesh, he was positively repulsive.

"I've matured into a man of faith," Victor confessed. "At the apex of the church I built in Germany is a crimson figure on a cross. The fat, muscle, bone, and connective tissue have been stripped away, leaving only the heart and the blood vessels. They are the essence of a man."

When Stewart said nothing, Victor fixed him with a stubborn stare. "Faith is important, Stewart, but it's not everything. Money also counts. Nothing in life is free."

"No. No, of course not," Stewart said, tensing.

"I'm glad you agree. It's time that we talked business." Von Sorge leaned forward and rubbed his hands together, a new fire burning in his eyes. "If you want to be my partner, you must grant me three wishes. You must help me complete three things before I die."

"If I can, Victor," Stewart said. "I'll do my best."

"You'll do better than that, Stewart. You must agree to our terms. Anita has prepared a contract for you to sign."

"Contract?"

"Of course, Stewart. We'll be investing heavily in you. Such an arrangement requires more than simple trust. It is natural that we want something back."

"Back?"

"Yes, Stewart," Victor said, doing his best to smile gently. "Do not worry. As my fairy godfather, it will be easy for you to grant my wishes. Here is the first."

Stewart swallowed but said nothing.

"I have nine exhibitions touring the world," Von Sorge continued. "The most popular features a giraffe, an oryx, and an ostrich. They are good, but the most important animal is still missing." He paused. "Like I told you on the telephone, it has always been my ambition to plastinate an elephant! Do you remember?"

"Of course I do. It's a very good idea, I agree, but it may not be as easy to get an elephant as you think. Since the police recovered elephant ivory from poachers in Asia last year, the Wildlife Authority is guarding them like hawks. The case was very famous."

Victor's mouth jerked downwards. "But Stewart. You know how much this means to me!"

"Yes I do, Victor," Stewart said, rubbing his forehead. "Don't worry. I'll find a way, I promise. I'll put some feelers out, but I must be careful to find the right people. One of the poachers escaped, but there are still people at the Wildlife Authority who will help. You've got to give me some time to feel them out."

Victor raised his shaking hands. "As you can see, Stewart, time is something I don't have."

Stewart cleared his throat. "Then you might have more luck in Central African Republic or Chad. Any country with a civil war. The rebels are taking elephants from them like crazy."

"I thought of that, Stewart, but decided against it. The elephants in those countries are too small," Victor complained.

Stewart nodded. "Zambian elephants are masterpieces, I must admit. Let me think about it a little more. I'll come up with something."

"Victor dreams of plastinating a blue whale, Stewart," Anita said languidly. "Thank God you don't live near the ocean."

Victor glared at her. "I dream of many things, *Liebchen*. The elephant is a small beginning. I plan to do much, much more. But it's something I can only do here, in Africa, with you, Stewart. We will make history, you and I."

"History," Stewart said resignedly. "It will be the Crown of Your Career."

"Yes, Stewart! The Project of a Lifetime."

Stewart sighed and rubbed his eyes. Victor held out his glass. "May I have a little more brandy? I must sleep soon, but first I want to tell you what my other wishes are."

Stewart filled their glasses. Victor lifted his in salute. "Here's to God, that Bloody Bastard! He never gives you what you want in life, only what he thinks you deserve!"

They touched glasses and tossed the amber liquid back. Von Sorge closed his eyes. The silence deepened and his breathing became regular. Stewart looked over and saw no life. He was afraid Victor had fallen asleep. "The rest of your wishes, Victor. What are they?" he prompted.

Victor's eyes jerked open. "They are spectacular, Stewart, I assure you, but I cannot realize them without your help."

"Of course, Victor. I'll do everything I can. Together we can make your dreams come true. The world owes it to you." And to me, Stewart thought, if the profits are as big as Victor seems to think they are. He smiled.

"Thank you," Victor murmured. "You'll make my life's work complete." The anatomist sighed and shut his eyes. When he snored, Stewart's heart sank. He inched forward and peered down. Victor was sleeping, deeply and completely, the drool running down his chin and his legs pumping as though he were running from an enemy.

Maybe he's being chased by an elephant, Stewart thought. He thrust out a hand to shake the man's shoulder, but drew it back when Victor cried out. Stewart knew he couldn't wait until morning to hear the rest of Victor's demands, but did he dare wake God's Chosen One in the middle of a dream?

10 | Quiet as a Leopard

The chicken hit her windscreen a second time, its poop splattering everywhere. Malinga shook her head.

Great. First Bertha's fundamentalism and now assault with a filthy chicken. I should have stayed in bed.

When the *sangoma* drew his arm back to strike her windscreen again, Malinga opened her door and grabbed his wrist. The chicken took off with an outraged squawk, leaving a white streak across her car's bonnet.

"What do you think you're doing?" she asked, twisting the *sangoma's* arm behind his back and pushing his body tight to the fender. The man was strong, but when she realized that he was also very old, she eased up. "You must be careful. You nearly broke my windscreen."

He glanced back at her with glassy eyes but said nothing. There was no struggle left in his wiry body, dirty and barely covered by ragged western clothing. His face was painted like a traditional healer, circles drawn with ashes around his eyes.

Bertha cried out when Malinga turned him over. "Madam! That's Kaseka Chelwa!" she cried. "Our *sangoma*! What is he doing here? Something must be wrong. The doctor gave him medicine, but he is sicker than before. We must help him or he will die! He has helped so many of us in the compound."

"Let's walk him to his house," Malinga suggested.

"No," Bertha said. "He lives too far away! Sit him on the bench near my door and I will give him some water. He's a very old man. He needs something to drink." One look at his dilated pupils told Malinga that he needed more than something to drink. He was showing the effects of a very strong hallucinogen.

Reflexively, she flipped open her cell phone to call the station for backup, then remembered the department's non-existent petrol budget and snapped it shut. It's better not to call them anyway, she thought as she and Bertha braced the man between them and walked him to the bench. The police would assume Bertha was associated with the healer, and Bertha would become an automatic suspect whenever there was trouble in the compound.

I don't want to be without a maid again.

The old man's knees gave out. Malinga pulled him up from the ground and braced him against her side. He smelled rank, and he was surprisingly heavy, weighted down by a sack slung across his back. When she reached for it, his small hand snaked out and his fingernails bit into her wrist. He twisted hard, then pushed her away.

"No," he muttered, fixing her with an icy stare. More alert than she expected, he was surprisingly strong for someone so old.

"Madam, you go," Bertha urged Malinga. "I will take him to his place."

"Thanks, Bertha. I hope he feels better," she said although she doubted the effects of the drug he'd taken would wear off soon. As Malinga put her arm around Katanga's shoulder and turned toward the car, she heard the *sangoma*'s voice.

"Inspector Malinga," he cried. "I must tell you something!"

She hurried Katanga into the car and turned back to him. "Old man," she said, "how do you know my name?"

"Your picture is in the newspaper," he said with a soft croak of laughter. "You know our troubles, it is true, and we are grateful. But those you are seeking are Big Men. Very, very big. Too powerful for you. You must stop or they will bring you great trouble."

"Do not worry, old man," Malinga replied. "We police are trained. We will get the killer, not the other way around. We have powers of our own, just like you."

"Yes, you are powerful," the old man said, "but watch out. Stay out of the newspapers. Do not be so loud saying what women need from their husbands. These are *muti* murders, nothing more. Very bad magic. Do not shout about it."

"But who will speak for these girls?" she demanded.

He shrugged. "Their parents, if they are lucky. But few parents will speak out for girl children. They are more interested in finding someone who will buy their girls as wives. Look at the Archbishop. He sold his own niece for *muti* to defeat a rival witch." When he saw the skepticism on her face, he nodded vehemently. "It is true. Even the Archbishop. Every businessman wants *muti*, every student, every man who can't sex his woman enough to keep her. Stay out of it and you will be safe."

Malinga shook her head. "Nonsense, old man. This monster is killing girls, threatening my children, my neighbors' children, and the children of this compound. I must stop him."

"He will kill again. Each time his victim will be younger. I have one word of advice for you, Mama Policeman. Be as quiet as a leopard if you hunt him. Stay out of the newspapers or he will come for you and your daughter." He smirked in Katanga's direction.

Malinga grabbed his shirt and pulled him up. "What do you mean? Do you know more than you are telling me?" He shook his head so hard, his necklace rattled and the feathers in his scrappy headdress nodded wildly.

She scowled at him. "You must get rid of your dangerous superstitions, old man."

His head fell back and his eyes fluttered shut. He was limp, almost comatose. Bertha knelt and pressed a cold cloth over his eyes. She looked up at Malinga and scowled.

"Leave him, Madam. You must go. He is telling you crazy things. You must go." When Malinga didn't move, Bertha stood and put her hands on her hips.

"You are cursed, Madam. Cursed. You must stop acting like a man."

11 | Noah's Ark

Stewart tugged gently at Von Sorge's sleeve. "Doctor!" he whispered. The man flinched but snored on. Stewart raised his voice. "Doctor! Wake up!"

Victor opened his eyes with a jerk and scanned the room frantically. Stewart patted his shoulder. "Everything's all right, Victor. You're in my home. You arrived just a few hours ago, remember?" Von Sorge looked doubtful.

Anita raised her voice. "Victor, you're in Zambia. It's all right. You're in Stewart Bleming's house."

Victor saw her and a smile crooked across his face. "Ah, *Liebchen*. It's so good to hear your voice. I was dreaming that I was dead."

"No, Victor. You are not dead."

"I would gladly die for the dream I was having," Victor said, chuckling. He began to choke and cough. When Anita reached to wipe the sputum off his jacket, he pulled back.

"Don't touch me!" he roared. "I will take care of it myself!"

"Of course, *Liebchen*." Anita looked at Stewart and rolled her eyes. He nodded sympathetically.

"I dreamt I was leading an anatomical safari," Victor said.

"A hunting expedition?"

Victor's face clouded. "No, Stewart. A safari. It was like Noah's Ark." Stewart raised his eyebrows. Noah's Ark meant lots of animals, two of every kind.

"Just think of it, Stewart! We will recreate Noah's Ark, a great plastinated pageant of beings. Everyone who sees it will have a vision of God's grand design."

Anita smiled wryly. "I think his grand design is very apparent, Victor. Just look at you!"

Victor cackled dryly. "I'm serious, *Liebchen*. The elephant will be the crowning touch. It will be inspirational, spiritual, metaphysical! Like a message from God himself," Von Sorge crowed. "It will be the Crown of My Career. The Project of My Lifetime. And yours, Stewart." He smiled, his eyes wide and unblinking.

Stewart sat back and grinned despite himself. "It's a jolly good idea Victor, but . . ."

Von Sorge frowned at him and jerked his body forward. "No 'buts', Stewart! You are so English with these 'buts.' Stop being so timid! The animals will be wonderful. You'll see what I am saying once we assemble them." Victor's cheeks spasmed as he tried to grin. "But first, you must find the elephant. It's central to the final tableau."

Stewart thought about how shocked Malinga would be when she saw the show. She'd spent months going after the poachers who had ruthlessly murdered ten elephants in Kafue National Park. When her children were threatened, she'd rescued them. Her love affair with Eitone had been strengthened by a shared commitment to save elephants' lives. Although Eitone had abandoned her and run off with the tusks she'd retrieved from the Asian bandits, she still believed in his innocence. Plastinating one of Kafue's beloved elephants would challenge everything she believed. It would shake her very world.

Stewart laughed. "Like I said, Victor. It's a bit difficult, but I'll find a way."

Victor snorted. "The elephant is the easy part, Stewart. Wait until I tell you my second wish!"

"Easy? The elephant is easy?" Stewart said, laughing nervously. Easy for you to say, he thought, eyeing the anatomist skeptically. "Okay, Victor. I'm all ears. What's the hard part?"

12 | William's Warning

Bertha's condemnation startled Malinga, but she suppressed her anger and forced a smile. "It seems, Bertha," she said softly, "that we'll have to agree to disagree about that. Enjoy your time with your children. I'll see you on Monday." She dusted off the legs of her pants and walked to the car. Katanga's eyes were wide. "Don't worry," Malinga told her as she opened the car door. "This old man is like all *sangomas*. They help people but sometimes they go too far. Myth and magic hold Zambia back."

"I know that's true of most witch doctors, Mummy," Katanga said, turning toward her on the seat. "But this one is different. He's Redbone, the witch doctor on the telly. He can cure absolutely anything!"

"I'm sure he can, but he's not going to cure anyone right now. Let's get out of here. Put on your seatbelt. The road is bad."

The fact that witch doctors enjoyed a flourishing business annoyed Malinga profoundly. Advertising flyers handed to motorists stopped at intersections proclaimed their powers to find you a wife, make you sexually potent or fertile, get you a promotion or a new car. Even some of the chiefs, trained in the arcane arts, exploited the gullible to earn pocket change. Malinga was too far removed from village life to believe in supernatural powers, but she respected witchcraft's social power.

"I laugh at the stories, but I still knock on wood," she'd once told Davison.

"And you should, Boss," he'd replied. "These guys know how to make their predictions come true."

Asedi had shuddered. "They speak to the spirits of our ancestors. How can we ignore them?"

As Malinga drove toward the main road, William the Bicycle Man waved her down. She lowered the car window to greet him. "Mum, can I speak with you a minute?" he asked. "In my workshop? Let Katanga stay here."

Malinga got out of the car to follow him, flipping the door locks closed. She looked back at her daughter. "Stay here, Katanga. I won't be a minute. William probably needs a loan for some family problem."

He drew her to the back of his workshop, where they could not be seen or heard from the street, and pretended to show her a bike. "Mum," he whispered. "When I saw you with Redbone, I was frightened. I hear there will be more killings. More girls and women will die, and you will be one of them."

Malinga laughed and patted his hand. "If I had one hundred dollars for every time I've been threatened, William, I would be a very rich person."

"No, Madam. No." He shook his head, frowning. "This time it is different. There is something very, very evil here in Kalingalinga. Redbone is part of it, and so is his son, Kivuli, who is back from South Africa. Even the son's name is evil. It means shadow, or ghost. The man who is dead but still looks alive. No one calls their child Kivuli unless they want to invite trouble. Only a man as arrogant as Redbone would do such a thing."

"Okay, William. We'll look into it. Thank you for warning us." She smiled. "Now, how is your fam . . . "

"No, no, Madam," he interrupted, leaning closer. "Do not make light of this. I have heard things. You must be careful. Do not pretend this is not real. Pay attention or you will be dead. If not for yourself, do it for your daughter."

Malinga felt a cold shiver run down her back. She pulled her card from her bag. "Here's my cell phone number," she'd said. "Call me immediately if you hear anything else."

William nodded. "Be careful, Madam. Don't play with these people. They are very, very dangerous."

13 | The Second Wish

Victor was gloating. Stewart's frustration amused him.
He drew in a deep breath and spoke patiently, like he would to a
child. "Every show must have a theme, Stewart. There must be
one tableau that hits the visitor between the eyes. I see the Heights
of Paradise: Eve and Her Children, Riding on the Back of an
Elephant!"

Stewart frowned. "Not only do you need an elephant, you
need a mother and child. Am I hearing you right?"

"Yes, Stewart. That is my second wish. We must
plastinate a mother and her child."

Stewart laughed nervously. "Has someone volunteered?"

Victor laughed with him. "No, Stewart. Most of my
donors don't come to me until they are well past child-bearing age.
I have no volunteers for this job. You'll have to find them."

Stewart couldn't hide his surprise. "I don't understand,
Victor. Where do you think I will 'find' these 'volunteers'?"

"You'll find them the same way you've found your other
women, Stewart."

Horrified, Stewart shook his head. "But Victor!
Harvesting a mother and child would be unethical."

Victor smiled. "That's where you're wrong, Stewart. It
would be an invaluable contribution to science, to our knowledge
of children's anatomy. If we could plastinate a few African
children, we could help millions!"

"But Victor . . ."

"No buts, Stewart," he said, wagging a shaking forefinger.
"So many of these African children will never survive. You said
yourself that you were doing these girls a favor because they were
bleaching their skin. Many of these small African children never
even get that far."

Stewart paled. How could he help this man kill the very children he'd come to Africa to save?

"Stewart! Don't look so distressed!" Von Sorge said. "You know as well as I do that scientists – reputable ones – have been experimenting on African children for decades. Polio vaccines, AIDS, Ebola. They still do it. And if we exhibit a mother and child, people will see how traits are inherited."

Stewart stopped shaking his head. "What you say about the experiments is true. I've seen some myself. From that perspective, I suppose you're right."

"The mother and child are critically important, Stewart. Our viewers will be walking through paradise and it will be incomplete without them!"

"The show you describe would be enormously successful. I just don't know if we can get the specimens you want."

"Please be more optimistic Stewart, more determined! In the interest of science if nothing else. My critics call me Dr. Death, but I bring new life to every creature in my exhibits. Forty million people have seen them already, but I promise you, Stewart, Noah's Ark will break all records!"

Anita stood up and put her hands on her hips. Stewart thought the pale woman, flush with anger, looked rather pretty. "Really, Victor! Stewart must focus on supplying bodies for medical education. We have unfilled orders from universities all over the world. Cyprus, Ghana, and India are still waiting for exhibits! You can follow your dreams once we are financially independent, *Liebchen*."

Victor glared at her. "You are right, my darling, but I'm pressed by time. Soon, this disease will overtake me completely and without warning. If I am too practical, it may be too late. You know this is the Crown of my Career."

Stewart grinned. "The Project of a Lifetime."

Anita sighed and extended an arm to help Victor to his feet. He coughed and struggled for breath, but he waved Anita away for the third time. When she looked at Stewart beseechingly, he realized that if he played Victor right, he could take over his entire empire. Including Anita.

Victor's voice drew his attention back from his vision. "You know, Stewart, I saw a Zambian woman on television during our layover in Johannesburg. A policewoman, very beautiful, who would be perfect. Her body is divine! Fit and well proportioned, and she has very large eyes and a small crown of soft hair. Maybe we could use her." His eyes jerked toward Stewart's face. Von Sorge tried to wink, but his lid stuck halfway. Irritated, he reached up and shoved it up.

"You said you often work with the police. Do you know her, by chance?"

14 | A Ghost Before Death

As Malinga threaded the Cruiser back onto Thabo Mbeki Road, the sky opened up in a torrential downpour. Thunder rumbled and lightning lit the underside of the lowering clouds. She turned down the air conditioner. William's warning had chilled her, but she found it hard to take Redbone seriously. He was a man who enjoyed his own dramas.

William was serious, a solid Christian, and head of his compound watch association. His implication that Katanga, if not both of her children, could be targets for the murderer panicked her momentarily, but she knew she had to stay calm. The girls' murders were frightening, but she couldn't be carried away by rumor.

She breathed in deeply and took her daughter's hand. "I remember when Arcades was a cow pasture and Manda Hill a tiny huddle of shops. Before you were born, there was nothing here. We all shopped in the traditional markets downtown."

Katanga smiled. "I like going downtown. Levy Junction has some great stores. But I want to check out the 3D cinema in Manda Hill first." Lightning struck the field next to them. "I think it hit the Parliament Hotel," Katanga said, straining to look back.

As Malinga turned into the car park at Eco Bank, the line of cars she was following came to a standstill. The Arcades Mall parking lot was a giant puddle. The street kids' drum and kazoo band ran for cover, and flea market vendors were pulling down the sides of their tents.

Ignoring the rain, Katanga flipped her seat belt open when the car came to a stop and was out the door before Malinga could pull the key from the ignition. She caught up with her daughter inside Celestin's Palace of Luxurious Beautification, behind the first strip of shops off the car park.

The shop was buzzing. Its Paris-trained owner, Congolese-born Celestin Kabila, his wife Josephine, and six other hairdressers catered to a salon full of women, providing elaborate weaves and long, flowing Brazilian extensions. Josephine ushered them toward the back of the shop. Hip hop music blared, competing with the din of women comparing hairstyles and clothing. Hair and nail products perfumed the air.

Katanga's friend Margaret and her mother Patricia's elaborately braided copper and brown styles were still under construction when Malinga and Katanga walked past. Realizing their hairdos were a mirror image, Malinga smiled. "It looks like you two are going to a party."

Patricia sighed with great satisfaction. "We are preparing for our regular mother-daughter shopping trip to Jo'burg. We go to South Africa every few months to get out of this dreary place. You should go. It would do wonders for you."

Malinga shook her head. "Not on my budget." She fingered her short hair. "I just need a trim," she told Celestin, "but I think Katanga wants something more elaborate." While the natural Malinga had worn ever since she noticed her hairline moving steadily upward from constant braiding earned her the frequent criticism that she'd 'gone bush,' it was better than going bald.

When they reached the end of the line, Katanga jumped in the empty chair and smiled up at the owner. "I bet Celestin agrees with me, Mum! He told me last time that I would look nice if I had lighter skin like you."

The Congolese grinned broadly, swirling a cloak around the girl's shoulders and fastening it firmly in the back. "I can speak for no one else, but I am so happy to be white," he said in a booming voice. Many of the women in the salon smiled in agreement and nodded. He winked at Malinga. "Right now, Katanga looks more like Josephine's daughter than yours."

Josephine gave her husband a playful slap on the shoulder. "Malinga is *café au lait*. Katanga is like me. The darkest, most expensive *chocolat* you can buy."

"Katanga's father is light," Malinga said, "and so are her grandparents. So it skipped a generation, but it must be somewhere on the family tree."

Josephine laughed. "It's still no reason to bleach. Your skin is beautiful and so is Katanga's."

"Ah, but look how beautiful bleaching has made my skin," Celestin said. "Four years I have been faithful with the injections. Each one lasts a month. They are *tres chere*, so very expensive! But worth every Rand I pay!"

"When your face falls off, you'll pay an even higher price!" Malinga said.

"That won't happen. The injections are so much better than the pills or creams," Celestin argued.

Malinga shook her head. "Either way, it's like braiding your hair all the time. Sooner or later, all of it falls out, so what good does it do?"

He tossed his head. "For me, it is a godsend. When I was a boy, every day I ask the Lord, 'Why you make me black?' I never liked my black skin. One day, God, he send me the answer. I read about that beautiful singer in Cape Town. She is three shades lighter. How is this possible? Injections! So I get them. God finally gives me the skin that is truly mine."

He did a little spin behind Katanga's chair. "God helps those who help themselves," he continued. "My mother bleach me when I was a baby boy, like Michael Jackson. Now I am gorgeous. Black skin, people think it is dangerous. People treat me good now because I look white."

He laughed at Malinga's frown. "Do not worry! I am still black on the inside. I think black. I have black kids. Me, I am a boy of the compounds. But I love the white skin! Like that singer from South Africa."

"Giselle?"

"Yes, yes. That is her. She bleaches, and so do half the dark ladies in South Africa."

"Giselle is Zambian, you know."

Celestin laughed. "That explains why she is so beautiful. That and the bleaching. You see those Nigerian movie stars? The highest bleaching rate on earth . . ." His voice trailed off when Malinga's frown deepened.

Celestin ruffled Katanga's hair and winked. "But, my girl, you must wait. This place, this Lusaka, it is so small, so pro-veen-chee-al" – he drew out the word for its comic effect— "that any decision you make here will seem like the wrong one once you are in the beeg world! In Europe, they like us dark. The darker the better. When you go to London, you will be glad you never bleached."

Josephine wagged her finger at Celestin. "This husband of mine. He want me to bleach, but I tell him if he want a white woman, marry one. That man will learn his lesson one day with his bleach. It is a wish for death."

She leaned forward, her voice dropping to a whisper. "Being white is like being a ghost before you are dead. *Mzungu*, you know? White, aimless. A little bit crazy. They think they are gods, doing good for mankind! They don't know the evil they do."

15 | Eve and Her Children

When Stewart realized that Victor was talking about Malinga, he nearly laughed. This was a comeuppance beyond his wildest imagination. "As a matter of fact, Victor, I know her quite well. I work with her."

"You work with her?"

"As a forensic consultant. But she's raising such a fuss about these girls, it's getting very difficult to collect new specimens. She'd really beginning to annoy me."

"Ah! So this is the bloody woman you told me about." Victor smiled. "Then it's settled. Once she joins our group of cadaver-volunteers, she won't bother you anymore."

Stewart laughed. "Right as usual, old man. It'll be hard for her to bother me if she's dead. I know her very well. The entire family trusts me."

"If they trust you, it will be even easier."

Stewart frowned. "That's true, but she's a Deputy Inspector of Police. An extremely visible person. And her children are so young, I would hate . . ."

"Don't worry. Eve needs Her Children."

Stewart could see Katanga and Shiko in his mind's eye. He knew that if he agreed to this, he'd be crossing the final line. He shook his head again. "Malinga's one thing, but the children have done nothing to me. They visit me. I'm like an uncle. It doesn't seem quite right."

"Would it be better to leave them orphaned?"

Stewart looked up, startled. "I suppose not."

"We would, in fact, be doing them a favor. They'd be with their mother for eternity."

"I suppose," Stewart said. "They would certainly be easy to capture. My maid, Bertha – the woman who served you tonight

– works for Malinga, too. A Trojan Horse, so to speak, is already in Malinga's stable." With a little bit of cunning, Stewart knew he could throw the witch doctors under the wheels of the bus at the same time.

"If you think about it," Victor said, narrowing his eyes and grinning slyly, "it's the perfect crime, not only for us, but for the victims. They'll disappear completely, and no one will be the wiser. At the same time, they will fulfill a much higher role."

Stewart nodded enthusiastically. "It's true. As a policewoman, Malinga's bound to meet a violent death sooner o later, and her children will be left destitute. We will save them the anguish of their destiny."

Victor beamed. "Eve and her offspring, riding on the back of the elephant, immortalized forever but completely unrecognizable. The perfect crime and the perfect exhibit at the same time."

"This deserves a toast," Stewart said, raising his glass. "To Malinga, the Perfect Eve, Victim of the Perfect Crime. It's perfectly fitting!"

Anita laughed and raised her snifter. "White, black, yellow or brown. Without their skins, they all look the same."

Stewart looked at her, a smile slowly forming on his face. "Once she's gone, I'll be able to grow your business in southern Africa without limit. It will be easy once we get rid of her."

Victor finished his brandy and set down his glass. "You look very happy, Stewart."

"For good reason. Your idea is wonderful, Victor."

"Bloody wonderful," Victor agreed. "But time is of the essence. How soon can we assemble the specimens?"

"It will take a few weeks. I'm sure you appreciate how risky it is, attacking a Deputy Inspector of Police."

Victor shook his head and waved his hands as though he could banish trouble from the air. "I don't have a few weeks, Stewart. I only have a few days."

"A few days? I can't possibly move that fast."

Victor shrugged. "I don't care how you do it, but we must move quickly. I need to gather all the specimens and return to Germany within a week. No longer."

Stewart frowned. "That's impossible. If we move too fast, we're bound to make mistakes. You don't want to spend the rest of your life in a Zambian jail."

"I know it's dangerous, Stewart, but we can do it, I'm sure of it. We just need a plan." They sat for a moment, thinking. Then Victor's face brightened. "What is the one thing any mother would kill for?"

Stewart's eyes widened. "Her children, of course."

"Of course. We can lure her into a trap if we baited it with her children. Invite them here, Stewart. You said you know them well and they have visited your home before."

"I could invite them for tea," Stewart said, nodding. "Bertha can bake their favorite sweets, so their last few hours on earth are happy. I'll put something in the biscuits, so they'll never know a thing." He smiled at Victor and Anita and felt enormously pleased.

Suddenly, he sensed something new in the air, like the national stadium after Zambia won an especially important match. It was the smell of victory. Malinga and her children would come in an instant if they believed they could meet Giselle. He clapped his hands for joy. "I have a very good idea, Victor, but let me think it through a bit more before I tell you."

"Don't take too long, Stewart. We only have a few more days."

"I think I've got the answer we need," Stewart said. "I'm sure it will work."

"I'm sure it will," Anita said, catching Stewart's eye as they helped Victor straighten up in his chair. Stewart returned her gaze. "You catch on very quickly, *Liebchen*," she said, winking.

Stewart blushed as he returned her wink. She was really quite lovely. If her husband was out of the picture, he just might win her along with the rest of Victor's empire. He tilted his brandy glass toward her in a discrete salute.

"Yes I do, Anita. Yes, I do."

16 | She Dropped the Boys

Katanga looked up at Josephine, suddenly thoughtful. "Ghosts, eh? Let me think about that." Then she looked at Malinga and grinned. "If I can't bleach my skin, can Celestin bleach my hair? Please, mum? Please? Just the tips?"

Celestin laughed. "I can braid the sides, twist them into a Mohawk, and bleach the very top bright orange!"

Katanga squealed. "Celestin! That hairdo's in my magazine," she said, rummaging in her backpack. "Here it is! Look!" She showed her mother. "It would be great on me. Please please please!"

"Okay, okay, okay!" Malinga said, laughing and patting her daughter's knee. "Won't you miss your dreadlocks? They took so long to grow."

Katanga shook her head. "I know, Mummy, but they get so heavy."

"Well then, Katanga! Let's see what a Mohawk looks like on you. Celestin, work your magic!"

Malinga sat down in front of Josephine, who gave her a scalp massage, staving off a nascent tension headache, one of the many she'd had since they'd discovered the first girl's flayed body dumped in a Lusaka side street. She tilted Malinga's chair back and lifted her head to cushion her neck with a soft cotton towel. Placing cotton pads over her eyes, she began brushing a warm, soft wax and acid mixture on Malinga's face. Celestin looked over and grunted.

"Eh. Malinga! While you are getting your face peeled, tell us about these poor girls. All so beautiful! All so busy getting peeled, but not *voluntaire* like you."

Josephine glared at her husband. "Celestin! Enough joking!" She lowered her tobacco-stained voice and whispered. "But he is right, Malinga. You must tell us what is going on. We are all so frightened. Everyone thinks Zambia is so peaceful. That is why we came here from the Congo."

Malinga kept her eyes firmly shut and said nothing.

"Malinga, you must tell us. The presidential election put everyone on tension. He is so against foreigners. If the President doesn't stop, we Congolese will be in trouble, targeted by copycats. "

Malinga tried not to listen, but Josephine persisted. "You Zambians blame everything on us. You think we are all murderers. You think we play with *muti* all the time. No. We are ordinary, just like you, working and taking care of our kids."

"The outbreak of petty violence in Kitwe frightens me," a second woman said. "Why should a man be allowed to take a woman's skirt because he thinks it is too short?" Malinga agreed, but knew it wasn't the time or place to discuss police business.

"It is like the Taliban!' Josephine said. "Here in Zambia, women should not be hurt because of what they wear!"

One of the customers looked over at her. "These Lusaka killings are not the same as the problems in Kitwe. They are well organized, not random like taking girls' skirts. Here, there is one killer, and he is making a coat from the women's skins, like the movie."

When everyone gasped, Celestin laughed. "I hear that many women are buying human skin for transplants. If you bleach too much, your skin gets weak and you need trans . . . No, no, not transplants. How you say it in English?" He snapped his fingers. "Not transplants. Grafts! Like patching a bicycle tire."

Malinga glanced at her daughter, sitting oblivious under a dryer. "Celestin, for heaven's sake," she whispered. "Katanga shouldn't hear this. I'll come back later to talk with you in private. For now, it's better to say no more."

"You will be surprised by what I tell you," he murmured. "It is true. Some of the very women you know, some of your friends. Maybe even some of the women who are seated here," he hissed.

A few of the women in the salon looked down, earnestly perusing their magazines, while others searched their purses. Malinga decided to break the tension and cleared her throat. "Did you hear that Thandiswa Mazwai is coming to town? Are you going to the concert?"

"Thandiswa," one of the women cheered. "I'm so glad she split with Bongo Maffin."

"When she dropped The Boys, her career took off," agreed another. "Maybe we should take a hint!" The women laughed and chatter in the salon returned to a normal level. As if on cue, the sun broke through the clouds. Malinga's microdermabrasion started to itch. Josephine removed the wrap and rinsed her face gently with cotton balls.

"Here. Put on a little sunscreen," she advised. "You must be careful or you will have an orange face like women using those cheap peels. Yours will be beautiful if you are careful in the sun."

Malinga caught her daughter's eye and smiled. "Your hair looks great, Katanga!" The girl looked down at her toes, suddenly bashful. Malinga reached out and lifted her chin so she could look into her eyes. Her smile deepened.

"Come on, Katanga. It's time for lunch at the Mint Café. Let's go before all the best tables are taken."

Katanga jumped down from her chair and grinned shyly up at her mother. Malinga's heart flip-flopped.

My job takes me away from the children far too much. Their childhood is slipping away too fast.

She grabbed her daughter and hugged her tight. When Katanga didn't pull away as she usually did, dread crept through Malinga's body.

The girls he's killing aren't much older than Katanga.

She shivered, then pushed the idea out of her head. "Let's go get some lunch," she said, throwing her arm around her daughter's shoulder, wishing it were an invincible shield.

17 | My Third Wish

Stewart wrenched his gaze from Anita's face and tried to compose himself. She giggled and pulled on Victor's arm. "Let's go to bed, *Liebchen*. I'm tired. We need to sleep," she said, gazing all the while into Stewart's eyes.

Victor yanked his arm from her grasp and shook his head angrily. "It's not time for bed yet, Anita. Stewart and I have one more thing to discuss." He jerked his head toward the doctor. "Something is missing, Stewart. Can you tell me what it is?"

"Missing? What's missing?" Stewart tried to focus, but he could think of nothing but Anita's full lips.

Von Sorge started to laugh. "That's what I'm asking you, Stewart. What's missing from our image of Paradise?"

"Missing? From the tableau?" Stewart's eyes flicked back to Anita and she winked provocatively. "I'm not sure, Victor. What's missing?"

"It's easy, Stewart. In our Vision of Paradise, one person is missing. Who is it?"

Stewart scratched his head. "Sorry, it's a bit late and I've been up all night."

"So have I, my friend! We won't be much longer, so don't spoil things. You must guess!" Victor said in his butterfly voice, humor shining in his eyes.

Stewart swallowed his annoyance. "Sorry, Victor. I can't."

"Eve, the children, and . . ."

"The elephant?"

Victor broke into a choked guffaw. "No, no! Stewart! You're not thinking."

Stewart was growing increasingly impatient. "Just tell me Victor. Please. Who's missing?"

"Ah, Stewart. I'm so disappointed in you. Who was in the Garden with Eve? Who created her?"

Stewart gasped. "God?"

"Well, yes, technically that's true. But whose rib did he use to make the first woman, Stewart?"

Stewart rubbed his eyes, looked at Anita and shrugged. "I don't know, Victor."

"Adam, Stewart. Adam!"

"Oh, yes. Of course. I'm so tired, I'm afraid I'm not thinking straight," Stewart said, enormously relieved that the game was over.

"And who will be Adam, Stewart?"

The doctor shook his head wearily. If Victor didn't stop asking questions, he might die sooner than his doctors had predicted. Stewart exhaled. "I have no idea."

"Remember what I told you earlier," Victor coaxed. "About what I want after my death?"

Stewart rubbed his eyes again and let his shoulders sag. "Honestly, Victor. I can't do this anymore."

Victor started to laugh. "You bloody idiot!"

Stewart looked at him sharply.

"Stewart, Stewart. Isn't it obvious? Adam will be me!"

"But you're still alive!"

"Not for very long," Victor answered. "My doctors give me six months at the most."

Stewart felt a mix of pain and relief and ducked his head so Victor wouldn't see his face. "Sorry, Victor. I had no idea."

"Don't be sorry. We all have to die sometime."

"I guess."

"I'm more fortunate than most. I have a vision of my own life after death."

"Yes," Stewart said. "You would." He was weary to the bone, but knew they wouldn't finish until Victor was done. He rubbed his face with both hands and sank back into his chair. "Life after death, Victor?"

The corners of Victor's mouth jerked upward. "Yes, Stewart. Yes. When you are plastinated, you live forever!"

Stewart shrugged. "In a way I suppose you do, Victor."

"There's more, Stewart. When the visitors look at our tableau of Noah's Ark, they'll see a sea of animals and naked bodies. I alone will be clothed."

"Clothed?"

"I want people to focus on my genius, not my genitals."

"Victor will be the Crown of Creation," Anita said dryly.

Stewart suppressed a smile. "He certainly will."

"I will symbolize evolved man. Man the scientist, man the creator." Von Sorge said. "That is, until they walk around behind me. Then they will see me as God created me. They will see my back side, naked as the day I was born."

"Naked?" Stewart said. "Really? You want them to see your bum?"

Victor chortled and began choking again. Controlling it, he sighed. "I wish I could take credit for this wonderful idea, but it was Anita's." A smiled played around Anita's mouth, but she dropped her eyes when Stewart looked at her in surprise.

"You're sure you want that to be the last thing the public sees of you?" he asked Von Sorge.

"I never wanted to be God, Stewart. Adam is much more my style. The experimenting sinner who gives Mankind a gift: knowledge of who they really are. It's the legacy I want to leave."

Stewart nodded, thinking of Victor's naked bum retreating into destiny, and tried to keep a straight face. "Your legacy, Victor. That's quite extraordinary!"

"You understand me so well, Stewart. I have just decided that when I die, I want you to plastinate me. I must be in the hands of the very best!" Victor's head began to shake and Stewart realized the anatomist was crying.

"Of course, Victor. You can count on me." He placed his hands gently on Von Sorge's shoulders. "Why don't you two get a nap? Bertha will show you to your room. We can discuss this further over dinner."

"Not yet, Stewart," Victor said, holding up his hand. "I haven't finished. That is not my third wish, being Adam. That is a given. My third wish is quite different."

Stewart turned wearily and stood, hands at his sides. "Third wish. Okay, Victor. What is it?"

"My third wish is to exhibit an albino. I've been reading about the albino cases in Tanzania, Stewart. It would be really nice to have one for our exhibit."

Stewart's mouth dropped open. "An albino?"

"Yes. Range of human variation and all that kind of thing. We'll have to leave some of the poor bastard's skin on so people know what they're looking at. If I am not mistaken, your beautiful Deputy Inspector works with one."

"That's right, Victor. But it might be a little tricky to take two Deputy Inspectors at once." When he saw the disappointment on Von Sorge's face, Stewart hurried on. "It's not entirely out of the question, however. Let me think about it and we'll discuss it later. I have an important operation today and a meeting with Malinga's team. I've got to get some sleep."

He stood and stretched, hands at the small of his back. "One thing is certain. Once we've collected all your prizes, we'll have to disappear quickly."

"No problem," Victor said. "That's why we came in my private jet."

Chuckling in disbelief, Stewart bent to help Anita pull Von Sorge up from his chair. When he saw her nipples hard against the cashmere, he was embarrassed by the reaction below his belt. Anita is the exact opposite of my wife, he thought. An absolute strumpet! Not my type at all. But it had been so long since he'd been with a woman, he could barely take his eyes off her.

He blew out a long sigh, and noticed Anita's eyes on him. She looked almost hungry. With Victor in decline, it had been a long time since she'd been with a whole man.

He pulled his eyes away and straightened up. "Why don't you two relax and get some rest? I'll be back here as soon as the meeting at the police station is over," he said.

His eyes were drawn back to hers and Anita smiled. "Come as soon as you can, Stewart! We will miss you! We need your help so much!" Anita winked and wet her lips suggestively.

Stewart backed away. "I'll be back around eight." He nodded at his maid. "We'll have cocktails. Bertha's preparing dinner for us."

"I can't wait," the blonde said as she helped her husband straighten. Bertha took Victor's other elbow and they walked him to the door. Anita signaled Bertha to wait and rushed back to Stewart. She stood on tiptoe and brushed Stewart's cheek with her lips.

"I can't wait," she whispered into his ear, giving his arm a light squeeze.

18 | Skin for Grafts

Katanga kept her head down as they edged around the
puddles in the car park. Malinga leaned toward her. "You look
like you just came from London. Except," she said, grabbing her
daughter's shoulders to give her a quick hug, "you need some
jeans from X-Factor to go with your new look."

Katanga looked up at her, doubtful. "Do you really like it,
Mummy?"

"I love it," Malinga said. "I'd have mine cut like that if it
could fit under my uniform hat."

The Mint Café was bustling with noontime traffic.
Malinga chose a table for two on the terrace as far away from the
hookah-smoking teenage boys as she could get. It was all the rage
in Lusaka, along with the latest track shoes, smart phones, and 3-D
movies. Zambia's traditions were being replaced by fads from
abroad. The country's borders were so porous that anything could
enter, Malinga thought, including serial killers.

She was yanked from her daydream by Katanga's voice.
"Mummy, after we eat, can we go back to the store next to
Celestin's for my jeans? I only hope they have my size! I'm
always too tall!" When the waiter brought Katanga her Slimy
Dragon, Malinga started to tease her about the green health drink,
but stopped when the girl's face took on an expression of awe. She
glanced over her shoulder to see what she was staring at.

The woman was beautiful, stately as a queen, tall and
ethereal, her wide straw hat and the scarf beneath it flowing with
the rhythm of her walk, sunglasses covering her thin face. When
she walked up the terrace stairs, her body, pencil thin, was
outlined by her dress. The tiny grey dog tucked under her arm
was asleep.

As she drew closer, Malinga realized the face behind the
dark glasses was splotched, her knife-sharp features melted and

almost grotesque. Other people were staring, too. The woman pulled her hat brim down to shield herself from their prying eyes.

Katanga whispered, "Mummy, that's Giselle, the singer. She . . ." Her voice drifted off in confusion.

"Yes, Katanga," Malinga interrupted, reaching out to cover her daughter's hand with her own. "Let's not stare. It's never nice to do that to another person."

Katanga ducked her head. "I heard she was back from South Africa for a while," she whispered. "She had problems on her last concert tour and needed to see her doctor here in Zambia." She shook her head and her eyes grew even larger. "Do you believe we're actually seeing her? But what's wrong with her face?"

While some Zambians criticized Giselle for her ambition and fast living, almost every female Malinga knew secretly envied the star. But her daughter was right. Something was dreadfully wrong with the woman's face.

"I think she bleached too much." Malinga said quietly. "She's still lovely, don't you think?"

Katanga looked at her in surprise. "I thought you didn't like bleaching. Giselle has bleached forever. Even when she was here in Zambia."

"What happened to her in South Africa?" Malinga asked, knowing Katanga faithfully kept abreast of the tweets and gossip columns.

"I heard her band broke up, Mum, and her lead singer quit. They said she . . ."

Malinga's cell phone rang and she fished it out of her bag. It was her mother-in-law. Her ex-mother-in -law. Reluctantly, she opened the phone and put it to her ear. It was always bad news when Vivian called, and this was no exception. Malinga's ex-husband was supposed to take Shiko for the weekend, but something had come up at work. Vivian couldn't pitch in. She had bridge club all afternoon and then a kitchen party for one of her nieces.

"I can't possibly miss it," she breathed, "and Shiko can't possibly tag along. Can you imagine, Malinga? That cross-dressing gay dancer, Jones, is coming!" Malinga rolled her eyes. Jones was more important than her grandchildren, to be sure.

"I am so excited! Homosexuality may be illegal in Zambia, but who else could tell women so many things they didn't know about pleasing a man?" Malinga held the phone out from her ear and mouthed the word "Vivian" at her daughter. Katanga suppressed a giggle.

"And oh the dirty jokes that she-man tells! You know I'll have to stay there half the night. They will never let me go home sober," her mother-in-law cried. "And they take away our cell phones so we can't call for help. Or a taxi. One woman tried to walk home by herself last time and she was set upon by a gang of boys. It took her months to recover, but in confidence she told me she hadn't had such a good time in a long while!"

Malinga cut in. "Yes, Vivian. Thanks for calling. I can see that you're very, very busy. Let me try my parents and see if they're free."

"Ah yes, your parents. They live such a simple life, and they love the children, don't they?" Before Malinga could respond, Vivian pressed on. "Well then. It's settled. I'll tell Herbert to drop Shiko off at your parents' place."

Vivian hung up before Malinga could protest. She was fuming. "Katanga," she said, turning to her daughter. The girl had slipped from the table and was approaching Giselle for an autograph. When Malinga saw that the star was sitting with Stewart Bleming, the well-known English surgeon who helped her with forensics from time to time, she quickly paid the bill and walked over to their table. She wanted to talk with Stewart about the case and ask him if splitting Bertha's time still worked for him.

"Mummy, look!" Katanga said, holding up a menu with Giselle's signature.

"I hope she hasn't been bothering the two of you," Malinga said, putting her arm around her daughter's shoulders. "She's such a fan of yours, Giselle. So am I." Malinga smiled at the doctor. "Nice to see you, too, Stewart. I was meaning to call and remind. If you have some time this afternoon, I'd appreciate it if you'd drop by the station and talk to my team about this case. We found another body last night."

Stewart nodded. "So I've heard. What a terrible shame. Giselle, allow me to introduce Malinga Mutende, Deputy Inspector with the Zambian Police." He looked up at Malinga. "Giselle's visiting, so I'm a little short of time today, but I'll try to come over later this afternoon. I'm always interested in your work."

Giselle's head drooped but she forced a smile. "Stewart is reviewing my case today and grafting donor skin on a few of my lesions, but it shouldn't take long." She patted the doctor's hand. "Help them, Stewart. Help them as much as you can. It's not right that all those young women are being killed."

Giselle looked up at Malinga with a tender smile. "Every woman in this city feels vulnerable right now," she declared, dabbing lightly at her mouth. "Even me. My dear, you must catch this killer as soon as you possibly can."

Malinga was flattered in spite of herself. "You can be sure I will. Sorry we interrupted. Enjoy your lunch. See you later, Stewart." She steered Katanga toward the stairs.

"Wow, Mummy! I got her autograph!" Katanga crowed. "She's the most famous Zambian woman alive."

Malinga smiled down at her daughter. "She's my hero, too. But fame and fortune aren't everything. She's worked very hard to get where she is. She's as lovely as ever, but . . ."

"Yeah, I know, Mom. Her skin is funny, isn't it? It looked grey, and there were big brown spots near her ear."

"Don't think about it anymore, Katanga," Malinga said, afraid her daughter would start having nightmares. Malinga knew that Katanga was almost as susceptible as she was to voices from the other side.

"But Mummy . . . "

"Really, Katanga. I'm serious. There's nothing to worry about. Stewart will help her, I'm sure. He's a very good surgeon." She glanced back over her shoulder at the doctor and the music star and frowned.

It's nice that Stewart is helping Giselle, but where does he get the skin he uses for the repairs?

A terrible feeling surged through Malinga, but she pushed it aside. Stewart was probably taking skin from another part of Giselle's body to repair her face.   She couldn't suspect everyone.

19 | That Chicken Needs Socks

Malinga drove east from Arcades past Zambia's national university to the second roundabout, where Zamchick had recently installed a huge pullet as an advertising gimmick.

"Take a right at the giant chicken," Katanga said in her best imitation of her grandfather's gravelly voice.

"The chicken's legs are too fat," Malinga said. "It looks like he's wearing sport socks."

Katanga grinned. "We should get him some. We could dress him up like a famous football star."

"He could be Santa Claus for Christmas."

"We could dress him like the President," Katanga said, giggling. "He's got the right shape!"

Malinga's mother and father, Joe and Iris, were waiting at their front door. "Shiko will be here, too," Malinga told her mother when they were unpacking the groceries she'd brought. "Vivian can't take him today, and Herbert's too busy at work."

Her mother rolled her eyes. "That man! He works so hard to keep his Benz. But I hear he has a new car, a fancy BMW. My neighbor saw him at the supermarket." Iris lowered her voice to a whisper. "I don't think the woman with him was his secretary. She was white. Gertrude said it might be a client."

"Gertrude always had an eye for those things," Malinga said, sighing. "I can't believe how crazy I used to be about that man. I was so young!"

Her mother laughed and shook her head. "It's not your fault, Malinga. He used to be a very handsome man." She shrugged. "Not anymore. Gertrude tells me that he's a bit fat around the middle these days."

"Like the chicken at the roundabout," Katanga said as she came into the kitchen. "Did Mum tell you that he's going to run for Presi . . . "

Her voice was cut off by the sound of screeching tires. Herbert's BMW was at the gate and he was honking the horn. They looked at one another and grinned.

"Said chicken has arrived," Iris intoned. When Katanga raced out to open the gate for her father, her mother patted Malinga's shoulder. "Let her love him," she said. "Her illusions will be lost soon enough. For now, let her have all the joy they bring her."

Malinga nodded and looked away. "You're right, Mum, as usual."

Her mother smiled at her. "It's hard to extend compassion to someone who's hurt you, but it's always worth it in the long run." Malinga returned her smile. At the sound of running feet, she grimaced and turned toward the door. "I hope Shiko doesn't eat you out of house and home," she said, patting the little boy's head as he ran through the door to hug his grandmother.

"You're growing so fast! Look at how tall you are!" Iris exclaimed.

Malinga threw her arms around them both. "I'm so glad you can keep the children for a few days. The long weekend will give me the time I need to crack this case."

Her mother nodded. "You catch that killer, Malinga. I'll feed the children. I think that's a fair deal. Besides, it's no trouble. You know your father and I love to have them stay with us." She bent to kiss Shiko's head. "Go see your grandfather. He's been waiting for you."

She turned back to Malinga. "I know you can catch him, and when you do, I'll thank the God that made you! This is no ordinary killer. He's giving us all nightmares." Iris walked to the porch with her daughter and opened the door for her. "Malinga?"

"Yes, Mum."

"Be careful."

Malinga nodded. "You know me."

"Yes, I do, and that's what worries me!"

Malinga laughed and walked down the driveway, opening her car's locks as she went.

"Malinga," Herbert called to her from his car.

She walked over to the BMW, thought about a smart comment, but decided to ignore it. "You can't even come in and say hello to my parents?"

"I'm in a rush," he lied. Iris was right. He had put on some weight, most of it around his midsection. His face was puffy from too many late nights. At least you're not doing it on my time anymore, Malinga thought.

"I wanted to ask you about the children," he said. "Do you think they're safe staying with you? The latest murders are making me very nervous."

"You say that every time I have a new case," Malinga said. "Maybe you should be concerned for me. This killer is targeting women, not children. The kids are fine where they are." She turned her back on him to open her car door.

"Malinga," he growled. "I'm not stopping until I get my children back. They are rightfully mine and you know it."

"Custody might make sense when you decide to settle down," she replied, turning toward him. She put her hands on her hips. "How would you take care of them, Herbert? Hire a housekeeper so you can have time with your girlfriends?"

He narrowed his eyes and started a retort, but she cut him off. "At least the children have a mother they can count on. They could never count on you and they still can't. You haven't paid child support for two months. Do you think they live on air?"

"Don't provoke me, Malinga. I can take the kids away from you anytime I want. I know all the judges."

"Maybe you do. But until you bring your support payments up to date, I don't think you can make a very good case for custody."

Shiko was standing near the front door, and Malinga hoped he hadn't heard their exchange. "Shiko," she called. "Come and get your suitcase and your schoolbooks." The boy ran to the car. His father opened the trunk and Malinga helped him remove his bag.

"Daddy! Daddy!" Shiko called, running for the driver's side door as his father started to reverse. "I miss you so much! Can we stay with you on school break?"

Malinga frowned, but remembered her mother's words and repressed the sarcastic comment she was about to make. She didn't have to worry. Herbert couldn't stand the kids for more than four hours at a go. Too lazy to get out of his car, he shook the boy's hand through the car window.

"Bye Daddy," Shiko called, running toward the gate as the BMW continued to reverse. As the car accelerated, Malinga's heart dropped. She ran to grab Shiko's hand. In his rush to escape, Herbert nearly pinned the boy against the gates. Shiko was frightened and started to cry. Malinga picked him up and cuddled him, tickling his smooth midsection until he giggled. Herbert slowed and lowered his window.

"Do you always have to make a scene?" he asked.

Malinga glared at him.

"If you keep overreacting," he persisted, "you'll spoil a lot more than our marriage. This killer knows how weak you are. He knows how weak all women are. He's going to get away with all these murders and more. You won't be able to stop him. He's too sophisticated. You'll probably be demoted."

Malinga's face burned like it had been slapped. She shut the gate and turned toward the house. "Come, darling," she said to Shiko. "Let's go find Minnie Mouse. He's our favorite dog, remember?"

Shiko squiggled from her arms and ran toward the house, calling Iris's dachshund. "Here she is, Mummy," he cried, grabbing the dog around her midsection and lifting her from the flower bed where she'd been sleeping. He grinned up at his mother.

How quickly children forget. And forgive, she thought, grabbing him to her. She'd lost Eitone Mazoka, her ranger captain lover, kidnapped by elephant poachers only a few months ago. Their blossoming love affair had been all too brief. So brief she often wondered if it was actually an illusion.

It didn't matter anymore. The most important thing in her life was her children, and she wasn't going to lose them. Not to Herbert. Not to anyone.

I couldn't stand it. They're all I've got now.

By the time Malinga reached the police station, she had a raging headache. Herbert had little talent as a husband and his skills as a father weren't any better.

What right does he have to threaten me with a custody suit?

She swallowed a few painkillers with some bottled water. Under Zambian law, Herbert had every right to claim the children. He was their biological father, after all. Few things trumped that under the law. More importantly, he was well connected in the country's legal establishment.

Yes, he fooled around, but so did every other man in Zambia. Even those with no money in their pockets left their children hungry so they could buy a beer for some young floozy. She rubbed her temples, thinking of Redbone's warnings. Witch doctors helped men keep the upper hand.

Despite what Redbone said, Malinga knew her visibility was an asset. It would keep Herbert at bay. If he sued for custody and she spoke out, the newspapers would make his comings and goings around town even better known than they already were. While part of the thrill for him was notoriety, he still had a law practice to run.

But if Redbone's right, the killer may come after the children.

She shook her head. I can't let that old man scare me, she thought. She rested her aching forehead in her hands, thinking about the lack of security at her parent's house. She could still see the fear on Shiko's face as Herbert's car closed in on his tiny frame.

I'll never let Herbert take the children from me again. They'd never be safe in his care.

20 | Trust Me

As she prepared the doctor's instruments for Giselle's surgery, Bertha could hear the old *sangoma* scratching at the dead skin on his feet. The noise was annoying and the man was filthy. "Go outside when you do that," she told him. "You sound like the old dog you are, leaving dirty skin everywhere. I must keep this room very clean." Redbone shuffled out the door, glaring at her over his shoulder. She looked away. The *sangoma's* special powers still frightened her.

So did his beautiful son's.

Kivuli, like Redbone, could reach into the grave and across time and distance to make other people do his bidding. She was no exception. As hard as she tried, she couldn't resist him. When he returned from South Africa, she'd fallen in love with him even though she was a baptized Christian.

He'd taken terrible advantage of that love.

On full moon nights, she still relived every second of her baby's death. The image of her son's arm, sticking up from the rubbish tip, still haunted her. Bertha clutched at the cross on her chest, saddened by what she'd done for this beautiful man and his aging father. Their power was irresistible. When she'd given them shelter, things had turned for the worse. Her biggest mistake, she knew, had been trusting Redbone to take care of her boy while she was working at Malinga's.

She fingered the cross again. What she felt for Kivuli wasn't really love, she knew. Not the way Jesus had said it should be. Not the love of man and wife. No. She'd been bewitched. She knew that now. She'd come under his spell and her son's proximity had given Kivuli ideas. His claimed that the ancestors told him that if he killed the boy, they'd be rich enough to go to South Africa. Horrified, Bertha argued with him for a week, but it only made matters worse.

She tried to escape, but Kivuli caught her and forced her to watch while he took the baby's genitals, then slit his throat so the medicine would be stronger. After the child bled out on the rubbish tip, he'd locked her up with what remained of her son's tiny body for two days. That's when I went crazy, she thought. I have to bite my heart to live each day, but I must go on.

Not only was suicide forbidden by her religion, but her other children needed her. If she abandoned them now, her sins would be compounded. Kivuli would catch her if she tried to run. She'd thought about asking Malinga for help, but now that her baby was gone, nothing mattered anymore.

Even the killings. When Kivuli had butchered two women to get more money for his start in South Africa, he did such a crude job the doctor insisted on finishing the next two girls himself. They hadn't suffered as much under his knife.

He was a decent man, the doctor. He'd taken very good care of her. Why he was involved with the *muti* killings – and now with this strange man from Germany – puzzled her. She shrugged. What greed did to people was beyond her understanding. Even a good man like the doctor.

She started when Stewart entered the surgery, and turned to greet him. "All ready for Giselle, Bertha?"

She nodded, wondering what he intended to do to the beautiful woman from South Africa, asleep on the operating table. The doctor hummed as he prepared for the operation, and when Giselle opened her eyes, he leaned over her. "Don't worry my dear," he said gently. "We'll make that lovely face of yours look just like new. You are too beautiful to be so despondent."

Her eyes were wet, but she smiled bravely. "Thank you, Stewart. I know you'll make me perfect again. I hope the samples you have are flawless."

"Only the best, only the youngest," Stewart said, smiling. "I've built up quite a store of them, and I've also been practicing a new technique to reduce recipient rejection. This job will be the best I've ever done. You have my word on that."

She smiled up at him sadly. "I wish there was something I could do for you in return."

"You help me every time you smile, my dear," Stewart said. He knew that Giselle would agree to invite Malinga's children to tea if he asked, but decided to wait until the operation was finished. If it was as successful as he planned, she couldn't refuse him the favor. "I might need your help on a small matter once this is done," he said. "But for now, just relax. We're ready for the operation. I know you'll be pleased with the results."

Stewart began the meticulous process of hand washing that preceded every surgery. Opportunistic infections were a problem in third world environments, even in an outpatient suite as clean as his own. He glanced at the clock, and scrubbed faster. He wanted to get to the police station quickly, so he could learn firsthand what Malinga was planning.

Once Giselle was sedated, the surgery went quickly. Bertha handed him the instruments as she'd been trained to do. Halfway through, Stewart stretched and looked over at her. "Bertha, my dear, did you learn anything from the Deputy Inspector's case file?"

She shook her head. "There's very little in the file, Doctor, and Malinga is angry because there is so little evidence. Only the skinless bodies. So far, only one witness has come forward. A boy saw the Archbishop's driver dump the first body, but no one has seen you or the witch doctors, so the police think the Archbishop is behind all the murders."

"Good work, Bertha. It's a shame they're blaming that poor old man, but better him than us. Kindly tell Redbone and Kivuli to continue taking every precaution." When the doctor had removed Giselle's damaged skin, he looked down and sighed, hoping the new graft would take. Giselle trusted him implicitly, but the damage from bleaching was extensive.

He smiled. How ironic to meet DI Mutende and her daughter at Mint Cafe just when he was about to try the new skin graft procedure on Giselle. By inviting him to participate on the case, Malinga unwittingly helped him thicken the smokescreen hiding his work. Stewart grinned as he rinsed his hands. Giselle would have to rest for quite a while. He'd check the graft after his dinner with Victor and Anita.

Tonight Anita would probably give him 'dessert', he thought. His cheeks colored. He could tell the German woman wanted him, and he wanted her. It had been a long time for both of them, and the coupling would relieve their longings. It was delicious to feel so alive again, and he knew Anita felt the same.

It would be a relief when Victor was dead. The bossy little man with his shopping list made Stewart furious. Women, children, elephants, albinos. Was there no end to the bastard's greed? To his hubris? Imagine! Exposing his bum to posterity!

Anita was another story. Stewart's flush deepened. She was the Crown Jewel of Victor's Empire, no doubt about it, and Stewart could hardly wait to knock the crown from Victor's head. If he played his cards right, she would be his when Victor died.

Smiling, he dried his hands on the crisp towel Bertha handed him. He'd been patient for a long time, and now the clouds that settled around him after his wife's death were lifting. He tossed the towel in the hamper and Bertha heard him whistle as he headed toward the door.

"We've a lot of work ahead of us, Bertha."

"Yes, doctor. I'll clean while you're out."

"I wasn't talking about cleaning, Bertha. You heard the doctor. He has very big plans for us. In addition to the elephant, I must get him Malinga and her children – and the other DI, what's his name . . ."

"Wilson, sir."

"Wilson. That's right. There is so much to do, you must help me."

"I will sir, of course," she said as she followed him to the driveway.

"For now, Bertha my dear," Stewart said as he climbed into his car, "please keep an eye on Giselle. Make sure she is hydrated and stays quiet. She should sleep until I return. When you hear the Germans stir, kindly see if they want tea. Tell them I'll be back for dinner at eight."

Bertha smiled back at him in a way she hoped was convincing. She'd help him fool Malinga, but she didn't like the idea of hurting the children. Stewart was more refined than the witch doctors, sure, but in the end, the results were the same.

Although he helped people like Giselle, in the end, he was motivated by greed and power just like them.

Stewart waved as she closed the gate, then turned toward downtown and the police station. Victor's idea for the final tableau was sensational, he had to admit. It was outrageous, but so was the man who'd proved to the world that dead bodies could be more than subjects of superstition and medical study. They were awe-inspiring in and of themselves, beautiful and strange under the skin, inspiring a deep ecstasy in Stewart since the first time he'd peeled a girl.

The more he thought about it, the more he couldn't wait to get started on Victor's final project. If he called in a few favors, he could get the elephant. It would be tricky, but Stewart knew a man who could do it. The rest would be easy.

It would be child's play to lure Malinga's children into his lair and make Victor's second wish a reality. Once he had the children, Malinga would follow. Giselle was perfect bait and Bertha would make sure it happened in time to meet Victor's schedule.

Stewart was still uncomfortable with murdering the children, but it was better than leaving them orphaned. Wilson was a different kettle of fish, although the albino might be as attracted by the idea of meeting Giselle as Malinga and her children. He'd have to think about that one further.

Stewart relaxed, tapping his fingers on the steering wheel in time to a popular Zambian song. If he committed the perfect crime against DI Malinga, he could do anything he wanted to grow the business in southern Africa. He swerved to avoid an on-coming motorist who turned across traffic to beat the red light, exhaling in relief when his vehicle cleared the man's bumper by centimeters. Angry, Stewart gestured at him through the windscreen. And then he smiled.

When Victor died, he'd get Anita, and what a prize she'd be. He felt himself stirring at the thought. She was so young, so vivacious. He licked his lips and his gaze melted into the near distance. The driver behind him tapped his horn when he didn't notice the light change.

Love. Imagine! At his age! The future would be better than he'd ever dared believe, and it couldn't happen soon enough. In the meantime, he'd build Victor's trust by seeing that everything happened according to schedule, no matter how demanding. Everything.

Stewart smiled. Everything. Including Victor's death.

If Victor wanted to be Adam, there was no time like the present.

21 | Wilson to the Rescue

Malinga jumped when Wilson's bag hit the top of his desk. The racket was deliberate, she knew, because he was grinning at her when she looked up. A big man who smelled of breath mints, garlic, and light perspiration, his daily practical jokes irritated her. He was four years her junior and much less experienced, but outranked her, made more money than she did, and earned more vacation time.

She hated him on principle, but right now she needed him. She forced a smile. "Welcome back, stranger."

"It's great to be back," he said. "But you look terrible."

"For good reason. I've held the fort single-handed all this time, but now all hell is breaking loose. It's going to finish me." Wilson ignored her, whistling as he sifted through the papers on his desk. "It pains me to see you in such a good mood, Wilson. It hasn't been easy without you."

"Thanks for the warm welcome," he said with an annoying half smile. "Keep it up and I won't give you the gift I bought you in Zanzibar."

"Keep it. You left us shorthanded just when God decided to send Lusaka a new string of serial murders. No matter how hard I pleaded with your mother, she wouldn't give me your contact details." When Wilson's smile broadened, her anger rose. "We needed you, Wilson. You're supposed to call in."

"Sorry, Malinga, but the Mailonis almost finished me. I needed a break after that ordeal. I was on edge all the time, afraid those guys would sneak up on me and cut my throat. I didn't want my kids to see me murdered on YouTube. My family was afraid I'd never come back from the Luano Valley." He drew in a breath and looked at her speculatively, annoyed by the frown he saw forming on her brow. "Relax, Malinga. I'm back now, ready for action. By the way, how's everything at home? Heard anything from Eitone?"

Malinga averted her gaze and began sorting through the files in front of her. "Let's not talk about that."

"I'll take that as a no."

"Then you'd be right. When the poachers took him over the Congolese border, the trail went cold. After I exhausted all the leads I had, Chikanda handed me the new case."

"What is it?"

Malinga looked up at him. "Haven't you read the papers? We've got a new serial killer. *Muti*, I think."

"I thought we were done with those."

Malinga laughed. "Not by a long shot. These are so gruesome, at first we thought the Mailonis had a younger brother," she joked. "But their MO is totally different." Malinga shook her head. "To be honest, I'm not sure if we're dealing with just one serial killer. There are some substantial differences in the bodies we've found, so there may be more than one killer, but they're all *muti* killings. The bodies are flayed, stripped of organs, and dumped by the roadside, so there are very few clues. Only missing parts."

"These days, it seems like every murderer who wants attention takes a souvenir body part."

Malinga laughed. "True, but these victims are something else. The worst one was last night. The killer removed her skin, breasts, labia, vagina, heart, eyeballs . . ."

"Sounds like an anatomy lesson," Wilson muttered. "I hope they're not reporting that in the press."

"We haven't been able to keep much back from the reporters. The story is as sensational as any Lusaka's likely to see outside of some of the shenanigans of our politicians. This killer never rests. Five girls, stripped of their skin, dumped in the hedgerows of Lusaka all hours of the day and night for almost a month now. The press is all over us."

Wilson stopped rooting for things in his bag and looked up at her. "I didn't know it was so bad."

"That's why I was trying to reach you. There's no end to it. Last night the call came in at three a.m. If you catch me napping, just give me a nudge."

"What does the boss say about it?"

"What boss? I don't think Inspector Chikanda lives in Lusaka anymore. He's a one-man traveling show for Zambian police work. As soon as he came back from replacing me on the President's special ivory poaching mission to China, he left for Interpol training on trafficking in France. He hasn't been here since this thing started and I don't expect him back for another month."

"Then it's just you and me."

Malinga nodded. "We're stuck, big brother. It's up to us to restore peace of mind to Zambian women. And we have no time to waste. If we get copycat killers thrilled to imitate the originals, then no woman in Zambia will be safe anywhere."

"Parading them through town in their underwear seems quite tame by comparison. Where do I start?"

"Settle in and have a look at the file. The team briefing is at fifteen hundred hours. Our new forensic pathologist from France is coming, and Danise said she'd turn up, too."

"We have a forensic expert from France? How'd that happen?"

"It's the boss's idea," Malinga said, shrugging. "Since we don't have one in Zambia, he leaned on Interpol for assistance."

Wilson whistled. "Lot of help that will be."

"He arrived a few days ago from Interpol's Marseilles office." Malinga shrugged. "Who knows? He may be more useful than we think. He's already examined the bodies and the little evidence we have. The victims were dumped in residential compounds around the city, so we have no actual crime scenes and damn few clues."

"Who else is on the case?"

"Davison and Asedi, of course, but you know how they are. Nothing but arms and legs when I need another brain. We've had some help from local police, but with four murders already this month, it's been tough to adequately investigate them all.

"And a fifth last night."

"Yeah, but we don't have much on her yet. Danise is running a psych profile of the women and the killer and Stewart's helping with forensics. He'll be a little late. He's doing surgery as we speak."

"As usual. That man works too hard. And he's so generous. He never refuses anyone who needs his help."

"Especially when the supplicant is our own Giselle."

"Giselle?" Wilson grinned. "Stewart's coming up in the world."

Malinga smiled, thinking of the look on Stewart's face when he met Jacques. "In some respects, yes. He seems a little jealous of our Interpol friend, but there's nothing I can do about it."

She relaxed back in her chair. "I'm sorry I'm so grouchy. My migraines have kicked up ever since this started. I'm glad you're back, brother. A fresh look at the evidence will help us rally."

"If you want, I can do more than that." The big man grinned and eyed her speculatively. "Let me take over the investigation so you can concentrate on the rest of the workload."

Malinga's mouth dropped open and then she started laughing. "I don't believe you're serious, Wilson! I can't believe you said that!"

"Just trying to help!"

"Fancy that! How nice of you to think of me, but you can forget it right now. The answer is no."

22 | What Bertha Heard

Bertha pulled back from the door like she'd been slapped. It was clearly the sound of two people making love, and it was clearly being made by Stewart's visitors. Bertha shivered. Making love? The man had barely been able to keep liquid in a teacup or walk down the corridor to the guess room. How was he able to make love?

Bertha's eyes narrowed. When she pressed her ear against the guestroom door for a second time, her eyes snapped open. She heard the woman's muffled scream, followed by a jolt of satisfaction from the man and more muffled giggles from the woman.

"Ah, Victor," she heard Anita murmur. "You were wonderful, as usual."

"And you, my dear, you never fail to enchant."

Bertha still couldn't believe what she was hearing, although one thing was certain. It was not time to invite them for tea. But it was an excellent time to get information she could use to increase her value to Stewart in the coming days. She held her breath and leaned in again. She hadn't meant to eavesdrop. She'd come to deliver the doctor's invitation to tea, but stopped when she heard the pleasure of lovemaking coming from within.

Victor's voice had changed. It was deeper, more demanding, sexy. He was laughing. It was not the strangled, shaky laugh she'd heard from him earlier, but the laugh of a healthy man in his prime. Bertha leaned closer to catch what Anita was saying. The door swung open slightly and she pulled back, holding her breath, afraid of discovery. She needn't have worried. Stewart's guests were too engrossed in their post coital play. Bertha leaned forward so she could just see the two figures entwined on the bed.

The woman stood, shook on a peignoir and lit a cigarette. "Let's plastinate him," she said vehemently. "He's an arrogant, nasty Englishman. I'd like to see him suffering for eternity!"

"Ah, *Liebchen*! Don't be so angry! Besides, I've got a better idea. We'll get what we need from the bloody bastard and let him take the heat," he said, laughing again. "He's ripe for the picking. He'll never suspect us."

Anita inhaled the smoke from her cigarette and tilted her head to blow it toward the ceiling. "Humm . . . I get you, Victor. If he's caught after we've disappeared, he'll sound like an idiot if he tries to implicate us. As far as the authorities are concerned, we were never here. We never registered the plane or cleared immigration."

"It will be easier than I anticipated," Victor agreed, laughing. "My dear, I must say you were masterful playing the role of a tempting little trollop."

Anita was laughing, too. "He was drooling so much I thought I'd have to mop the floor. But *Liebchen*! You were wonderful as well, so brittle I thought I was watching Dr. Frankenstein's monster!"

Bertha's almost stopped breathing. She brought her hand to her mouth, shocked at what they were saying. Had it all been an act?

"That English clown!" Victor gloated. "That simpering, posturing English snob."

Anita was snorting with laughter. She put on her very best English accent. "'I say! I'd planned to return to England by the end of the year, old chum.' You exposed him for what he really is, Victor. He's nothing but a prick! He acts high minded, but he is just as greedy as the next man."

"As we are!" Victor said.

Anita laughed appreciatively. "As we are."

"God, I hate the English," Victor shouted. Bertha peeked around the edge of the door when she heard a clatter. The man had thrown his cane to the ground for emphasis and was pacing the floor. Clearly not a cripple. It had all been pretense.

"I'll teach him to elbow in on my markets!" Victor said. "I can't wait to see the look on his face when he realizes we're going to plastinate him! He can be the ape man following Adam, smelling all his farts!"

Anita wagged her finger in mock dismay at Victor. The amusement shone in her eyes. "Don't get too excited, *Liebchen*! We must wait until he gives us what we need – the elephant, the mother, her children, and the albino Adam – and they are safely loaded on our airplane."

"And we are back in Germany, designing our next exhibit."

"Oh, Victor! It will be your best yet!"

Victor nodded. "I wasn't sure we had to kill him, but now I know we must. He expects too much."

"But offering him the partnership was a stroke of genius. When he realized its profit potential, he was hooked!" Anita held her cocktail glass out in front of her, admiring its color. "I suppose we could just let him retire. He said he . . . "

"Too late for that," Victor said. "I'm afraid the bait we dangled in front of him was irresistible. If we let him live, he'll always be a threat to us. Besides, the sheer pleasure of turning that arrogant English wimp into a Body Works volunteer is too delicious to forgo."

Anita sipped her drink. "I agree with you there. These English are insufferable. It was a good idea to accelerate the deadline. Making him think we have to get out of here by early next week was a stroke of genius."

"Once we kill him, we've eliminated our biggest source of competition. Nip it in the bud, so to speak." Victor leered at his wife. "Come here, *Liebchen*. I want to nip your buds."

She leaned toward him and jiggled her breasts invitingly. He pulled her supple body close. "But first we have to build a relationship with his suppliers so we can ensure a steady stream of manikins, animal as well as human."

"Oh, Victor! Do we have to deal with the Chinese again? I don't have the stomach for it after what they did to you." She grabbed Von Sorge, accidentally tearing one of the fake electrodes from his skull, and kissed him passionately. "We have plenty of time to talk about this later. Right now, he's gone, so let's take advantage of it."

Victor had cleaned some of the makeup off his face, but left the electrodes in his hair. He rubbed the spot on his skull where they irritated his skin. "They itch. I don't like the Chinese, either, darling, but if I'm not mistaken, Stewart's working with a couple of local witchdoctors to get the girls." He rubbed a patch of skin irritated by the theatrical glue and looked at himself ruefully in the mirror. He touched the spot on his head lightly. "You'll have to stick this on again when we finish. Don't forget."

Anita came up behind him and threw her arms around his shoulders, nuzzling his neck. "Oh, Victor!" she exclaimed. "I can't stand you in that make up! Get that cleaned off immediately and then come to me! I need you now!"

Victor smiled at her. "All things in their time, Anita. You must take me as I am or not at all."

She looked up at him slyly. "No choice?"

"We can't risk it. If he finds out we're fooling him, he will be insane with rage. Just think of me as Frankenstein's monster!" He growled and pawed the air. "What a great idea you had, Anita. Pretending I have Parkinson's! It's so much fun, fooling this local rube."

"Fun, Victor?" Anita said, pouting. "That's the last thing I'd call it. If that man simpers at me one more time, I don't think I can stop myself from retching!"

"It will be over soon. We only have to keep it up until we get what we want. Only a few days. Less than a week at the most."

"It seems like forever." She sighed, and turned her face away from him. They went quiet.

Bertha pressed herself against the door of the guest suite, hoping for more details of their conspiracy. When the springs on the bed start to creak again, she turned on her heel and made her way back to the kitchen with the tray of ice water she'd planned to give them. Her heart was pounding furiously. They were fooling the doctor. What could she do? She had to tell him everything, that was sure.

When his arm shot out to grab her, she almost dropped the tray. He helped her catch it. "Come with me," he whispered, pulling her into a side room. He grabbed the tray from her and put it on the sideboard. She submitted, and hated herself for it. He smelled like he'd rubbed himself in animal dung, and his skin was rough against her. She struggled to free herself from his grasp on her neck, but he held her against the wall like a lion.

"What do you want?" she asked when he was done, pulling her skirt down with a jerk.

"I saw you listening," he whispered.

She turned her head away. "You are starting to smell like your father," she said. "I will run you a bath."

"Not now. I want to know what you heard the *bazungu* saying."

"The German doctor and his wife?"

"Who else do you think I'm talking about! What were they saying?"

Bertha shut the door quietly, leaned back against it, and caught her breath. She narrowed her eyes, looked at Kivuli, and decided to keep the secret to herself until she'd thought about it more. She didn't have to tell him everything. There may be a way to use this information to her advantage to get away from him. Or see him dead like he deserved.

This was the man that killed her son. Not just killed him. Brutalized him. If she played her cards right, she might just get the revenge she'd prayed for.

"I don't know."

"What do you mean? Did they speak in German?"

"No, she's English. She uses a little German here and there but they weren't talking in it."

"Then what was the matter? Why couldn't you hear?"

"The man is ill. He speaks in a very strange way, very quietly, so I can't make out what he's saying."

"Could you tell what they were doing?"

She swallowed. "I think they were resting. It was very quiet."

He snorted. "That's all? Just resting?"

"Kivuli, he's a sick man. I don' think he can do anything else."

"Too bad for him," Kivuli said, turning her face to the wall again and snatching up her skirt. She gritted her teeth, glad she'd kept the secret to herself. It angered her when he forced her against a wall from behind like an animal. Kivuli was an animal, she thought. She had to be free of him. Keeping what she knew about the doctor and his wife secret might help her do that.

But what about Stewart? The guests planned to kill him and put him into one of their exhibits. Should she tell him? She'd been close to him once, respecting him and respected by him. He'd taught her many things, and often complimented her on her help in the surgery. She could never hurt him, she knew. He trusted her. But she was frightened of what he'd become.

With his wife gone, sadness had consumed him and changed him. Greed had turned him into an animal, closer to Redbone and Kivuli than he liked to believe. It was the greed that was consuming them, leading them to murder these girls.

At least Malinga was trying to help. Maybe Bertha should tell her. If she did, she could stop the killings and put an end to the *muti* murders. Bertha knew that no other mother should suffer like she had for her son, like she was sure these girls' mothers were suffering now.

But her son was gone, so what did it matter? If she told Malinga what she knew of Stewart, she doubted the detective would believe her. She was a new girl, new to the city. She herself might be arrested for the crime, for helping her master peel these bodies, the bodies of these poor girls. They wouldn't hesitate to blame her. The saintly English doctor, who's spent his life helping the poor, would go free and she would end up in jail.

Bertha put her hands to her temples and moaned, hardly noticing that Kivuli had finished and she was alone. She pulled her skirt down again and stood tall.

She could align with Malinga and use the knowledge she had to ensure that Kivuli and Redbone were put in jail for life. That would be good. Very good. But she'd have to be careful she wasn't drawn into it. If she told Malinga, Dr. Bleming might be implicated. She had to be very careful about what she said.

If she spoke out, she'd probably lose her job with Malinga, and have nothing at all in the end. Better to say nothing, better to keep what she knew to herself, and hope it would be over soon. Before she was killed, or lost any more of her children.

Her shoulders slumped. She stepped quietly out of the side room and turned toward the kitchen once again. She was a smart woman, but she was nothing but a woman, after all. Malinga had beaten the odds, Bertha knew, but it was unlikely she would be as lucky. Or that Malinga's luck would hold.

23 | The Coffin Found the Killer

"But Malinga," Wilson said, grinning, "you could use the help." Malinga stood shakily and rubbed her temples. Her migraine was worsening. She forced herself to return Wilson's grin, raising her head high, placing her hands on her hips, and shaking her head to signal her refusal.

"No, you don't, Wilson. You got the Mailonis and the raise that went with them. This one is mine. You'll hear all about it at the briefing. I expect you there in about an hour." She turned back to her computer screen to hide her scowl.

Wilson's grin thinned. "I am Acting Inspector whenever Chikanda's out of the office. If I want to take over the case, you have no say in the matter."

"That's true, Wilson. You're absolutely right. Your seniority is a fact you'll never let me forget. But if you do that, you'll always have to watch your back." Malinga wagged her index finger at him. "Give it up, Wilson. It would take too much time for you to get up to speed. We have to catch this guy before more girls die. Until we do, I'll never get any sleep. Or get rid of these migraines."

She sighed and sat down. "Besides, the public expects me to handle it. I've been very visible in the press. They'll worry if we change lead investigators at this point. Our informants and witnesses will be confused, and it will drag things to a standstill."

He started to speak, but she put up her hand. "Stop, Wilson. I won't stay silent about it, and we can't afford any infighting right now. The public is already pretty dubious about our ability to solve these crimes and find the killer."

He grinned. "I was just teasing, Malinga. Relax."

"You've been a good friend and partner, Wilson, and I welcome all the help you can give me. You're a first-class investigator."

"You're right, Malinga. I am. And so are you, but I still think these murders are getting the best of you." Wilson shook his head. "I know what it's like. After a few days in the bush chasing the Mailonis, I started seeing things."

"Wilson!"

He laughed again. "We're surrounded by superstition, Malinga. Sometimes it's catching."

She nodded. Even the educated middle class wasn't entirely immune to superstition. Even the police were susceptible. "Just last week, after we found the second body, Asedi and Davison were talking about the resurgence of coffin bashing in Northwest Province. They'd helped with a case up there last year."

Wilson knit his brows. "Not that again. I thought it was over."

"It's picked up again. In the case they witnessed, the local witch doctor used a dead baby's coffin."

Wilson grimaced. "Like the finder on a Ouija board."

"Davison insisted that the coffin moved on its own and the six men carrying it had no control over its direction. It took them right to the grandparent's door. Of course, the witch doctor had given the men hallucinogens to heighten his power of suggestion over them. The baby had died of AIDS when the grandparents couldn't get medication. The crowd bashed them to death with the baby's coffin, and buried them underneath it."

Wilson grimaced. "If police coverage was better, people wouldn't take the law into their own hands like that."

"Davison and Asedi thought it was the ancestors' revenge, even though they knew the grandparents had done everything they could to keep the baby alive. I tried to argue that it wasn't the grandparents' fault, but they wouldn't hear it."

"'The spirits always guide the witch doctor to the guilty party,' Asedi insisted. When I asked if God was guiding the coffin, they looked at me like I'd grown a second head. 'It was another kind of power, the power of the witch doctor's spirits,' Davison said.

"I told them that as Christians and police, they couldn't condone coffin bashing and they should have stopped the crowd before they murdered the old people. They avoided my eyes, and Davison finally said, 'If we'd tried to stop them, Mum, they would have killed us.'"

"He's right, of course, but we'll never stop witch doctors if we're afraid to intervene!" Wilson said.

"You're preaching to the choir." Malinga glanced at her watch. "We have ten minutes before the team meeting. I'll see you up there." She gathered her files and headed for the stairs, then turned back. "We have to catch these killers, Wilson. You and I have to cooperate or more women will die."

He nodded. "Don't worry, Malinga. I'm behind you."

"I want to push the team harder. Help me do that."

"Of course. It will be good for them. They just don't know it yet."

She laughed and headed up the stairs. Innocent lives were at stake. Solving the case would make her eligible for a raise, but more importantly, it would save more innocent girls from horrible deaths. They had to try harder. She had to try harder. Frustrated by the witchcraft and superstition so common in Zambian life, she knew she had to keep speaking out against them so the public would eventually understand and put an end to the worst abuses of their traditions.

Malinga pushed the conference room door open with her hip and slid her files down on the table. She was angry that *muti* killings were still going on in Zambia, angry that women like her feared for their safety, angry that most police were too frightened and intimidated to help. And she was angry that Wilson, who knew the effects of superstition and witchcraft better perhaps than anyone, a policeman who would never be frightened or intimidated, would stoop to making her feel unsteady as a woman so he could take the case from her. She'd trusted Wilson as a friend, and hoped he'd back off and not challenge her leadership again.

A thought hit her. The man who was responsible for these murders should be dumping the bodies in places where they'd never be found except by scavenger animals who would make short work of the remains. Instead, he was leaving them in public places, to be found by innocent passersby on their way to work or school. He was deliberately fanning the fires of public outrage. It felt personal, like he trying to humiliate her. He was willing to take the risk of being seen in order to make her – and the police more generally – look bad.   Could it be someone she knew, someone who wanted revenge? Someone from a previous case who felt slighted or injured by the police?

She knit her brows, thinking back, but no one came to mind. She tried to shake the thought off. It was her own paranoia and it would lead nowhere. On the other hand, her own daughter might be a victim if she pushed the case too hard and the killers felt threatened.

She sank into a chair and started flipping through her notes, trying to get a grip on her emotions. Not only was she exhausted and frustrated, she was more than a little heartbroken by recent events in her own life. If she was going to take charge of this case and catch the bastard responsible, she had to let her grief go. She'd never admit it to Wilson, but she wondered if Eitone's disappearance had been entirely against his will. She could think of too many ways her lover – her ex-lover – might have benefited from disappearing with the ivory from ten dead elephants.

The tusks were worth millions, true. But benefitting from the animals' deaths went against everything he held dear. She sighed, doubting she'd ever bring the poaching case to a satisfactory conclusion. Or see Eitone again. He's in the past, she thought, dead to me. Time to move on.

She stood and stretched, trying to relax. Her migraine was finally letting up. When her team arrived, she had to be strong and focused.

This case was a perfect opportunity to speak out against gender violence and the superstitions holding Zambia hostage to the past. It was the perfect opportunity to stop the criminals who were profiting by terrorizing law-abiding women, killing girls in horrible and shameful ways.

Yes, the case was difficult, but no more difficult than others she'd dealt with. In fact, it might be a little easier because the perpetrators were probably local medicine men, not connected to international gangs with unlimited resources or to corrupt government officials like the poaching case.

Muti murders wouldn't end. Too many big people profited, and little people were afraid to speak out. But if she could identify the witch doctors who were responsible and confront them, it would be a huge step forward protecting women and girls. And it would help her challenge the practice of *muti* killings, no matter who the victim was.

I won't stop speaking out, and I certainly won't turn the case over to Wilson. I won't let a witch doctor intimidate me. I'm going to catch these killers before they kill one more girl, I swear it.

24| Find Me an Elephant, 1

Downtown traffic was a tangled mess, so Stewart used the time spent crawling toward the police station to work on Victor's shopping list. With less than a week to find the human and animal 'volunteers' to make all of Victor's dreams come true, he'd have to move fast. Locating an elephant, although difficult, was comparatively easy compared to the list of human beings Victor wanted to recruit. So Stewart decided to start there.

He tried Stefan Bwalya's number, but wasn't surprised when he got no answer and left a message. No one in his network had seen or heard from Stefan or any of the other poachers in months. The police had reported Stefan's disappearance – with Elvis, Eitone, and the elephant tusks – last year, but Stewart suspected he was still in the city. If he couldn't locate Stefan, his replacement at the Zambian Wildlife Authority might be persuaded to help for enough baksheesh.

Stewart jumped when his cell phone rang. "Stefan! So glad to hear from you! How can I lay my hands on an elephant? I need one fast."

"I can't help you with that one right now, Stewart. Things are still too hot. I expect they'll stay that way for at least another few months."

"Can some one else at ZAWA help?"

"Not now, Stewart. They're watching us like hawks. By the way, don't bother to call me again for the next little while. I'll be out of the country."

"Stefan!" Stewart cried, but he'd had already hung up. Stewart scowled and drummed his fingers angrily on the steering wheel. Without Stefan, there was no hope of getting an elephant from one of the national game parks. And there were damned few other places where their disappearance wouldn't be noticed.

Victor had the money and the plane to make it work if Stewart could just get the beast. A private jet wouldn't be searched as vigilantly as a public aircraft when it left the country. If they managed to find an elephant, they'd have to move fast, but it wouldn't be impossible to get it out of Zambia before someone noticed. Stewart thought hard, then brightened. There was not just one, but two elephants within easy reach of the Lusaka airport.

The first possibility was at Chaminuka, a 10,000-acre private game ranch half hour northeast of the Lusaka airport. The ranch had three elephants: a bull named Duff, his mate, and their baby. If he could find someone inside Chaminuka to arrange the bull's death, the body could be moved onto Victor's jet at night and no one would be the wiser. Finding a reliable contact was the problem. Too many people loved Duff and would protect him. It was doubtful that the owners, ardent conservationists who were extremely proud of their elephant 'herd' and the rare animals they raised for other game parks, would be willing to sell.

There was another possibility closer to hand. Stewart thumbed his phone's contact list and tried the number, but it rang through to voice mail. This wasn't the kind of request he could leave a message about. It would be fatal if someone else heard it. "Call me," he said. "It's urgent." He pocketed his phone and sighed. His search for an elephant carcass had ground to a halt, just like the traffic he was sitting in.

What of the human specimens Victor needed? Stewart drummed his fingers on the steering wheel once again, mind as jangled as the traffic jam in front of him. He leaned on his horn, but the traffic wasn't moving. The normal afternoon snarl had been aggravated by a fender bender in the left-hand lane. Stewart swore under his breath. He had to get downtown fast or he'd miss part of Malinga's meeting. That wasn't good. He needed to know everything the police were planning,

He stopped cursing under his breath when he remembered his earlier inspiration to make good on another of Victor's wishes. He put a call through to Bertha. "I'm inviting Malinga and her children to my house for tea so they can meet Giselle next Saturday. Start planning the tea – and preparing the operating room," he ordered.

"Tea?"

"Yes, Bertha. We'll invite them for tea, and plastinate them immediately afterward. Tea, as they say in American crime movies, will be our cover story."

"I see," Bertha said. "Yes, of course." She hesitated. "Do we really have to kill the children, doctor?"

Stewart smiled. Nothing he'd like better than to do away with Malinga's brats, but he couldn't express that sentiment to Bertha, who'd just lost her youngest child. "I'm afraid so. It's part of Victor's grand scheme, Bertha. You heard him talk about it today. I'm afraid we can't dissuade him, but don't worry. It won't take that long."

"Yes, Doctor." She hesitated again, thinking of what she'd overheard from Victor and his wife. She decided to tell him. "Doctor?" she began shakily.

"Yes, Bertha," Stewart said impatiently.

"I need to speak with you. Something's changed . . ."

Stewart swerved to avoid an oncoming truck. "It will have to wait until I get home, Bertha. Traffic's terrible. I've got to go."

When he broke the connection, Bertha slumped against the kitchen counter. Although Malinga deserved everything she'd get, the children did not. They were innocent, and Bertha couldn't knowingly lure them into a trap that would lead to their deaths. She was haunted by the thought of Shiko and Katanga's grandparents. Iris and Joe wouldn't survive the deaths of their only daughter and their grandchildren at the same time.

Bertha knew she couldn't burden another mother, another woman, with the same grief she still felt so deeply. But could she prevent it? The doctor was determined that if one scheme failed, he'd find another. The only way Bertha could stop the killing was to tell him what Victor and Anita were plotting. If he knew they planned to leave him empty-handed, he'd call a halt to the killings. She'd tell him this evening, after dinner, she decided. Would he believe her? A mere servant? Worse, a woman? Stewart had long admired Victor, and was sure he'd get rich off this scheme. If he didn't believe her, who could she turn to?

Should she tell Malinga? Malinga could stop the
Germans, but once they talked, Stewart would be arrested and so
would she. Her surviving children would be left under her
mother's protection, a woman so poor that she could provide only
the thinnest of blankets. More than likely, her children would not
survive.

Tears streaming down her cheeks, Bertha thumbed her
phone's contact list frantically. She was not an animal. She was a
Christian, and a good one, a good woman who had worked hard
all her life for her family. A good Christian who had watched her
own baby die. She had to stop this horror, but she had to do it in a
way that wouldn't expose her or threaten her children.

Who could help?

Bertha stopped thumbing her contact list when she saw
the number. There was one possibility, a group she knew could
help without calling in all the dogs of law, a group that knew how
to solve problems quietly and completely with a minimum of fuss.
Her heart rose, but when the voice answered, Bertha froze. She cut
the connection when she realized she didn't know what to say.
How to explain the crazed plans underfoot to a total stranger,
someone who might be so shocked she would turn away?

Bertha pocketed her phone. It wasn't time yet. She had to
know more.

25 | The Before and After

The psychologist tapped her pen on the table and frowned at Malinga's case summary. "Five victims. The first two were murdered by a different killer than the last two, and the third one, the pharmacy student, by yet another pscycho," Danise said. "I get the sequence, but I'm still puzzled. This kind of killer is rare, so to find three in a city the size of Lusaka is statistically improbable. Frankly, I think . . ."

She broke off when the door flew open and Wilson rushed in with a tray full of takeaway cups. "Sorry I'm late. I couldn't keep my eyes open without a cappuccino. I must be jet lagged."

"Jet lagged? From Zanzibar?" Malinga scoffed, reaching for one of the cups Wilson placed on the table. She was annoyed but couldn't afford to alienate the him. He was Acting Chief and could bump her off the case in an instant. She gave him a half smile. "Poor excuse. But since you brought us coffee, you're forgiven." She gestured at the empty chair across from her. "Sit down so I can introduce you."

Wilson grinned at the neat woman who sat on Malinga's left and extended his hand. "It's great to see you again, Danise," he said, shaking her hand vigorously. "I never got a chance to thank you for your help with the Mailoni brothers. Your idea that they were hiding in plain sight was brilliant. They were in the village the whole time we were chasing them in the bush!"

Malinga gestured across the table at a pale, white-haired man who was observing the proceedings with amusement. "And this is Dr. Jacques DuClaire. He's the forensic specialist I was telling you about who just joined us from Marseilles."

"Great to meet you! I'm Wilson Mwiinga," he said, reaching out to shake the Frenchman's hand. Although he was seated, Wilson knew the doctor was well over six feet and two hundred pounds. "I'm a DI like Malinga, but Acting Chief while Inspector Chikanda is away in France. Pleasure indeed." Wilson tapped the case folders lined up along the table's edge with a long, neatly manicured index finger. "Should we go through these one at a time, or do you want to give us your overall observations first, Dr. Hatchitapika?"

Danise shot Malinga a sideways glance. "Call me Danise, Wilson. You don't need to be formal here. We're all on an equal footing," she said pointedly, gesturing for him to sit down. "Malinga and her team have already heard my analysis. I'd like to hear from Jacques now. Many of my psychological observations are derived from the physical evidence, and I want to know if he's got anything new."

Jacques switched on the projector and turned down the lights. The room fell silent. "I've taken the liberty of numbering the girls in order of discovery, from 1 to 5. Is that okay with everyone? Info on the girl who was killed last night, Victim Number 5, is cursory. She has yet to be identified."

"That's fine, Jacques. Please continue," Malinga said. He turned toward the screen and flicked the remote. Pictures of the first four victims trailed across the screen. Girls posed in family photos, smiled happily at graduation, hugged babies and puppies, posed in formal head shots. "These are our victims," the Frenchman said. "Before they were killed."

He touched the remote and a sequence of grisly photos replaced the 'before' pictures. He cleared his throat. "And this is what the murderers have done." Malinga flinched. She'd seen the victims' photos before, but not projected, vibrant, nearly life-size.

"I reviewed each victim's case file," Jacques said. "The evidence points to two, possibly three killers, confirming what Dr. Hatchitapika – sorry! Danise – says. Here's why I think she's right." He clicked the remote and a postmortem close-up of Victim 1 appeared on the screen.

"This is our first victim, and this" – he clicked the remote again and another image appeared next to the first – "is our second. "The skin of the first two victims was removed with a knife, and the work was not careful." The beam from his laser pointer traced the reddened edges of what had been a face. "Skin was removed from both victims while they were still alive, judging from the amount of blood around the wounds and the state of their capillaries. The suffering was immense, but shock would have set in to mitigate the pain before the killer went too far."

He pressed the remote and a close-up of Victim 3 appeared on the screen. "The third victim was exhumed after burial by her family, so the tissue had deteriorated. The facial skin, eyeballs and tongue had been removed with a non-surgical knife." He outlined scars on the victim's body with his pointer. "As you can see, it was also rough work. The scars are ragged along the edges. But the victim was dismembered after death, with little bleeding around the lacerated areas."

He turned to the group. "All three were dismembered using rough knives, the first two while they were still alive and the third after she died." Malinga looked away from the screen and gulped hard. The fingers of her hands, pyramided in front of her, tightened.

"We can contrast this with the last two victims," Jacques said, bringing two more images up on the screen. "There's no bleeding around their incisions, which were made with a much finer instrument, probably a surgical scalpel." When Jacques brought the next image up, Malinga flinched again. "Body parts were removed from all the victims, but in the last case, some of the blood vessels had been cauterized."

Jacques flicked to another set of images. "Less skin was removed from the first two victims, and they were missing fewer body parts. The last two victims were missing almost all of their skin. It had been removed in one piece, or close to it. A formidable surgical feat. They were also missing several major organ groups. Liver, heart, and spleen." He looked around the group. "Victims 4 and 5 were dismembered by a trained killer with access to medical instruments. The first two were done by amateurs."

He brought up a new image and used the laser pointer to highlight variations in skin tone and texture visible in what remained. "All the girls were bleaching their skin, and some of the tissue had been treated after their deaths with what looks like white glue or plastic. I've sent samples of the residue to the Interpol lab in Nairobi to determine which chemicals were used. The last two girls had lingering signs of skin grafts in places where their skin didn't peel completely free."

Malinga leaned forward. "Skin grafts?"

"Another sign that we are dealing with a sophisticated killer," Jacques said, "although his reasons are puzzling. These were surgically applied grafts, but they were applied after death, possibly to experiment with fit or to match tone."

"Any other physical trauma?"

"The first two victims had subcutaneous head trauma, and the third showed signs of strangulation."

"So they were physically assaulted before death?"

The Frenchman nodded. "The first three girls, yes. But there is no sign that they resisted their killer. No skin or hair under the fingernails, for example. The last two victims showed no external signs of violence, but they were drugged before they were killed."

"So they knew the killer?"

"I think so, although they may not have known him personally. The killer might have been someone they knew or respected because of his status."

Danise sighed. "A sophisticated man, no doubt. Someone who could completely change their lives. Potential sugar daddy. Polished, respected, and completely mad."

"What drug was used?" Malinga asked.

"I suspect Roofies – Rohypnol, the date rape drug – although I have to wait for lab results before I can say for sure." Jacques nodded at Asedi and Davison. "Your detectives tell me that the drug has become popular in Lusaka over the past few years."

Asedi beamed and Davison sat up, ready to speak, but when Malinga raised an eyebrow, he sat back. "Anything else, Doctor?" she asked the Frenchman.

He drew a deep breath and frowned. "I'm afraid so."

26 | It's a Tall Order

Stewart's phone rang as he waited for the traffic to reach the downtown turn off. He answered irritably, but focused when he heard the now-familiar voice purring in his ear. "What progress have you made, Stewart?"

"We'll have Eve and her children by Saturday. I'll plastinate them on Sunday at the latest."

"Good work, Stewart! That's very good news! Anita, we'll have Eve and her children very soon!" he shouted.

"We've already got Adam," Stewart said grimly, hoping Victor wouldn't hear the distaste in his voice.

Victor paused, then laughed loudly. "Yes, of course. I'm a willing volunteer. You are very funny, Stewart. For an Englishman, that is. But what about the other two? The elephant and the albino?"

"I've got to go, Victor. I'm in the middle of downtown traffic and it's starting to move."

"I'm very worried, Stewart. I'm worried you can't fulfill all your promises."

"Don't be. I'll tell you the rest of my plans at dinner."

"But I am worried, Stewart. We are pressed for time and we are still missing the most vital elements of our tableau."

Stewart shook his head, exasperated. "All we're really missing is the elephant. It won't be any trouble getting Wilson."

"I'm glad you're so sure of yourself, Stewart." Anger was creeping into Victor's voice. "I would like to be sure, too. I want you to tell me when and how you will get the elephant and this Wilson fellow by the time we meet for dinner tonight. All the bodies must be plastinated before we go back to Germany next weekend, so we must finish gathering them this week."

"That's a tall order, Doctor."

"Ah, Stewart. I told you to call me Victor."

"Victor."

"Of course it's a tall order, Stewart. But it's better if we do it quickly, all at once, so we can be out of this God-forsaken country before anyone suspects us. My reputation cannot suffer another forced exit. Especially over an elephant. The public wouldn't tolerate it. Humans are one thing, but an endangered species? No one will worry where it came from once it is in the exhibit, but we have to get it to Germany very quietly."

"You're right, Victor. We have to be careful in Zambia. Public sentiment is running very high at the moment. But I'm making arrangements with a source that no one can question – official or unofficial."

"That is tantalizing news, Stewart. I look forward to hearing how you will get the elephant. I know you are plotting right now," he said playfully. "And I know you are going to succeed! You are so greedy," he laughed, "almost as greedy as me! And so resourceful! You must know some bloody government bastard who can be corrupted."

Stewart paused, annoyed that this man – this fiend – had called him greedy, but decided to let it pass. He drew a deep breath. "You might say that, Victor. I can't promise you, but I think it will work and I'll know by this evening. My old contacts have gone to ground, I'm afraid, but there are two other possibilities."

"What are they, Stewart."

Stewart took a deep breath. "I can't tell you just now. I can only say that they're both close at hand."

"That's good, Stewart. It will reduce the risks in processing and shipping. But what could possibly be so secret, Stewart? Tell me! I might be of some assistance."

Stewart scowled. The last thing he needed right now was Victor running about on his own. No, he'd have to keep his plan to himself until he was ready for action. "Before I tell you, Victor, I need to make a few more calls. I'll tell you tonight at dinner."

"You must tell me now, Stewart! I am getting so excited!" Stewart thought he heard Anita's stifled giggle in the background, but decided it was just line noise.

"No, Victor. I'll tell you tonight."

"I can't rest until I know. It will make my Parkinson's worse."

"I'm sorry, Victor. Try to relax. Trust me. I'll tell you the details tonight."

"I can't wait."

"I'm afraid you'll have to." Again, Stewart thought he heard Anita's voice. "Victor, is Anita there?"

"No, she went for a dip in the pool."

Stewart's focus dissolved instantly into thoughts of the woman's lovely body floating seductively in the warm water of his swimming pool. He jerked himself back to reality when he saw traffic starting to move. "I've got to go, Victor. Say hello to Anita and enjoy yourselves. You don't have much longer," Stewart said as he hung up.

Especially you, you revolting German freak, he thought. He pressed speed dial again. No answer. Later, he thought, after the meeting with Malinga.

Stewart sighed as his mind filled once again with an image of Anita floating in his pool, nipples hard above the water, ready for his kiss Soon, her body would be his, and when he had her, he knew his life would begin again. Not just beautiful and sensuous, Anita was a very clever woman who would make any man a proud partner

Soon Victor would be gone for good, a permanently lifeless manikin staring at them from beyond forever with vacant eyes. A butt-naked Adam, the laughingstock of the world..

27 | Wash Away Evil

"Let me preface my remarks by saying that the evidence is puzzling across the board," Jacques began. "I'm not sure of the significance of what I'm about to tell you, but it surprised me. The third victim suffered a botched abortion. The last two victims were raped, and since there are no signs of bruising on the genitals or thighs, we assume that the rapes were post-mortem."

Malinga looked up. "Postmortem?"

No wonder the girls were trying to get her attention. They'd been violated in death by someone they trusted. What could be worse?

"I'm afraid so. The semen comes from one man, but Interpol can't find a match on international or national DNA data bases. This confirms that we're dealing with two killers, possibly three, because the last two murders occurred after two suspects had been arrested in the third girl's murder."

"We've had two arrests?" Wilson asked.

Malinga turned to him. "We picked up two guys spotted dumping the third woman's body," she said. "The killers may have mutilated her so it looked like *muti* in order to cover the fact that she'd had an abortion."

"That' what I think," Danise said, nodding. "She died from a botched abortion and the killers tried to cover it up. If we include the third victim with the others, it might throw the investigation off track on all of them. Let's question the two suspects we've arrested only for the third."

Malinga nodded. "You may be right, Danise. Anything else, Jacques?" He shook his head and Malinga was about to thank him when Wilson stood up.

"Thank you, Doctor," he said. "Your summary has been very useful, very useful indeed. The differences suggest at least two killers. I only hope we can catch the others before they kill Victims 6, 7, and 8."

Malinga bristled.

Wilson may be Acting CI in Chikanda's absence, but I'm still lead investigator on this case.

She glared at him, but he ignored her. "Let me clarify a few things," he continued. "You're saying that Victims 1 and 2 were flayed and dissected while they were still alive?"

"Right."

"You're saying that the killer took the girls' skin and privates and some of their internal organs?"

Jacques nodded.

"And you're saying that all the girls were bleachers?"

Jacques nodded. "That's right."

Wilson frowned. "Interesting! That's the typical *modus operandi* in albino *muti* murders." Startled, everyone looked up at the light-skinned man. His lash-less eyes didn't blink. "Maybe these are *muti* murders plain and simple, committed on victims who were light-skinned but not albinos by birth."

Jacques nodded. Malinga said nothing.

"Contrary to what Malinga might tell you," Wilson said, smiling pointedly at her, "My trip to Tanzania was not just a vacation. As chair of Zambia's Albino Persons Association, I met with the police in Dar es Salaam to get an update. In Tanzania, albino murders are much more prevalent than in Zambia. They reached such epidemic proportions three years ago, the Tanzanian parliament finally declared them illegal so the police could strengthen enforcement and prevention. That drove incidence down quite a bit."

"I'm glad to hear that, Wilson," Malinga said in a strained voice. "But what does that tell us about this case?"

"It may tell us a lot. In albino 'skin killings,' as they're called, the victim is kept alive for as long as possible while their body parts are removed. It's supposed to increase the potency of the magic."

"Like the first two killings!" Jacques exclaimed.

Wilson nodded. "Exactly! When the killers finish, they're supposed to leave their victims' bodies in flowing water to wash away lingering traces of evil, but in reality, they usually dump the bodies in rubbish tips with their tongues cut out so they can't call for help." Wilson said. "Besides, albino tongues are valuable."

Jacques shook his head. "Who buys these wretched things?"

"Lots of people," Wilson said. "Prices are high, so the clients have to be rich. Dealers make a tremendous commission. Especially for genitals, brains, tongues, and skin."

Jacques frowned. "Why are the prices so high?"

"It's simple. Albinos are rare and buyers are desperate for the power they are fabled to possess. The *sangoma* gives the customer a shopping list of body parts and sends them to a middleman, who commissions a killer."

"So there's a system?"

Wilson nodded. "*Muti* killing is a major international business. Dead albinos make powerful medicine. When you're killed for *muti*, the buyers gets your power. He – or she – puts paste or powder made from your remains on their clothing, smears it on cuts in their skin, or eats it. Buyers wear your bones as charms, bury them in the foundations of new houses or businesses, or plant them in their fields to increase their crops. Fishermen weave albino hair into their nets. Miners bury albino bones or splash their blood on the ground to attract gems and gold to their claims."

"*Incroyable*! Jacques exclaimed. "So primitive! People still do this?"

"Not so much in Zambia," Wilson replied, annoyed by the European's distaste. "It's a lot worse in Tanzania and South Africa."

"But why albinos?" Jacques asked.

"Because they're white!" Wilson said, grinning. "Almost Caucasian, like you. Many Zambians – many Africans, in fact – still carry old biases. It's the same reason woman bleach their skins. White is good, black is bad. Albinos are rare, somewhere in between. Full of magic."

"Some people even believe that sex with an albino cures HIV," Danise said.

"Is it just albinos?" Jacques asked.

"Not originally," Wilson said. "The first Tanzanian victim was pigmented, a twenty-year-old farmer who was clubbed and skinned alive. The murderers were caught when the gang leader laid the skin over bushes at his hotel to dry. About ten years ago, there were so many skin killings that Tanzania, Malawi, and Zambia deported all foreign witch doctors. When local witch doctors took up the slack, they started the craze for albino skins."

"Market differentiation," Danise said dryly.

Wilson nodded. "There's a lucrative pan-African market. In 2008, so many Tanzanian albinos were murdered that the EU and UN protested until the government banned all traditional healers. They still operate, but under cover, of course. They meet needs no one else can."

"Do you think our killers have international connections?" Malinga asked.

Wilson nodded. "I'm sure they do. Demand is still growing. Two years ago, a fisherman on Lake Tanganyika tried to auction his albino wife at a Congolese border crossing. A man carrying an albino baby's head in a sack was arrested at the same place a week later. This past year, a gang slit a five-year-old girl's throat while her siblings watched, then drunk her blood from her skull. Then they sold her legs, arms, and head."

"Drinking blood is supposed to boost your vitality," Danise explained, "and eating brains increases political savvy. That's why people believe politicians use *muti* magic."

"An albino's grave must be guarded so the body isn't stolen," Wilson said. "In Tanzania, albino children are sent to specially guarded schools."

"*Incroyable!*" Jacques exclaimed again.

"No albino in Africa ever feels secure inside their skin. There aren't enough police to protect us and the laws are weak. The reward for our skins is too high."

"Our opinion leaders aren't helping," Danise added. "The *Post* used *muti* to boost their reporters' morale and increase circulation. When the Zambian national football team traveled to the Africa Cup, each player had his own personal *sangoma*. They used lion and hippo grease to enhance their performance."

"And they won!" Wilson said, laughing.

"Maybe so, but endorsements like those create havoc," Danise said testily.

"I was only joking, Danise. I am, after all, personally affected by this wave of superstition."

Malinga shook her head. "I'll never let Katanga say it's nice to be white again. She's on a bleaching kick these days and nothing I say seems to make a difference."

"These Nigerian movies about witchcraft are not helping," Asedi said. "They are full of horrible things that look real."

"Nigerians are bringing many terrible ideas to Zambia," Davison pronounced. "Nollywood, it's called, the place where they make the movies. I have to fight with my children not to watch them. All about greed and superstition and jealousy . . ."

Malinga cut him off. "Okay, team. Let's refocus. We've got a crime wave in Lusaka, and it's going to get a lot worse unless we catch these guys soon. What else have we got?"

28 | Find Me an Elephant, 2

The traffic light near Parliament seemed interminable. Stewart thought he'd crawl out of his skin if he had to wait a second longer and pressed speed dial again. The number rang several times, but no one answered. He began to close his phone but lifted it to his ear when it rang. He heard a familiar voice answer.

"Stewart?"

"Yes, it's me. What's wrong? You sound breathless!"

"The President's going crazy about these *muti* murders. The press is trying to implicate him. Can you imagine? Who would think our fearless leader dabbles in *muti*?" The voice raised with false incredulity, then dissolved into laughter.

Stewart laughed with him. "I certainly can't. *Muti*? Our President?"

"Do you know anything about these murders? I'm trying to get through to the police to find out what's going on, but I've had no luck."

"As soon as I get through this traffic jam, I'm going to a police briefing on the case. I'll find out what's going on."

"Good. Call me as soon as you have something."

"I will."

"Perfect. I want a full report. But you called me. What's on your mind?" the voice asked.

"I need an elephant," Stewart said.

"An elephant! You're joking! Whatever for?"

"About a year ago . . ."

The voice interrupted. "Present day, Stewart. I don't have time for a history lesson right now. What's in it for me?"

"What's in it is money, a lot of it."

"I see. An elephant, you say. Baby or adult?"

"It has to be an adult.   You have one in the menagerie, don't you?" Stewart asked.

"We have a fine old bull.   You know that.   Let me ask the grounds keepers and see what I can arrange.   I'll get back to you."

"Okay, but don't take too long."

"How long do you have?"

Stewart sighed. "I know this is short notice, but I've got to have it by Wednesday, Thursday at the latest."

His listener whistled. "Do you want me to float it down the Zambezi River while I'm at it?   Or should I load it on the Presidential jet?"

Stewart laughed. "I knew I could count on you."

"Just how do you propose to do this?"

"I hear cyanide works nicely."

"It certainly killed a lot of elephants in Zimbabwe a year ago.   But where do I get it?"

'I'll take care of that, no problem," Stewart said. "If I give you the poison tomorrow, can the elephant be dead by early next week?"

"I'm not sure. I'll let you know as soon as I can.   The timetable's a real problem.   I'm not sure the elephant I've got in mind can get sick that fast."

"It has to," Stewart said.

"What's in it for me?"

"Like I said.   Money.   Lots of it."

"I heard you the first time.   Will you tell me how much, or are you going to surprise me?"

"I'll tell you as soon as you give me a fixed delivery date. The faster you get it for me, the higher the reward will be."

"I'm still not sure."

"What are you talking about?   You've got one right there. It can get sick and die pretty quickly, can't it?"

Silence.

"Don't take too long," Stewart repeated, and hung up. He waited for the red light to change again, regretting that he'd been so abrupt. He had to step more carefully, he thought. Paul was a blackmailer, and a good one. He had his hands in every pie and knew every secret worth knowing. Including Stewart's deepest, darkest secret. He'd seen him rape the corpse, and he'd taken a picture.

And then he'd laughed. "Pitiful" he'd said. "I can't believe you've fallen so low. It's time for you to go home, man. Just as fast as you can."

Stewart grimaced at the memory and steered through the traffic light. Paul had no idea just how far he'd fallen, but Stewart would have the last laugh. If Paul had one fault, it was greed, and Stewart planned to take advantage of it. Once Paul delivered the elephant, Stewart would be on the plane so fast Paul's head would spin and his empty pockets would flap in the breeze. He'd get nothing, and there'd be no retaliation. Paul would only incriminate himself if he tried. A lot of good old file phone images would do him then.

Stewart's phone rang again. It was Victor. "What have you learned?" his voice purred.

Stewart winced at the sound. "I've started the wheels turning. The first possibility I thought of is at a place called Chaminuka. It's a small private game ranch east of the Lusaka airport that has an absolutely fabulous young bull named Duff."

"That sounds marvelous. How much will Duff cost?"

"He's way out of your price range, Victor. In fact, I don't think Duff is for sale at all. He's become something of an icon, a national treasure. But don't worry. I have an even better idea."

"Everything is for sale if the price is right, Stewart. Look at you! What's the other possibility?"

"I'll tell you later, Victor. I've got some urgent police business to attend to now. I'll tell you everything at dinner." Stewart shut off his phone. He'd had it with the insane little German, all he could stand for the moment. Things were looking up, however. Paul was ready to play ball.

Stewart turned right at the last intersection and entered the police station car park in a considerably better mood. His plans were laid for Malinga and the children, and it sounded like Paul could land him the elephant. Now, all he had to do was grab the albino. He smiled. Maybe Wilson would enjoy tea with Giselle as much as Malinga and her children.

He slipped into a parking space and was whistling by the time he pulled open the station door. He'd remembered someone in the lab who could get the cyanide to him fast, no questions asked.

29 | When the President Calls

Malinga looked at her acting boss. "Anything else, Wilson?"

"Most *sangomas* make their medicines out of plants, not people. Zambians visit with them for minor illnesses or illnesses that Western medicine can't cure, and for good luck charms."

"It's not always the *sangoma's* fault," Davison said. "Children are killed by their own relatives. Their sacrifice is considered honorable because it brings money into the family. Mothers are told that a child who is sacrificed will have a better life and a new soul."

"It's true," Asedi agreed. "A woman in my village was forced to hold her daughter while killers drank her blood. Her relatives collected the money."

"This must frighten those of you with children!" Jacques exclaimed.

Malinga looked up at him sharply. "It's worse than you can imagine. Before she came to work for me, my maid Bertha's infant son was kidnapped. The killers took his heart and genitals, and left him in a rubbish tip in Kalingalinga. Stewart examined the body, but we never found the killers."

"Lusaka may look sophisticated, but the village is right on our doorstep," Danise said.

"Tell me, Jacques," Wilson broke in. "Was the Atlas bone removed from any of the victims?"

"The Atlas bone?" asked Danise.

"It's the vertebra connecting the neck and spine, the higher and lower parts of the body. Witch doctors think it's very powerful, and it's often removed in *muti* murders," Wilson said.

"I saw no obvious damage to their spinal cords, but I'll check again," the Frenchman said.

Malinga remembered the gossip she'd heard at the beauty salon. "Do you really think these girls were victimized because they were bleachers, Wilson?"

He nodded. "They may have been chosen because they were the next-best thing to real albinos."

"It makes some sense psychologically," Danise said. "But if one in three Zambian women bleaches, it may not tell us much."

"That's true," Malinga said. "By the way, Jacques. Were you able to lift any fingerprints?"

Jacques shook his head. "The killer used gloves, and the bodies were washed after the skin was removed. Even if I could pull prints, they wouldn't help us much. Unless the killer's a foreigner, there would be a very small data base to compare them to. It sounds like most of your *muti* killers travel under Interpol's radar."

Malinga looked at her watch and glanced around the group. "Thanks everyone. Great work, Jacques. Let's take a short break before Danise reports her findings."

"A break? We don't have time for a break!" Wilson interrupted. "Let's move on to Danise's report now. But first, I'm sure I speak for all of us when I say thank you, doctor," he said, shaking Jacques' hand.

Malinga tensed, annoyed once again by Wilson's presumptuousness. "Yes. Thanks again, Doctor. Update us whenever you have something new. We'll take a short break for amenities and . . ."

The conference room phone began to ring and she checked the caller ID. "Sorry, team. It's the operator. It must be important or they wouldn't interrupt us. Let's convene back here in fifteen minutes," she said, opening the door so the group would leave the room before she picked up the receiver.

"Malinga Mutende here. How can I help you?"

"Malinga, I've got a call from the President's press secretary. He insists on talking to the officer 'in charge of the murdered girls,' as he puts it. Since Wilson hasn't been back long and you're probably still in charge of the case, I thought I'd put him through to you."

Malinga frowned. She wondered what Wilson was telling people. "I'm in charge of the case until it's solved. Remember that. Now put him through." She bit on a cuticle while she waited. It was never a good thing for the police when the President got involved. If a case was politicized, you ended up with one too many victims or one too few killers. And far too many fools.

But she was a pleased nonetheless. The President's involvement would increase visibility. It looked good that the team was led by a woman. Even Wilson could appreciate that. Finally, she heard a tenor voice on the other end of the line. "Hello?"

She took a deep breath. "Hello, Mr. Secretary. This is Malinga Mutende. I'm the Deputy Inspector in charge of the cases involving the young women."

"Yes, yes, yes. Paul Walusiku here. I want to talk to the person in charge."

Malinga flinched. "Like I said, that's me. The Chief Inspector is currently in France training with Interpol. He left me in charge of the case."

"A woman, huh? Isn't this case too important to be handled by a woman?" Malinga held her tongue.

"Okay, okay," the man continued. "So you're in charge. The first thing I want to know, Miss In-Charge, is why the press is implicating the President in this story. I quote today's *Times*'s headline: 'President In On *Muti* Murders.' What are they thinking? The man is their President!"

"I'm sorry they said that, sir, but it didn't come from us. We've given them nothing on this case."

"But *muti*? *Muti*?" His voice rose. "What possible connection could it have to the President? What do they mean?"

Malinga cleared her throat. "Well, sir, the murders resemble *muti* killings."

"But we don't have those in Zambia. And if we did, the President most certainly would not be involved."

"Yes, sir, I know. These cases resemble *muti* killings. There must be an international connection because this kind of thing doesn't happen in Zambia," Malinga said, aware of the political implications of her answers.

"I still don't see how the President's involved," the man insisted.

"The story didn't come from us. If it's any comfort, the press also blames us."

"Look, Miss In-Charge . . ."

Malinga flared. "That's Deputy Inspector Mutende, sir."

"Yes, yes. Whatever. I want you to come to State House with your team first thing tomorrow and update me on what's going on."

"Yes sir, of course. But with all due respect, do you mean Monday morning? Tomorrow's Sunday."

"I know what day of the week it is, thank you very much, Miss In-Charge. Yes, I do mean tomorrow. Come in the afternoon, after church. Ask for me, Mr. Walusiku, the President's Press Secretary. If the President's around, we'll talk to the Big Man himself, so come prepared."

"Yes, of course."

"Fine, fine. By the way, he's given you until Friday to take care of this problem."

"Friday? That's only six days away."

"Yes, I know. Look, Miss Malinga. I have to hang up. I have another call to make."

The phone went dead and Malinga frowned. The case was beginning to get visibility, all right. Maybe that was a good thing. The girls might get justice after all. But Friday?

Her frown deepened. There was little hope she'd find the killer by Friday when they'd managed to turn over so little in the last two weeks.

But it's worth a try. If we move quickly, fewer girls will die.

She broke into a smile.

If we can crack this by Friday, maybe I'll get that raise after all.

When the door opened, she looked up. Her team was back.

30 | We're in Big Trouble

Malinga was pleased to see Stewart Bleming slip into the conference room and loosen his tie as he took a seat between Davison and Asedi. He'd provided forensic insights on other cases, and had been especially useful on this one. Until Jacques showed up, that is. Stewart had been a bit uncomfortable when he'd had to play second fiddle to the more experienced Frenchman.

Malinga smiled at him warmly. "Stewart! Glad you could make it. Do you know everyone?" When he nodded, Malinga called her team to order. "The call I just received was from the President's press secretary. We have an audience with him, and possibly the President, tomorrow."

Davison's face broke into a big grin. "The President must be pleased that you are leading the investigation, Boss, after all you did for the elephants."

"Thanks, Davison, but the President wasn't pleased at all. The newspapers are saying he's responsible for what they're calling *The Muti Killings*. They're stirring the public up and the President is very unhappy. He wants us to find the killer and clear the air immediately. In fact, he wants us to do it by Friday."

"Not good," Wilson said, shaking his head.

"Not good at all," Malinga said. "I'm afraid that all we can do by Friday is tell the press that the President's not involved." She rolled her eyes toward the ceiling and put her hand on her heart. "The President may be a lot of things, but he has never been, nor will he ever be, a *muti* killer."

They all laughed.

"He prefers to kill us slowly," Stewart said, "and he doesn't get much for our remains."

"He tells us lies, starves us, and then eats us alive," Davison chipped in.

"He hasn't had any luck since he took office last year," Asedi exclaimed. "He needs all the good *juju* he can buy. Maybe he is in on this."

"Enough, enough," Malinga said, laughing. "Time to get serious! We've all got to be on the same page before we go to State House tomorrow."

Davison and Asedi groaned. "Do we all have to go?" Davison asked. "Even us?" Asedi echoed.

Malinga nodded.

"But my daughter's getting confirmed tomorrow," Davison protested.

"My niece is getting baptized," said Asedi.

Malinga laughed. "That's the holiest you two have been in a long time. Isn't there a golf tournament at the Lusaka Club tomorrow, Davison? And a fashion show at the Padmozi, Asedi?"

They looked down at their hands. Malinga smiled, secretly pleased that they didn't want to come. She had no money for overtime, and her deputies were loose cannons under the best of circumstances. "Don't worry. You're off the hook. Wilson and I will have to manage without you."

She glanced around the table, settling her gaze on Stewart. "Jacques just gave us a summary of the forensic evidence. We're about to hear from our psychologist." She nodded at Danise. "Your report, Doctor, if you please."

Danise passed out a printed table. "Here's a summary of their personal, social, and family characteristics. The empty rows on the bottom are for new victims." When the group protested, she shook her head. "I see no sign that this killer's slowing down." She pointed at the table. "You can read the details later. For now, I'll just give you the highlights.

"The victims were all young, between seventeen and twenty-seven. They were intelligent, judging from their school records and what Davison and Asedi learned from their relatives, friends and neighbors. They were fit sportswomen who worked out regularly, small by Zambian standards, and attractive, as you saw in the family photographs.

"They were known and respected by their neighbors, good students with extracurricular and volunteer activities. The last two worked at University Teaching Hospital as volunteers. They didn't live in the same compounds or go to the same schools, markets or churches, were not friends, and had few friends in common. They did, however, all frequent Celestin's Palace of Luxurious Beautification in Arcades."

Danise looked up from her notes. "Isn't that the place you go, Malinga?"

Malinga nodded, surprised to hear Celestin's salon mentioned. She hoped he and his wife weren't implicated in the crimes, but what she'd heard that morning suggested a connection. "I'm surprised they could afford it. It's expensive for students."

"Three of the women came from well-to-do families, and two also worked outside of school," Danise said. "I guess they thought their looks were worth the investment."

They were all bleachers, Malinga remembered. Light-skinned, beautiful women. Perfect targets for *muti* magic. And for older men who wanted young girlfriends. "Did any of them have sugar daddies? Boyfriends, current or jilted, who might be angry enough to murder them?"

"None of our witnesses reported boyfriends or sugar daddies," Davison said. "They went to the same nightclubs all young people in Lusaka frequent, and we know that the date rape drug was used in those clubs."

Jacques nodded. "If the killers approached them in a bar, they probably had to use chemical persuasion to get them to leave. These girls don't sound like the type who would go with just anyone who asked."

"All of them were small women," Asedi said. "I bet the killer is small, so he picks small women because they're easier to handle, easier to move about, alive or dead."

"That makes sense," Davison agreed.

Jacques nodded. "Yes. They would be easier to abduct, butcher, and skin in one piece. If the organs are being sold for *muti*, does it make any difference how big they are?"

"Not that I've heard," Wilson said. "In *muti*, innocence has a value, which is why they kill children. Were these young women virgins?"

"According to their neighbors and friends, they were," Asedi said. "Except the third one, of course. She'd had the abortion."

"I'll reexamine the others, but the postmortem rapes may make it impossible to tell," Jacques said.

"Did the killer take their brains?" Malinga asked. "They were all such bright girls. Perfect *muti*."

Jacques shook his head. "No, the skulls were intact."

Wilson sat back. "What if this isn't a single killer or even two killers," he said. "What if it's a copycat spree?"

The room went silent. "If you're right, we're in big trouble," Danise said.

31 | Small Killer, Live Chicken

Malinga shook her head. "It's possible, I guess, but I don't think so. First off, there's the physical evidence. The semen from the rapes is from the same man."

"I think Malinga's right," Danise said. "There are probably two, maybe three, killers. The postmortem rapes suggest that one man is in charge. If we can leave the third murder aside for the moment, the other four are the real thing, *muti* killings, possibly by two different killers. It looks like the third killer's motive and methods were not connected to the others."

Malinga raised her eyebrows and looked around the group. "Let's look at the third one carefully and see if we can rule it out of the pattern. Was she killed by the man who got her pregnant? Who was he? Her boyfriend? Former boyfriend? Sugar daddy?"

"An older man with status who needed to cover up her pregnancy," Wilson offered.

"Maybe it is the Archbishop. One of the guys we pulled in was his driver," Asedi said. "A witness saw him dumping the body."

Danise nodded. "If His Eminence got the girl pregnant, he'd surely want to get rid of the evidence."

"Maybe so," Jacques said, "but wouldn't he just pay her off? He didn't have to kill her."

"Unless she threatened to talk," Stewart said. "Or tried to blackmail him."

"I think Jacque's right. He'd just pay her and be done with it," Wilson said. "But then again . . ."

The group started to argue, and Malinga had to raise her voice to bring them back to order. "Let's look at the rest of the girls," she said. "Can we agree that they're real *muti* killings?"

"Yes, they're *muti*," the group agreed.

"What's the motive? Power? Magic?"

"Money," Wilson said.

"Money?" Asedi asked. "I don't think so. These girls had very little money. They were students."

Danise laughed good-naturedly. "Wilson didn't say 'robbery,' Asedi. Remember what he told us earlier? Removal of skin, eyes and other body parts suggests that the murderers already had buyers for what they took. My guess is that they sold a little in Zambia, but shipped more to Tanzania or South Africa, where the market's better."

Stewart cleared his throat. "I agree. But the first two murders were so crude, I don't know how anyone could sell the parts. The skin, at least. It's possible that the organs were not as damaged and could be sold."

"You're a doctor. What have you heard about this?" Wilson asked. Stewart regarded him gravely, but on the inside he was ecstatic. Wilson had just handed him the opportunity he needed to frame Redbone and Kivuli.

"All too much, I'm afraid. The market in human body parts is huge. But your report says that the last two victims were raped by the same man."

"The rapes look like an afterthought, like the killer was compulsively marking the victims," Malinga said.

"Since these are *muti* killings, we can assume the rapist was African," Stewart said.

"Why do you say that?" Malinga asked.

"It's hard to put a finger on it. I just have that feeling."

"Because a Zambian man will rape anything, including dead women? Because African men are like animals, and European men are not? Is that what you want to say, Doctor?" Wilson asked angrily.

Stewart shook his head sadly. "You paint me in a very bad light, Wilson. I don't think any of those things. I just have a feeling, that's all."

Wilson continued to look furious, but said nothing.

"I'll ask the Interpol technicians if they can give us a reading on that," Jacques said. "Until then, it's probably safer not to hypothesize about the rapists' race. If we are misled by our biases, we may miss something vital." Stewart and Wilson looked away. "Who do you think is behind this, doctor?" Jacques asked.

Stewart looked up. "No idea," he said, shrugging. "Witch doctors, I'd guess. I've heard there are three principal markets for body parts and skin. The biggest is run by powerful South African *sangomas*. It operates in Tanzania, Burundi and Malawi and is also a jumping-off point for the trade to Europe. It's primarily for albinos, but not exclusively so.

"Some time back, police at Heathrow reported a *muti* network bringing body parts from Tanzania into Britain and selling them through shops in Tottenham and Brixton. The investigator was threatened, and the rumors were never confirmed. This network functions in other European countries as well. There's a smaller, legal European market for museum exhibits and shows." Asedi flinched. "I'm sorry, Asedi, but it's true. Some people are just as interested in human trophies as animal.

"Over the past few years," Stewart continued, "those markets have been overshadowed by demand from Asia, especially China. There's a new network of Asian collectors who, like the Europeans, want skins or complete organ systems for display."

Asedi flinched again. "People display those things?"

Stewart smiled. "I'm afraid so, my dear. They're status symbols and museum pieces."

"The killers must be well connected if they're serving those markets," Malinga said.

"That's true, which is why I think it's more likely that they're connected to dealers in Tanzania and South Africa," Stewart said. "They're local *sangomas* trying to tap into the market here on the continent."

"If it was a criminal ring from South Africa or Tanzania, we would have heard something from the compounds," Wilson said.

Asedi nodded. "Our informants will sell each other out for a few *kwacha*, but this time, no one's talking. It makes me think the killer – or killers – are big men, Zambian politicians, maybe. Military officers. Wealthy businessmen."

"Don't forget the Church," Wilson said.

"It's possible. Our informants are too frightened to tell us anything," Davison said. "Someone must have seen something, but the parts from these girls disappeared into thin air."

"And no one knows where they were killed," Asedi added.

"Right. None of the victims were out of contact with their friends or relatives for very long," Danise said. "We've tracked them right up to the time they were kidnapped, but no one saw the kidnapper or the abduction."

"The victim's bodies were left near their homes. That's very risky," Malinga said. "If the remains had been dumped outside the city, no one would be the wiser. Instead, they're leaving them where they can easily be found. I have a feeling they're taunting us by dumping the bodies in public."

"You're right, Malinga," Danise said. "They are taunting us. They're sure they won't get caught and think they're beyond our reach."

Stewart looked at Malinga, suppressing an urge to grin. "Maybe the killer's warning you. Maybe the witch doctor you spoke to is right." Malinga's skin crawled. If she was targeted, nothing would keep them from going after Katanga, too.

"We know two things: the killer is very powerful, and he is very small," Davison said with a sly grin. "But one thing we forgot." He waited, looking around the group.

"Davison," Malinga growled. "This is a murder investigation, not a game show!"

Davison's grin widened. "There is one thing we forgot. His customers are carrying chickens."

"Chickens?" Asedi asked.

"For *muti* murders, anyone who comes to the *sangoma* must bring a live chicken. That is always the first payment. So we must look for people carrying live chickens!"

32| Redbone's Confessions

Everyone groaned. "That's every other person in Lusaka," Stewart said, laughing.

"Only every fifth person," Davison chortled. "That narrows our list of suspects."

"Stop joking, Davison," Malinga said testily. "We don't have time for it. Girls are dying. Asedi, let's hear your report on the third case. You said that the Archbishop and his henchmen made the girl's body look like a *muti* murder to throw us off a botched abortion. Let's hear more about the girl."

Asedi scanned her file. "Her name was Ruth. She was a good girl and a good student, but she made one mistake: she trusted her uncle. She visited him every Friday without fail because he helped her with school fees." Asedi looked up from her notes. "The uncle knew the Archbishop's driver and set up the meetings between Ruth and the Archbishop so she could earn her fees. "

"Her deflowering paid for her college?" Malinga asked.

"I think so. The Archbishop's driver told us that he took the holy man to the uncle's house every Friday, and the girl arrived shortly after by minibus," Davison said.

"The driver was very nervous when we picked him up," Asedi said, "and kept changing his story. At first, he claimed he'd never been in the Emmasdale compound where Ruth and her mother lived. Then we confronted him with the witness's statement."

"A neighbor boy told us he saw the car the night Ruth died," Davison explained. "He saw the driver dump something into the hedgerow, but he couldn't see what it was. He refuses to make a sworn affidavit because he knows the driver works for the Archbishop. We're trying to make him comfortable enough to identify the driver in a line up."

"Lean on the driver. Tell him we're going to question the Archbishop tomorrow," Malinga said. "Let him know we'll go easier on him if he testifies against his boss. Try to get something more from him tonight."

"We've got the uncle, too," Asedi said, "but I think we've got all we can get from him. He's more afraid than the driver,"

"Keep working on both of them," Malinga said. "they'll crack eventually. Good work, you two. Any more ideas on the other cases?"

"I have one, Boss," Davison said. "The killer must be very strong, even if the victims are small. Have you ever tried to skin an animal? It's not easy."

Jacques nodded. "That's true. It takes a lot of strength."

"We know the killers must work from Lusaka," Asedi said. "All the victims lived in the city, and all the bodies were dumped here. Not much time elapsed between when the girls disappeared and when the bodies were dumped. The killer's workplace can't be too far from here."

"He must have transport," Davison said. "Without a car, you can't carry a body very far. He couldn't hire a taxi."

"Maybe he has a pimpmobile like you see in the Nigerian movies," Asedi joked.

"That would be hard to hide," Stewart said, smiling. "What about the plastic in the muscle tissue, Jacques?"

"It's a new preservation technique, never used in Africa before. Interpol's checking for me."

"We already have some false confessions," Asedi said. "An old *sangoma* in the Kalingalinga told us he killed one of the girls. He's the one with the filthy dreadlocks and the *muti* hanging around his neck who carries a bag on his back."

"Redbone? That tiny old man? He said he killed one of the girls?" Malinga asked.

"That's the one," Asedi said with a grin. "I don't think he'd have the strength to kill a chicken, but that's what he told us."

"I saw him this morning when I dropped my maid off in Kalingalinga. He told me to stop talking to the press." Malinga smiled reluctantly at Davison. "He was carrying a live chicken, and it made a terrible racket when he smacked it on my windscreen. He wouldn't let me touch that bag. When he grabbed me, I realized how strong he is."

"See!" Davison joked. "A small man, very strong, carrying a live chicken. When we talked with him, he said he killed the second woman, but not the first one or the last two. He says the Archbishop killed the third one."

Asedi shook her head. "He's a very old man. I don't think he killed anyone."

"Don't count Redbone out so fast, Asedi," Stewart said. "He's a very powerful *sangoma*. He lives near me and he's always busy. He may not be strong enough, but his son, Kivuli, is. Kivuli just returned from South Africa, and probably has connections with *sangomas* down there."

Malinga straightened.

Kivuli. William the Bicycle Man warned me about him.

"Do you think Redbone and Kivuli are responsible for the murders, Stewart?" Malinga asked. "Bertha seems genuinely afraid of them. Why would she be so frightened?"

"One question at a time, Malinga," Stewart said, laughing. "Bertha lives near them in Kalingalinga, which may be enough to frighten her. It's never a good idea to point a finger at powerful witchdoctors. Most people are afraid of them."

"Redbone told me the killer would come after me if I keep speaking out against him in the press, but I don't believe much of what he says," Malinga scoffed.

"Especially when he claims the Archbishop killed the third girl," Asedi said.

Wilson shook his head. "I just can't believe that."

"I'm inclined to agree with Wilson," Stewart said. "I think Redbone's either setting the Archbishop up or telling stories to make himself look important. He probably has a grudge against him and he wants to settle the score. The Archbishop often speaks out against *muti* in his Sunday sermons."

"We need to bring both witch doctors in for questioning right away," Malinga said.

"That's not going to be easy," Stewart said. "Witch doctors can disappear into thin air."

"We've got to bring them in, whatever it takes. The tissue pathology suggests that the first two victims were killed by witch doctors, but not the last two. Do you have any idea which surgeons in Lusaka were skilled enough to remove their skin?"

Stewart cleared his throat. "I'm a bit out of touch with the university crowd, but I'll take it up with my colleagues and get back to you if I hear anything."

"Good, Stewart. That would be very helpful."

The others nodded and started to talk at once. Malinga called for quiet. "Okay, everyone, it's getting late. Let's finalize our plans for tomorrow. Wilson and I will go see the President. Davison and Asedi," she said with a thin smile, "when your church services are over, find the witch doctors and bring them in. If you can't find them, ask around and learn as much as you can about them. Put out the word in Kalingalinga that we want to question them.

"When you're done in Kalingalinga, split up. Davison, go to the Palace of Luxurious Beautification and talk to Celestin and Josephine. Try to catch them behind the salon or after hours so you don't bother their clientele or tip off a potential suspect.

"Asedi, see if anyone in Kalingalinga's women's association will talk, and double check your map of the dump sites for places you think our killer is hiding. Are there any surgeries, storefronts, workrooms, or warehouses in the area – other than yours, Stewart, of course – where this work could be done?

"Jacques, while you're waiting for the toxicology report on our latest victim, research the Atlas bone and let me know what you hear from Interpol about the plastic. It's very curious."

The Frenchman nodded. "No problem. With your permission, I'll brief Stewart on what I've got, and double check my notes to see if I missed anything on the first round."

Malinga smiled at her team. "Thanks for your hard work," she said, closing her file. "We'll meet back here tomorrow at sixteen hundred hours. Wilson and I should be done at State House by then." She laughed as heads started moving back and forth. "I know, I know. The President won't be on time, but we have to act like he will. See you tomorrow."

As Davison and Asedi gathered their papers and headed for the door, Jacques cleared his throat. "I'd rather not come with you when you visit the President. I have more work to do in the morgue."

Malinga laughed out loud. "Guess you don't know much about our President," Wilson said. "The bodies in the morgue will give you a better reception."

"Right now our glorious leader hates *bazungu* – white people like us," Stewart added.

"But his Vice President is white!" Jacques exclaimed.

Stewart laughed. "He really hates foreign *bazungu*, even people like me who've been here most of our lives. The Vice President is white, British-born like me, but he became a Zambian citizen years ago. It's us – foreign passport holders – the President hates. He says we're freeloaders who've been able to do whatever we like in Zambia for far too long."

"It started last year," Malinga explained, "shortly after the elections. He told the American Ambassador not to call unless he had an appointment. He said that Western ambassadors were dropping by to talk about human rights violations so often, he couldn't have a proper bowel movement." She shook her head. "He actually said that to the press. Can you imagine?"

Jacques raised his eyebrows, a smile forming on his lips. "Sounds like a very outspoken man."

"No question," Malinga said, smiling back at him. "Since you can't meet the President, let Danise and I take you to dinner tonight instead."

"I'll join you," Wilson said. "I need a good meal after all the horrible food on Zanzibar."

Malinga couldn't gracefully refuse him. "All that fresh seafood will be a tough act to follow."

"That's just it, Malinga. It won't be. I need a steak. A Zambian steak. I'll meet you all at the Carnivore later." He pushed his chair back from the table and stood. "Don't hang around here too late by yourself, Malinga. If you're being targeted, you don't want to give the killer any opportunities. I'll drop you at your hotel, Jacques. I don't want anything to happen to you, either."

"Jacques," Stewart said, "I'll send my taximan to fetch you a little before the dinner hour. Just wait in front of the hotel at nineteen hundred hours."

He looked in his briefcase. "Damn! I've forgotten a file in the lab. I'll be right back to pick up my papers, Malinga, so don't lock the door."

33 | Healthy Fear Is A Useful Thing

Danise stood and stretched. "Good meeting, Malinga. It's an interesting case."

"That's an understatement!"

Danise laughed. "We made some progress today, thanks to you. But you look very tired. How are you holding up? It can't be easy to see what's he's doing to these women."

Malinga nodded. "They're even talking to me in my dreams. I'm not getting much sleep lately, and it doesn't help that Wilson wants to take the case from me now that he's back." Danise groaned. "I may be paranoid, but I think Wilson and Chikanda are double-teaming me again."

Danise smiled gently. "Ah, Malinga. Talk to your boss before you jump to conclusions. You handled that case in Chobe brilliantly, and the elephant poaching case in Asia was even more complicated. You're tough, Malinga! And you've got brains. They're what got you promoted, don't forget."

"But the elephant poachers got away," Malinga said. "With the ivory."

Danise patted her hand. "You'll find them eventually. By the way, have you heard anything from Eitone?"

Malinga shook her head.

"He's a good man, Malinga. Just right for you. Keep believing in his innocence."

Malinga smiled weakly. "Thanks, Danise. With everyone else telling me otherwise, it's easy to forget." She frowned. "I have a lot of things on my mind. I saw Herbert earlier, and he threatened to take the kids away."

Danise groaned. "Not again!"

Malinga nodded. "Not only that, but after Redbone warned me off, another informant in Kalingalinga told me more women would die and I would be one of them." Malinga's shoulders sagged. "I'm tempted to let Wilson take over, but I feel strongly that this case should be handled by a woman."

"It should. What exactly did your friend say?"

"He said that Redbone and his son, Kivuli, are involved, but I don't believe it."

Danise nodded. "They may be involved, but the leader is much more sophisticated. Someone local."

"My feelings exactly, Danise! I feel like the killer's right around the corner and we're missing him by a mile! And I feel like I'm being watched. I'm anxious all the time. I'm even afraid the killer might come after Katanga."

Danise patted her hand. "Healthy fear is a useful thing, Malinga. It's probably smart to assume that something could happen, but it doesn't mean you have to run away. Danger's an occupational hazard for you, after all."

"There's something else here, something that doesn't quite wash. I can't figure out what it is, and it's driving me crazy. The killers are taunting us, embarrassing us. One of the killers is a very skilled surgeon, someone we know and trust. But he – or she – is committing these terrible acts of violence."

"Maybe it's not just the witch doctors who resent your visibility, Malinga. If the killers have international ties, there's a great deal of money involved." Danise grinned. "From my vast experience with millionaires, I know they'll do anything to protect their investments. But what do they gain by embarrassing you?"

Malinga shrugged. "They can get me kicked off the case or fired, if they keep it up."

Danise studied her, frowning. "Do you think they have ties with the elephant poachers? The poachers could go back to their old tricks if you were eliminated."

Malinga sighed. "I suppose that's possible."

"Cheer up, Malinga. It'll do you good to relax tonight. I'll see you at the Carnivore." Danise opened the door, then turned back. "Don't stay here too late, Malinga. Wilson's right. These killers will do anything to make sure the police don't catch them."

"You're scaring me, Danise."

"I don't mean to. I just don't want to see you or the kids at the mercy of a homicidal maniac. Why don't you leave with me now?"

"I have to wait for Stewart to come back from the lab."

Danise frowned. "Leave when he does, Malinga. Don't stay here alone." She smiled. "I'm looking forward to dinner. This man Jacques intrigues me."

"I like him, too. He's actually turning out to be a terrific help, and he's not arrogant like most Frenchmen."

Danise laughed and wagged her finger. "No racial or ethnic stereotyping allowed, Malinga. See you later."

Malinga rubbed her forehead, fretting about what Danise had said. Her friend was right. Extra precautions were in order. She opened her phone to check with her mother on the children's whereabouts, but shut it when Stewart threw the door to her office open, marched up to her desk, and leaned over her, scowling. She drew back, alarmed.

"Are you all right, Stewart?"

He shrugged and threw himself down in her visitor's chair. "It's that bloody Frenchman. I was doing a fine job on the case until he came along. Now I can't get near the lab. You have to do something about him, Malinga."

"Chikanda decided to bring him here, not me. Try to be understanding, Stewart! This isn't a competition. Since he's not a practicing physician like you, he has time to pour over the results. Don't you think he had some interesting points to make?"

He scowled at her again. "I can't see the value of all this analysis. Let's find the witch doctors and be done with it. We're wasting time while girls die."

"What witch doctors are responsible, Stewart? You've lived in Zambia for decades. You must have seen some very strange things. Any guesses who it might be?" Malinga was relieved to see Stewart begin to relax in response to her deference. His mania had become unsettling. She forced a smile to encourage him.

"It's obvious the uncle killed the third girl. I doubt the Archbishop's involved. In the first two cases, I think you're looking for one or several local *sangomas*, and in the last two cases, for a sophisticated, modern-day witch doctor, possibly foreign."

She frowned. 'If a local *sangoma* is connected with the international body parts market, he's bound to have some powerful Zambian partners. Big money always attracts big criminals, same as elephant poaching."

He laughed. "Crime flourishes in a country with borders as porous as Zambia. You and I both know it's laughably easy to take anything in or out of here. Befriend a few border officials, make sure they're happy, and everything will flow. You should probably check for connections with narcotics and guns."

"You're right. These international crimes are connected. I'll ask Wilson to take a look." Malinga narrowed her eyes. "Do you really think our border control is that bad?"

"I don't think so, I know so," Stewart sneered. "I worked in Solwezi at the Meheba refugee camp for seven years. We could get anything we needed if we greased the right palms."

She shook her head. "Corruption."

Stewart laughed. "I never minded the corruption, once I learned the rules. It's part of doing business, and it's not as bad as other countries. It gets things done."

"Any idea who's doing this, Stewart? You know a lot of people. Where should we look?" Head tilted to one side, Malinga appraised him. He looked away and coughed, knowing this was the perfect opportunity to throw her off course.

"I have a few ideas. Would you like to hear them?"

She nodded. "Of course."

"I think Redbone and Kivuli are connected to the Chinese network, and may have other international connections. Once Asedi and Davison find them, Malinga, bring them in for questioning. Better yet, lock them up."

She shook her head. "You know I can't do that until we have better evidence. Besides, it's so hard to believe. Redbone seems so harmless. It seems that the international body parts trade is much more sophisticated."

Stewart exhaled forcibly. "It may be sophisticated, but it's desperate. The supply lines were cut when the Chinese government forbid using prisoners' remains without their permission. At the same time, human remains have become more popular than rhino horn with many wealthy Chinese collectors. They're looking for new sources."

"You mean Africa?"

He nodded. "Zambia is opportune because border enforcement is so lax. They plastinate human remains and hide them in shipments of other goods."

"Plastinate? How?"

"Plastic is substituted for live tissue in a two-step process called plastination. The results are extraordinary, like you're looking at the insides of a living, breathing human being."

Her eyes widened. "Jacques said that these girls' remains had been partially impregnated with plastic. Why didn't you say something?"

Stewart looked away and cleared his throat. "He's been so helpful to you, I didn't want to one-up him."

"One-up him? How could you possibly do that?" Malinga regretted her words as soon as they left her mouth, but Stewart didn't seem offended.

He smiled thinly. "Easily. I may live in Zambia, but I know more than he does about plastination. I've been following developments in the field. It's the first major advance in preservation since embalming. It renders the subject lifelike, odorless, and strong enough for shipping."

"Plastination?"

"Here, let me show you what I'm talking about." Stewart pulled his cell phone out and thumbed intently through his photos. "Here," he said. "I took these pictures in Paris when I was visiting there a few years ago."

She looked at photos and gasped. "Stewart! You can't be serious! People actually collect these? Please don't tell me that Zambian women were killed for this!"

"It's possible," Stewart said, thumbing to a new photo and holding his phone out to her. "It's extraordinary, isn't it?"

She looked away. "Extraordinary? You call that extraordinary? Why would anyone want these?"

He smiled. "From my perspective, the work is visionary. These are true works of art."

"But Stewart! These were live human beings!" Malinga protested. "Shows like this encourage more body snatching. If our young women suffered and died to satisfy someone's obscene curiosity, that's abhorrent. How can people condone this?"

Stewart frowned at her and snapped his phone shut. "I knew you wouldn't get the point," he said, and started packing up his things. "The bodies on display were volunteers. The owners donate their bodies to science before they die."

Malinga wasn't sure she believed him, but knew it wasn't wise to argue. He was angry again, threatening. "To each his own, Stewart," she said. "But I know these girls didn't donate their bodies to science. If people like this are harvesting bodies in Zambia, it's our job to stop them. But first we've got to find them. Who do you think they are?"

34 | Fingering the Chinese

Stewart's eyes narrowed slightly. "My guess – and it's only a guess, mind you – is that Chinese surgeons connected with our traditional healers' network and have a clinic somewhere outside the city, maybe near one of the mines. They're dumping the remains in the city to throw you off."

"Do you think Redbone and Kivuli are collaborating?"

He shrugged. "I don't really know. Redbone doesn't have much of a grip on reality, but his son recently returned from South Africa. Speak with Kivuli when Asedi and Davison find him."

"Who else?"

"I have no clue. That mystery must be solved by your team, my dear," Stewart said.

"But you've been here so long. You know everyone."

He laughed and ducked his head. "My powers are in medicine, not detection, Malinga. I'm a simple doctor."

"You're too self-effacing, Stewart. You're one of the cleverest men I know."

"Perhaps your French pathologist – you said he was from Marseilles? A ghastly seaport, that – can lead you in the right direction."

"Oh, Stewart! You're jealous!" she said, laughing. When he frowned, she patted his arm. "No need to be. Chikanda sent him. He looks smart because he has a lot more time to spend on the case than you. You're a brilliant man, but you're too busy helping people to compete on the forensics."

He squeezed her hand and released it. "That's very kind of you to say, Malinga." His resentment was still strong. He turned away so she couldn't see it and started gathering his things. "I really must be going."

"By the way, do you know Celestin, the hairdresser at the Palace of Beautification in Arcades?" Malinga asked. "He told me that some of his customers want grafts to repair the damage they've done by bleaching. Would they be like the grafts that were on the victims?"

It's like the ones you're giving Giselle, she thought, remembering the damage she'd seen on the women's skin."

Have you heard about it here in Zambia? Celestin claims there are doctors in Lusaka who are performing miracles with grafts. Are any of your colleagues involved?"

She noticed him tense ever so slightly, but he shook his head and continued collecting his papers. "Sounds shady to me. I don't think the science is sufficiently advanced to make that kind of tissue repair routine. It's used for burn victims, but the threat of infection is enormous. You need the best sort of equipment and clinical conditions, and you certainly can't find them here in Zambia."

"Maybe there's a doctor who's trying something new?"

"I'll ask around." Stewart shouldered his bag. "Sorry, Malinga. I do have to go. Giselle will be anxious if I'm away too long. I'd join you for dinner tonight, but I'll still be working with her. She's in the middle of treatment, so she feels very vulnerable right now."

Malinga eye followed him to the door. He was still in good shape for an older man, she thought. Lean and strong. She wondered if his relationship with Giselle was more than professional. "No apologies!" Malinga said, drawing in a deep breath. "How's the treatment going?"

Stewart looked away. "Much of it's palliative. More I can't say. Patient confidentiality and all that."

Malinga flushed. "Oh Stewart! Of course! I bet it's doubly true when your patient is as famous as Giselle!"

"It's important for every patient," Stewart said. "I just don't get many as famous as she is." He laughed. "Sorry! I'm a bit overprotective, I guess."

"Don't apologize, Stewart! I should apologize to you. I'm so grateful you're helping us." She smiled sheepishly. "I hate to bother you because I know you're really busy, Stewart, but

Katanga asked if we could see Giselle again. She won't shut up about it. You know how teens are."

The doctor laughed. "I know how Katanga feels! Giselle still mesmerizes me and I'm fifty years older than your daughter."

"I was surprised to see you two together at The Mint," Malinga said. "I didn't know you knew her."

"Giselle and I have known each other for years. We went to neighboring private schools here in Zambia. I was much older, so she adopted me as a surrogate brother."

"She couldn't have chosen a better one. Could you use your influence so Katanga could see her again?"

Stewart smiled at her. "Flattery will get you everywhere, Malinga. I'll try for Saturday. Would that work for you?" he asked, restraining himself from rubbing his palms together and gloating. "Would Shiko like to come as well?"

"He'll be ecstatic! They both will!"

"We'll have a proper high tea. Can Wilson join us?"

"I'm sure he would!"

Stewart's smiled carefully. "It's up to Giselle, of course. I'll ask her as soon as she's fully conscious."

Malinga took his hand. "Thanks again, Stewart. Your experience throws a whole new light on our meager facts."

He nodded, his face gentle. "We'll have a lovely tea for Giselle next Saturday. She's returning to South Africa the day after, so we won't have another chance."

Malinga grinned. "That's great, Stewart. Katanga and Shiko will be thrilled. I won't tell them yet – they'll bother me for the entire week. And I'll check with Wilson."

"Good, good. In the meantime, call me if anything else comes up. You know I'm always ready to help." He glanced back at her as he turned the doorknob.

"Be careful, Malinga. Whoever is doing this is very, very dangerous. Call me on my cell if you need me." She nodded. "If I don't see you before, I'll be expecting you and the children – and Wilson – for tea late Saturday afternoon."

"That's just lovely, Stewart. You're so kind!"

35 | Isn't He Dead Yet?

When Stewart left, Malinga sat for a moment, thinking. She frowned. Stewart had been like an uncle to her, but he'd changed so much since his wife died. He was preoccupied, cold, and distant. Maybe it was inevitable. Losing a life partner was not easy. She'd only had hers for a few months and the loss was palpable.

Before Jacques arrived, Stewart had been a willing collaborator, eager to share information and ideas, but now he was resentful and evasive. She couldn't put a finger on why his current vagueness bothered her so much, but it did.

Take the business about Giselle. If Stewart wasn't performing skin grafts, what else could he be doing to repair the damage to her skin? She shrugged. There was a lot about medicine she didn't know. It was possible that there were other treatments. Plastination?

But why was he being so secretive? If Celestin was right and there were other physicians performing skin grafts, wouldn't he know about it? And it made no sense that he was jealous of Jacques. He was a family practitioner in a small country. Jacques had an international reputation, but Stewart still insisted he prove his worth.

She flipped off the overhead light and locked the door to her office behind her. Stewart was probably reluctant to cast suspicion on fellow physicians providing experimental treatment to women who'd bleached. Medical societies could be so conservative, and these women needed help. Most of them could not afford to travel outside the country to get it, either. Physicians doing pioneering work in Zambia would be in demand in the future, when even more women who bleached would need help repairing the damages.

By the time she descended two flights of stairs to the car park, it had started to rain. She paused under cover of the station's rear exit while she searched for her car keys. The rains had started for real. They were beautiful, but they made life so complicated. I must remember my umbrella, she thought.

The sound of wipers on the windscreen relaxed Malinga and she settled back in her seat and turned the key in the ignition. Today's meeting increased her confidence about the case. Asedi and Davison had done a good job questioning the driver and the uncle and were likely to get more information – if not full confessions – soon.

She hoped against hope that the Archbishop himself was not involved. A close friend of the President, it would be very sticky indeed if he was implicated in the murder of a college girl. While they had no suspects in the other murders, she doubted the Archbishop and his crew were involved.

It was unlikely that Wilson could persuade Chikanda to replace her on the case, but it annoyed her that he would try. She smiled when she thought how Danise – someone she could always count on, a woman leader who struggled against the jealousy and prejudices of men – had put him in his place.

She was happy with the progress her team was making, although they had nothing definitive yet. Asedi and Davison were more useful than she'd hoped. They'd collaborated closely with neighborhood associations over the past year and would get more information tomorrow. Asedi's analysis of the dumpsites was narrowing the killers' possible location. Even Davison was rising to the occasion, despite his tedious jokes.

Danise and Jacques provided critical insights from completely divergent directions, while Wilson's insights from Tanzania about albinos and Stewart's knowledge of the body part trade and plastination explained an otherwise inexplicable set of crimes and showed the potential of a tie-in with international criminal activity. She frowned. If the murders were indeed the first in a rash of *muti* murders with connections to Tanzania, South Africa, Europe, and Asia, the killers might prove more difficult to catch than she'd bargained for.

Stewart's hunch that local *sangomas* were feeding a Chinese network centered at one of the mines was brilliant. Redbone's son Kivuli might be key. Zambians often returned from

South Africa with new ideas, and he could be collaborating with Chinese and South African buyers both.

Once the case was solved – and she was confident it would soon be – Malinga would use her increased visibility in the press to gain more lasting legal protection for women and children. She'd persuade Home Affairs to strengthen border controls and advocate for stronger licensing laws and regulation of the Zambian Traditional Healers Association. Good healers were a boon to the community, but without supervision, anything could happen.

She thought about Katanga and Shiko, safe and warm with their grandparents under the big chicken's wing, no doubt watching telly with Iris's dachshund curled at their feet. She tried her mother's number, but it was engaged. Maureen so liked to catch up on the news with her sisters every night.

By the time her parents dropped the kids back home on Tuesday after the long weekend, Bertha would be back to care for them. Malinga felt grateful to the woman and admired her strength. She was strict, but she hadn't been corrupted by the city. Malinga could count on her to take good care of Shiko and Katanga while she tied out the case.

Herbert didn't have a leg to stand on, and if he took the children on another unauthorized vacation like he had last year while she was chasing the poachers in Asia, she'd make good her threat to press kidnapping charges. He knew that if she did, he'd be disbarred, and she banked on his love of cars and girlfriends to keep him in line.

Malinga swerved to avoid drenching a group of pedestrians with rainwater. She sighed, feeling a sudden surge of vulnerability and self-doubt. And loneliness.

If I'd never met Eitone, my life would be perfect right now. I miss him so much, and I'm sure he had nothing to do with the disappearance of the ivory. I should give up on him, but I can't.

She brightened at the thought that something might come to light while she was working on this case. It might suggest new ways to block illicit trade in living beings once and for all.

It's all about borders, after all. So many innocent creatures – human and animal – kidnapped and sacrificed for profit.

Malinga reached the restaurant early and grabbed a table for four. Relaxing in a dark corner, she thought back to the afternoon's meeting. Watching Danise and Wilson go at it was always fun. Danise had no trouble debunking Wilson's patronizing attitudes. For all that, he was very clever, and she wanted his thoughts on the case now that he'd heard all the evidence. For all his arrogance, Wilson was a lot smarter than he let on.

Danise gained some new insights, too. She probably knew something about the Archbishop's background through her work with families in the parish. Malinga was excited about the prospect of getting to know Jacques better, and wanted to pick his brain about Stewart, who seemed unnecessarily protective of his role with the department. Malinga hoped Stewart felt better about Jacques now that they'd talked because she needed his full, open cooperation.

Yes, they'd made great headway and were likely to gain even more ground over the next few days when they had full forensics on the latest killing. She felt strong, competent, and confident that she'd soon give her nighttime visitors the answers they were looking for. All that said, what should she do about the President's demand to close the case by Friday? They were making great progress, but the last thing she wanted to do was implicate an innocent, especially a powerful innocent like the Archbishop, because she was being pressed. She'd been pushing her team hard, but now, with the pressure coming from a man they couldn't refuse, would they unite and come through in extraordinary ways? They'd done it before and could do it again because they took their responsibilities for the wellbeing of the nation to heart.

When she looked up from her wineglass, she spotted Wilson dodging puddles in the parking lot and waved to him through the window. When he reached the table, he shook the rain off his umbrella and leaned it against the window. "The traffic is terrible. The streets in town are overflowing." He threw his jacket over the back of the chair and sat down. "By the way, The Husband called me."

"Herbert? Isn't he dead yet?" Malinga asked.

Wilson laughed. "Afraid not."

"He's just what I don't need right now. He's threatening to take Katanga and Shiko away from me because of this case. We had a fight at my parent's house earlier this afternoon when he almost ran over his own son. Why did he call you?"

"I was surprised, but I think you just explained it. I'd just arrived home and took the dog for a walk when the phone rang. He talked like he was my long-lost friend. Then he asked me what we're doing to ensure the safety of his children."

"Whose children?"

"'His' children, he said. He said that since I'm Acting Inspector while Chikanda is in France, I should make you give the kids to him until this case is done." Wilson cringed and ducked. "Don't throw anything, Malinga, especially the knives."

She glared at him. "It's not funny, Wilson."

He looked over the table at her and smiled. "I know that. Don't kill the messenger, Malinga. Not every man in Zambia is a chauvinist pig. I'm on your side, remember?"

"When The Husband calls you again, be sure to tell him to get lost. He dropped Shiko off at my parents even though he'd promised to keep him for the weekend. I'm sure it breaks his heart every time he has to dump the kids so he can keep his heavy dates. He should spend more quality time with his children."

"Yeah," Wilson smiled. "Quality time. Herbert's definitely looking for quality time with his kids. That's why he bought the new BMW sports car. Have you seen it? And the white woman sitting in the front passenger seat who so loves to let her blond hair flow in the wind? I'm sure she'll give them a lot of quality time."

She felt her face flush. "Tell me you're joking. I thought my mother was delusional."

36 | The Old Beast Should Die

Stewart waited fifteen minutes before he could squeeze his way into main road traffic, snarled by the torrential rain. Even on high, the wipers could barely keep up. He was anxious to see how Giselle was doing, but happy with the way he'd switched Malinga's road signs so they pointed in all the wrong directions. In pursuit of the witch doctors and their Chinese collaborators, she would be chasing her tail for the rest of the week until it was time for tea with Giselle.

Stewart cursed the lorry that cut him off at the next intersection, but relaxed when he remembered Anita. He gave his imagination free rein, mesmerized in part by the steady beat of his windshield wipers. Anita. He couldn't wait to see her beautiful, sinuous body and voluptuous breasts again. A stupid smile crossed his lips. She'd be a lot better than a cadaver, and might cure him of the crazy urges he'd been unable to curb on his own. Women could do that. They were powerful in so many ways.

Fortunately, their naïve, trusting natures made them easy to fool. Look at Malinga. He'd given her quite a bit to chew on, enough misinformation to keep her out of the way for some time to come.

Stewart smiled, imagining Anita's naked body surfacing in his pool, water cresting over her lovely breasts. She was gorgeous, a throwback to the tantalizing women of the Forties and Fifties, real women who knew how to please their men. Like Marilyn Monroe. Yes, that was it, he thought, feeling the crotch of his trousers tighten. That's who she remined him of. A beautiful kitten waiting to nip you with her tiny teeth, or catch you with her tiny talons. Playful, luscious. Slightly dangerous. Once Victor was dead, he'd . . .

Stewart swerved to avoid a car making its way up the verge to his left and swore. If anything, the traffic was worse than it had been a few hours ago. As he waited at the next red light, he fretted at how long it would be before he saw Anita again. Maybe tonight, after Victor went to bed, he would finally get the chance to tame her. He smiled. He would give Victor a little something to help him sleep.

Anita's animal eyes and luscious lips sent Stewart drifting in a world of delight. When he had the woman herself and everything that came with her, life would be incredible. Imagine becoming her personal and professional partner! Owning part of her empire! Owning the woman herself! It was the dream of a lifetime.

He'd stay in Zambia long enough to get the African side of production going, then they could be together forever in Germany. Or England, which allowed internet sales of body parts. Things were going better than he'd hoped. While Malinga chased the witch doctors for a few days, he'd collect Victor's elephant. Malinga and her children would walk into the trap he'd baited with Giselle next Saturday. With luck, Wilson would walk in with them, but if an opportunity to snatch the albino DI came earlier, he'd take it. If he were to meet Victor's timetable, he'd take all the opportunities that presented themselves.

Including killing Victor himself.

But no. As much as the thought pleased him, it would have to wait. They had to get out of the country as fast as they could and killing Victor now would only delay things. Malinga, her children, the elephant, and Wilson would disappear with no trace left behind. He would wait and help Victor into his grave once they were safe in Germany.

When his phone rang, Stewart's foot slipped off the brake pedal and he nearly smashed into the car in front of him. He fumbled for the phone angrily, but smiled when he saw the caller ID. It was Paul. He probably had good news.

"Hey Stewart! Paul here!"

"Thanks for calling back! Any news about the elephant?"

"I won't . . . "

The connection broke and Stewart threw his phone on the seat. It rang again, and Stewart had to reach it on the passenger side floor, swerving dangerously into the left-hand lane and getting an angry warning from the truck next to him. But he was grinning.

"Stewart."

"What's the news, Paul?"

"It's all good. Why else would I call? You're in luck, friend. It just so happens that our most famous pachyderm is on his last legs. A big one. Lots of tusk. I think you'll like him. I'll tell you more as soon as you tell me what's in it for me."

"Money, of course.

"You already said that, Stewart. How much?"

"I don't know yet. I'll find out tonight. I know it will be substantial."

"How substantial, Stewart?"

"Fifty thousand US?"

The caller laughed. "Fifty thousand, Stewart? Fifty thousand? Are you out of your mind? Do you know what kind of risks are involved? Double that and you may get your elephant."

"Be reasonable, Paul! There's no risk for you. All you have to do is ensure the elephant dies. It'll be out of Zambia before anyone knows it's gone. You just have to persuade the public it was a mercy killing and it's gone to the glorious elephant burial ground in the sky."

"Nothing to it, eh Stewart? It's that easy, huh? The President won't be happy. What will I tell him?"

"That the beast was old and died of natural causes, like the President himself should be gracious enough to do."

"You shouldn't say things like that."

Stewart laughed. "How many times have you said it yourself? Look, Paul, I'll get you the poison in a few days. It'll arrived pressed into blocks of feed. No one will suspect anything until it's too late. Not the President or the elephant."

"Sorry, Stewart. You talk a good line, but it's one hundred thousand US or nothing, half up front."

"I don't know if my sponsor is willing go that high."

"Willing or not, he'll pay. Or he'll get nothing." Paul's voice was serious. "This is risky business, Stewart. You know that as well as I do. It costs a lot to kill an elephant these days – even when it's legal! Look at what those American hunters pay!"

"I know, Paul. But I'm not sure I can talk him into it."

"Do you best, Stewart. And tell him I need half up front. I have expenses. We'll need a helicopter."

"We can just truck it out."

"That won't work. If you come in a truck, security will be alerted and pretty soon everyone will know what you've done. We've got to get in and out of the President's park fast, and take all the evidence with us. You're not just talking about a couple of tusks, Stewart. He wants the whole thing, right?"

"Yes, he does," Stewart said, weary of the whole business. "I suppose you'll have to pay the helicopter pilot not to talk?"

"I trust him, but I will have to pay him. By the way, where to you want it delivered?"

Stewart blinked. Delivered? The word seemed rather harsh. "Lusaka International Airport."

"Are you crazy? There are too many people there!"

"The private side, Paul. My sponsor has his own jet."

Paul thought for a minute then chuckled. "Perfect. Remember that I need half up front, Stewart, and I won't do anything until I get it. I don't have to remind you what it would mean for your career if I told anyone what I saw."

"I know, I know. You remind me every time I speak with you." Stewart leaned on his horn. The man ahead of him in the right lane retaliated by swerving in his direction.

"When, Stewart? When?"

"The money?"

"What do you think we're talking about here?"

"I'll know late tonight. I'll call you in the morning."

"It all depends on you, Stewart. Once I have half the cash in my hands, it will take three days from start to finish. We'll deliver it to your friend's jet at night."

Stewart tapped his fingers on the steering wheel while he waited for the next light. His plan was shaping up nicely. There'd be no evidence left behind. Once Paul got his money and the poison, the elephant would be dead, rather conveniently, toward the end of the week. He'd load the carcass on the plane and pack the other bodies around it. He'd need a good source of dry ice. There wouldn't be time to plastinate the beast until they reached Germany.

Once in Germany, he and Victor would have all the time they needed to plastinate their 'volunteers' properly and create the effects Victor was looking for. After Stewart set up the lab in Zambia, he'd settle his affairs with Victor for good. And he'd make sure Paul got his share of the cyanide so there was no one left to tell the story. He smiled.

He couldn't wait to climb on the jet and be out of there. With Anita clawing at his crotch.

37 | Too Close for Comfort

Wilson shook his head. "No. I saw Herbert in his new bomb at Manda Hill with a very sexy lady – *mzungu* – in the passenger seat. Maybe he borrowed it for the afternoon. Maybe she was the sales agent. Who knows? Who cares?"

"I care," Malinga said. "He hasn't paid me child support for a couple of months. He says he's broke, paying for repairs on the house we still own jointly. Sounds like he's investing his money in other things."

"Who knows?" Wilson repeated. "Maybe he got it as a bribe. You know how lawyers are in Zambia. I think everybody has their hand in the till but us."

Malinga nodded. "Sometimes I wonder why I decided to become a cop," she said. "You remember Gillian? My best friend from university?" she said. "She's vice president of Lusaka's newest Nigerian bank and makes more money than the President. They make her buy a new car every year with company funds. The latest one cost at least $100,000. And we can't get enough for petrol!"

Wilson laughed. "Let's face it, Malinga. You're a cop because you like helping people. She likes robbing them."

Malinga eyes widened and then she started to laugh. "You're right," she conceded. "Sorry I let it get to me. No more talk about Herbert. Or cars, or money. Let's talk about the case. For starters, the third murder doesn't look like it's connected to the other four."

"Absolutely. You said you have two men in custody."

"That's right. The uncle and the driver. We know the broad circumstances of her disappearance. She was at her uncle's one minute, on the bus the next, and called her mother to say she was almost home. Then she disappeared into thin air until she was found the next day in a hedgerow. They were trying to prove she was in certain places at certain times," Malinga said. "Probably forced her to call. In the other cases, the timing is less clear. We don't know if they were missing for hours or days."

Wilson nodded. "Then there's the 'coincidence' that the Archbishop visited the uncle at the same time as the girl. In my book, he's as much of a suspect as the uncle and the driver."

"We have to talk with him as soon as possible. Let's do it tomorrow, after we finish with the President. By the way, Wilson, let's not say anything to the President about the Archbishop. They're old friends."

"No problem." Wilson glanced toward the entrance and waved. "There's Danise. Speaking of forgetting, weren't you supposed to pick up Jacques?"

"No. Stewart said he'd have his taxi man pick him up," Malinga said. "But let me check with him." She called Jacques' number, but there was no answer. She tried again, but after a few tries, she shrugged. "I guess he had something better to do."

"He's pretty new in town to have outside interests."

"It doesn't take a willing man long to find a willing friend."

Wilson grinned and picked up the wine bottle to fill her glass. "Don't condemn all white people because your husband is sleeping with one." She grabbed the cork from his hand and tossed it at him, laughing.

"Looks like the tension's getting to you," Danise said as she came up to their table. "Or am I interrupting something?"

"Not a thing," Malinga said. "Besides, if you don't interrupt Wilson, you'll never get a word in edgewise."

Laughing, Danise shook her jacket out and put it on the back of her chair with her umbrella. "I feel like a wet dog." When the waiter left to fill her drink order, she leaned toward Malinga and whispered. "I was serious about my warning this afternoon. This killer is flaunting these deaths. He's making it too easy to find the bodies. He's trying to ruin your reputation."

Wilson nodded. "Or he's trying to threaten you. Either way, he's coming way too close for comfort."

"I'm more confused than worried," Malinga said. "The witch doctor, Redbone, warned me to lay low. The bicycle man told me the same thing. Stewart thinks the killer may be Redbone or his son, in cahoots with Chinese buyers. What would they gain by humiliating me?"

"They can slow you down, keep you out of the way, maybe even get you fired from the case," Danise said. She raised her eyebrows. "What Stewart's saying makes a lot of sense. They might have tried to butcher the second girl and when they failed, they linked up with a professional for the next two."

"Stewart thinks the Chinese are dissecting the bodies at a facility near one of their mines. Outside of the hospital, there's no other facility in the area that could handle it. They're dumping the remains in Lusaka to confuse us. He says Zambia's borders are so porous, we practically welcome this kind of atrocity."

Wilson chuckled. "Everyone thinks Zambia's so peaceful, but there's always been a good deal of international crime and lots of rural violence we never hear about. Look at the Mailonis."

"But that's not like this," Danise said. "The elections made everyone tense. I'm afraid there may soon be other copycat killings."

"The smooth execution of the last two murders suggests they're not copycat. They were probably committed by the same man, and they were professional," Malinga said.

"I think we can operate on the presumption that these are not random acts of violence, but systematic body part harvesting," Danise said. "Davison and Asedi are right. Someone's paying husbands and fathers to deliver the goods. It won't be the first time we've heard of a man selling a woman for quick cash. The Short Skirt War in Kitwe worries me. Not a day goes by when some woman isn't beaten to death by her husband or father."

There was a sudden crash and they looked toward the entrance of the restaurant. Malinga saw what was going on, rose and hurried over. When she reached for the man, the hostess stopped her.

"We can't let this man in, Madam!" she protested, eyeing his torn suit jacket with disdain. "He's been in some kind of fight and he's probably drunk."

38 | Taxi from Hell

"I'll vouch for him," Malinga told the hostess. "Please take his raincoat and umbrella and dry them while he's having dinner." She grabbed the big man's elbow and whispered, "I called, but your phone was off. You're not drunk, are you?"

Jacques smiled ruefully and shook his head. "I wish I were, but we didn't have time for that. I'm sorry to be late," he said as they walked toward the table. "I've had quite a ride."

Malinga chuckled. "I can see that. It looks like a long story. Let's get you a drink first." Wilson and Danise settled him at their table and put a large glass of burgundy in his hands.

"What happened?" Wilson asked. "I thought Stewart sent his taxi man to fetch you. Have you been out of cell phone range?"

Jacques shook his head. "Out of range doesn't begin to describe where I've been." He took a long pull of red wine and set his glass back on the table. "All the taxi drivers know where this restaurant is, no?" When they nodded, he grinned. "All but the one Stewart sent! This one, he took me through the worst part of town. He said it was called Kalinga…"

"Linga," Wilson supplied.

"Kalingalinga. Yes, that's it! He wanted me to buy a prostitute and share her with him. Then he offered me drugs. I was beginning to worry for my safety. No offence, but I thought maybe he wanted my skin."

Malinga winced.

"When he took me to a small gambling place and insisted I go in with him, that was the end of it. They were fighting cocks and it was very bloody. There were many Chinese, very drunk, betting large sums of money. I showed the taxi driver my identification and explained that I worked for the police. He drove me a short distance away and pushed me out of the car."

He shook his head. "I couldn't see anything. The night was very dark and the corner was very wet. Fortunately, Dr. Bleming was passing, and offered me a ride."

"Stewart?" Malinga said. "What was Stewart doing there?"

"He said he lives near there. He was going home, but he turned around and dropped me here so I would be safe. He felt responsible for what happened to me, but it wasn't his fault. I described the man who picked me up. It wasn't his man. He thought there had been a mistake."

Malinga poured him a second glass. "Don't worry, Jacques. I'll make sure your ride home is a lot safer." She handed him the menu. "After your introduction to Zambian night life, I think you're going to prefer the cuisine."

Jacques laughed. "In that case," he said to the waiter, "give me the largest steak you have. Make it rare. Then bring a bottle of wine for the table."

As they ate their appetizers, Malinga explained their working hypotheses about the killers. "When you told us how the third case is different from the others, Jacques, it brought everything into focus. The *muti* connection seemed much too obvious. Like you said, the killers were probably trying to hide the abortion."

"I'm relieved that most of the evidence points at the uncle, working with the Archbishop's driver, and not at the Archbishop himself," Wilson said. "We can't finger such a well-known person unless the evidence is very tight."

"Don't rule him out too quickly just because he's a churchman," Malinga said. "We can't let anyone off the hook because of who they are."

"But since he's one of the President's oldest and dearest friends – and his priest," Danise said, "you'll have to go slow on this one."

After dinner, Jacques bought them all brandies. Malinga lifted her glass. "I can't tell you how grateful I am to all of you for your work," she said. "We're making great progress. All we have to do now is keep the pressure on. Lusaka is talking about nothing else, including how grossly incompetent we are because we haven't found the killer yet."

"We've got to start tracing the international connections," Jacques said.

"I asked Davison to take a look at the Chinese coal mine a few hours south of here first, then at large Lusaka businesses," Malinga said.

"Good move, Malinga," Wilson said. "We'll systematically rule out the possibilities."

"Don't worry, Malinga," Danise said. "We'll find the bastard who's behind this. At the rate we're going, we'll find him soon." She put down her drink. "But for now, I've got to go. I've got some student papers to correct and an early lecture on Monday."

Wilson offered to drop Jacques at his hotel. On the way to the parking lot, Malinga pointed at Mika Hardware on the opposite corner. "The only people who've benefited from these murders so far are the hardware stores," she said. "Everyone is adding deadbolts and tripling their locks."

"The killers have taken poor, innocent Lusaka by surprise," Wilson said. "We haven't seen anything like this in years." He flicked the locks open on his Cruiser. "Make yourself comfortable, Jacques. I'll just walk Malinga to her car."

When Malinga had settled into the driver's seat, Wilson shut the door and leaned into her window. "Let me take this case, Malinga. I have much more experience with serial killers than you do."

"I'm sure you do," Malinga said, shoving her key into the ignition. "But I'm going to see this case through. It's personal for me. I don't want any more women to die. Besides, the Mailonis were very different, so your experience doesn't apply." She started her engine, and looked up at him. "Wilson, I already told you that I intend to make my name with this case, just like you did with the Mailonis." She winked. "If you really want to help, make all the other stuff on my desk go away so I can work on this full time."

He pulled back from the window, laughing. Then his face suddenly sobered. "See you tomorrow. Be sure your doors are locked. And be prepared for a struggle, Malinga. I still don't think you can handle it."

"I know I can. I've got really good connections, Wilson. It's me the President wants to see, so don't try to take over at tomorrow's meeting. By the way, speaking of connections, would you like to meet Giselle on Saturday?"

"Giselle? Sure! Are we catching the early flight to South Africa?"

"No, silly. She's here at Stewart's, and he's invited us all for tea late Saturday afternoon."

"That would be great. Let me check with Bernice and get back to you in the morning. Can she come too?"

"You'll owe me, Wilson."

"I know. I suspect I already do."

39 | A Little Cottage in England

Stewart tooted three times for his gateman, who looked like a drowned rat when he finally heaved the gate doors open and closed them after Stewart accelerated up the driveway, slippery with mud. Rain, Stewart thought. Now that it had arrived at last, it changed every game plan in town, including his own.

True, farmers needed the rain; without it, people would starve, especially after the President's unpopular decision to sell the maize surplus off to Kenya last year left the poor struggling with high prices. Infant and child mortality rates had skyrocketed.

As the gates clanged shut behind him, Stewart sat thinking about Anita and smiled. He ached to kiss her full, luscious mouth, to stroke her breasts and enter her as hard and rough as he could. She'd like it after being without sex for so long. So would he. He shook his umbrella out as he entered the house and headed for the kitchen, hungry after chasing Jacques and returning him to the restaurant before something truly horrible happened to the Frenchman.

"Bertha!" he called as he rounded the corner to the kitchen, "I need . . ." That she was there was no surprise. That Anita and Victor were with her, cocktail glasses in hand, was.

"Hello, Stewart," Victor called huskily. "We were teaching Bertha how to mix the latest German concoctions."

"Have one!" Anita urged, flashing him a welcoming smile. "They'll pickle your liver instantly! We can plastinate you for the very next show!"

Stewart's head jerked up in surprise. When he saw she was joking, he forced a laugh. "Don't do it until I grant Victor his three wishes! Let's take our drinks into the library, shall we? I need to dry out by the fire."

Stewart closed the library door and turned to Victor and Anita. "My man wants one hundred thousand for the elephant," he blurted, "fifty thousand up front and fifty thousand when he delivers it to your plane. He can do the job in a few days once you make the down payment."

Victor's eyebrows jerked upward and Anita started to laugh. "*Liebchen*, did you hear what Stewart just said?" he asked and started laughing himself. "Is it me or the cocktails, *Liebchen*?"

Anita's snort sent a shower of spray onto her hand. "Neither, darling. I heard it, too. Stewart said one hundred thousand, darling, and it looks like he is serious. One hundred thousand . . ." she shrieked, breaking into giggles.

Victor stopped laughing. "Your friend is dreaming, Stewart. I might have to go to Central African Republic and deal with Boko Haram after all."

"You don't have enough time, Victor, and you know it. Besides, the CAR's in chaos, and you would never make it out of there alive in your fancy airplane. We could get you an elephant cheaper from Zimbabwe, but it takes time, and you don't have that. This price includes delivery to the airport and a guarantee of complete confidentiality. I don't think you can do much better. Tourists who come here to hunt pay more than that in licenses and taxidermy fees, and they still have to pay for their safaris, taxes and shipping."

"Bloody hell, Stewart! I don't care what they pay! Your bloody bastard supplier wants too much."

Stewart looked hard at Victor and shook his head.

"You're getting a cut, aren't you?" Victor said in his butterfly whisper.

Stewart shook his head again. "That makes no sense, Victor. Now that we're partn . . ."

"Some partner you are! You've backed me into a corner! It's too late to look elsewhere. This this will come right out of your profit!"

"Victor, you said yourself that Noah's Ark will be your best show yet," Stewart said. "You'll make millions."

Victor turned away from him, sulking, but the thought of potential glory calmed him. He turned to Anita. "What do you think, *Liebchen*? Can we afford this investment?"

Anita smiled slyly, half to herself and half to Stewart. "If Stewart holds up his end of the bargain, Victor, we'll be in the black within the year. But he has to produce the volunteers we require. The elephant alone won't be worth as much."

"Which means . . ."

"He has to stay here."

Stewart gasped. "Not a chance! I'm going with you!"

Anita laughed and winked at him. "You can come and visit us in Germany after a while, Stewart, but for now you have a contract to manage our eastern and southern African facilities. Besides, you'll become a suspect if you disappear at the same time as the bodies."

Stewart shook his head. "But I have to go with you, at least until I'm sure the police haven't identified me. Then I'll come back and open the business."

"I'm afraid that won't work, Stewart," Anita said, studying her nails. "We need immediate start up or we can't stay afloat. We need the first autopsy specimen next week, then we'll place a firm order for others."

Stewart swallowed hard. If any part of this operation failed, he'd carry complete responsibility for it. The Germans, back on their home soil, would never suffer any consequences. He looked at Victor thoughtfully. "It seems I do all the work, bear all the risk, and you get all the profits."

Victor patted Stewart's hand and settled back in his chair. "Let us talk about timing first, Stewart. How soon can I have the elephant?"

"Wednesday, Thursday at the latest."

"Are you sure?"

"It depends on when you give my friend the down payment. He won't do anything until he sees the cash."

"*Liebchen*, can you arrange this for Stewart?"

"Of course, Victor." Anita pulled Stewart to the side and leaned close so Victor couldn't hear. "Come and see me later, Stewart, when Victor's asleep, and we'll work out the rest of our arrangement." She lowered her voice even further. "We have a problem, darling," she told him after a lingering kiss. She could feel his temperature rise. "It's Victor! He wants to cheat you!"

"I'm not surprised," Stewart said, shaking his head. "We'll talk about it later. Right now, I have to take care of a bit of business. Put Victor to bed and come back here. I'll be with you momentarily."

Anita gave him a quick kiss on the cheek and walked back to her husband. "Come, darling Victor. Let's go to bed."

Stewart hurried toward Giselle's room, anxious to check her progress. Bertha stopped him as he neared the door. He motioned her to step aside. "Let me pass, Bertha. I want to see how she's doing."

"I just changed her bandages," Bertha said, pulling the door shut behind her. "She's sleeping well, breathing easily. I did just as you said. I cleaned the stitches carefully, and put on the cream you left. Let her sleep."

Stewart straightened. "Good work, Bertha. As long she's comfortable."

"Of course she is. You taught me well. Now go to bed and get some rest," she told him.

"Not just yet. Where's Redbone and Kivuli? I need to speak with them."

"Redbone is here. I haven't seen Kivuli, but since it is raining so hard, he is probably here. Make yourself comfortable and I will fetch them both."

Stewart dried off by the fire in his library, relieved Giselle was safe and that Anita was settling Victor in the guest wing. She'd soon be back. The sound of the storm relaxed him, and he poured himself a brandy. The rains have started full force, he thought. Tomorrow I'll have to check the storm drains. He sat up suddenly. Tomorrow. Right. Malinga and Wilson were meeting with the President. He flipped his cell open.

"Paul," he said when the press secretary answered. "We're in the clear. I convinced Malinga that Redbone and Kivuli are responsible for the murders, working with the Chinese at the coal mine in Southern Province. That'll keep her out of our hair for a while."

"Good work, Stewart. We have to deflect suspicion from ourselves at all costs."

"It won't be hard to lay the blame on Redbone and Kivuli," the doctor said. "Everyone already thinks these murders are the work of witch doctors. I just had to connect them with someone with a surgical facility. I'll plant some evidence at the Chinese clinic early tomorrow and lead Malinga and her team right to it."

Paul grunted. "Just keep that old man and his son as far from me as you can until she arrests them."

"Are you afraid of Redbone and Kivuli?"

Paul said nothing, and the doctor laughed. "No need to be. It's easy to keep them in the dark. They're blinded by money. Bertha keeps track of them and Malinga both. No worries, Paul. No worries."

"And my latest payment?"

"I'll have the first half for the elephant on Monday."

Paul chuckled, "That's not the payment I mean."

"I thought the payment for the elephant would take care of it."

"It's not enough," Paul said.

"You'll have to wait for the other one. I won't have more until I finish this job. Would you like to watch the next one?"

Paul snorted. "Catching you with one cadaver was more than enough." He held the receiver away from his ear. The memory made him feel dirty.

Stewart laughed. "Don't be so squeamish, Paul. It's made you a very rich man. This is my very last payment. You can't milk me forever."

"No worries," Paul said, sighing. "After the deal with the doctor, anything more would be tempting fate."

"I don't know where you'll go, but a little cottage in England is all I need," the doctor said. "I'm leaving here as soon as I get the laboratory at the university set up and running."

Bertha clapped her hand over her mouth to keep from crying out, but Redbone chuckled. He was standing behind her at the doctor's door in bare feet, with Bertha at his elbow.

"Did you hear that?" she whispered. "England!"

Redbone stiffened and put a finger to his lips. He was on alert, like an old dog with one last bit of fight in him. They stared at each other, and then he smiled. He signaled her to follow him down the corridor where they could talk.

"Get Kivuli," he told Bertha. "Get him now and bring him to the kitchen. I will meet you there."

40 | The Pit Latrines of Kalingalinga

When she'd gone, Redbone rambled back to the library. Stewart was just closing his phone. He stood and clapped Redbone on the back. "Well done, my man!" he exclaimed. "That fat French pig! We certainly gave him a ride. This should keep him out of our way until we're done."

Redbone nodded. "It was good. But the police are getting too close. How many more women do you need?"

Stewart shrugged. "I need at least three to fill the orders I've got now. That should give you and Kivuli enough to go to South Africa when I leave for England." He glanced around the library with regret. "Unfortunately, we'll have to tear this place down and destroy the evidence before we leave."

"Burn it to the ground," Redbone said. "All of Kalingalinga would be entertained." When he smiled, his face looked crooked in the fire light. Stewart felt a sudden surge of fear.

Redbone laughed and the doctor forced himself to chuckle. "You may be right. I hate to destroy my museum, but a fire would make quick work of it."

Redbone rubbed his hands together. "We can set it as soon as we lay in some stocks of petrol."

Stewart snapped his fingers. "Tell you what! We'll have a bonfire to celebrate when the President fires Malinga on Friday."

Redbone chuckled. "How you hate that woman," he said, wagging his finger at the doctor. "Your hatred has caused us to make many mistakes."

"What do you mean?"

"We should have hidden the bodies when we were done. There are many pit latrines in Kalingalinga, and many hungry dogs. But you had to show that policewoman how smart you are."

"She's ruined everything for me, Redbone. I must pay her back."

"She's not worth the trouble."

Stewart shook his head. "We had a solid relationship with the police until she came along. We'll need it again when I establish the lab here. I'm not afraid of her."

Redbone leaned closer. "I see fear in your eyes, doctor."

Stewart looked away, and the witch doctor began to laugh. "Kivuli and I do not fear her. We will make sure she cannot hurt you. She is only a woman, after all. This is the way my father taught me. We have no fear of women."

Anita pushed the door open without knocking, a large cocktail glass in either hand. She stopped short. "Stewart! Sorry! I didn't realize you had a visitor."

"This is Redbone, Anita. He helps me with the work."

Redbone spit into the hearth. "You and your women," he growled under his breath and turned to shuffle out the door. Stewart called to him. "Do me a favor, Redbone, and ask Bertha to come here, please."

Stewart settled Anita in a chair. He felt suddenly tired of the woman. Did her temperature ever drop?

Bertha appeared silently at the door. "Yes, doctor?"

"We'll need dinner, but bring another round of these cocktails first, would you?" He smiled at Anita. "Special German cocktails, are they not?"

In the kitchen, Bertha found Redbone glaring up at his son. The boy was staggering slightly.

"Kivuli," Redbone growled. "What have you done?"

"Nothing a little ganja won't fix," Kivuli said, grinning. He fell into a chair and started to giggle. "I took Giselle," he said. "I hid her in a very safe place, just like you told me," he said, laughing wildly.

Bertha's heart sank. So that's why the woman was missing when she'd gone to check her dressings earlier. She grabbed the front of Kivuli's shirt and shook him. "What have you done with her?"

Kivuli laughed harder.

Redbone pulled Bertha back. "Stop it, woman. It's no use. He'll tell us everything when he sobers up. Put him to bed and lock the door to his room. Don't let him have any more drugs."

She nodded. "He'll pass out soon."

"He can see me when he wakes in the morning," the old man said. He crooked his finger. "Once you put him to bed, come to my room."

She grimaced. Fortunately, the old man rarely had the strength to do anything physical, but he smelled like a hyena. "I'll draw you a bath first," she said, turning away.

He snorted and grabbed her arm, twisting it hard. His eyes drilled into her. "You're ours now, Bertha. To serve us in any way we want. There's no escape."

She pulled away from him, suddenly defiant. "You're wrong, old man. I'll find a way to leave, wait and see. You'll never hurt me again! What if I tell the doctor that Giselle is missing and that Kivuli took her?"

"He'll find out soon enough, Bertha." The old man's laughter emerged in a grating rumble. "Quit your chatter and get ready for me."

41 | Believe Only What You See

The party never ended in Kalingalinga, but the compound's eastern rim, along Alex Nkata Road, was quiet when Malinga drove home through the downpour. Jacques' detour through the compound puzzled her. *Bazungu* didn't usually get the Cook's tour of Lusaka vices unless they asked for it. When they did, it was of more notorious parts of the city, not Kalingalinga.

She shrugged. It was a shame that Jacques had missed Stewart's taxi man, but he was no different than any other *mzungu* she'd ever met. He probably misunderstood what the cabman said, but wouldn't make that mistake again while he was in Lusaka. She'd speak to him in the morning.

She turned off Bishop's Road, nosing her car down the side street to Martin Luther King Drive. Most of the streetlights were out and she drove slowly to avoid a string of cavernous potholes, filling fast with the hard-driven storm. She was grateful when she reached her gate.

Time to relax. A quiet bath will do me good.

There was a time in every investigation when it paid to look for a breakthrough in the warmth of a nice deep tub. With the children staying at her mother's, the house would be peaceful and quiet. She shivered as she waited for her gardener to open the gate. The chill had set in with the rain. It was torrential and would collect at the bottom of her garden where it met the neighbor's walls in a narrow V. She'd need to check the drains after her bath.

She tapped her horn a second time. Spotting her through the gates' peephole, Mr. Phiri pulled them open. He was wearing tattered shorts under his long overcoat, and gave her a wide grin and half salute. She shivered and thought of her bath again, promising herself to rummage through her father's closet for some old trousers Mr. Phiri could wear.

Benny pelted around the corner of the house as she parked in the carport. She brought him his kibble and flipped on the radio in the kitchen. While she warmed the mealie meal and beef stew Bertha had left for Mr. Phiri, she hummed along to Giselle's new release.

"Men are like strangers," the singer crooned in a low voice over a pulsing dance beat, "you will never know them well."

"Thank you, Madam," Mr. Phiri said when she brought him his dinner. "It is a very good evening, is it not?" She laughed obligingly and sat with him near his small charcoal heater, inquiring about his children and gossiping about the neighbors. The rain was rhythmic and strong. "This will do the mealies good," Mr. Phiri said, nodding at the downpour. "But too much and it will flood my house in Bauleni."

By the time they'd agreed that the President had waited too long to replace the surplus maize he'd sold to neighboring countries -- it had rotted before it could be redistributed to the poor – the rain had slowed and bright clouds were racing across the sky. When the full moon broke through the clouds, lighting up the front garden, Malinga sighed with contentment. Her frangipani's blossoms shown ghostly pale in the moonlight, and frogs called from the rock-edged pool near the front entrance. A few cars moved slowly by, but traffic on her side street was light. Most of the houses in her compound were rented to foreigners, transient *bazungu* from embassies and aid projects staying in Lusaka a year or two at most.

She gathered Mr. P's dishes, wished him a goodnight, and slipped back into the house she'd rented there three years ago when she left her ex-husband. While Herbert rattled around their old house with whatever girl or girls he was dating at the moment, she and the children huddled here. She knew there was no long-term benefit in renting and filling a stranger's pockets with money, but she had no money to build. With the government performing poorly, the President cut the police and security budgets.

Malinga was cautious with her salary, saving half of it as insurance against downsizing. One mistake on a high-profile case like this could mean her job. She sighed. The house was peaceful without the children. Sinking onto her bed, she slipped off her shoes and wiggled her toes in relief. Her divorce had shown her how tough she could be. When Herbert kidnapped the children last year and she thought she'd never see them again, she'd stayed strong until he brought them back.

How difficult can this killer be compared to my ex-husband?

She smiled and stretched. The investigation was finally going somewhere. Not that it was headed for quick closure, but the lead on the Archbishop was strong. If they had more leads on the other girls from the compound women's groups by Friday, she was sure they could buy more time from the President. Tomorrow, they'd start searching for local *sangoma* with connections to foreign middle men. Asedi and Davison would identify clinics with the necessary equipment while she interviewed Redbone and Kivuli.

She'd review what they had on the Archbishop and speak with him on Sunday after they met with the President's press secretary. She didn't like to think of the church man as a murderer, but the power of *muti* was just as strong among church people as anyone else.

Just last week, a Zambian panhandling for a bus ticket to Johannesburg claimed to be a South African witch doctor so weakened by combat with a well-known Lusaka pastor that he didn't have the strength to fly home on his broomstick. Local churchmen often claimed to win battles with the devil to attract churchgoers, so the panhandler's story wasn't so farfetched. He soon had enough for his ticket.

Nighttime battles between witches could be more sinister.

The stink of a young woman's corpse, straining the walls of a makeshift coffin in a village just north of Lusaka, returned to her nose. "Her body fell from the sky," witnesses insisted. "We found her flattened among the rows in the maize field. Her mother refused to come or prepare her daughter's body for burial."

The villagers took charge, but every coffin they made was too small for the ever-expanding corpse, bloating quickly as it decomposed. Running out of wood, they decided to force the corpse into the last coffin and nail the lid shut.

By the time Malinga arrived, the entire village was hysterical, terrified by the power of the mother's *muti*. While the police loaded the girl's coffin on their pickup, the minister, a small, well-fed man with a very bald head and a very white goatee, distracted the villagers so Malinga could talk to the mother.

"My daughter and I were flying on our broomsticks, when a rival witch came along," the old lady said. "Her energy wave knocked my daughter off her broom. When I tried to save her, the witch grabbed me by the throat. She said I would die if I ever tried to see my daughter again."

When Malinga shook her head, the old woman laughed. "I knew you wouldn't believe me," she'd said. "You police only believe what you see."

Malinga tested the water running into her tub with her pinky and opened the hot water tap as wide as it would go. The rain had chilled her. She frowned. Police were meant to observe what they saw and find the truth by sifting through the evidence, not listen to fantastic stories or dream up things that were not there.

Like talking corpses.

She prayed the girls would leave her alone tonight so she'd be fresh for her meeting at State House in the morning.

42 | The Smell of Frangipani

Malinga lowered herself into the bathtub gingerly, relaxing in the hot suds. There were few things more pleasurable after a day of hard work. Her pleasure was multiplied by the quiet of the house. No children tonight. She eyed the fresh towels Bertha had stacked at the end of the tub.

Thank heavens Stewart recommended the woman. I'd be frantic without her.

Even the two days she'd spent between maids had been a major strain. Affordable nannies, cooks, and maids made it possible for African professional women to work full time after the birth of their children. Good ones were hard to find among the thousands of village migrants looking for work in the capital city.

When the doctor offered to share Bertha, Malinga had immediately agreed. The recommendation of a friend was an invaluable credential, a warranty of safety and reliability. Not only was Bertha quiet and neat, by some miracle she also spoke good English, unusual for a village girl.

Malinga propped her ankle on the edge of the tub, admiring her new pedicure, and smiled. Was it only this morning that she and Katanga had visited Celestin? He was expensive, but salon prices were still a bargain in Lusaka. She thought of Katanga's new hairdo and chuckled. Her children were growing up fast, but they were still as innocent as bumbling puppies. Relaxed in spite of Herbert's threats, she closed her eyes and let her mind drift. Men are like strangers, she hummed, but the voice cut through.

Help us! Every day there will be another one of us unless you stop the murderers!

Malinga stiffened. Damn voices, she thought. She ran a bit more hot water and snuggled into the suds. Let it go, she thought. It's just nerves. She closed her eyes and started humming Giselle's new song.

There will be another one tonight.

Malinga hummed louder to drown out the whisper. When the muffled pounding started, Malinga assumed it was her neighbor's son. He was always working on some kind of project. She chuckled. Katanga could now match his hairstyle point for point with her new Mohawk. Her thoughts drifted sleepily. It would be delicious to have an uninterrupted night's sleep. She desperately needed at least one night of sound sleep.

The pounding noises grew louder. They were close. Her eyes fluttered open and she sat up.

Had she dozed? The water was turning cold and she needed to go to bed. She pulled herself upright and opened the drain. As she dried off, she heard the pounding again. She lifted the window curtain to look for the source, but couldn't see through the blanket of trees.

She smiled at the wet cloud of frangipani petals glowing below her in the moonlight and opened the window a bit wider to let their scent into the bath. Truly heaven, she thought, inhaling deeply. The pounding started again.

It's heaven, all right. Except for that noise.

She listened closely, and realized it wasn't the neighbor's son. The sound was coming from her side of the fence. Was Mr. Phiri cutting kindling for a fire? The carpenters refurbishing the house next door for an American couple gave him the scraps from their packing crates, but he had to chop them up. But not at night. The neighbors would be angry if he chopped them up at night.

Time to have a talk with Mr. Phiri.

Malinga finished toweling off and grabbed her robe. Shoving her feet into her slippers, she hurried to her closet and pulled on some trousers and a t-shirt. It wouldn't do to lecture Mr. Phiri in her bathrobe. And it won't do to trip over my slippers, either, she thought. She slammed on some tennis shoes and hurried down the stairs.

My gun, she remembered, pulling it from her purse. Loaded, safety on. Mr. P. had remembered to turn on the security lights, glowing through the curtains. She preferred the steep darkness of the village, but crime in Lusaka dictated the perpetual twilight of safety.

She pulled on a jacket and stuck her revolver in the outside pocket. Stepping toward the back door, she heard a different noise: scraping followed by a thud so loud it resonated through the glass. She lifted her hand to the curtains, but stopped, adrenalin pumping. She couldn't decipher the sound.

Why wasn't the dog barking? Why hadn't the guard cried out? She froze, fear washing through her. It could be him. It could be the killer. Malinga knew the first rule of police work: Call for back up. She hated looking vulnerable, especially to Wilson, especially now.

Rules are made for a reason.

Malinga punched in Wilson's number and put the phone to her ear. Danise's warning came back to her, and she told herself she was being strong, not weak. "Wilson?" she said when he answered. "Are you anywhere nearby? I need your help. Someone's prowling outside my house."

"You're in luck, Malinga. Jacques and I had a drink at the hotel and he just went up to bed. I'm headed toward Leopard Hill. I can be at your place in fifteen minutes."

"Come as fast as you can. Something's going on outside. I'm going to take a look."

"Be careful, okay?"

"I'm always careful," she said, snapping her phone shut. Her fingers tightened around her pistol. She grabbed the torch hanging near the back door and pulled the patio curtains wide.

You're a policewoman. Act like one.

Unlocking the slider, she stepped out, pausing while her eyes adjusted to the shadows cast by the security lights. The night air was balmy and filled with the scent of frangipani, strong in the rain. She looked upward at the tree's soft pink blossoms, bejeweled with raindrops, and felt herself relax a bit.

It's probably nothing. A tree limb blown loose by the storm.

Flicking on her torch, she swept the light across her garden. She squinted, trying to make out a form near the back fence, obscured by the gloom, puzzled that there was no dog and no guard. Watching her feet so she wouldn't slip on the wet ground, she picked her way through Shiko's toys, strewn along the path. I've got to get that boy to pick up his things, she thought, smiling. But this time, I'll give him a reprieve. He's so disappointed by his father. Too often her son had sat on the steps, waiting for a father who never came, gloomy for days.

She blinked the moisture back from her eyes and squinted, straining to see the fence. There was something outlined against the wood. At first, the image she focused on didn't register. Then it came into focus with a terrible force. Malinga gasped and staggered back.

My God! What is it? It looks like . . .

Malinga forced herself to lift her torch and look again.

43 | A Special Bone

The body festooned across her fence was still dripping blood, every drop thrown into high relief by the security lights and Malinga's torch. Malinga gulped back her fear and took a few steps closer. Her eyes widened in disbelief.

It was Giselle, the mysterious star she'd seen only a few hours before, hidden behind her sunglasses and wide-brimmed hat — that she was no longer wearing, no longer capable of wearing.

Not by a long shot.

Someone had arranged the singer's remains in a ghastly tableau covering more than three meters of fence. The woman's torso was nailed through the neck to one post. Legs and arms were nailed in no particular order to the adjoining posts. Hanging off another post, further to the left, was her beautiful print dress. Her hat skewed off another. Both were soaked in blood. Her sunglasses were fixed on what remained of her nose. Below them, her ghoulish grin was framed by random patches skin, sewn on by a crazed doll maker.

Malinga dropped to her knees and bit off a scream, hand over her mouth, eyes fixed wide on the barbaric, insane patchwork that had been Giselle. She vomited hard into the grass and struggled frantically with the dry heaves that followed. Jerking upright, she scanned the garden in panic, wide-eyed and panting.

The killer might still be here.

Rising to her feet, she wiped her eyes and caught her breath. Gripping her pistol with both hands, she swung it in a wide arc in front of her as she inched backward toward the patio. When she reached it, she flipped open her cell phone.

"My God, my God, my God," she muttered, fumbling at the keypad. She hit redial and Wilson's number lit the screen. "Pick up, pick up, pick up," she whispered into the device. "Pick up! Pick up! Pick up!" she screamed under her breath. "My God! Where are you? Wilson! Answer me, goddammit!"

The ringing stopped and she heard Wilson speak. It was his voicemail. "This is Wilson Mwiinga. I can't get to the phone right now. Leave a message at the beep."

She dropped the phone as though she'd been stung, grabbing her pistol tighter as another wave of horror rushed through her. She took deep breaths as she scanned the garden with her torch, gun held rigid in front of her. That's when she saw a flicker in the shadows.

Something's moving.

She lifted her gun and craned forward, staring into the darkness. The hair on her forearms bristled with fear. Drawing in a couple more breaths, she forced herself forward, eyes scanning the hedges and the fence, ears straining to pick up any sound. She peered into the shadows, to see what it was that was moving.

"Dammit," she cried out softly when she realized what it was. "Damn," she whispered again.

It's Benny. He's alive but something's wrong.

Her dog was whimpering softly, lying on his side, cut from scrotum to sternum, his entrails covering the grass around him. She ran to him and lifted his head gently. He looked up at her with sad brown eyes, whimpering. His tail wagged, and he struggled to lick her face. She patted him, tears rolling down her face as his tail wagging slowed, then stopped.

When his mouth relaxed, the bone he'd been carrying dropped to the ground. It was circular. It was human. A ridged ring with open knobs like handles left and right. A vertebra, she thought, and then she remembered what Wilson had said.

An Atlas bone.

The smell of blood, salty and elemental, gagged her. She took long deep breaths through her mouth to steel herself against the dizziness that threatened to overwhelm her. A sense of imminent danger engulfed her. She struggled against it. She wouldn't give in.

Get up, for God's sake. Get up!

She stroked Benny's ear one last time and lowered the dog's head to the ground. As she forced herself into a standing position and the Atlas bone fell from her hand, a fresh wave of fear coursed through her.

Oh my God! He might still be here. The killer who did this might still be here.

44 | Flying Witches

Malinga stifled the urge to scream. She had to reach the safety of her house and wait for Wilson. She looked up the garden pathway. Only twenty steps to safety.

She forced herself to take a few deep breaths as she wiped the tears from her cheeks. She had to be strong, but the fear still gripped her. A chill slid down her back to her pelvis. She swayed and nearly crumpled to the ground, but fought back the overwhelming desire to faint. Moving forward, she thought of Danise's words and found herself smiling grimly.

Healthy fear is good for you. But it's also damned inconvenient.

Malinga kept whispering encouragement to herself and willed her knees to work. Only ten steps to go and she'd be safe in her house.

Wilson is coming. Just let me get in the house.

A woman in this line of business has to be a whole lot tougher than her own fear, Malinga thought. You can't be controlled by it.

I can do this. I can do this.

The light droplets of rain on her upturned face roused her. Malinga's primal mind screamed at her to run, but she forced it to quiet and looked carefully around her. She wiped her jacket cuff across her mouth as she looked down at the mangled body of her dog and up at Giselle's body, festooned across the fence.

What kind of monster could do this?

Malinga fought back another wave of terror. The bastard will get you if you don't snap out of it, she thought. She shook her head and renewed her courage. Revulsion and shock would have to wait.

She'd seen Giselle only a few a few hours before, at noon, at the Mint. She rubbed her forehead, forcing herself to think. It was just before midnight, just twelve hours later. The killer had done this in less than twelve hours. Granted, the butchery was crude, not the careful peeling the last three girls had endured, but it still took time. The killer must have dismembered Giselle somewhere else, and nailed her body to the fence while Malinga was dozing in the bath. That didn't give him much time to get away. A cold sweat beaded her brow.

He might still be in the house, waiting to kill me. Did he lure me out here so he could get inside?

Her eyes scanned the path as she strode toward the house, her gun held steady in both hands. Reaching the porch, she felt inside the door and flipped on the kitchen lights. Her hands were shaking so badly, she drew her pistol close to her chest and pushed the door open with her foot.

She entered quickly, eyes flitting from side to side, ears alert. When she was sure the kitchen was clear, she locked the door behind her and edged toward the pantry. Her phone started to ring, startling her so much she lost control of her bladder. Swearing, she grabbed the phone and lifted it to her ear.

Wilson's voice broke through her daze. "Malinga! I'm just pulling into your driveway. What's going on? Where are you? The gates are open and the guard's not here!"

She dropped the phone and ran to the door. Flinging it open, she ran to meet his car. "My god, Wilson! Giselle's been killed! Her body's in my garden! The killer may still be here! He hung her on the fence! Giselle's been skinned, Wilson, skinned! And mutilated!" She stopped babbling when she ran out of breath, but couldn't stop the tears coursing down her face. And she hated herself for it.

Wilson eased the car door open and grabbed her wrists gently. "Calm down, Malinga," he whispered. "Calm down. Let me close the gate. Your neighbor's lights just went on. It's better if we kept this to ourselves right now. Go inside. I'll be right in."

Malinga clung to him. "I can't, Wilson. I can't. He may still be here. I didn't get a chance to search the whole house. Come with me. I can't face it alone!"

"Okay, Malinga, okay. Sit on the steps while I shut the gate. Put your head between your knees and try to catch your breath." Malinga stumbled to the stairs and sat for a second, catching her breath. Then she looked dowr. and realized she had to change her pants. Wilson hadn't seen the wet stain yet, so she could save herself that embarrassment. She ran into the house and raced up the stairs. When she reached her bedroom and had stripped off her pants, her blood went cold.

Oh God! He could be right here! What am I thinking of?

She took a quick look around and started to laugh.

If he were here, I'd be dead already.

Exhausted and angry, she pulled on a fresh pair of panties and clean trousers and took a deep breath, struggling to control herself. She straightened as anger triumphed over exhaustion, pulled on her jacket, and stormed toward the stairs.

I'll kill you, you bastard. I know you're laughing right now, but I swear to you, you won't be laughing once I find you. I've had it with you and all the bastards like you!

She paused, sweeping the hallway with her pistol, finger on the trigger. And then she heard it.

Footsteps.

She froze. They were male, heavy, coming around the corner of the staircase. She raised her pistol and braced her elbows against her sides. "Freeze!" she commanded. When the figure came into view, her stomach turned to jelly.

"My god, Wilson. Don't do that. I thought you were the killer!"

He forced a laugh and reached out to turn the barrel of her gun toward the ceiling. Her wrist went slack. "It's a good thing you can stop yourself as quickly as you start," he said. "I'd be a dead man otherwise."

"I've never been happier to almost shoot someone," she laughed, trying to control her hysteria. "Sorry, Wilson. The last half hour has been . . ." The front door burst open against the wall and they both jumped.

"Police!"

Wilson and Malinga raced down the stairs. Rounding the corner, they stopped short. Malinga's deputies were towing a small man in a very large raincoat between them. When they spotted Wilson and Malinga on the staircase, they let go and the man fell to the floor, a crumpled bundle of cloth.

Davison grinned at them. "Asedi and I caught the prowler! We heard Wilson on the radio, and came as fast as we could." He nudged the bundle he'd tossed to the floor with his boot and it slowly began to unravel.

"Go easy," Davison growled, pointing his gun at the pile. "I've got you covered." The bundle moved again and began to rise, tugging a body up behind it. A tear-stained face emerged and Davison's gun twitched.

Malinga blinked. It was an old face. One she knew. "Don't shoot, Davison! That's my night guard!" she gasped.

"Your night guard?" Davison sneered. "Your night guard? If he's your night guard, what was he doing hiding behind the compost pile?"

"Hiding, Davison. That's what he was doing. He was probably afraid for his life." She bent over to help Mr. Phiri to his feet. He stood as tall as his tiny frame allowed.

"Madam," he cried. "I have failed you! When I saw that thing flying over the fence, I lost all strength. It was not human! It was a witch! I am sure of it! And he shed his skin on the garden fence!"

Malinga thought her heart would break. His frail body was shaking uncontrollably, tears drenching his coat collar and T-shirt. The old man was terrified, and for good reason. Flying witches could unhinge anyone. She put her arm around his shoulder and guided him to the couch. "Sit here, Mr. Phiri. I'll get you a cup of tea. It was an awful fright, I know."

Davison stood to the side, looking sheepish.

"While I make tea," Malinga whispered to him, "calm the old man down and get him to tell you what happened. Asedi, tell the medical examiner and the crime scene crew to get here as fast as they can."

At full voice, she added, "it's chilly out there and tea will help us think. My headmistress always said tea was a sure cure for everything." I don't think she had this kind of thing in mind when she said it, she thought to herself.

45 | The Way Witches Do

"We have a long night ahead of us," Malinga said when they were all settled in the living room with their steaming cups. "While we wait for the medical examiner, I'll describe what's in the garden. Then you can tell me what you know."

They looked at her and waited. She drew in a deep breath. "First, there is a body on my fence, but it's not a flying witch. It's Giselle."

"Giselle!" Asedi gasped. "Madam! What are you saying?"

"Malinga," Wilson managed. "Are you sure?"

"I couldn't make a hard and fast identification, Wilson. I wanted to catch the killer if he was still around. But I'm sure it's her. Her face is distorted, but the clothing nailed to the fence matches what I saw her in today. The large hat and designer sunglasses she always wears are still there, too."

Asedi and Davison were staring at her, wide-eyed. Asedi looked as though she was about to cry. Malinga cleared her throat. "Her body was cut into pieces."

"Madam!" Asedi clapped her hand to her mouth to muffle her cry. Davison gaped, and Wilson was staring at her. He shook his head. "Malinga. Are you sure?"

Malinga pulled in another deep breath and steadied her voice. "Her remains are nailed across three meters of my back fence. Her skin was removed, so we'll have to do a positive identification from her dental records. She was. . ." Malinga hesitated. "Placed there during the rainstorm, so there probably won't be any fingerprints on her body or her clothing. Not only was she flayed like the other victims, but she'd been butchered."

Tears ran down Asedi's face. "Giselle! Butchered?"

"Cut into pieces. The pieces are nailed to different parts of the fence. It was a rough job compared with the most recent case, even rougher than the first.

"The skin on her face was intact, but it's partially bandaged and stitched. Stewart Bleming had been treating her for the effects of long-term bleaching. I think the skin grafts were part of it."

Malinga swallowed hard. "She was nailed out there" – she gestured toward the back garden — "sometime after I got home tonight. From the amount of blood, she may have been killed there, too, but the medical examiner will tell us more."

"Were any parts missing?" Wilson asked.

"I don't know, Wilson. I didn't have time to do an inventory. But we'll know as soon as forensics finishes." She drew in her breath. "My dog Benny was butchered, too, gutted but still alive when I reached him. When he breathed his last, the bone he'd been clenching in his jaws dropped on the ground. It was a ring, a vertebra. I think it might be Giselle's Atlas bone."

Wilson nodded, but said nothing. Asedi and Davison were grief-stricken, frozen in their chairs, speechless. Mr. Phiri continued his silent weeping.

"I'm sorry," Malinga said. "I know you were fans. We all were. I saw her today at the Mint with Dr. Bleming, so I knew she was in Zambia."

Wilson's eyes narrowed. "Do you think he killed her?"

Malinga shook her head. "He was her childhood friend. I don't think . . ." Malinga stopped at the sound of a van pulling in. "This must be the medical examiner and our lab guys. We'll finish our work as soon as they do the initial exam and photographs," she said as she walked to the door. Pulling it open, she gaped.

"Stewart! What are you doing here? I called for the medical examiner. Where is he?"

"Unfortunately, my darling," Stewart said as he brushed past her into the room, "Lusaka's medical examiner is under the weather. Today was his thirtieth birthday, and I'm afraid he was celebrating at the clubs."

He smiled. "When your men couldn't reach him by phone, they drove to his house. He'd passed out in his driveway. They put him to bed face down so he won't drown in his own vomit. All very thoughtful. Then they came and got me. I'm afraid that I'm as good as it gets tonight."

"We're glad to have you Stewart," Malinga said, "but there's something . . ."

"You're very lucky to have me, my dear," the doctor continued, smiling widely. "When your boys came to my place I was working late, so I'd only had one glass of wine with dinner."

"Stewart," Malinga said. "There's something you need to know."

He patted her arm. "No worries, Malinga. Admittedly I don't normally do this kind of work – it's too stomach-churning for my taste – but I do have training as a medical examiner, and I'm happy to be at your service."

"Stewart . . ."

"Now tell me, is this one like the other murders? By the way, thanks for the case files. I've been through most of them, so I'm prepared."

Malinga winced. She placed a hand on his arm and pushed him gently toward a chair. "Sit down, Stewart. There's something I have to tell you, and I'm afraid it's really bad news."

He looked up at her, puzzled. "These murders are all bad news, Malinga, but I . . ."

Malinga put up a hand to silence him.

"The body we've found is Giselle."

Stewart paled. "Giselle?" he whispered. "Giselle? That's impossible. She's at my house. I just checked on her a few hours ago!" His face reddened as his voice rose. He stood up, arms clenched into fists. "She was doing fine. I left her sleeping in my surgery. How could it be her?"

Malinga touched his arm. "Stewart, please sit down. She's in the garden, but I . . ."

He turned and ran toward the patio door.

"Grab him," Malinga shouted to Davison. "Stop him before he disturbs the scene." The doctor reached the door with

Davison and Asedi on his heels. They chased him down the lawn and Davison readied himself for a tackle, but they didn't have to use force to slow the doctor down. He fell to his knees in front of the fence and howled, fists raised to the sky, tears coursing down his cheeks.

Davison stood quietly behind him, and Asedi touched his shoulder. Malinga drew up with Wilson and Jacques close behind. The bright moon sparkled off the raindrops in a glittery, spectacular show.

"Asedi, Davison, take him back inside the house," Malinga said. "Give him some brandy. Wilson, call Jacques and get him here as fast as you can. Then see if you can raise Danise. The doctor's going to need a sedative."

Malinga helped Asedi and Davison bring Stewart back into the house and sit him on the couch. He was shaking, but the tears had stopped. He managed to drink some tea and began breathing more naturally.

Malinga sat on a footstool, facing him. "I'm so sorry, Stewart. I'm so very, very sorry. I know you were extremely close to her..."

He raised his head and let out strangled growl. "Save your words, Malinga."

"The crime scene crew will be here soon. I'll update you as soon as we hear anything."

"I'll get them," he said, his voice rising. "I will get them and make them pay. All three of them will pay!" He rose to his feet. Davison tried to restrain him, but he threw the smaller man's grip from his arm.

"Get out of my way," he shouted as he ran for the front door.

"Quick, Davison," Malinga yelled. "Grab him! He can't leave in this condition!" Davison started forward, but Stewart slammed the door in his face. Davison shook himself and yanked the door open. Malinga followed, but slowed when she heard the door slam on the doctor's Rover. The heavy engine turned over, and his tires screeched as he sped into the night.

Davison walked back up the drive. "I'm so sorry, Madam. I did my best, but that man had the strength of ten people. I could not control him. He got into his car and locked the doors. I had to jump out of the way before he ran me down!"

"It's okay, Davison," Malinga said. "He can't do too much harm. There won't be many people on the road this time of night. We'll catch up with him and get his statement as soon as we're done here." They turned to look at a police van pulling into the drive.

"Here's the forensic team now," Malinga said. "Asedi, show them where the body is. Davison, help me put Mr. Phiri to bed. He's fallen asleep here and I want to move him before we start our work in the back." They brought the guard to his room and laid him down on the bed. Malinga felt his pulse. "He's still alive," she said. "By the way, Davison, what did Mr. Phiri tell you when you spoke with him?"

"He said he was attacked by flying witches, Madam. He said they flew over his head while he was at the gate. He said there were two, a male and a female. The male was very large. and flew over the gate carrying the female across his shoulders like a bag of mealies. When he saw Mr. Phiri, he lifted him by the front of his coat and shook him." Davison shivered, struggling to go on.

"Relax, Davison," Malinga said. "There's nothing to be afraid of. We all know that witches don't exist, right? And we know that they don't fly."

He looked at her, startled. "Right, Mum. The witch . . ." – Davison looked at Malinga's frown and corrected himself – "this flying person told Mr. Phiri to leave, to never come back, and dropped him to the ground. Mr. Phiri was too frightened to see much, but he said the man who was flying had long hair and was wearing a leopard skin." Davison looked at his hands.

"The way witches do," he said apologetically.

"The way witches do," Malinga said in reply.

46 | A Man in Charge

The investigative team was so quiet that the neighbors soon shut off their lights and returned to bed. The team put Giselle's remains in the police van just as the first cock crowed. As experienced and professional as they were, all of them had a hard time with the gore. Giselle had been Zambia's biggest female star.

Jacques worked placidly beside them, instructing them in advanced techniques as they systematically recorded the scene and collected the evidence. Danise talked with Malinga and made notes. She spoke quietly with Asedi and Davison, who were staring fixedly at the remains, milling and muttering, fighting for self-control.

Malinga finally gave into her exhaustion and re-entered the house through the patio door. She was saddened by the sight of Benny and wondered what she'd tell the kids. When Mr. Phiri woke, she'd ask him to dig a small grave in the backyard. Killed by a cobra, she decided while he was finishing. The kids would understand that better than disembowelment at the hands of a deranged killer. Malinga shivered.

Wilson watched her as she shut the patio door and turned toward the couch. "You're making me nervous," she said. "Stop staring at me and tell me what you're thinking."

"I think I'm too tired to think," he said, shaking his head. "And I'm overwhelmed by the killer's ferocity."

"And you've only seen one example of his work."

"I don't know about the others, but this isn't witchcraft, no matter what Mr. Phiri says about flying demons. It wasn't done for body parts. This is blind violence. Cold blooded and savage. Rage and revenge."

"And systematic. And mocking. The way he cut that woman up was very, very personal," Malinga said.

"Don't you think that's the point, Malinga?" Danise asked.

"I know he's trying to scare us, but this looks like revenge against Giselle herself. Who were her enemies? Has anyone threatened her? Who would know?"

"Stewart will be a good place to start, once we find him," Wilson said. "We can talk to her producer and agent. Maybe Stewart has the contact number."

Malinga looked at her team, a sudden thought brightening her features. "I know that Zambia has lost an icon, but I think the killer's finally given us the advantage we've been looking for."

"I'm sorry, Madam," Davison said, scowling. "But I disagree. Killing Giselle is not an advantage."

Malinga half-smiled. "You misunderstood me, Davison. All I'm saying is that this is our first actual crime scene. Forensics agreed that the butchering was done here."

"I hope the rain didn't erase the killer's prints," Wilson said.

"Forensics will tell us tomorrow if they were able to lift anything," Malinga said. "Asedi, when it gets lighter, why don't you and Davison have another look out there and see if there's anything we missed. Be extra vigilant. If you see something, don't disturb it. Come and get me. We finally have the break we've needed, and I don't want to spoil the evidence."

"Do you think there will be more murders?" Asedi asked.

"I know there will be," Malinga said. "This killer's having too much fun to stop now. We need to move fast. Wilson, we need more officers on this. Can you arrange it?"

"No problem, Malinga. We have to do everything we can."

Jacques entered quietly through the back door. "We're done," he said, holding up his hands. "Can you tell me where the washroom is? I need to clean up."

Malinga walked him down the hall to the bathroom and reached in to flip on the light. "There are fresh towels on the rack. Take a shower if you'd like."

He laughed. "I'll save that for the hotel. Right now, I don't think there's enough hot water and soap in the world to make me feel clean again. If it's not too much trouble, I would love some coffee."

Malinga smiled. "I think the whole team could use some." When he returned to the living room, Malinga handed him a cup. "Drink up, Doctor. We've were just saying how shocked Stewart was when he saw Giselle's body."

"I know they were old friends, but he's also our prime suspect," Asedi said. "He was one of the last people to see Giselle. He operated on her. Maybe he bungled it."

"Did you hear what he said right before he left?" Davison added. "He said he would get them, all three of them. He knows who the killers are."

Wilson sighed. "He probably meant there was more than one killer. I don't think he meant anything more."

Malinga disagreed with him, but let it go. She shrugged. "You may be right, but we still have to find Stewart and talk to him." She shook her head. "He can't have killed her. They've been friends since secondary school. And he was at home when the forensic team called him."

"We can't rule him out, Malinga," Wilson said.

Malinga shrugged. "We can't discount him as a suspect, but I doubt he did it. Were you able to get any prints out there?" Malinga asked Jacques.

"We tried, but the rain and the blood took care of most of them. We got a few partials, and your men are going to try to run them. And we got this."   He tossed an evidence bag on the table. "It's the woman's Atlas bone. I think your dog fought the killer for it."

"Like I told you," Wilson said.

"She was butchered with an ax or some large cutting tool," Jacques added.

"Like the first two murders," Malinga said. She sighed. "Right now, we have a bigger problem. What are we going to tell the President in a few hours? Giselle is a famous Zambian star."

"I think they were also good friends," Wilson said.

"If it were my President," Jacques said, "I would be very careful about telling him there is another victim, especially a

famous one who is his friend."   He grinned. "In fact, I would tell
him nothing. Not yet. You still have to make a positive
identification. You have to manage him, or he'll ruin your
investigation."

"Maybe Stewart can tell him once he's recovered," Wilson
said. "After we've cleared him as a suspect, that is."

Davison looked at his watch. "It's eight o'clock, Madam. I
need to go home and get ready for church. My daughter is being
confirmed today. As soon as that is done, I will go to the Chinese
mine and look at their clinic. I should have answers by sixteen
thirty."

Asedi started and looked at her watch. "I, too, must go.
After my niece is baptized, I'll go back to the compounds where
the other bodies were dumped and find the witch doctors.
Davison and I will return here and have another look. If there's
anything more, we'll have it for you by the time of our meeting."

"By then, I'll know if we can process these prints," Jacques
said. "And I'll summarize what we've got from here while you're
meeting the President."

Malinga smiled. "Thanks, everyone. Asedi and Davison,
we'll see you later. Jacques, Wilson can drop you back at the
hotel." Jacques waved as he followed Asedi and Davison outside.

"Wilson," Malinga called out, "can I ask you something?"

He turned, his hand on the doorknob. "Anything,
Malinga, but make it quick because I'm drop-dead tired."

She caught his eye and held it. "I need to know you're
solidly behind me. I've built a good team, and I know the
evidence. Don't fight me on this."

Wilson shook his head. "I'm sorry, Malinga, but I can't do
that. You shouldn't be leading this investigation. You're not
holding up well. I saw you fall apart when I got here earlier."

"You were as unnerved as I was when you saw Giselle's
body. I've been first on the scene for the other four. Of course I'm
unnerved. You would be, too."

"Not as much as you are."

"Do you honestly think you can come in this late in the
game and be as good as I am?" Wilson looked away. "Wilson,

look at me," Malinga fumed. "If you take this case over from me now, it will slow us down completely."

He turned away from her. "I'll think about it, Malinga. I'll let you know after I've talked with the Inspector."

"Talk to the Inspector?"

"I have to, Malinga. Remember, I'm Acting." He opened the door and looked back at her. "With all due respect, Zambians may want to know that a man is in charge. It makes them feel better. You know how they are."

She glared at him. "I know how you are." Her frown deepened and she shook her head.

"I'll see you at the station," he said as he closed the door.

47 | No One Will Know

The tires on Stewart's old Rover squealed as he pulled through the gates of his compound. He ran into the house, shouting Kivuli's name. Bertha came out of the kitchen. She dropped the pot she was drying when she saw his face.

"Where is he?" Stewart bellowed. "Where is he? So help me, Bertha, if you are hiding him, I will kill you, too!"

"Kivuli went out just a short time ago," she said, cringing and backing away from his waving fists. "Redbone is here, sleeping. I will get him for you."

When Redbone emerged from Bertha's bedroom, scratching at his stomach, Stewart grabbed his shoulders and started shaking. "Giselle is dead! What has Kivuli done?"

"Dead!" Bertha exclaimed. "What do you mean? She is right here! I tended to her last night. I showed you. She was sleeping."

"What have you done with her?" Stewart shouted.

Redbone scratched his chest. "I did nothing. I was too busy satisfying this woman. Was I not, woman?"

Bertha ignored him. "Kivuli went out. We haven't seen him since Redbone took me to his bed."

Just then they heard a pounding at the door. Kivuli burst in, covered in blood.

"You bastard!" the doctor shouted. "You killed Giselle and cut her up like an animal! Don't deny it! You took her to Malinga's house and hung her on the fence!" Bertha gasped. What horrors had Kivuli committed with that beautiful South African woman? She shook her head. Nothing could be worse than what he'd done to her youngest son.

Kivuli glared at the doctor. "Yes, Stewart! I did it!" Kivuli shouted back. "I did it to hurt this detective woman. No one will believe she can protect anyone when they see what I have done. And she is frightened. I saw her face. All she did was scream." Kivuli started laughing. "Her gate guard will never be the same either. He pissed his pants. But that miserable dog of hers bit me." He held out his arm in Bertha's direction. "Woman," he said, "wash me and tend my wounds."

Stewart loosed a horrible scream and rushed at Kivuli with his fists flailing, but Bertha stepped in front of him and grabbed his hands. "Wait, Doctor!" she said. "We are all to blame. Giselle was already dead. Her heart stopped shortly after you operated this afternoon. We" – she glanced at Kivuli and Redbone – "decided to put her body to good use. If you punish Kivuli, you must punish us all."

Kivuli lifted his necklace of bones and held them in front of the doctor's face. "You see this, old man?" he said, yanking the collar of the doctor's shirt hard. "These bones are the first beneath the skull in every person. They hold our head upright." He grinned. "I take them so I walk straightest of all. Giselle's would be hanging here, but that dog fought me, and got it from me. He ripped open my arm, but I made him pay." He laughed. "That policewoman cried hard. She was very sad."

"I don't care about the damn dog! How could you butcher Giselle?" Stewart cried, tears streaming down his face. "You mutilated her," he said, falling to his knees. "I saw what you did. You cut her to pieces. It was horrible! I barely recognized her! How could you do that?"

Kivuli shook his head. "You killed Giselle. "You and your operation. Now no one will know that she died from your medicine. You should thank me for saving you skin and your reputation." Kivuli threw his head back and laughed at the shock on Stewart's face, then grabbed the doctor's shoulders and shook him hard.

"It is true," Kivuli said. He pulled Bertha forward and shoved her at the doctor. "It is as this woman said."

Bertha broke from Kivuli's hold, straightened herself, and cleared her throat. "It is so, Doctor. She was dead when you came in earlier, but I didn't know how to tell you." She looked away, avoiding Stewart's eyes.

"It can't be so!" he said. "I took every precaution."

Kivuli snorted. "Old man, you have made too many mistakes. From now on, I am in charge. I will listen to you no more." He raised his knife menacingly, and advanced on the doctor.

Bertha clung to his arm. "No Kivuli! Not the Doctor!!"

Stewart tensed for the blow, his eyes focused on the edge of Kivuli's knife as the man swung it toward him. He prepared for the blow. Kivuli was going to kill him. But when his cell phone range, Kivuli stepped back, startled, and began to laugh.

"Stewart. Victor here."

"Yes, Victor. What's up?"

"How's it coming, Stewart? Have you found those bloody bastards who can give you the elephant yet?"

"I'm working on it. I should know by later today. I can't talk to you now, Victor. I've been up all night. There's been another murder, and the police have asked for my help."

"Another murder? Anyone we can use?"

"I'm afraid not, Victor. The killer left her in pieces, so unless you've learned a way to piece her back together again, we're out of luck."

"Like Humpty Dumpty, eh? We can't get them all, I suppose!" He chuckled.

"I've got to go, Victor. I'll keep you informed."

"Can you join Anita and I for lunch?"

"I'll be busy all day, Victor. Why don't you and Anita take a car out to Chaminuka for their Sunday buffet? You'll see their elephant family. I know how much you love elephants." He could hear Victor laugh. "I'll speak to you later."

48 | Late for the President

"Did you hear him, Danise?' Malinga said as she came back into the living room and stood glaring down at her friend. "Did you hear him? Wilson still wants me to give him the case. I can't believe he'd do this to me!"

Danise smiled and reached for Malinga's hand. "Yes, Malinga. I heard him." She patted the cushions of the settee. "Sit down here a minute. Calm yourself. Let's talk."

"I can't believe it! Wilson won't give it up!" Malinga sat down next to her friend. "What should I do, Danise? He's going to call Inspector Chikanda."

"You can't stop him, Malinga. Maybe Wilson is right, and you should drop the case. If nothing else, it looks to me like the killer is after you. It's getting very personal."

Malinga jumped to her feet and started pacing. "That's exactly why I can't drop it, Danise. Every minute counts. Quitting now is the worst thing I could do. If the killer's after me, it means we're getting close." She stopped pacing and crossed her arms over her chest, frowning. "But I don't really think the killer's after me. I think he's just trying to unnerve us and throw us off."

Danise shook her head. "I'm a psychologist. I know what you're facing. He's not just trying to unnerve you, believe me."

Malinga sat down slowly next to her friend. "Do you think he'll try to kill me?" Her eyes widened. "Do you think he'll try to hurt the children?"

"I can't tell, but I wouldn't underestimate him." Danise looked at Malinga's pale face, and patted her hands. "Don't panic. Just be careful."

"You know I will. I've got the kids to think about."

"I'm here for you anytime you need help," Danise said, smiling. "But I can only give you advice. I can't make you take it. You're a grown woman and a veteran police officer."

Malinga squeezed Danise's hands and smiled. "Thanks, Danise. I need you standing behind me. The thought that the killer might be after me makes me very, very angry." She shuddered. "I feel so powerless. If he can do this to Giselle, he can have me anytime he wants with no warning at all. Me, or one of the kids. Or Wilson, if he takes over." She hid her face in hands.

Danise reached over and patted her shoulder. "He's terrifying, Malinga, like all psychopaths, and he's dangerous. He's everything in human nature that's twisted and perverse. But he also has a major weakness that you can exploit. He's arrogant. Overconfident. He thinks he's the paragon of human perfection, more intelligent than the rest of us."

Danise peered at Malinga over her half glasses and waited until she looked up. "Malinga, listen to me carefully. He's egocentric, so focused on himself that he lacks any empathy for other human beings. That's why he can treat his victims like objects. That's why we'll catch him in the end. "

"What do you mean?"

"He lacks empathy, right?" Malinga nodded. "So he sees everything with tunnel vision. There are many things he can't see, many things he'll overlook. Since he doesn't function like a normal human being, he can be outwitted."

Malinga frowned.

"I know this sounds a bit harsh right now," Danise continued, "but I'm glad he did this. It tells me he's so sure of himself that he'll keep putting his victims right in your face. He thinks that if he challenges you directly, you'll crumble."

"That's exactly what I'm doing," Malinga said, shaking her head.

"Malinga," Danise said. "Stop feeling sorry for yourself. There's no time to wallow in self-pity. The Inspector would have given the job to Wilson if he thought you'd be intimidated so easily."

Malinga drew in her breath. "Easily? Easily! You think I'm giving in easily, Danise? My life and my children are at stake here. If he can do this to someone as famous as Giselle, he can do it to anyone. What would keep him from hurting us? We're insignificant! She shook her head vehemently. "Maybe it's time I recognized that I can't be a policewoman and a mother, too. Maybe Herbert's right. Maybe it's too dangerous for my children."

Danise laughed. "Nonsense, Malinga. Policemen who are fathers are just as vulnerable. Besides, if you resign this case, you'll break the pledge you took when you joined the force."

"That may be true, but I have to do it."

"You'll lose everything you've worked for, Malinga, and your children will be so disappointed. Don't let them down. Don't let yourself down."

Malinga's face registered the shock she felt. "You're right. If I quit now, I'll have to resign my commission. Shiko and Katanga will never forgive me. But what's it worth if the killer gets me or one of the kids?" She shook her head. "I know I won't be able to stay on the force if I quit this case, but that's exactly what I've got to do."

"Malinga! You're giving in when you finally have the advantage!" When Malinga shook her head again, Danise smiled. "Don't you see how close you must be if he's willing to do something this risky?"

"What do you mean?"

"When he chose to dump the bodies in Lusaka, he knew he might be seen. This was riskier than dumping a body in the bushes in a distant village. When he came into your garden last night, he was taking a tremendous risk in order to frighten you. You must be very close on his trail."

"But I have no clues, no leads."

"Really? The evidence is piling up, Malinga. You'll have some very important answers by tomorrow afternoon after you interview the Archbishop."

Malinga looked away. "You're right, Danise, but . . ."

"You have a great team. Use them, but more importantly, use your head." Danise drew in a breath. "Listen to me. I f you give in to your fears, you'll regret it for the rest of your life. You're this close." She showed Malinga the tiny space between her thumb and index finger and grinned. "This close!"

Malinga laughed, thinking about the promise she'd made to herself not to let fear rule her actions. "Okay, okay, okay. You've convinced me. But what do you think I should do?"

"Exactly what you feel."

"What do you mean?"

"Pretend you're frightened. Announce that you've withdrawing from the case. Make it look like you're taking a break and are going on leave with your children."

Malinga shook her head. "But you just talked me into staying. I don't understand!"

Danise laughed. "Just pretend you are quitting. In reality, work behind the scenes and direct the investigation. Or . . ."

Malinga frowned. "Or?"

"Go in the opposite direction. Bait him. Be as visible and arrogant as he is. Challenge him. Call him out in the press again."

"I like that option. It's more or less what I'm already doing, and it's more like me. Hiding in the shadows was never my strength."

"You're right," Danise said. "I'll get results faster. But it will put you directly in harm's way."

Malinga frowned. "I want to get this guy, but I still have to put my kids first. Maybe the other route is better."

"If you choose that strategy, you have to convince everyone – everyone, including your house staff – that you've dropped the case. You'll have to leave the city and send the children to your parents' place in the village."

"You know I can't do that, Danise. I'm not that good a liar, and it puts too much responsibility on my parents."

Her friend smiled. "I was hoping you'd say that. Stand as tall as you can. Be brave and brash and obnoxious."

"That won't be hard," Malinga said, smiling sheepishly.

"These girls deserve the best, and it's you, not Wilson."

"I am the best. I want justice for these girls."

Danise laughed at the worried expression on her friend's face. "Stop feeling sorry for yourself, Malinga. You know how good you are. But you've got to remember one thing. This killer is ruthless. He showed us that tonight."

Malinga nodded, relaxing into the sofa's curves. She stifled a yawn. "Sorry, Danise. It's not the company, it's the hour. You've put me at ease again."

"I'm glad I was here. Call me anytime. Except in the next six hours. I'm dead out." Danise yawned and stretched, then rose and collected her things. "I have to get some sleep. You should, too. You have a lot to think about, but you don't have to do it all now. If you need someone to sort it through, talk to me. Anytime, Malinga, day or night."

"After tomorrow morning, you mean." They both laughed. "Chances are I'll have a lot to talk about after we see the President." They walked to the door.

Danise paused and turned back to her friend. "All of Lusaka is behind you. We know we're safe in your hands. It's one of the few times the public has actually believed in the police, and it's because you're doing all that stuff that isn't feminine. You're speaking out, refusing to accept persecution. It means so much, not just to women either. A lot of men are treated like slaves, like they're brainless and worthless, so they understand what it means to be peeled psychologically. Harness public opinion to your advantage."

Malinga smiled. "It's good to hear that people get it. Davison and Asedi have been working with neighborhood watch groups, so we can ask them for even more help. You know how they are – fervently ready to protect what little space society allows them to have."

Danise smiled. "Go to bed. And remember not to tell the President what you're telling me. He'll have you arrested for open rebellion."

Malinga watched Danise cross the front garden and waved as she pulled out of the driveway. She collected the tea things from the living room and put them in the kitchen sink. It was getting lighter, almost dawn. She'd had exactly no hours of sleep. She's right, Malinga thought. I desperately need to sleep before I see the President.

What a time for Bertha to be off. I could use a little of her coffee cake.

Malinga sighed, checked the door locks, and headed for her bedroom. When her cell phone rang, it took her a few seconds to get oriented.

"Malinga! Ready to see the President? It's almost noon."

Malinga looked at her watch. "My God, Wilson! It's a good thing you phoned! I'll meet you at State House as soon as I shower."

49 | Second Thoughts in Chaminuka

Anita licked her fingertips suggestively and gave Bertha a wink. "These scones are so delicious, they're sinful." Bertha had her back turned and said nothing, but scrubbed the pans in the sink with an extra vengeance. The minute she agreed to help the Germans cheat Stewart, she felt their evil slide over her and couldn't scrub hard enough to get their dirt off.

"I'm so glad you understand us," Anita said, when Bertha poured their morning coffee. She directed a high voltage smile in Bertha's direction and flicked her thick blond hair back. "It's good to know we can count on you to help us with Stewart. We only want the best for the dear man, after all, just as you do."

How could setting Stewart up to take all the blame possibly help him, Bertha wondered. How could leaving him disappointed and heartbroken help? They planned to pay him nothing, Bertha was sure. They would leave and return to Germany and Stewart would go to jail. If she helped them put him there, she'd have enough money to put her children through school. Through college if that's what they wanted.

But it left her feeling like the terrible traitor she was. Bertha thumped the pan she was washing down on the counter and turned her back. "Yes, madam," she mumbled.

"You're very quiet this morning, Bertha," Victor burbled. "I thought you'd be happy with the advance we gave you. I thought it was quite generous."

"Yes, sir. It was."

"What do you plan on doing with it?" Victor asked.

Bertha shrugged.

"It might be good for you to get your hair done," Anita suggested, patting her own.

"I will buy school things for the children."

"But, Bertha, you need to put yourself first sometimes," Anita insisted.

"I cannot do that. I have many children and they need many things. My family needs things, too. I bought food, as well. A chicken. It will feed us for many days."

Anita laughed uproariously, and Victor chortled. "A chicken?"

Bertha colored. She struggled to control her temper. "It is a very special thing when we get to eat a chicken, sir."

Anita reached for her bag and pulled it toward her. Rummaging inside, she exclaimed when she found what she was looking for. She dumped a wad of *kwacha* on the table and laughed again. "Here, Bertha. This should be enough for you to get your hair done and buy some new clothes. God knows, you need them."

Bertha looked down at her t-shirt and wrapper, stained with the remains of hundreds of hours of household work, and fought back the urge to slap the woman. She was mortified but needed the money badly. It turned her stomach to take it. She hesitated, but thought of how much food she could buy for the children and her elderly mother and reached for the bundle of notes. She stuck it in the band of her wrapper and turned back to the sink.

"Thank you, madam."

"Promise me you will do something with your appearance," Anita insisted.

"Yes, madam," Bertha replied, thinking of her other clothing, the dress she wore to church. She could wash it and the woman might think it was new.

"By the way, Bertha, whatever happened between the doctor and his witch doctor helpers last night? We could hear them screaming."

Bertha shrugged but said nothing and busied herself clearing the table. "I do not know, madam. You must ask the doctor."

Anita sighed and inspected her nails. She continued to buff them. "We expect the car for Chaminuka at nine. When it comes, would you fetch us from our suite?

"Yes, madam." Bertha removed her wrapper. "Now, if you have finished your breakfast, I must clean the doctor's office," she said, and walked swiftly to the door.

"That's quite all right, Bertha. Just be sure you call us when the driver comes."

Bertha nodded. "Yes, madam," she said, and left.

"That wad of money should ensure her loyalty," Victor said. "And a continuous suppy of these delicious scones. Can you pass me another, *Liebshen*?"

Anita pulled one from the plate and walked over to him, teasing him to take a mouthful. Then she kissed him on the lips, but pulled away when she heard a car in the drive. "I think that's the driver," she said. "I must grab a wrap." Victor watched her disappear and smiled to himself. Time to put on the Parkinson's act, he thought. The driver might say something to Stewart if he didn't look ill.

"I am Peter," the driver said, smiling broadly as he helped them into the rear seat of the Land Cruiser. "I think you will like your visit to Chaminuka very much. There are many wonderful animals there, and you can go on a game drive after you have your lunch."

The driver headed east toward the airport, turning left just before its entrance onto a dirt track leading north. In less than an hour, they pulled up to a gate in the middle of a vast stretch of farmland. One word to the guard and they were through.

"This is where they keep Duff," the driver said as they neared Chaminuka, pointing to their right at a deep hole in the ground. "They removed an old water tank and it's deep enough to keep the elephants in at night. Of course, their mahout stays with them to make sure they are comfortable and well fed so they don't bother our farmers."

"Where are the elephants now?" Victor asked with a note of disappointment in his voice.

The driver chuckled. "You will see them when you go on your game drive. The mahout must take them walking many miles every day so they are not restless when they come to sleep at night." He pointed to the left. "That barn houses our cheese making facility. I will show it to you before we return to Lusaka.

"Now," he said with a flourish, "we will stop to see the lions before we go for lunch." Victor and Anita cried out at the size of the male and female pacing the fence, their eyes gleaming. "What a fine animal! Is he for sale?" The driver laughed at the joke. "They had two cubs," he said, "but a hyena took one. There," he said, pointing at a large tree some distance from the fence, "is the mother and the other cub."

After a tour of the lodge's art collection, a sumptuous luncheon buffet, and a toast with the hotel's excellent wine, a Chaminuka guard helped Victor and Anita climb up onto the safari vehicle's high rear seat. Crossing the dam at the end of the lodge's lake on a narrow track, they stopped to admire a great heron among the reeds. As the vehicle labored up a steep incline, Victor forgot himself and whooped. Jumping to his feet, he shouted, "There, *Liebchen*! Look! It's the elephant! Get closer!" he called to the driver, who smiled and slowed the vehicle.

"Are they all so beautiful?" Victor croaked, struggling to regain his persona.

"Yes," the driver said proudly. "Zambian elephants are all beautiful. At Chaminuka, we protect them, so they will never become extinct."

"Ah, Victor!" Anita breathed. "He is so beautiful! Will the one we're getting be so large and magnificent?" she whispered.

"Stewart promised us, *Liebchen*. A specimen like this one would be so fine in our exhibit."

"I am so excited! Can you just see Eve and her children around him?"

The driver helped Anita step down and held her elbow as she tottered across the uneven ground toward Duff. "His mahout will make sure he will not hurt you," the driver explained. She gazed into Duff's placid face and his enormous lash-fringed amber eyes and sighed. "You are so beautiful," she said. We wouldl be so proud to own you." When she reached out to pat his leg, Duff growled. The low rumbled startled her and she ran back to the safari vehicle.

"Oh, Victor! I thought I was near God! I will not go back to Germany without one! How proud we will be when we finally own one!"

He smiled and touched her fondly. "You are right, *Liebchen*. We will be very proud. But there is something I must tell you." As the driver started the vehicle and turned back toward the lodge, Victor leaned closer to her and smiled gently. "I know you love these elephants, Anita."

"Oh, Victor! I do," she said, stroking his knee.

"I know you love them, but Stewart is having trouble finding one at a reasonable price. We may have to go to the Congo or CAR and try our luck with a forest elephant. They are equally as beautiful, but not so large."

"Oh, Victor! I will be so disappointed! You know how I like to have the best!'

"Stewart may fail us, *Liebchen*. Worse, I fear he is in danger of getting caught red-handed when he tries, and will incriminate us. We may have to leave sooner than we thought and drop the mess he is creating in his lap."

"Oh, Victor! Give him another chance! What about the lab? What will we do if we don't have the lab? Where will we get the volunteers we need?"

"We will find a way, my darling, but we can't do anything if we are in jail. We can always come back when things quiet down."

"I refuse to give up, Victor," she said with a pretty pout. "Maybe Stewart got the man to negotiate a better price. He may know something by now, darling. Why don't you call him?"

50 | Friends in High Places

"Thanks for your help transporting the giraffes," the President's press secretary said as he led Malinga and Wilson toward the front entrance of State House. "The sables I ordered from Chaminuka were delivered yesterday. Soon our menagerie will be complete." Paul smiled at them over his shoulder. "Our last President banned all animals from State House after one of his monkeys pissed on him during a press conference. The new President is willing to take his chances with uninvited animal commentary. He was also prudent enough to move the podium."

Malinga laughed. "Thank you for seeing us, Mr. Press Secretary."

"Call me Paul," he said as he ascended the portico's curved staircase into the first reception room. He glanced back at Wilson. "How many of your team are here?"

Wilson coughed. "Malinga's heading the investigation."

Paul looked at her disparagingly. "Really? A woman? I told you we wanted a man!"

Malinga held her ground. "There are several of those on my team. We have six full time detectives, a UTZ professor developing psych profiles of the killer, and a forensic specialist from Interpol with expertise on serial killers. Inspector Chikanda sent him."

"So where are they?"

"At the station, working day and night to stop this killer."

"Not a moment to waste," Paul said, nodding. "This is the first crime to catch the attention of the international press since the new President came into office and could have a major impact on tourism. Move quickly." He swatted a bit of lint from his sleeve. "We've been so busy redecorating State House that we scarcely noticed the killings. But the number of girls being murdered rose so fast that the press is all over us, accusing the President of colluding with the murderers. How many bodies are there now? Ten? Thirteen?"

"Five," Malinga said.

"Really? So few?" Malinga drew back, startled by his insensitivity. Paul rushed to correct himself. "I mean, or course, that I'm relieved to hear it's a manageable number." When she said nothing, he straitened his jacket and gestured to the portico.

"A fresh coat of paint has improved the looks of the place, don't you think? Our President's house must make Zambians proud." A tiny moue of disdain crimped his lips. "Our former president left it looking very grim. I don't know what he was thinking, bringing foreign dignitaries to this dingy old house."

"You've done a good job, Mr. Press Secretary . . . ah, Paul" Malinga murmured with a little smile. "It looks very nice."

"Let's hurry," Paul said, starting up the stairs. "The President is in quite a state about the murders and the accusations he's suffered." He waved them past the scanner and police guard to a second garden courtyard and gestured toward some overstuffed chairs pushed against the wall facing a tiny fountain trickling through a dry bed of papyrus. "I'll get you some tea," he said, disappearing down the corridor to the right.

"I've got to find out who his decorator is," Wilson said, pointing at the 1950s-era copper map of Zambia hanging opposite them. "I thought my parents had the last one one of those. Look at the ashtrays. Fake elephant feet, probably from China."

"I hope they are," Malinga said. "It would be a shame if an elephant died for that sin."

Paul returned, trailed by an aged butler with one milky, glaucoma-blotted eye. "I must apologize," he said, flashing his biggest campaign smile as the man arranged tea things on the table. "The President will be a bit late. He likes to greet the crowds at church after the Archbishop finishes the service. Since this is an important feast day, we may not see him for some time." Malinga and Wilson exchanged glances. Paul looked at his wristwatch. "I'm finalizing plans for Zimbabwe's Presidential visit next week, but I'll be back as soon as I can."

When he'd left, Malinga looked at Wilson. "Let's not talk about about the Archbishop, shall we?" she said, sipping her tea. "He's probably saying mass right now."

Wilson nodded. "No one will be happy to hear that. Especially the President. The First Lady gave the Archbishop a specially minted medal honoring the accomplishments of his reign. It cost a fortune." They relaxed into silence, sipping their tea and enjoying a view of the animals wandering free in the President's compound.

"Look at that elephant, Malinga," Wilson said excitedly, leaning forward to point.

"He's the biggest one I've ever seen!"

"A monster!"

"I heard he's on his last legs, but he sure looks good," Malinga said.

"He does." Wilson glanced at his watch. "It's already noon. Maybe we should come back another time."

"If we leave without permission, Paul will have us removed from the force and stationed in some tiny village near Mwinilunga."

"But we have the staff meeting before we talk with the Archbishop. We'll be late."

"Might be just as well," Malinga said. "If we're late for the Archbishop, the Sunday afternoon crowd will have thinned out. I don't want to raise unnecessary hackles."

She glanced at cell phone. "It's The Husband. Excuse me for a minute." She stood and put the phone to her ear.

"Malinga," Herbert growled. "Where the hell are you? It's Sunday. I'm at the house. I want to get a few things."

"I'm at State House, Herbert. I'm working, for heaven's sake. We're waiting to give the President a special briefing on the murders."

"But I can't get into your house! There's a policeman at the gate and he won't let me in."

Malinga smiled and made a crackling sound. "I can't hear you, Herbert" she said. "I'm losing the signal. I'll call you back later," she promised as she hung up. When the phone rang again, she sighed. Herbert never gave up that easily.

"You think this is funny, Malinga? You think you're a big deal because you're talking with the President? If this case is as serious as it sounds, I'm going to take my children away from you."

"Keep your shirt on, Herbert. My housekeeper watches them while I'm at work. Which I am right now, so I have to hang up." She turned her phone off.

Wilson raised an eyebrow.

"Herbert again. He wants to get into my house."

"Not just now," Wilson chuckled. "Let's hope he doesn't alert the press."

"Don't worry. He won't. He'll have to answer too many questions." Malinga walked to the edge of the veranda, where the courtyard gave way to a wide bank of stairs descending to the ceremonial lawn. "This is where I was sworn into the force," she said, gesturing to the grass below.

Wilson whistled. "You're lucky! I was sworn in downtown. No pomp or circumstance."

They turned at the sound of Paul's footsteps bustling across the courtyard from the President's private quarters. "He's coming! He finally got away from a delegation of women from his home village." Next to witch doctors, Malinga thought, family matriarchs were the most intimidating Zambians you could possibly meet.

"He wants to see you right away. He wants to walk in his garden with his new giraffes, so he doesn't have much time."

Malinga and Wilson exchanged glances. She rolled her eyes and rose from the bench. "Ready."

Paul turned to Malinga. "What did you say your name was again? I want to get it right when I introduce you."

"Malinga. Malinga Mutende."

The press secretary grunted and turned toward the garden, then hurried to the edge of the veranda and pointed. "Look! There they are! You can see three of them very clearly.

Come! Look! Aren't they the most beautiful things you ever saw?"

"The most beautiful *giraffes* I ever saw," a gruff voice rumbled from behind them.

Their heads swiveled around.

"Mr. President," Malinga gasped.

51 | Results or Else

"Don't be alarmed," the President said, smiling. "I've just returned from church, so I should be quite harmless for the next few hours." His laughter boomed. "Come. Let us sit out on the veranda. Paul will see that we have tea."

"The giraffes are beautiful, sir," Malinga said.

"I'm so glad you like them. Animals are so important to our heritage and traditions as a country."

He turned to his press secretary. "Now, Paul," he said, "introduce these people, will you? I hate talking to strangers in my home." He took Malinga's hand, raising his eyebrows at Paul.

"This is Malinga Mutende, head of the investigating team," Paul said.

"The policewoman of my dreams," the President joked, and held her eyes as his smile broadened. "I may make you head of my personal guard once you're done with this case. Let's get it over with soon, shall we?"

He chuckled and patted her hand. "I'm glad we have a woman competent enough to handle this. Your leadership sends the right signals to Zambia women and to the international community." He leaned back and looked Wilson up and down as though he were a museum specimen. Then he mock charged him, grabbing his hand and shaking it roughly. "And this big white man. Who the hell are you?"

"Wilson Mwiinga," he said, standing up to the President's bluff. "I like to pretend I'm Malinga's boss, but she's in charge on this one."

"Glad to hear it. We men have to get along with the women who run our lives," the President joked. He motioned them to take seats. "Let's get down to business, shall we? I don't have much time, but this case is bringing so much negative attention to Zambia that I can't afford to ignore it. Tourists already think Africans live in the dark ages and they can't visit here without an elephant gun. Even when they're not hunting."

He chuckled, but his face darkened and Malinga's blood ran cold. His hand shot in the air and he wagged his finger menacingly. "*Zambia Watchdog* is hinting that I have a role in this, that I believe in witchcraft and use it to shore up my position in this country. Nothing could be further from the truth."

As quickly as they had assembled, the thunderclouds disappeared from his eyes and his face relaxed. He paused for a dainty sip of tea. "As I was saying to the Archbishop this morning after mass, witchcraft is setting this country back hundreds of years. I couldn't be more against witchcraft and charms. Any intelligent African is."

They nodded and his face brightened.

"Which is not to say that sometimes it isn't useful to pretend you believe in it, as every intelligent African politician also knows." He chuckled. "Enough of that. Tell me what you've got on the killers."

Malinga cleared her throat. "There have been five murders in Lusaka, one in Mongu and one in Chipata, but we don't think the ones outside of Lusaka are related."

The President nodded. "Go on."

"We have a strong lead in third case, but not on the others."

The President sat forward, eager. "Who is it?"

"Since the man is only a suspect, it would be remiss of me to release his name, even to you Mr. President."

"I see," he said, taking another sip of tea and scrutinizing her over tented fingers. "I would prefer to hear that you've arrested someone and are close to putting the mind of the public to rest."

"We are very close, Mr. President, I assure you. We have a team of experts from here in Zambia, and Inspector Chikanda enlisted the help of Jacques DuClaire, a pathologist from Interpol. He arrived in Lusaka a few days ago and has been of enormous assistance. The brutalities committed on the third girl are substantially different from those inflited on the others, suggesting a different killer using a different weapon, but . . ."

She broke off. The President had rested his chin on his hands and his head was down. He had fallen asleep. When she stopped, he jerked awake and looked around.

"I know I can count on you find these monsters. Both of them. The three of them," he scowled. "As many as there are. I want these killings to stop." He rose and his scowl deepened. "This can't continue. If you find any other girls, hide them. Keep them quiet! These bodies are frightening the public, not to mention tour operators."

His voice rose. "What do you think people say about a country where people are skinned? We are supposed to be doing that to the animals, for heaven's sake! Not our own people!" he shouted, bringing his fist down on the table with a crash.

"Listen to me. Listen very carefully or you will regret it. If I don't get results, I'll have your jobs in a heartbeat. I thought I'd give you a week, but I can't wait that long. You have five days. If you don't have the killers in hand by Friday, I will replace you. Is that clear? In the meantime, say nothing to the press, even if there are new cases. Until we have some answers, I want you to say nothing."

He walked to the edge of the veranda to admire his menagerie. His face darkened. "Paul? Paul!" The venom re-entered his voice. "What the hell happened to my giraffes? They must be here where we can see them when the Chinese minister comes for tea. Where is Madam, the President's wife?" he asked, and strode off.

Paul scurried after him, glancing back at Wilson and Malinga. "Don't move. I'll be right back."

The detectives resumed the seats. Wilson looked a little grey. "We can't possibly solve the murders in five days!" he said. "Some of the lab work won't be done that fast. He's going to take our jobs."

"I doubt that, Wilson. Who would he give them to?"

"He'll find someone, I know it! Let me take over, Malinga. If I'm heading the investigation, we might have a chance."

52 | Presidential Directives

"Relax, Wilson," Malinga said. "He's just blowing off steam." She grinned stiffly. "Don' worry, he can't take our jobs. Who'd want them? Who in Zambia is qualified to do what we do? Name one person."

"Someone from the provinces would be happy to take our jobs, qualified or not."

"That may be true, but it won't happen any time soon," Malinga said. "It would take too long and the press would be on high alert if he swapped horses on this case. Just relax. The President does this all the time to intimidate civil servants. He's famous for it."

"He's famous for firing people at whim," Wilson insisted.

"Ministers, yes. Political appointees, yes. But he's nobody's fool. He'd be cutting his throat in the international press if he sacked us." She nudged Wilson's elbow and pointed down the hall. "Let's talk about this later. Paul is coming back."

"The President has issued some directives," Paul said, clearing his throat and puffing out his chest. "The first is to all priests, ministers, and preachers in Zambia. They must speak out against witchcraft at least once a week." He shook his head and gave a short snort of laughter. "Not that it will make much difference."

He glanced at his paper and continued. "Perhaps the next two directives will be a little more useful. First, the President will speak out against these crimes at a press conference tomorrow, when he will announce that he is personally offering a five-thousand-dollar reward for any information leading to the capture of this fiend."

He looked up at Malinga and Wilson. "Not fiends in the plural, please. Just one. We can't upset the public." He scratched his head. "Just to clarify, in case there are two or more fiends, we will give three thousand dollars for each of them. But only for testimony that directly leads to their identification and capture. Nothing less."

"That's a good start," Malinga said. "People who were too afraid to speak may come forward . . ."

"Maybe," Paul said, cutting her short. "Prepare yourselves for a flood of new informants. You'll need more men" — he glanced at Malinga – "sorry, more officers, to handle them. Come to me if you have budgetary concerns."

Malinga nodded. "Thanks."

"The final thing the President wants you to do is go to the people. He'll tell the cadres to support police in any way they can. That should help considerably."

"My deputies are already working with neighborhood watch groups in every . . ."

Interrupting her, he said "At our press conference tomorrow – yes, this will be a joint effort between the police and the President's Office – the President will emphasize how everyone must help. Shops must lock up early, schools cannot allow children, especially girls, to walk home alone, and women should never travel alone, especially after dark. The people will be directed to report anything unusual. Then the President will symbolically deputize them."

"Good idea," Wilson said. "It reinforces self-reliance of the local groups we've been working with, but please ask the public to go through their neighborhood committees or central station will be overwhelmed with calls." Malinga was annoyed at how easily Wilson took the credit for her deputies' work, but decided to take it up with him later. Paul nodded and turned to leave. "That's fine. Call me if you have any other ideas before the conference."

"I will. Thanks, Paul," Malinga said before Wilson could open his mouth.

"One more thing." Paul turned back to look her full in the face. "Don't turn this into a political spectacle with any remarks about women's rights. If you do, you will suffer more than the loss of your badge. Do you hear me?" She nodded.

"At the end of the press conference, reporters will interview the President about his concerns for women and children – the usual thing – and take them for a tour of his new menagerie. By the way, the President asked me to talk to Inspector Chikanda. He wants to be sure you're competent to lead this investigation." Malinga flinched.

"We must be sure we have the best person for the job," he said, glancing at Wilson. Malinga nodded again, forcing herself to remain calm. "One more thing. Our President tells me that his brother Presidents from neighboring countries have offered help from their detective squads."

Malinga bristled and Paul held up his hands to cut off her complaint. "Don't get excited. I've suggested that he hold off until Friday. Asking for their help signals weakness to the international community and may frighten the people even more. When they get frightened, witchcraft escalates. We don't want this to turn into some face peeling free-for-all."

When he started to laugh, Malinga and Wilson looked away. It only increased his delight. "Not to mention the calls we'll get from ambassadors," Paul continued. "Too many interruptions, fewer bowel movements, unhappy President. I must keep him happy, and you must do everything you can to help me accomplish that goal."

Paul's smile turned into a scowl. "If you want to keep your jobs, catch the killer. You have five days. Use them wisely. The President is becoming impatient. You've had three weeks already."

He wagged a finger at them. "Don't fail us. I warn you. Don't fail us or I will personally make you the laughingstock of Lusaka and see that both of you are fired in disgrace." He stalked off. "Show yourself out," he called over his shoulder. "You're nearly there. Out, that is."

Malinga drew in a deep breath and put a hand on Wilson's sleeve to calm him. "Relax, Wilson. Let's get back to work. Can you make sure Davison and Asedi are at the station in half an hour and pick up Jacques on your way there? I'll see if Danise is available and stop at Stewart's on my way in. See you downtown."

53 | Starting to See Things

"It wasn't Giselle, Malinga. Giselle is sleeping right here. That's all I can tell you right now. Besides being my patient, she's an international celebrity and her medical details must remain confidential."

"I'm so glad she's all right, Stewart, but I still can't believe you left the scene with no explanation. You scared us all to death. I know you don't work for me officially, but we have to coordinate when something like this happens. It could mean life or death."

The doctor stared at his hands and said nothing. His face was deathly pale.

Malinga sighed. "It makes you look bad, Stewart. And you gave me a fright." When the doctor looked up at her again, there was nothing left of the bold Englishman Malinga once knew and loved. The man she saw before her was confused, distracted, close to panic.

"Stewart, talk to me. What's going on here?"

He rubbed his brow. "I'm exhausted, Malinga. You can't imagine how these past few hours have affected me. First, your men wake me in the middle of the night to cover for the medical examiner. Then I find what I think is the body of my patient – my friend, for God's sake! – nailed to your back fence. I drove like a madman to get here to check. Fortunately, there aren't many people moving about at three a.m. in Lusaka, and very few cows. It would be disconcerting for anyone, don't you think?"

"Maybe, Stewart, but you left us with no explanation. Who were the three people you said would pay?"

He looked away. "I was in shock, Malinga. I was probably thinking of the three killers we talked about earlier. I'm not sure what I was thinking, to be frank."

"Are you sure Giselle is all right?"

He looked up. "Malinga, I told you that already."

"Can I see her, Stewart?"

He looked away and picked up his coffee. "No, Malinga. I can't let you do that. It violates her privacy, and I'm afraid if I wake her and she sees a strange face, it will impede her recovery."

She nodded. "Okay, Stewart. I understand. Just tell me what happened when you got here."

"I don't remember everything. I do remember running from my car and shouting for Bertha. I woke her, and she came stumbling from bed. She followed me down the hall to the room where Giselle was – is – sleeping soundly. She seems to be recovering well from the anesthetic. At that point, I completely broke down, crying with relief. Then I collapsed. I woke up just before you got here."

"Can I talk to Bertha?"

"I've sent her to find out who stole the clothing we found on your fence, and look for Redbone and Kivuli. I wouldn't be surprised if they had something to do with this. I want to find them as quickly as I can."

"Tell her to be careful, Stewart. They're dangerous men. Davison and Asedi will be looking for them, too. Why do you think they're involved?"

"I know them only slightly, mostly by reputation. I've seen them here and there in Kalingalinga, and I've heard that they're up to no good. I think they're behind a lot of shifty stuff in this compound. Why they would do something like this is beyond me."

"Does anyone else have a grudge against Giselle and want to do her harm?"

The doctor sighed. "When you are as famous as Giselle, many people want to hurt you. Her band broke up before she came back to Zambia. Maybe it's one of them."

Malinga nodded. "Katanga told me about her band. She follows all the tweets. Is there anyone who might want to cause a problem for you?"

"That's a very good question, Malinga, and the answer is really quite complicated. After our new President was elected, many Zambians who were my friends expressed their true feelings about whites. I have been disappointed – no, I should say, gravely hurt – by their reactions."

"I'm sorry Stewart. That happened to many of us. He's a controversial figure."

"It's more than that, Malinga." His voice tightened as he continued. "These were people who'd been my friends for many years. Many of them harbored deep seated feelings of resentment toward me that they never expressed." He covered his face with his hands.

"I'm sorry, Stewart. You and your wife served this country well for decades. It must be a terrible disappointment."

He sniffed. "The less said about it the better."

"I understand." She paused. "Come to the station, Stewart. The way you left the scene and what you said about knowing who did it makes you a suspected accessory, so I have to take you in anyway. There'll be some formalities, finger printing and the like, but don't hold it against me. I have to play this very straight. If you don't clear all the hurdles, my team won't trust either one of us."

He nodded. "Of course, Malinga. Let me finish my coffee. I'll be there shortly."

Malinga stood. "If you think of anyone who has a reason to harm you or Giselle, let me know. I want to find the person responsible for the travesty on my fence as soon as I can and make a positive identification of the victim. That may tell us more."

Stewart nodded when she finished but didn't look up. Malinga left him, discouraged by what she'd heard. She felt sorry for the man. He'd served Zambia well.

As she walked toward her car, she thought she saw Bertha disappear into the side door near the kitchen. She blinked and rubbed her eyes, took a few steps toward the house, then shrugged and climbed into her car.

I'm so tired, I'm starting to see things.

54 | Witch Doctor in Fancy Dress

"Well, Malinga?" Wilson said. "You haven't said much. Do we have enough evidence to nail His Excellency, or don't we?" She was seated across from him but continued to stare at her hands. Her mind was elsewhere.

"Malinga!" Wilson called, rapping his knuckles on the table. "Is anybody home in there?"

She jerked her head up. "Sorry, Wilson. I'm a bit tired from last night." Her smile was forced. Her meeting with Stewart had been frustrating, and she was still angry with the President's press secretary. His parting words revived her worries for her job and her children. She had to pull herself together.

If I let political flunkies affect me, I'd never have come this far.

Despite the President's mandate to move females up in the police force, not many women succeeded. It was more important than ever that she did.

Young women need my example. I'll show them what I'm made of one more time.

She cleared her throat. "Before I say anything, I want the team to hear what Stewart told me earlier."

She looked at the doctor and he nodded, considerably more composed than he'd been earlier. "Thanks, Malinga. Let me apologize to you all for going off the rails this morning at the crime scene, but I'm sure you understand what I was going through.

"When I left you, I rushed back to my home. Much to my relief, Giselle was resting comfortably right where I left her. I questioned my staff, but no one knows how her clothing ended up at the crime scene or who the victim really is." He looked around the table. "I'll do everything in my power to help you find the men responsible for these ghastly crimes."

"Thanks, Stewart," Malinga said. "Asedi, Davison, as soon as we finish, I want you to find Redbone and Kivuli and bring them in for questioning. Stewart believes they had access to his compound and they might have something to do with the murder. Oh, and for form's sake take a set of prints from the doctor."

She turned toward the Frenchman. "Jacques, can you rush a positive identification of the remains we found last night?"

"I'll push the work on the dental records as fast as I can," he said.

She turned to her deputy. "Davison, let's hear what you learned about the Chinese clinic."

"The clinic at the coal mine in Southern Province gives basic first aid for minor accidents like broken bones and scrapes, but there's no operating room. It's a dead end. I'm checking other private clinics and hospitals near Lusaka, and our plain clothes men are nosing around for anything unusual."

"Good plan. Keep going," Malinga said. "We have extra staff coming in from the Copperbelt, so work with them. Asedi?"

"I haven't learned anything new from the compounds," Asedi said. "No one in the drop site compounds remembers anything, and they're still very frightened. The President's reward should bring some witnesses forward, but so far no one's talking."

"Do we have enough evidence to bring charges against the Archbishop?" Malinga asked.

"Arrest, maybe. Conviction, no, but definitely enough to warrant a visit," Davison said.

"After we review what we've got," Malinga said, "Wilson and I will call on him. If we can rule him out, we'll have only two murderers to catch by Friday."

Jacques cleared his throat. "I learned two things that might help."

Malinga laughed. "Let's hear it, Jacques. By the way, I'm glad you're holding up so well. I was afraid you'd be on the first Air France jet back to Marseilles after last night!"

The pathologist laughed. "Not a chance. Things are just getting interesting. I had another look at the bodies. The last three had skin grafts and traces of a plastic-like substance on their skin, as you know."

Malinga noticed Stewart was staring at Jacques.

"They were recent skin grafts, like the body we found last night," Jacques continued. "The first victim had none, but all the later ones did. None of their family members reported any surgery, so the killer may have been practicing grafting techniques and experimenting with preservative compounds on the captured women before he killed them."

Malinga caught Stewart's eye. "Doctor, do you know of anyone doing that kind of work locally?" He shook his head.

"There was grafting on my vic's face," Malinga said, sitting back to fan herself with one of the case documents. The station house was poorly ventilated and air conditioning limited to the Inspector's personal office. Lingering heat despite the November rains made the place muggy and fungus ridden.

"I found one more thing when I double-checked the bodies," Jacques said. "All but the third girl was missing her Atlas bone. That's the cervical vertebrae just at the top of the spinal column that Wilson asked about."

Malinga remembered the feel of the bone in her hand and shivered. "That's the bone my dog had in his mouth. Apparently, the killer tried to take it, but Benny wouldn't let him have it." She paused and looked at Davison. "So we're on the lookout for a witch doctor with a fancy necklace. Maybe Davison will spot him carrying a live chicken." The group laughed, and so did Davison, although he looked a bit sheepish.

"Only joking, Davison," Malinga said. "Let's hear your rundown on the Archbishop."

Davison straightened, visibly relieved. "We've told you about the evidence linking him with Victim Three, Ruth Moyo. She was a nineteen-year-old second-year student at the National Institute for Public Administration. As Danise mentioned, she was a model student and lived with her widowed mother, Victoria, in Emmasdale, a relatively well-to-do section of town. The morning after the murder, a neighbor boy visited the mother to ask if Ruth was home. Mrs. Moyo had worried all night because her daughter called at eighteen thirty to say she was on the bus, close to home, but never returned.

"When Mrs. Moyo told the boy that her daughter was not home, he asked her to come and see something. A woman's naked body had been dumped three houses away. The mother followed the boy to the place and identified Ruth from her flip flops and a scrap of underwear still fastened around her middle. I went to question her. When I arrived to question her, she was wailing inconsolably.

"There was no hope left in this woman. Ruth was her oldest child. Her promise to care for her family once her studies were done had been a great source of comfort and pride for her mother. She told me that Ruth was very committed to God and had asked her mother to attend fellowship meetings with her.

"Neighbors and church members had already gathered around the mother by the time we arrived," Asedi added. "Among them was the uncle, Nimbus Malomo, who was the last person to see Ruth alive. He told us that Ruth had taken a minibus to Kabanana to visit him when she knocked off school the day before. She typically did this on Fridays after school because he was her favorite uncle.

"The uncle said Ruth came to his home in high spirits. She'd finished a major set of exams at NIPA and was very enthusiastic about her results. He told us he never imagined he wouldn't see her alive again when she left his house at eighteen hundred hours. She didn't call him when she got home to reassure him she was safe, as she usually did, but he assumed she forgot because she was so happy.

"As we know, she never reached home. Sometime after she left her uncle's house, the killers grabbed her. After they finished with her, they wedged her body into the hedgerow nearby. Her facial skin, eyes and tongue had been removed, along with her breasts, vagina, and exterior genital skin. As Jacques just reported, the killer did not take her Atlas bone."

"The cause of death was a cranial contusion," Jacques added. "The girl had been hit on the head with a heavy object. There were no signs of struggle, no skin under the nails, no broken fingernails, and little disturbance around the body. That and the relatively small amount of blood told us that the murder had been committed in another place. There was no bleeding around the wounds, so she was butchered after she died."

Malinga remembered the public outrage when the murder was reported in *The Times*. "The culprits of this gruesome murder must be brought to book," tweeted a reader named Mbili. "That is why the death penalty must be upheld, to serve such characters right." Madu warned the killer that while he thought no one had seen him, "Almighty God has seen you and you will pay the price." Idah captured the feeling of many when the number of murders increased: "These really are the last days mentioned in the Bible. God save us all!"

"Fortunately, we have enough evidence to continue to detain our two suspects, the driver and the uncle," Davison said. "We brought her favorite uncle in for questioning after the funeral, and he hasn't given us a straight story yet."

55 | Every Confidence in You

Malinga's cell phone vibrated. "It's the Inspector. I've got to take this," she said, ducking into the hall.

"Malinga!" her boss said. "Paul called me from State House. He wants you off the case. What happened?"

Malinga's pulse quickened. "Sorry he bothered you, Inspector. I thought we had reassured him."

"He said that you didn't know what you were doing, and that he wanted a *real* inspector – a proper policeman – leading the investigation."

"Yes, he told me that, too, Inspector. I thought he was just threatening me. I never thought he'd call you in France or I would have called you first."

"Did you have words with him?"

"No sir. I bit my tongue. He seemed satisfied, and I thought he was dropping it. That's why I didn't call you." She paused. "Look, Crispin. I know how embarrassing this is for you. I'll step down if you want me to."

"You know I don't want that, Malinga."

"I'm glad to hear that, sir, because I don't think it's a good idea. The President gave us five days. If you remove me, it will double everyone's workload and delay us even further. Wilson is still coming up to speed. We're stretched, but the President told us to add detectives from the Copperbelt. He's giving us the money. They owe it to us after raiding our budget for the campaign."

The Inspector chuckled. "That's true. Paul told me they're offering a reward. Do you think that's a good idea?"

"It always brings people out."

"He also told me that the President plans a press conference to encourage the compound watch groups."

"We're on it. There's no harm in warning people to look out for themselves, although I'm a little nervous about vigilante justice," Malinga said. "I don't want to encourage a second wave of vengeance killings or witch hunts."

"That won't happen if you're careful and work closely with the local committees."

"Asedi and Davison have worked with the compounds since last year. Danise and I – she's the psychologist from UNZA that helped us with the Mailonis – are discussing how I can bait the killer and force him out into the open."

"That's always tricky."

"But it will get quick results. Besides, I think he's already got it in for me."

"Why do you say that?"

She cleared her throat, unsure how to proceed. "Last night, he nailed pieces of his latest victim to my back fence. We thought it was Giselle at first."

"The singer? Giselle the singer?"

"We thought so at first, but Stewart says it wasn't her, that she's still alive and well at his place. The body was draped with her clothing, hat, and sunglasses. We don't know who the victim is and how the killer got Giselle's clothing, and neither does Stewart, but we should know by the end of the day."

"My God, Malinga. How many does this make?"

"Six."

"That's peanuts in a European city, but it's a catastrophe in Lusaka. Funny Paul didn't mention it."

"I decided not to tell him about last night's victim until we know more. I'm glad we didn't, because now we know it wasn't Giselle. We're going to keep this one quiet for now. The President's worried about Zambia's image and the impact of the murders on tourism."

"People are too willing to believe Africans are serial killers anyhow."

"Black magic and all that. The style of these murders feeds that myth for sure. If we identify the international dealers, we can share some of the blame with the buyers."

"I know how badly you want to catch him, Malinga, but do you really think you should bait a guy like this? He's a psychopath."

"Danise thinks it will draw him out and he'll start making mistakes. I'm going to challenge him at tomorrow's press conference."

"Be careful, Malinga. You know how dangerous this man is." He paused. "I'm still not convinced it's a good idea, but you're in charge on this one. I'll call Paul and tell him that I stand behind you 100 percent. You've proven yourself so many times I have no question about your competence, no matter what Wilson says."

Her heart sank. "He called you, too?"

"Yes, shortly after Paul. I didn't take it seriously. If anything, I was a little impatient with him. He's had his day in the sun, but that doesn't mean he's as experienced and tough as you are."

Malinga held the phone away from her ear.

Then why did you give him the promotion?

"Thanks Inspector. I appreciate your support. There's one more thing that I need to talk to you about."

"What is it?"

"The Catholic Archbishop may have something to do with the third murder."

Inspector Chikanda drew in his breath. "You have my attention, Malinga."

"I didn't mention it to the President, but we're reviewing the evidence right now. Wilson and I will pay the Archbishop a visit later this afternoon."

"Call me the minute you learn anything. He's one of the President's closest friends."

"I know. I'll get back to you as soon as I can."

"Good luck, Malinga." He paused. "You know I have every confidence in you. Get in there and do your job like you always do and don't let these guys unnerve you."

"Thanks Inspector. I'll call as soon as I have something."
She smiled ras she closed her phone.

Wilson had the Mailonis. This is my chance to shine.

"The Inspector wishes you all well," she told her team as
she re-entered the conference room. "He knows we'll have this in
hand well before Friday."

The group brightened.

"But if we're going to make it by the deadline, we have to
keep moving. He wants to be the first to know about any new
developments, so we have to be sure there aren't any leaks.
There's another reason to be absolutely discrete: we're setting a
trap for the killer and it won't work if he learns what we're up to.
Don't say anything to your wife— or husband," she said, grinning
at Davison and Asedi. "Don't e-mail, text, or say anything to your
kids. If they're like Katanga and Shiko, the news will be all over
town in an hour."

She looked at each of her team members in turn.

"This is critical. If I find that anyone has leaked
information about the case, intentionally or accidentally, it will
mean your job. Understand?"

They nodded and she took a deep breath.

"Okay, let's wrap up our review of third case so we can
get moving. Davison?"

56 | Hiding a Botched Abortion

"We detained two suspects the same day we found the body," Davison said. "The first one was the girl's uncle, the one she'd visited, Nimbus Molomo. The second suspect was a complete surprise." Davison paused. "It was the Archbishop's driver.

David Jere, Lusaka Province's Police Chief, picked the driver up after the uncle mentioned his name. Both men claimed they were following the Archbishop's orders, but we haven't talked with him. It would be a disaster if we picked up the Archbishop and he had nothing to do with it."

Malinga nodded. "We'd never hear the end of it. Tell the group what Jere said."

Davison drew a big breath. "The Archbishop's car was spotted in the compound just before dawn, a few hours before the neighbor's boy found the body. He saw a man removing something from the car's boot and shoving it in the bushes. He'd snuck out of his house to go nightclubbing against his parents' orders, so he won't swear an affidavit.

"He'd seen the car in the compound many times. The Archbishop had visited Ruth and her mother at their Emmasdale home more than once. The uncle says the Archbishop also visited with Ruth at his house once a month. The driver says he brought the Archbishop to the uncle's house and waited in the car for two hours while the Archbishop was inside."

Wilson shook his head, smiling.

"The uncle told the driver he was saving the money the Archbishop gave him for Ruth's college tuition and fees. He said he did it so the girl didn't have to troll the bars to find her sugar daddy.

He came to her," Wilson said.

Jacques held up a finger. "If I might? There is another complication. The girl was pregnant, victim of a botched abortion."

"That's why I don't think the Archbishop is our serial killer," Davison said. "I think the abortion went bad and the driver and the uncle tried to cover it up by making it look like a ritual murder. By the time this happened, the first two murders had already occurred."

"They made a dreadful mess of it," Stewart commented. "Looks like they tried to cover up her identity and went too far."

"Maybe they got paid for the body parts, in addition to the murder," Wilson said. "They thought they could get away with it because the big man had a hand in it."

Malinga smiled. "You've always hated the church."

"I do. Let's go talk to him," Wilson said.

Malinga started loading files in her briefcase. "If we leave now, we can get there before tea."

"Before you leave, Malinga," Asedi said, "how should we handle all the confessions we'll get after the President announces his reward? As soon as you have that press conference tomorrow, the switchboard will be flooded with calls."

"Let's ask people to report to their compound groups first. The President said he'd increase their budgets so they can sort it out. Can they do it?"

"I know they can, Mum," Davison said, smiling broadly. "We've worked hard with them."

"If we tell callers to work with their compound group first, then come into the station personally to fill out a report and sign an affidavit, it will cut down on the nuisance calls," Asedi added.

"I'll pull two traffic cops off the street to process calls for the next few days," Malinga said. "After the reward is announced, compound officials will want a tangible sign of our appreciation. If a reward is given to only one person, it will make things tricky."

"Don't worry, madam," Asedi said. "The groups will help us whether they get a reward or not. They want to make life in the compounds better. They're better organized than the politicians. And they deliver on their promises."

Davison sighed. "This case is becoming a political football. Saturday morning, Emmadale's Parliamentarian staked a fifteen-million-*kwacha* reward for the killers. A few other bigwigs promised to top it up."

Malinga was encouraged. Her team was still upbeat, which was good because there wasn't much time left. "Thanks for the great job. These were real women, dying in piteous and horrible ways. We can stop the killer now. Asedi, Davison, find those witch doctors. Start at Stewart's house in Kalingalinga and talk to Bertha again. She may have seen them. See if she knows anything about the clothing on the body on my fence while you're there."

"Once you and Wilson have the Archbishop in hand," Stewart said, "you can focus on the witch doctors."

"It can't happen too soon," Danise agreed. "All Lusaka is in an uproar. I can't turn on the radio without hearing call-in talk show complaints about us."

Malinga straightened. "Let's turn that around, shall we? Wilson, thank Police Chief Jere and tell him we're taking the case over from him as part of our wider investigation."

She looked at the group and smiled. "We're going to be putting in some long hours for the next five days. I hope you're ready."

Davison grinned. "Let's go the President one better and solve this thing in two days, not five. The faster we do it, the more lives we'll save."

"That's the spirit," Jacques said.

"Time to pay the Archbishop a visit, Wilson," Malinga said. "One less killer prowling Lusaka."

Stewart motioned for them to stay. "Malinga, before you leave, tell us about the trap you're going to set for the killer."

"I haven't worked out all the details yet, but at the press conference tomorrow I'm going to challenge him to meet me face to face. I want to make him so angry he wants to kill me. When he comes after me, we'll catch him."

"Do you think he'll fall for that?"

"I hope so. Danise thinks he's so arrogant he doesn't believe we can catch him, and that he'll make a fatal mistake when he comes after me."

"Unfortunately, my dear, the mistake might be fatal for you," Stewart said. She doesn't have a clue, he thought. He held the door open for her and smiled down at her as she passed through. "Good luck," he said.

Malinga smiled back at him. "Hopefully I won't need it."

Oh, Stewart thought to himself, you will. Now that you've baited me, Malinga, I'll be happy to finish you and those lousy brats of yours off. "We're still on for tea this coming Saturday, right?"

When Malinga grinned happily and nodded, he almost laughed out loud, but managed to confine himself to a smile.

"Off you go, Malinga. Give my regards to the Archbishop."

57 | Leave the Archbishop Alone!

The second-story gables of the Archbishop's Dutch colonial house were visible through the mango trees topping the high fence. The gates were open, but an armed guard eyed Wilson and Malinga as they pulled past the gatehouse. He waved them through when he saw they were police.

"Do you see the Archbishop's limousine?" Malinga asked Wilson. "Davison said it was probably an old Benz, pure black."

"No," Wilson said, "but it might be in one of the garages."

"The driver claims that the Archbishop ordered him to kill Ruth," Malinga said as Wilson drew into a parking space, "but I doubt he'd take such a risk." She shook her head. "I have no doubt he bedded the girl – he has a history of much more erratic behavior than that – but he'd be crazy to kill her just because she was pregnant. He would just pay her mother to keep quiet."

"I think the driver and the uncle panicked and did the dirty work themselves," Wilson agreed. "When we get back to the station, I want to lean on those guys."

"Good idea. Let's clear the Archbishop and get back to the station. I don't want to embarrass ourselves or a venerable old churchman."

"Venerable? He gave up venerable when he allowed one of his bishops to marry that Asian woman," Wilson retorted.

"He's still official leader of Zambia's Catholics, all three million of them. If we get on the wrong side of him, he'll be more trouble for us than a hundred *sangomas* full of *muti*."

Wilson laughed. "We can't let that bother us. He's a murder suspect. At the very least, an accessory. What's our strategy here?"

"Let's tell him the driver and uncle have implicated him and see if he admits anything. He's been speaking out on the telly, calling for the public to unite against the *muti* killers so no one else is hurt."

"Catholics have always been good at promoting their own innocence, but it's possible the driver and uncle did act without his knowledge," Wilson mused. "Although we can't assume anyone's above *muti*."

"Even you, Wilson. Remember the time you put the snakeskin in your drawer?"

"Oh, Malinga. You know that was just a joke."

"Some joke, Wilson. When the cleaning lady opened it, I thought she'd have a heart attack.

"She got me back," he said, laughing. "She didn't clean my office for a month."

Malinga laughed with him. "I thought you were going to be buried in teacups and breakfast leavings."

She opened the car door and looked up. The daylight was disappearing fast, taking the color with it. There were no bird sounds. What had chased them off? It was chillier than usual this time of year, but it was still winter, early November, five months past the summer solstice, and yesterday's snowfall in Johannesburg set a record. Malinga reached her suit jacket out of the car and pulled it on, snugging it over the service revolver in her shoulder holster.

The house, tucked against the cathedral's nave, had a grim, determined air and badly needed a coat of paint. Didn't the President's own personal priest deserve something better for his efforts? As she and Wilson crossed the parking area she whispered, "We've chased all the way down here to accuse him of murdering poor Ruth, and his taste probably runs to boys."

Wilson grinned. "That's the Catholic track record. Girls just don't seem to be their cup of tea."

"Did you hear about that case in Kabangwe?" Malinga asked. Wilson shook his head. "It happened while you were away. On a tip from a neighbor, the police rescued three naked boys from a shallow covered well at the local church. They had deep bruises on their buttocks. The priest insisted he found their clothes near the well and heard the boys calling for help. After he rescued them, he beat them so they wouldn't play there again. He was arrested on child abuse charges but released five days later." That night, the parents beat the priest.

"A lot of Zambians think that a misbehaving teenager needs a good helping of intimidation," Wilson said.

"I hope Shiko never 'needs' that kind of treatment. I never thought I'd say it, but I think my mother's right," Malinga said, pressing the Archbishop's doorbell. "All our public officials should be spanked."

"Integrity's out the window. Vows and commitments – forget it. I think that . . ."

The door was pulled open by a flat-faced butler. "What do you want?" he growled. "Can't you leave the Archbishop alone? It's almost dinner time and he hasn't had a break from people all day." His scowl deepened. "What if I told you people to go away? What would you think of that?"

Before they could respond, he slammed the door in their faces. "He just made me mad," Malinga pressed the doorbell again, harder this time, then held it for few seconds, but got no response. All they heard was the wind beginning to stir in the trees. "I hope we don't have to get a warrant," Malinga said, stepping back to search for movement in the windows, "but if he doesn't open this door soon, I will."

Wilson glanced over. "You might want to soften your approach a little. I hear he really hates women."

"I heard that, too."

She looked at her watch. "Let's go get that war . . ."

The door flew open and the Archbishop peered out at their faces. "I hope you haven't been waiting long. I didn't hear you ring. I was listening to the radio. How can I help you?"

"Your Grace!" Wilson said. "Sorry to disturb you! I know it's late, but could you spare some time for two poor cops?"

"Of course," the old man said, flinging the door wide open. Malinga was surprised at how vital and handsome he was for a man in his late seventies. The wool cardigan covering the tab collar of his black shirt set off the grey flecks in his eyes.

"Come in, come in. My butler must be sleeping. Again." He smiled at them.

"He answered the door, then slammed it in our faces,"
Wilson said.

The Archbishop frowned. "Let me apologize for him.
Sometimes the man is over-protective, and this recent situation has
made him very grumpy." He chuckled. "Those of us who serve
the Lord accept that the way is not always smooth." He gestured
for them to step inside. "Please do come in. I'm Archbishop
Mwanza," he said, extending his hand to Wilson.

"Wilson Mwiinga, Deputy Inspector with the CID."

"Ya, ya. Weren't you the one who caught the Mailonis?"

Wilson nodded. "This is Malinga Mutende, also a Deputy
Inspector." She smiled and extended her hand. He ignored it.

"I see far too much in the press about you," the cleric
grumbled with a dismissive wave of his hand. "It's not womanly,
the police. Not womanly."

"I joined the force because of my aunt," Malinga said with
a half-smile. "Her husband beat her so many times when he got
drunk that she finally had him arrested. I realized that police
work might be the perfect career for a woman."

He stared at her, then shook his head. "What happened to
Love, Honor and Obey?" he said with a smile. "A man in my
position must agree to disagree with many people." He turned
down the hallway. "Come. Join me for a cup of tea in the kitchen.
I gave my housekeeper a week off to visit her mother in the
village. She's not been feeling well – the mother, that is – and
Miriam's been very worried. Until she gets her mother sorted, she
won't do her job properly, so I let her go."

How generous of you, Malinga thought. And how
convenient that you sent her into the bush, away from the police.
If anyone knew what really happened to Ruth, it would be
Miriam.

"Where does Miriam's mother live?" she asked.

"In Luapula. Way off the road, I'm afraid. Out of reach of
cell phones, I'm afraid. That's why Miriam had to go personally.
Her cousin brought the message just yesterday."

The Archbishop gestured to a farm table set beneath the
kitchen's wide windows. Doors opened onto the garden. "Sit

please." He poured their tea and served them fresh-baked Irish soda bread. "I can't abide the stuff," he confessed, "but Miriam learned the recipe from the last Archbishop, Father McMahon, and I can't bring myself to tell her that not everyone's taste buds are Irish," he said, eyes twinkling.

Malinga relaxed. She was tired and reluctant to break the pleasant mood. And she liked the old man. He was charming even if his gender beliefs were antiquated.

He is the Archbishop, after all. Innocent until proven guilty.

She forced herself to remember how Ruth looked when they found her under the hedge. "My dear Archbishop," she said. "I'm reluctant to bother you with more questions, but we brought your driver in for questioning about the murder of Ruth Moyo and we'd like to check some facts with you."

"Caleph? You're questioning Caleph?" The Archbishop rose from his chair. "Caleph wouldn't hurt a fly!"

"I hope that's true, Archbishop," Wilson said. "But your limo was seen by a neighbor in Emmasdale with the boot lid raised. The neighbor couldn't tell who the man was because he was wearing a ski mask, but he saw him pull a heavy object from the trunk and push it under the hedgerow." He paused for effect. "It was Ruth's mutilated body."

The Archbishop's hand flew to his mouth. "My God!" he said. "No! Caleph would never do a thing like that!"

"That might be true, but we had to take him in for questioning," Malinga said. "We've also detained Ruth's uncle."

The Archbishop's face grew pale, his large eyes locked on her own. "Not the uncle! He's not a killer!"

"There may be some other explanation, but both men are being evasive. That's why we came to you."

"Very well," the Archbishop said, standing and straightening the crease in his pants. He paced the room, hands behind his back, his sizeable stomach pushing ahead of him. His color slowly returned. "This is terrible. It cannot be true."

"I know you're shocked, Archbishop," Wilson said. "We were shocked as well. That's why we came to you immediately. To learn the truth."

Malinga knew Wilson was working to win the Archbishop's confidence, so she walked to the sink for a glass of water. Wilson was good, she thought, and he had a great advantage. Most Zambians wouldn't look directly into an albino's face. If they had enough courage to look, his pale eyes, squinting owlishly behind his horn-rimmed glasses, disconcerted them.

She filled a glass with water and Wilson passed it to the older man. "Please sit down, Excellency. Have a bit of water. It will make you feel better." The Archbishop slumped into his chair, his golden crucifix hanging askew on his broad paunch.

"I'm sorry, sir," Wilson said, "but since your driver won't talk, we have to ask some awkward questions. Police procedure, you know. Please forgive us."

The Archbishop nodded. "Ask me anything," he said meekly. Then his voice rose. "I can't believe you arrested my driver. He'd never hurt anyone. Neither would the uncle."

"How well do you know the uncle?"

"He is a parishioner, a friend, and very good man."

Malinga knew the time was ripe to spring their trap. "Your Excellency, we need to know where you were two Friday evening's ago."

The old man took a sip of water and began to choke. "Wilson!" Malinga shouted, "help him, for God's sake!!" The Archbishop's health wasn't good, and no one – not even the Inspector – would forgive her if he succumbed under questioning. His face was ashen. There was no time to lose.

58 | The Alibi

When Wilson thumped the old man's back, he swallowed, and they settled him gently back at the table. He shook an enormous white handkerchief out to its full extent and blew his nose. "I was here, of course," he said. "I'm here every Friday night. I said evening mass and ate my supper, then watched a little football. I always watch a bit of television. I wrote a letter to my sister in Britain and then I went to bed. I said my prayers, of course, and checked with the night guard to make sure the church was locked."

"Who can confirm that?" Wilson asked.

"My guard could have, but I let him go last week. My housekeeper thought he was stealing from us. We didn't want a confrontation, so she let him go."

"Do you know where he is now?" Malinga asked.

"No, I'm afraid I don't. My housekeeper might, but she's away. As I told you, her mother is quite ill."

"Is there anyone else who can confirm your alibi for Friday night?"

"Alibi? Since when does an Archbishop need an alibi? Only God can confirm my alibi."

Wilson hid his smile. "Did your driver ever use your car for personal business?"

"No, no. Quite the opposite. He treated it like a holy relic."

"Is it possible he took the car without your permission?"

The Archbishop nodded. "It's possible. The garage, as you saw, is on the opposite side of the lot, behind that tall hedge."

"The dead woman, Ruth," Wilson asked, "Did you know her?"

The Archbishop shook his head. "Only what I read in the papers. I prayed for her. We know these things happen for a reason. I suspect she had a bit of the devil in her." Malinga glanced sharply at Wilson, who gave an imperceptible shake of his head. The Archbishop's gaze went heavenward and he opened his hands to the ceiling. "Let us pray that she is resting in peace." He crossed himself then rested his hands on his broad stomach. "Thanks be to God the Almighty, who covers us all with his love."

Malinga shivered. If he's faking this, he's doing a really good job, she thought.

"Her uncle invited the girl to visit him in Kabanana," Wilson said. "She visited him almost every Friday afternoon, the neighbors said. So did you, apparently, because your car was seen there. A shopkeeper opposite the Uncle's place told us that each week, your car arrived just after the girl, and remained there for several hours."

The Archbishop's eyes widened and he drew a shaky breath. "I have no idea what you're talking about. I don't know the girl, although I read about her in the papers, like everyone else. A terrible crime, indeed, but I didn't know the girl."

"Your driver told us that you visited her," Malinga said. "His story is the same as the shopkeeper's. Who are we to believe?"

"The whereabouts of my car and my whereabouts are two different things," the Archbishop insisted testily. He sighed. "I would like to prove it to you, but since my housekeeper's not here, I'm not sure I can."

"Why would your driver implicate you?"

"I have no idea," the Archbishop said. "I always believed he was loyal. I can only assume he wants to blame me so you'll let him go." He drew himself up. "It is possible he borrowed my car for these escapades. Caleph took my housekeeper to the market on Fridays. I saw little of either of them until later in the afternoon, right before I said mass. They returned so my housekeeper could prepare my supper."

"He says you killed the girl," Wilson said. "He says you paid him and the uncle to help you. He also told us the girl was pregnant, and that you were giving her money to pay for her school. The uncle confirmed his story. He said he was friends with you and they arranged for you to meet the girl."

The old man scowled and brought his fist down on the table. "Lies," the old man said. "Lies, all lies." He stood shakily. "I'll say this one last time, and then you must go. I didn't know the girl, so why would I kill her?" He put his hand to his brow, closed his eyes, and fell heavily back into his chair. "You are upsetting me greatly. I'm feel very faint."

A minute passed and Malinga was beginning to worry, but he opened his eyes with some effort and turned to her. "Do you mind getting my medicine? It's in the bathroom near my bedroom. That way," he said, pointing down a long corridor, "to the end of the hall."

Malinga hurried down the hallway at a jog to get him the medicine before he fainted. Her head was down as she entered the Archbishop's bathroom, and she never saw it coming.

59 | Lousy Chinese Matches

"Not all men of the cloth are fallen," the Archbishop told
Wilson when he could speak again. "I know it hasn't been a very
good time for us, what with all the sex scandals and the
excommunication of our dear friend, Archbishop Milingo." He
shook his head. "It's a shame Emmanuel married that Korean
acupuncturist! By the Reverend Moon, no less. Imagine! I
couldn't believe it. Frankly, I think he went a little senile. He was
just excommunicated, you know."

Wilson nodded.

"It's such a shame. He was a very fine man. But the Pope
had no choice. He asked him to stop performing exorcisms in the
church, but Emmanuel was stubborn and held them in the
vestibule. He saw himself as a rising star in the African church.
Sure, the Pope was angry, but he turned a blind eye because we
need all the clergymen we can get.

"But when Emmanuel installed four married men as
bishops to kick off his Married Priests Now Movement – in
Washington, D.C. no less! – you can imagine the scandal. The
Pope had to get rid of him." The Archbishop shook his head.
"Even though he'd really let the church down, they showed him
plenty of mercy. The Vatican said that they'd watched his case
with 'vigilant patience' –whatever that means—and I . . . "

Wilson was desperately seeking a way to steer the
conversation back to the investigation when the Archbishop
paused in mid-sentence and turned his head toward the hallway
where Malinga had just disappeared. His face was quizzical.
"What's that noise?" he asked Wilson.

"I don't know, but it's coming from the direction of your
bedroom. Stay here and I'll check."

Wilson hurried down the hall and turned into the Archbishop's bedroom. Curtains flapped in the open patio doors opposite. Wilson hurried to the bathroom.

"Malinga?" he called. Rounded the corner, he bumped into a man. A rather large man, wearing a ski mask. And holding a gun to Malinga's temple. Wilson drew back.

"Put your hands up, inspector," the man said in a deep voice, "and I won't kill her. Now back up and let me out of this toilet. Slowly, now, so I don't have to shoot either of you."

Once he'd tied up Malinga and Wilson in the kitchen, the man turned to the old cleric. "Come along, Archbishop" he in a strangely strangled voice. "We're taking you with us."

The Archbishop started.

"Caleph. Caleph? Is that you?"

The man nodded sheepishly. Then he drew himself up and nudged the old man with his gun. "Come along, sir. We need to get out of here."

"What do you mean by this, Caleph?" the old man asked. "What have you been doing behind my back?"

"We'll talk about that later," the driver said. "Right now we have to get out of here. Come along, boss. I need to get you to safety. Ruth's uncle is already in the car."

"Get me to safety? What can you possibly mean by that? I need my pills. That young lady was getting me my pills. I haven't had one in hours and my blood pressure is rising."

"We'll get your pills on the way out, Archbishop. Just come with me." Caleph shoved the old man through the door and closed it before he could turn. Then he yanked on the handle of the jerry can he was carrying, spraying a petrol in a ring around the police officers' chairs.

"Sorry I have to do this," he told them. "But I'm sure you can understand why."

"They'll catch you," Malinga said. "And hang you."

"They won't if you two disappear. The only other man who seems to know anything about Nimbus and I is that small policeman who works with you. Davison? Is that what you call him?" They nodded. "I'm pretty sure he's dead," Caleph said casually. He got in our way when we were leaving the station."

He threw down the can and struck a match. "Sorry to leave you like this. I'm taking the Archbishop with me. You're the only ones who know we've been here, and pretty soon you won't know anything." He threw the lighted match in the petrol and slammed the door behind him.

Malinga and Wilson stared at the flame.

"Well," Wilson said.

"Well," Malinga answered.

"I've always meant to tell you . . ."

His voice broke off. He was staring hard at the floor. "Never mind. Look, Malinga. I think the match burned itself out before it ignited the gas."

She jerked her eyes open and squinted down. "You're right. How lucky for us."

"Lucky, yes. Yes, we are. Let's get out of here before he notices the house hasn't gone up in flames and comes back to finish the job. Thank heavens for lousy Chinese matches."

When she jumped to her feet, the chair slipped loose and fell with a crash. The jerk on the ropes was strong enough to release the bindings on her hands. She bent quickly and unfastened her feet.

"He may be a great driver, but he makes lousy knots," she said, grinning at Wilson. "Maybe it's the lousy Chinese ropes."

"Thank heavens for the Chinese," Wilson answered, shaking off the last of his restraints. "Let's go."

As they ran to the car, she pulled her service revolver from her shoulder holster. "I hope we can stop this guy without too much of a problem."

"Yeah," Wilson said. "I don't want anything to happen to the Archbishop." He turned the key in the ignition and backed out.

"I didn't want to have to chase him." Malinga said.

"Yeah," he said, "I know. I hate this part. I'll call ahead to the first roadblock on the North Road."

The driver had jammed a large screwdriver in the outside gate to slow them down, but Wilson pulled a very large hammer from the boot and in less than a minute they were out of the compound. "It works every time," he said when he jumped back into the car, tossing the hammer into the back seat. "At least the Chinese make great hammers." He grinned at Malinga and turned out of the gate, accelerating hard.

"How do you know he's headed for the North Road?" Malinga asked. "I'd guess he'd head south toward Zimbabwe. He can slip into South Africa pretty fast from there."

"North Road, I'm telling you. He's heading for the Copperbelt. His mother lives up there."

"Okay, then. Let's go. I'll alert the roadblocks on all the other roads out of the city. We can't let him get away."

"Don't worry, Malinga, we won't. I'm putting the light and the siren on. Brace yourself."

"Let's go. We needed an arrest in this case and we're about to get one!"

60 | Up in Smoke

Wilson slowed for the lights at the roadblock and wound his window down. "What's going on here? What's the hold up?" he asked.

"An accident," the officer said. "This guy was traveling so fast, he couldn't keep the car on the road."

When he stepped back to let them through, Malinga gasped. "Oh, no, Wilson! It's his car."

"And from the looks of the wreck, they won't be talking with anyone ever again." The Archbishop's car had flipped, skidded on its roof into the right front fender of an oncoming bus and ricocheted, bursting into flames when it hit a *kapenga* tree.

"Damn," Wilson said. "I guess I shouldn't have pushed him so hard."

"It's not your fault, Wilson. We were way behind him. Besides, the tar here is so soft he probably started flying when he hit the bumps. Let's see if there are any witnesses."

Wilson had to brake suddenly to avoid the line of cars and trucks backed up behind the wreckage. The police car skidded on the oil-covered tarmac, and Malinga was thrown hard against the seat belt. The car started to wobble, pulled by the soft earth of the shoulder, but Wilson flipped the wheel and kept it righted. They came to a stop inches from a pedestrian pushing a bike who had been ogling the wreck of the Archbishop's car and was now staring wide-eyed at them.

"That was a close one," Malinga said, coughing. "This seat belt pinned me. I can't breathe. Help me out of it, will you. Gently, now. I picked up a couple of bad bruises."

"Sorry, Malinga. I didn't expect that line of cars."

"Let's get out and talk with the bus driver." She winced and clutched her side, pointing out the window. "Too late, I think. He's leaving."

"I'll see if I can flag him down." Wilson ran out into the road,, waving his arms for the driver to stop, but had to dodge the bus as it swerved to miss him. "He wasn't stopping. He's got a schedule to keep and doesn't want to be held up talking to us."

"Right." Malinga said, her eyes following the bus until it disappeared at the top of the hill. "You didn't happen to get his license plate, did you?"

"Are you kidding? I was too busy getting out of the way," Wilson said, "but I bet one of the bystanders knows who he is. "These busses usually follow the same route and he's bound to have bought some booze or a girl somewhere near here."

Malinga shaded her eyes and squinted at the wreck. "The Archbishop didn't stand a chance. His driver was going too fast."

The crowd was gathering. A small man nudged his way in front of Malinga, stopping her in her tracks. She clutched at her side and held out her badge. "Excuse me," she said, but he persisted in blocking her way.

The man pressed closer, and the crowd began to form behind him. "Are you the police officers who were chasing this car?"

Malinga shook her head. "We weren't chasing the car. We were following," she said loudly so others in the crowd would hear.

"That's the Archbishop's car. I know it," the man said, raising his voice. "He comes up here to visit his mother every other week. Is he in it?"

"I think so," Malinga said.

The crowd started to grumble. Police and their high-speed chases. Now they'd even killed the Archbishop. Malinga raised her voice another notch and turned to address them. "The driver of this vehicle had kidnapped the Archbishop and was fleeing. He killed someone earlier, and we were sure he was going to kill the Archbishop. We were trying to save the old man, not kill him."

Wilson raised his arms to signal to the crowd that they should disperse. They moved a little way off, but continued to stare. "This is tense," he murmured. "Let's make this quick. We need to get out of here before they decide to turn on us."

"I can't blame them for being angry," Malinga said. "A little boy was killed just a few days ago by a policeman chasing a speeder through this town. It happens all the time. I know how angry I would feel if someone killed Shiko or Katanga. But we still have to take a look at the Archbishop's car."

Malinga and Wilson walked closer to the flaming vehicle. She shook her head. "Whoever was in that car is finished. There's no point risking our lives to pull the bodies out. We'd better get these people back. The petrol tank may explode." They subdued the crowd and moved them out of range just before the petrol tank caught, causing a tremendous explosion. Bits of debris flew high into the sky, burning bright against the coming darkness.

"There goes our evidence," Wilson said. He shook his head and sighed. "We're back to square one."

Malinga gave him a worried smile. "Don't be so gloomy," she said. "Let's go. This fire won't be out for a long time. In the morning, we can send someone up here to sift the ashes. I'll give the Inspector a call early tomorrow before he sees it on the news. There'll be a lot of blowback from the press."

Wilson nodded. "Let me see if I can take some statements." Their conversations with the onlookers didn't reveal much. Few people were along the roadside when the crash occurred. Any passing vehicles that had witnessed the crash had already disappeared to avoid involvement with the police.

The strobe on the top of their vehicle lit the night sky, blinking eerily over the undergrowth. Wilson shut it off and reached for the radio. "I'll alert Lusaka to send someone to the bus station to get that driver. Tomorrow, I'll ask the Copperbelt police to talk with the Archbishop's mother."

"I doubt she'll have much to add, but it's worth a try." Malinga tried to get comfortable as they turned around and headed back to Lusaka. She leaned her head back, felt gingerly along her collarbone and flinched. Her ribs were tender, too.

"How bad is it, Malinga?" Wilson asked.

"I'll hurt in the morning, but at least we didn't crash. It's going to be hard enough to explain this to the President as it is. And Inspector Chikanda."

Wilson grinned and shook his head. "Right on both counts, Malinga. I wouldn't want to be in your shoes."

61 | In Bed with the Devil

Bertha leaned on her elbow so she could look down in Kivuli's face. He was so beautiful, she felt her heart ache. "She is coming to Kalingalinga today," she told him. "She is coming to talk to the women so they will find the killers. Stewart said she has sent a man to arrest you and Redbone."

"What concern is this to you?" Kivuli's lazy eyes were half-open. Bertha bent her head to kiss him, but he pulled away from her, scowling.

While his rejection always hurt, in a strange way she loved him more for it. He was extraordinary, an exceptional being, so powerful and different from the other men she'd been with. He spoke with the ancestors. He summoned the spirits, and made the impossible come true, like going to South Africa. How exciting it would be, when he was famous in Johannesburg.

She sat up and stared down at him, her eyes glowing with warmth.

"Ah, lie back, will you?" He groaned. "I was just dropping off to sleep again. That neighbor's rooster will be the next one off my knife if they don't do something about his crowing. I was up most of last night. Go back to sleep," he mumbled, turning away from her. "Go back to sleep."

"I think you must be more careful," Bertha said. "Everyone in Kalingalinga is afraid of your father, but they are more frightened of you. They watch what he does, and they watch you. Someone may know what it is you do."

He looked up at her. "No one knows what I do at night. No one knows where I go. Only you, and if you are talking, it will go badly for you."

"I am not talking. You know I am not talking," she said, getting up from the mattress. "But there are those who watch and I hope they are too afraid to speak of you to the police. You may be clever, oh so clever" – she leaned down and kissed him before he could turn his head – "but you are not invisible."

"They're afraid of us. Both of us. My father and I. They know our power. They will not talk against us."

"Of course. But the police are not afraid. What you did Saturday night did not frighten that policewoman. No. She is not frightened. She is angry. You butchered Giselle. Stewart is trying to mislead her, but Malinga will soon find out. She is a very smart woman. And you killed her dog."

"She can never know who that woman was. I cut her into too many pieces. How will she know?"

Bertha shrugged. "The police can know. From their laboratories."

"What can their laboratories tell them? She recognized the dress, but you will tell her someone took it from Stewart's house and you don't know who it was. Stewart told her Giselle is here and she trusts him. How can they tell it was her? Or me? Her house guard was so frightened, he couldn't even look at me when I jumped down from the gate. He thought I was flying."

Kivuli rolled back to face her. "You must be quiet. I need some sleep. This woman is not clever enough to catch us. Our *muti* is too powerful," he said, lifting the baby's skull nestled at the center of his necklace of bones.

Bertha flinched and turned her eyes away. Kivuli forced her to look.

"You paid for this dearly, woman. If we want the money we need for South Africa, we must give the doctor enough bodies for his work. You must keep this policewoman away from here, away from him. And you must get her children for Victor They will come for tea on Saturday as long as they believe Giselle is still alive." He gloated. "South Africa will give us many chances like this one. This is practice. I will be very famous there."

Bertha sighed. "I know, Kivuli, I know. You will be very famous in South Africa. I want to go. I want us to go. But we cannot make any mistakes, or she will catch us."

"Since when is a woman strong enough to trick a witch doctor with *muti* as powerful as mine?"

He lifted the skull to look at it again and frowned.

"I will make some spells to throw dust in her eyes. She will not see us. She will not see anything. She may stand outside our door, but my *muti* will blind her. Come back to bed now. Come."

He patted the mattress next to him and she lay down. As he touched her and took her again, she could think of nothing but her dead son, how she held him as he died. She'd done it for this man, and now there was no other place to turn. She had to keep working for him, spying, helping him no matter how many women he killed. He would kill her if she tried to get away. She was sure of that. He would kill her like killing a fly. She closed her eyes and sighed.

He finished and rolled off her. "Now I can sleep," Kivuli said. "I have the *muti*," he said, a smile etching his sculptured mouth, "and I have someone who tells me everything." He grabbed her chin and pulled her face roughly toward him. "You'd better be telling me everything."

Bertha pulled away from him and sat up. "Yes, of course. You always have my help."

The young man snorted with laughter. "Your help is too small," he said. "The man who helps us is much bigger than you. You keep track of the police mamma at home. Stewart keeps track of her at work. But this big man watches from State House. He will be sure we do not fail. Our networks are powerful and tell us everything she does."

Bertha shook her head. "She has many people helping her, many police, even one *mzungu*. Now she is reaching out to the people who live here in the compound. She is asking all the poor to help."

Kivuli closed his eyes and sighed. "You are such a stupid woman. What do the poor ever know? Which one of them would ever dare to cross me?"

Bertha felt her anger rise. She frowned. "I am not stupid, and neither are these people. We are not as weak as you think." She rose from the bed and picked up her things. She turned back to him as she neared the door.

"I cannot stay. I must go. Today I must pick her children up from their grandmother, take them home, get them ready. But first I must clean her house and make sure all the blood stains are gone so the children are not frightened. All things must look normal."

Even me, she thought.

"You have proven that you are one of us, but that is not enough." He laughed and rolled over, pulling the covers over his head.

Bertha sighed. This man. Yes. She could not resist his power, his spells. She proved that when she helped him kill her own son. She must continue to help him, and go with him to South Africa so he can become the great man he was.

He pulled the covers down and scowled.

"Get out of here, woman. Bring those children to me like we planned."

62 | Like It's Never Hurt Before

It's Giselle. She's with us now. She has so much to tell you.

Malinga swatted at the women in her dream like they were flies circling her head. The movement pulled at her ribs, bruised by the seatbelt, sending pain shooting across her back and down her right side.

She tried to go back to sleep. Bertha was with the doctor and the children were still with her parents. She was grateful she didn't have to check on them tonight. Wilson had dropped her and gone to talk with the bus driver, but phoned a short time later to say that the man had nothing to add to his original statement. The Archbishop's car had swerved in front of him and he'd braked but couldn't stop in time to prevent the collision. It had happened too fast.

As she lay back on the pillow, Malinga found herself wondering about the dead girls. Her body twitched when she'd realized that they'd been laid back, just as she was now, before they were butchered. The thought was disturbing, and almost sensual.

She pushed herself up slowly and rubbed at her ribs, wandered into the bathroom, flipped on the light, and found the bottle of painkillers in her bag. She unscrewed the top, unsure of when she'd taken the last pill, and stared at the bottle for inspiration. Her ribs spasmed and she shook out two pills, swallowing them with a glass of cold water.

As the pain in her ribs subsided, she smiled, happy that Shiko and Katanga were safe with her parents. With Minnie Mouse, her mother's dachshund, to protect them, nothing could go wrong. Thinking of her children's sweet faces, she fell back to sleep almost immediately and started to dream again, walking along the roadside at her grandparent's farm.

She laughed when she realized that Eitone was there, calling to her. As she started running toward him, into his waiting arms, a wail rose up and red, ghastly corpses, stripped of their flesh, closed in on her from either side, blocking her way to her lover's arms.

They were carrying a woman toward her, braced up because her limbs didn't seem to be working so well. At first Malinga thought she was too weak to walk, but she realized that her limbs were too loosely attached to her torso to support her. A dog trotted toward Malinga, stopping occasionally to lick his hindquarters and his belly.

It was Benny. Benny and Giselle!

They came closer, close enough for her to see their bodies clearly, and stopped. For a moment they just looked at her, six supplicants, six women who had been as young and strong and smart and beautiful as she was. They raised their arms to besiege her. Benny whined as he licked his shredded belly, then sat and tried to lift his hide leg to scratch underneath his ear.

Help them! Hurry, or they will kill your children. It's too late for us, but not for them.

Malinga's body jerked and she cried out in pain, fear and frustration. Lifting her torso from the bed, she sat on its edge, tears streaming down her cheeks, sweat glistening on her skin. "It's not too late! It's not too late!" she shouted, then looked around, frightened by the vehemence of her own voice.

Jumping up, she pulled her bathrobe tight around her shaking body and wiped the tears from her face with one of its cuffs. You bastards, she thought. I'll get every one of you! She shoved her feet into her slippers and picked up the clock from the nightstand. Four a.m. She shut her eyes and rubbed her temples, then stalked into the bathroom. Fumbling with the switch, she turned on the light and splashed water on her face. She toweled it roughly, then gazed at herself in the mirror.

It's up to you now, up to you!

The singsong voices rang in her head. She clapped her hands over her ears to stop the noise, and as it gradually subsided, she knew. She knew the truth. She knew the body on her fence was Giselle, brought by a flying witch doctor just as Mr. Phiri had claimed. At least one of the killers was a witch doctor, she was sure, maybe more than one. Asedi and Davison had to find Redbone and Kivuli as fast as they could.

As the pain in her ribs subsided, she knew she was sure of one more thing. Stewart knew more than he was saying. He knew Giselle was dead and which three people were to blame. He was lying, and it was time for her to find out who he was protecting. It was probably the second killer, who they knew had medical training. That was it! Stewart knew him. It had to be one of his colleagues.

Malinga decided to tell Jacques about her hunch and ask him to take advantage of his professional bond with Stewart to probe him and learn more. She was sure Stewart was burdened by the knowledge that the latest victim was Giselle. But what did a professional doctor have to do with witch doctors? How did the first two cases tie into the last?

Satisfied that Jacques could get the answers she needed, Malinga turned off the lights, lowered herself to her bed, and snuggled into her duvet. The voices were gone, and she nodded off to a pleasant dream of Eitone, returning to their charmed encounter at Balancing Rock, when they were investigating the murder of ten elephants. Before she'd gone to Asia, and before Eitone had disappeared.

When the alarm sounded, Malinga opened her eyes and rubbed her temples, aware of the pain shooting through her body. It was 6:30, time to wake up. She had to call the Inspector before she met the team and pulled them together around a new set of facts. Monday. Friday was only five days away.

She inched herself from the bed. She'd had no idea that so many parts of her body could hurt at the same time. So far, the painkillers she'd taken barely touched it. The sensation was new to her, like having a migraine all over her body, an ever-present reminder that she'd lost the Archbishop, his driver, and the uncle in a ghastly car crash. Anything they might have added to the team's store of knowledge about the third murder had gone up in smoke.

What am I going to tell the Inspector?

She pushed herself up from the knotted sheets gingerly, so the movement wouldn't pull her shoulders, waist, abdomen, or ribs. The seat belt had cut deep into her now-aching chest. "Shite," she said to herself. Her jaw muscles ached too much to speak. She groaned.

Maybe it's just as well the Archbishop was dead, and she had to take the responsibility. The press would never believe that she and Wilson had been trying to slow the driver down, although she intended to make that very clear to the Inspector. But there'd be no way to defend herself from the press. They'd never believe her.

I've failed. I made a mess of things and I'm going to pay.

No sense putting it off, she thought. She nearly shrugged but caught herself in time. No sense inviting any more pain. It's worse than the time when the Kenyan hunter died in my arms, she thought. She tried to stretch a little to loosen up, but decided a hot shower would be better.

Glancing at her watch, she realized that she had to hurry. She had to call the Inspector before he heard it from someone else. If I get to him first, I can reassure him that we weren't the cause of the Archbishop's death, she thought. We have bystander testimony to prove it. But she had to hurry. She had to talk to him first. It would be harder to catch his sympathy and support if the press got to him first.

She turned the shower on as hot as it would go and let it steam up before entering. One eye was still closed but opened slowly with the moisture. Maybe my black eye will get a sympathy vote from the reporters, she thought wryly. She stretched each muscle in her torso and legs and turned her head slowly side to side to loosen her neck muscles. Her head hurt the most, but her spirits were improving as her muscles began to loosen.

Nothing broken. You expected this kind of thing when you join the police force.   Not a job for sissies.

She felt her body relax and strengthen. She had to get dressed and send someone to the scene of the crash, then go back to the Archbishop's house to speak with the guard and find out where the housekeeper and the gardener lived. I'll send Davison, she thought, her head clearing. Yes, that would make sense.

She frowned. In truth, whatever her suspicions might be, they'd probably never know for sure who'd killed Ruth. Now that the main suspects were dead, they had to rely on circumstantial evidence to rule out the Archbishop, his driver, and uncle in Ruth's death or any of the other murders.

Then she thought of Jacques and smiled. DNA from the Archbishop, the uncle, the driver, and Ruth's womb would tell most of the story, more than any living witness could.

Closure, she thought. Now I can focus on the other murders. I'll call the Inspector in an hour, get ready for the press conference, have a quick team meeting, then go to Kalingalinga to speak with the compound's neighborhood watch group.

63 | An Inside Job

"What were you thinking, Malinga?" the Inspector demanded. He raised his voice but was too much a gentleman to shout. "This is a catastrophe, Malinga. We were trying to improve our image in the press, not ruin it."

"Wilson was driving," she said, cringing at her own cowardice.

"That's no excuse," he answered. "You were in charge of this investigation, and now you've killed someone who might have been a star witness. And not just anyone. The Archbishop of Lusaka. The press will go crazy with this."

Malinga winced at his use of the past tense: *were* in charge of the investigation. Was he going to hand the baton to Wilson? If it was going to happen, she wanted to be sure it was for the right reason. The lie that she'd killed a witness infuriated her, but it had to be tactfully countered, both for the official record and to save her pride.

"Let me clarify, sir," she said, "It isn't as bad as it looks. Yes, Wilson was driving fast, but we were trying to save the Archbishop, not kill him. As far as we knew, two desperate men had kidnapped him. It was very dark, and we came on the scene just as we rounded that curve north of the farm stand. There were cars and people all over the road, and no one set out flares. There wasn't much Wilson could do. I'm just glad we didn't roll or hit anyone"

"So the accident happened before you got there?"

"The bus was leaving when we arrived."

"The bus hit the Archbishop's car?"

"The other way around. The car went out of control and swerved into the path of the bus."

"Have you questioned the bus driver yet?"

"Yes. One of our men detained him for questioning when he pulled into the bus park in Lusaka last night. Wilson went straight there, but driver's testimony wasn't very helpful. It happened so fast, he didn't see much."

"Go on, Malinga."

She felt herself calming and took a deep breath. "When we saw there was nothing we could do for the Archbishop or his driver, we told the bystanders that we were pursuing his kidnappers. If the press reports that, the story will be neutral at worst. At best, it will be favorable to us."

"I hope you're right, Malinga."

"The driver and uncle had already confessed to the murder of the girl," she continued, "but they blamed it on the Archbishop. That's why Wilson and I went to his house to talk with him. After we left the station, they escaped lockup. I suspect it was an inside job. Davison took a bad knock on the head when he tried to stop them. They came directly to the Archbishop's house. I suspect they were afraid of what he'd tell us about Ruth, the third victim, if we pressed him.

"They tied us up and the driver would have burnt the house down with us in it if he'd had better matches. We freed ourselves and pursued them as fast as we could," she went on, aware that she was running out of steam. "The press can't fault us for that. I'll explain it again at the President's press conference this morning. His press secretary has already called the reporters in, so it should make tonight's paper."

"Right," Chikanda said. She could hear him breathe more easily. "It sounds like you've done everything you could," he said. "And what you did was exactly what I would have done. Be sure to call the President's office to explain it to them as soon as you can. With luck, you may be able to avert a disaster."

"It's better than that, sir. We can tie off this murder with the genetic evidence, and now that he's dead, the Archbishop's role will never be made public. It would have been a very damning investigation if he'd lived to tell us what he knew. Even if he was only a silent witness, not a perpetrator, it would have been bad."

"That's true enough, Malinga," the Inspector said, "but I see one remaining problem."

"What's that, Inspector?"

"You have no suspects for the other four murders. Once you tie this one off, it's a dead end. I don't see any connection to the other ones."

"If I can find out who released the men from their cell yesterday, it may be a start. I have some ideas where to look." Malinga sighed, wondering if she should tell him what she was thinking about Stewart Bleming. She decided to wait until she had more evidence to support her growing suspicions.

"That's a good idea, Malinga. One suspect may be tied to all the murders."

"Right, Inspector," Malinga said, although she didn't agree. "We're beating the bushes for other suspects, especially the two witch doctors I told you about, Redbone and Kivuli. They've gone to ground, so the President told us to ask the neighborhood watch groups to help us. Asedi and Davison are starting in Kalingalinga this morning when the press conference is over."

"That's great, Malinga."

"Stewart thinks the witch doctors were responsible for the other murders. He thinks they have connections to international criminal networks through local Chinese businessmen. Hopefully, when the President announces the reward, people will be willing to come forward."

"I'm not sure that people trust the police enough to come forward," the Inspector said. "The reward will help, but you're going to get a lot of cranks."

"Asedi's worked out a way to screen most of them," Malinga reassured him. "My only hope is that people are more attracted by the reward than afraid of the killers. If we approach them in groups, a single informant won't be so obvious."

"Good thinking, Malinga. It still bothers me that those two men got out of jail so easily.

"Me, too."

"Like you said, someone at the station must have helped."

"I'll find out who it was."

The Inspector cleared his throat. "May I make a suggestion, Malinga?"

"Of course, sir."

"Look carefully at the people on your team. You can't assume they're all on your side. Don't go on appearances. It could be the person you trust the most."

A shiver ran up her spine. She thought immediately of Stewart. She'd trusted him implicitly, but she was convinced the girls had told her the truth. What could his motive possibly be?

On the other hand, could she really believe spirits who spoke to her in dreams when she was taking heavy painkillers? She couldn't reveal her dreams or her doubts to the Inspector, because if he thought she was compromised, he'd take her off the case immediately.

"One more thing, Malinga. Would it help if I called the President's press secretary and spoke with him directly?"

"I'm sure it would," Malinga said. "He'll insist that you replace me."

The Inspector laughed. "Don't worry, Malinga." He chuckled. "It's still my decision, right?"

"Right," Malinga agreed, holding her breath.

"It will never happen, not while I'm in charge."

Malinga drew in her breath. "You mean that?"

"Of course, Malinga. You've had your setbacks, but I think you're on the right track."

"Even without evidence?"

"You'll get it, now that the President has shown his interest and given you some resources. You'll get it, Malinga. I'm sure you will. Besides, who would he get to replace you? Some detective from the Copperbelt? None of them can hold a candle to you – to anyone on my team."

"Thanks, Inspector. Thank you, sir."

"Malinga," he continued, "I forgot to mention one thing. I'm coming back immediately. Please tell the President when you see him later today. It doesn't look good for me to be away from Lusaka at such a critical time."

Malinga sighed. "As much as I'd like to prove that I can tough this one out alone, I'd love to have you back. The political fallout has pushed me to my limits. When will you get here?"

"I'm on an early flight Wednesday. With all the connections, I won't get to Lusaka until late Wednesday night, so I won't be back on the job until Thursday morning."

"Thanks, Inspector," Malinga said. "That's a great relief,"

"I've got to go now. My training's about to begin. Call me tonight and let me know how things are going. I'll call the President later today."

Malinga started to close her cell phone.

"Malinga," he said, "one last thing."

"Yes, Inspector?"

He chuckled. "Try not to kill any more of the President's friends. Things will go better for you if you don't."

64 | Call Him Again!

"I don't know what you expect me to say, darling!" Victor snorted. "It's so unfair of you to get angry with me because Stewart won't answer his telephone!"

Anita's pretty little mouth formed a seductive pout. The hand she put on her chest to underscore her distress called attention to her curves. "But we've got to know, Victor. If we're leaving, we have to know within a few hours."

"There's no "if", *Liebchen*."

"Victor!"

Victor held his arms out to her. "Oh, *Liebchen*. You know I only want the best for us. But you heard the President's press conference. So much attention is being brought to bear on these murders, I'm afraid we'll be implicated. We must leave now, before we are thrown out! Or worse, thrown in jail!"

"But Victor! Will it really be better for us in the Central African Republic? They are killing each other right and left there."

"We will be safe. I spoke with the Boko Haram colonel. He laughed when I asked him if it would be difficult to get an elephant. He said they already have one waiting. We just have to bring the cash."

"How much?"

"He only wants twenty-five thousand."

Anita's mouth dropped open. "That is such a deal! How can he possibly deliver an elephant for so little?"

"It will be a little elephant."

Anita sighed. "The elephants here are so much nicer, Victor. Maybe you should call Stewart again."

Victor laughed and ruffled her hair. "Okay, *Liebchen*. I will do it, just for you."

She grabbed his hand and brought it to her lips. "I love you so much, Victor."

"I know." He picked up the cell phone and punched in Stewart's speed dial number.

She looked up expectantly. Victor frowned.

"No answer, *Liebchen*. This is a bad sign. We must pack our bags and tell the pilot to be ready immediately."

She pouted again. "The elephants next door are so small."

"That is true, *Liebchen*. But the colonel promised me one more thing."

"What was that, Victor?"

He smiled slyly. "He said that for another five thousand dollars, he could throw in a mother, two children, and an albino to sweeten the deal."

65 | He Fails the Test

"The press is calling you 'the Archbishop Killers'," Asedi
crowed when Malinga and Wilson entered the station's briefing
room. She wagged her finger at them, laughing. "You guys
couldn't be in a worse jam."

"Asedi," Davison said. "Ease up. They were doing their
best to catch the kidnappers. After they almost set them on fire!"
He lifted the ice pack, showing off the welt he'd gotten when he
tried to stop the driver and uncle from escaping. "Look what they
did to me!"

Malinga smiled at him sympathetically. "Sorry for that,
Davison. Fortunately, I think most of the reporters were on our
side."

"Most importantly, you're both still in one piece!" Jacques
said. "In French police chases, the cops seem to die more often
than the crooks."

"Jacques is right. I'm just glad you're both alive!" Danise
said, hugging Malinga. When Malinga winced, she held her at
arm's length, studying her face. "You are okay, aren't you?"

"Yes, we're both fine," Malinga said. "Once the second
painkiller kicks in and I can't feel my ribs anymore, I'll be one
hundred percent better."

"Be careful," Danise warned. "You shouldn't drive while
you take that stuff."

Malinga nodded. "I won't have to. We have a lot of work
to do here, and then Asedi and I have to go to Kalingalinga for the
first community meeting. In the meantime, Stewart volunteered to
help us find the witch doctors he thinks are responsible for
Saturday night."

"The President announced the reward in the papers this
morning," Asedi said. "We're getting a huge volume of calls
already, but the extra staff is handling it well."

"Good to hear, Asedi," Malinga said. "The President devoted most of the press conference to the memory of his friend the Archbishop. He blamed the tragedy on the killers and called on all Zambians to stop them. He expects all citizens to work with their neighbors to run the murderers to ground."

"I thought it was particularly exciting when you offered yourself up as bait," Stewart said dryly.

"Bait!" Asedi said. "Malinga, what is he talking about?"

"I told the killers to come after me instead of picking on helpless women. I promised them the justice they deserve."

Jacques whistled. "That was brave, Malinga, but was it wise?"

"I discussed it with the Inspector and he approved it. The killers are coming after me anyway, so I hope this will draw them out so we can grab them."

"You'll draw them out, all right," Stewart said, shaking his head.

"The Archbishop was very good friends with the President, wasn't he?" Davison asked.

Malinga nodded. "He was. That may mean we'll be fired sooner than Friday, but I doubt it. The reality is, we're all the President's got. Who's he going to put on this case if he fires us?"

Wilson shrugged. "I can't see him bringing cops in from other provinces. They'd have to start all over again. But we have to move fast and coordinate carefully."

"That's right, Wilson. That's just what I intend to do. In fact, would you work with Davison to close the investigation into the Archbishop's death? While Davison sifts the remains of the accident scene for evidence, ask the Luapula police to find the housekeeper and get her testimony about the Archbishop's whereabouts on Fridays and her visits to the market with the driver. I want to find out who was in his car when it made its regular Friday afternoons visits to Ruth's uncle in Kabanana.

"Jacques, can you find out if the DNA from Ruth's vagina matches the driver, the uncle or the Archbishop, and review all the evidence you've got so far with Stewart? And we need a positive ID on the woman on my fence as fast as we can get it."

She started to smile at them but winced and held her side. "If we close the loop on Ruth's murder, it will free us up to go after the other killers." She caught a quick breath, trying to hide the pain in her ribcage.

"Asedi and I will go witch doctor hunting in Kalingalinga with the neighborhood association." She drew in another shallow breath. "Today is Monday and we have until Friday to get this thing closed out. If we don't, it's our jobs. It makes the President look bad, and now, with this crash, it's even worse. The press will be following us around. We'll have to be twice as careful about everything we do."

She coughed and winced again. "Are there any leads we've overlooked on the other murders?"

"No one in the compounds remembers seeing anything," Davison said.

"Keep trying," Malinga said. "If we turn up another eyewitness, like the boy who spotted the Archbishop's car, it'll help."

"The bodies were all dumped in a one-kilometer radius," Asedi volunteered. "It's skewed toward the east side of the city, from Kalingalinga on the south to the American embassy on Ibex Hill. The girls we've been able to positively identify all lived in neighboring areas. The time between when they disappeared and when their bodies were found was short, four days at the longest. This tells us something about the killer that we've overlooked so far."

She paused until everyone's eyes were on her. "What's that, Asedi?" Malinga finally asked.

"The killer is lazy," she said. "He isn't straying far from home because he assumes we can't keep up with him. And the fact that he hung the latest body on your back fence tells us that he's arrogant."

"I agree. He's a game player," Wilson said. "He finds it entertaining to stuff this up our noses and watch us sweat."

"How can he do that? How can he know that we're sweating?" Davison asked.

Danise smiled. "Asedi and Wilson are saying what I've suspected for a while. The killer knows we're sweating because we've only made two arrests and they were for the third murder, which he probably didn't commit. He must be laughing, because the men we arrested – our only suspects in any of the murders – escaped yesterday. They had to have help from inside this station. Who was here? Who could have helped them?"

Malinga frowned. "I don't know, but we've got to find out. If we've been infiltrated, the killers will anticipate everything we do." The room went suddenly silent. Everyone averted their face as though they were ashamed except one, who forced himself to hold her gaze.

All of them – all but one – looked very guilty, although Malinga knew that none of them was. Except the one who was determined to look innocent.

She felt sick. The test had worked. Everyone – but one – had passed.

66 | Woozy from the Pain

To cover her shock and disappointment, Malinga laughed. "Cheer up, everyone. I don't think any of you are responsible. I just thought you might have some ideas about who it could be." she looked around the table. "Can you find out who was here, Danise?"

"Of course. I'll start right now," the psychologist answered. "It won't be that hard to find out who it is."

"The press doesn't know that we detained the driver and the uncle here before they kidnapped the Archbishop. Let's keep it that way. Their escape looks very bad for us. Someone is due for major discipline." She looked around the group again. "Think about it. If you have any idea who helped them escape, tell me or Danise. Even if you just have a hunch. I promise to keep it completely confidential."

She stood slowly and straightened her jacket. "Okay, Asedi," she said. "Let's get out to Kalingalinga and speak with the compound watch group about surveillance. Stewart, any ideas where we might find Redbone and Kivuli?"

The doctor looked dazed, as though he'd been startled from a thought he wanted to keep to himself. He cleared his throat. "You can start at Redbone's house. If he's not there, I'm sure the women will tell you where he's gone, and they might know where Kivuli can be found."

"Good. I'd like to check in with each of the compound groups once a day. Davison, when you're done combing last night's accident site, visit the group in George Compound and work out a plan for surveillance. Figure out how they'll report to us. Asedi and I will do the same thing in Kalingalinga. Once we work out a plan with those two groups, they can seed the other compounds."

Malinga's cell phone rang. She looked at the screen. "Sorry. It's the President's office. I've got to pick up." She walked toward the door and put the phone to her ear.

"You're in some trouble now," Paul snarled.

"Good morning to you, too, Paul."

"This isn't funny, Malinga. It's terrible."

"I know it isn't funny. I know it's terrible. Those things are not lost on me."

"You killed the Archbishop. You and your cowboy sidekick. Do you have to drive so fast all the time? You police are causing more accidents than you prevent!"

Malinga cleared her throat. "Paul, you know we didn't kill the Archbishop. His driver did. He had such a lead on us that we arrived well after the accident happened. We were late because the driver tried to set us on fire in the Archbishop's house before he drove away. He tied us up and it took us a few minutes to get loose. We took our best guess about where he headed, but showed up on the scene after he crashed."

"So you say, Malinga, so you say. If it's true, it's only shows how incompetent you are. I'm going to call Inspector Chikanda and ask him to replace you."

"Don't trouble yourself, Paul. He's cutting his trip short and coming back to Zambia. He'll be back on the job Thursday morning. You can speak to him in person."

"I'm glad to hear that, Malinga. Something will finally get done."

"Paul, I've got to get back to my team. Tell the President that the Archbishop wasn't the killer. His driver was paying the uncle for the girl's favors every Friday, pretending he was the big man. We'll know for sure once we get the DNA results tomorrow."

"As far as the President is concerned," Paul said, "the Archbishop is blameless. If you learn anything to the contrary, no one should know about it. Do you understand?"

"Of course."

"The President's best friend can not be implicated in these murders. If you learn anything to the contrary, spin it so it looks like the Archbishop was giving you the information you needed to catch the driver and the uncle. Got that?"

"I do."

"Anything else I should know?" Paul asked.

"Stewart suggested that the Chinese might be flaying the women at their new clinic near the Chimwemwe mine and dumping the bodies in Lusaka to throw us off."

Paul sighed. "Ah, Malinga. You really know how to pick them. It's also a really bad idea to implicate the Chinese in anything illegal right now. We're finalizing a new investment and trade deal with them. If you do learn anything incriminating, tell me immediately, before you tell anyone else."

"Of course. Our preliminary investigation was negative, and I doubt we'll learn anything from the local hospitals."

"Anything else?"

"Yes. We don't think the third murder, the one involving the Archbishop, is connected to the others. We've tying it off now, and we're moving fast to identify the other killers. We should be close to an arrest by the end of the day."

"Great. I'll tell the President."

"By the way, Paul," Malinga said, "don't tell anyone but him what I've told you. If the killers think we're still in the dark and get overconfident, we can catch them in the act before they harm another girl. With any luck, we'll get enough evidence to convict."

"Sure. My lips are sealed. By the way, the Archbishop's lying-in is tomorrow. Be there." He laughed and hung up. Then he dialed another number.

"Hey," he whispered when Stewart answered. "The police may be on to you."

"Give me a minute," Stewart said, and walked to the men's room. "I'm meeting with them right now. I've given them so many false leads, I don't think they have a clue what's really going on."

"That could change. You should be more careful."

"Careful? I'm always careful. Thanks to me, our police friends will be too busy with wild goose chases to notice me at all."

"Just keep your eyes open, okay? Malinga may be smarter than you give her credit for." Paul said.

"She's not smart enough to take bribes, is she? And she doesn't scare easily, which will make her easy to catch. We've already seen that. But I'm going to try a new strategy, my friend, a little diversion. I'm going to throw her a bone. A Redbone."

Paul laughed. "That's the best thing you've said yet," he said, hanging up.

Before she reached the squad room door, Malinga's cell phone was vibrating again. It was her husband. "Herbert, I'm pretty busy right now. What do you need?"

"I don't care how busy you are. I just heard what happened last night. How could you make such a fool out of me? Do you know how this will make us – my family— look? It's why I divorced you in the first place." Malinga frowned, but stayed silent, waiting for Herbert to blow himself out. "You never learn. I think the killers enjoy toying with you because you are so stupid. You are no proper mother to my children. I'm starting proceedings this morning to take them away from you as fast as I can."

Malinga sighed and flicked her phone closed. The pressure was becoming unbearable, and she was beginning to feel woozy from the pain. She needed another pill, but had to put it off as long as possible. It dulled her senses too much. She needed everything she had for what she was about to do next.

Shake it off, Malinga. Shake it off.

67 | Under Cover Lying-In

"Paul gave me an idea," Malinga told her team when she got back to the conference room. "And so did my husband."

"Your husband?" Wilson scoffed. "And Paul? The President's press secretary? Those two haven't had a good idea between them for a long, long time. And they're not exactly on your list of favorites right now."

"Paul is my brother-in-law," Stewart said, "but I must admit, Wilson's right. He's not the brightest light in Zambia."

"Paul mentioned that the Archbishop's state funeral will begin with a lying-in tomorrow," Malinga said. "He thought we should post someone there to see who turns up, but I don't think that will give us much. Besides, we don't have enough officers to devote one or two of them to a four-day official funeral."

"We can review the guest book and scan the surveillance videos," Davison suggested.

"Good idea. Set it up, Davison."

"I know where we can get some help with this," Asedi said, tapping her pencil on the desk. "Since he's being buried from the church in Kabulonga, let's ask the neighborhood watch group there to keep an eye out for us. They know the area and people better than we do. They'll see more than we ever could."

"That's a good idea, too," Malinga said, smiling her approval. "Do it. Stewart, since you're going to the funeral, can you see if anyone will talk?"

"I can try."

"You knew the Archbishop for a long time, didn't you?"

"Almost as long as the President," Stewart said. "At least thirty years. We both campaigned for him when he first ran for Parliament."

"That's before most of us were born," Wilson said, laughing as he stood to leave. "Come on, Davison. We have work to do. We'll have to catch up on Stewart's stories about the good old days some other time."

Impervious to Wilson's dig, Stewart continued. "I've been friends with the President since he was barefoot in the bush. My parents came to Zambia from Kenya during the Mau Mau Rebellion and my father was in Kaunda's first government. He was Chief Medical Officer in Northern Province. That's where we became friends with the President's family. Those *were* the good old days," he said with a rueful smile. "We were all such idealists then. We believed we could do great things, and that Zambia's wealth would be used for the good of its people."

"Times have changed, haven't they?" Danise said. "It's been a long time since we've seen that kind of idealism."

"You're right, of course. It was another era entirely. Now we're all so cynical, out for ourselves." Stewart looked down at his hands.

Malinga felt a surge of compassion for the doctor. "Not all of us, Stewart. We can win public trust back if we all put our minds to it."

"I'm afraid not, Malinga," Stewart said. "The social contract we believed in has collapsed. Now that the Archbishop's gone, there aren't many of us left." Stewart looked positively morose, Malinga thought.

"We'll make a new contract," she said. "When will you go to the lying-in?" she asked, anxious to get back to the subject. Reminiscences of the colonial era old guard always made her a little impatient. That had been an entirely different world, and they had to be willing to live in the new one.

"I'll go as soon as I can," he answered, "but first I've got to tend to Giselle, then try to find Redbone and Kivuli. I won't be there until tonight."

Malinga was confused. She'd been so sure Giselle was dead, but Stewart insisted she was recovering in his home. So far, there was no evidence from the autopsy. She frowned. "Is Giselle all right?"

"Medically, she's fine, but she's all nerves. She's very high strung to begin with, and her life has been very stressful these days. In fact, I need to get back to her now." He pushed back from the table and stood. "I'll phone you later if I learn anything about the witch doctors. Please excuse me." He grabbed his papers and left.

Malinga shook her head, convinced now more than ever that Stewart was lying. That could only mean he was somehow involved with the killers. Maybe Bertha could help her find out why. "We have to get going, too," Malinga said. "We're due in Kalingalinga – oops! – past due! Asedi, let's get rolling. We'll meet back here late this afternoon."

"I'll see what I can learn about the prisoners' escape, and keep working on these profiles, although I'm going around in circles a bit at this point," Danise said, frowning. Then she smiled. "By the way, Malinga, what idea did you get from your husband? You don't often credit him with anything useful. In fact, I don't think I've ever heard you pay Herbert any sort of compliment."

Malinga turned back from the door and into Asedi. "Sorry, Boss," she mumbled when Malinga winced, and stepped past her. "I'll meet you at the car."

It took Malinga a few seconds to catch her breath. "He claimed the killer was toying with me, Danise. I've thought that, too, but his comment convinced me that we have a leak on this investigation. I feel like the killers know what we're thinking and anticipate our movements. The suspects who escaped yesterday were being watched by the best guards I've got on the force. I still don't know how they got past them. Someone had to be helping them."

"The guards claim they were drugged, and I believe it," Danise said. "Even so, I don't think a stranger could pull it off."

"I don't either," Malinga said. "A stranger couldn't get past the entrance, or drug the guards. As unreliable as you are, Danise, I don't think it was you."

They both laughed. "But if it wasn't me," Danise said, "who was it?"

Malinga held up her hand and extended her fingers. "Davison and Asedi weren't in the office." She bent two fingers down. "Wilson was with me, and Jacques was in the forensics lab at University Teaching Hospital." She bent two more. "That only leaves one person on this team besides you.

Danise paled. "The guards already think Stewart's part of the police force, and he has access to drugs and knows how to use them."

"I'm also convinced the body on my fence was Giselle."

"So he's lying about that, too." Danise shook her head. "I don't know, Malinga. I can't believe Stewart would do a thing like that," Danise said. "Why would he?" Her frown deepened and she shook her head again. "It would implicate him in the killings."

"I don't want to jump to conclusions, but someone let those suspects loose. We just have to figure out who. Stewart's the most likely candidate."

"True." Danise laughed nervously. "On the other hand, there are at least fifty doctors in Lusaks. I bet every one of them wanted to let our suspects go."

Malinga's mouth dropped open, and she started laughing, too. The pain caught her again and she winced. "I get what you're saying, but I can't believe it's Stewart. He's not that kind of man and he's done so much to help this country and this investigation. He's just not capable of it."

Danise shrugged. "What did you tell me once, Malinga?"

Malinga struggled to shrug off her suspicions. "Only believe what you see."

Danise smiled at her and raised her shoulders. "Well?"

"I know, I know. I may need new glasses."

68 | Compound Alliances

"I am poor and I am a woman, but I dare these monsters to come after me!" Albertina said, clenching her fists at her sides as she walked along. "The President is right, Malinga. It is time we solved our own problems. We are ready to help you solve this one. Our members are waiting in the community center," she said, pointing to a neat brick building just ahead of them. "We built it ourselves and rent it for weddings and meetings. We do many things to make our lives better. I built my house and two of our members also built houses with loans from the savings fund."

She stopped and put her hands on the detective's shoulders. "Malinga, these men are threatening everything we have worked so hard to build. We will find them and bring them to justice. Just tell us what to do."

"Do what you have been doing all along," Malinga said. "But if you do find them, contact us. Don't go after them yourselves. We will bring them to task. We can't encourage vigilante justice, Albertina."

The big woman shook her head and smiled. "I would like to deal with them myself. But of course you are right. Let us go to the others."

Malinga and Asedi followed her through the entrance to the meeting hall. Albertina welcomed them into a room crowded with women in bright, colorful wrappers, many of them with babies on their backs. "You can relax now," she told them. "We are all working for you. By tomorrow, you will know where these men are. And the best news? We do it for free." She chuckled as she led them toward the front of the room.

Fifty women stood as one when they entered, their throats opened in a joyous ululation. "You are welcome," one woman shouted and the others echoed the sentiment.

Albertina gestured for Malinga and Asedi to sit at a small table center front. "Greetings, Federation members," she shouted, and called the women to order. "Thank you for coming. These policewomen need our help to stop the killers threatening our young women. Every woman must help." Malinga looked up just as Bertha slipped into the back of the crowded hall. She tried to catch her eye, but Bertha lowered her head as she slid silently onto one of the crowded benches.

After Alberta's introduction, Malinga raised her voice so all the women could hear her. "We are looking for two witch doctors, Redbone and Kivuli. Do you know them?"

"Who does not know them?" one woman shouted back. "If they are the men you want, we will find them for you and keep them here until you return."

"We will help! We will catch these men!" the others shouted.

Albertina called them back to order and Malinga continued. "We think these men may be involved in the girls' murders here in Lusaka, but we need to talk with them before we are sure."

"We do not have much time to find them before they kill again," Albertina added. "We must hurry, but be very careful, too. We believe these men are ritual killers. Do not approach them, and do not let them know if you see them. Tell me immediately and I will call the police." Fifty heads nodded and the women murmured among themselves.

Malinga had decided not to tell Albertina about the latest murder in her compound until they could determine the woman's identity. If these women heard what the killers had done to Giselle – by now, Malinga was sure that Stewart was lying to her and that it was Giselle – they would take vengeance into their own hands.

"Call us immediately if you see them or hear anything about them. Do not act on your own. I repeat. Do not act on your own. These are very dangerous men."

"They will claim more victims if we do not stop them," Albertina said. "They will grab you in the night! They will take your daughters! More young women will be lost unless we act.

We will search them out. We will not stop until we find them. We will hunt them down like dogs, and we will bring them to justice."

The women cheered wildly. "Hunt the dogs! Protect our children! We will find the ones who did this!"

Bertha listened with a growing sense of dread as the crowd around her cheered. Her eyes widened when Malinga explained what they knew of the killers. Her heart felt like it had stopped in her chest. Was this true? Was this what Redbone and Kivuli were doing? Did Kivuli catch these girls when they were traveling? Did he grab them from their beds? Did he find them alone in their houses after dark?

He'd told her they were all bar girls, fallen women, or that their bodies had been left unclaimed at the morgue. But Malinga was telling the women that these were good girls, working to help their families. They were girls who were studying hard to make their homes and communities better. They were being killed and butchered like meat, their bodies left with no respect in public places. The killers were challenging everything the women's association had worked so hard to build, and they were outraged.

"We will find them before they kill any else!" the women began to chant. "We will find them!"

Bertha was mortified. She hung her head. Redbone and Kivuli were doing the devil's work. They were terrorizing these women's very existence and hers as well. Greedy men, they would stop at nothing to get what they wanted. They created suspicion and fear and savagely destroy what little peace these women had wrested from the world around them. They challenged everything with meaning and order in her world.

"We must stop them," she heard herself say. "I must help you," she said in a louder voice, adding to the furious strength of the women's chorus.

As the noise grew, so did Bertha's understanding. Redbone and Kivuli were helping the doctor find women and dumping their bodies when he was done. The German and his wife were urging Stewart to 'harvest' even more women, and she knew that Stewart would help them build a factory – what did he call it? A laboratory! – to increase the number of women they could take. More women would die, and it would be Bertha's fault unless she spoke up.

The realization of her guilt overwhelmed her and held her hands over her mouth. Kivuli would take more of her children if he could sell them to the Germans. She might be the next victim. She jumped to her feet and waved her fist in the air. "I will help you stop them!"

The anguish overwhelmed her and she collapsed in wrenching tears. She was helping the killers, all of them, and women were suffering because of her. Women were dying so Kivuli could get enough money to go to South Africa. She was helping the very man who had oppressed her, who had already committed unspeakable acts of violence against her.

Why? Why was she helping Stewart capture Malinga's children, who were almost as dear as her own? How could she give them to the killers, who were making enormous profits and increasing their ability to kill more women just like her? Women like those who were now coming to their feet around her in a frenzy of desire to protect themselves and the little that was theirs.

"Tell us how to stop them!" the women shouted. "Tell us how to help you! Tell us what to do!"

Bertha looked down at her hands, wet with the tears that were streaming from her face. These were the hands that held her son while he was murdered, the hands that passed the doctor his scalpel and cleaned his instruments. The hands that touched Kivuli's face when they made love.

As the crowd's outrage grew, Bertha looked around her in panic. What would these women do to her if they knew she'd helped the killers? Had any of them seen her with Redbone or Kivuli? Malinga's gaze searched her out. Bertha glanced away, looking nervously around as Malinga continued to speak.

"The President has asked for your help," Malinga said. "The killers are hiding somewhere in the compounds. We need to root them out. There are not enough police to find them."

"We are your eyes!" Albert bellowed, raising her fist high while the Federation members cheered. "We are your ears! We are your hands and feet!"

"Halala!" the women cried in response. "We are with you!" the voices called. "We will stop them before they kill any more of our children!"

Malinga grinned as she held her hand up for quiet. It took some time for the women to settle down, but soon the room was quiet again and Malinga raised her voice to caution them one last time. "The killers are dangerous, so never travel alone or let your children go by themselves. Stay in at night. Report anything unusual that you see. Yes, women are suffering. But it will not be for long! We will catch the killers by the weekend."

"God guides our efforts," Albertina said and motioned them to silence. "Let us pray." The women took one another's hands. Bertha felt a hand grasp her left hand. She took the hand of the woman on her right just as Malinga and Albertina raised their joined hands heavenward.

She listened as Albertina prayed for strength and guidance. Eyes screwed shut, Bertha found herself praying with her. For justice. And for vengeance. And for the redemption she so desperately needed in order to find happiness again.

"We are one!" Albertina finished.

"Halala!" the women exclaimed in reply and then quieted, dispersing into groups to talk.

Albertina turned to Malinga. "They are making their plans. That is good. We will cover every inch of this compound. If the witch doctors are here, we will find them."

"Thank you, Albertina. I know they will succeed. I'll check with you tomorrow," Malinga said.

"I will call you if we learn anything new before then," Albertina promised. "We can move very fast. There are not many places where a killer can hide – especially one who is waging a war against women."

Bertha had edged toward the front, anxious to hear what the women were planning, stirred by their determination to keep themselves and their families safe from the most vicious and horrible threat they'd ever faced. Worse than Kalingalinga's floods, worse than the crowding, worse than the poverty. As she listened, she made her decision, and pushed forward toward the front of the room. She would find a way to put an end to it, a way to bring all of them – Stewart, the horrible Von Sorges, even her own lover, Kivuli, and his father – to task for what they had done to her and her child, and the horrors they intended to perpetrate on other women in the future.

Malinga, startled to find Bertha at her elbow, was even more stunned when the woman took her hand. She smiled. "Hello, Bertha. I'm surprised to see you here."

"Madame, I am part of the Federation. It is for all poor people. I cleaned the house before I came, and now I will go to your parents' to fetch the children. It is not far."

She smiled and Malinga smiled back at her.

"They will be fed and happy by the time you get home, Madam. They will be clean and in bed. You have nothing to fear."

Malinga nodded. "Thank you, Bertha. It means so much to have a friend I can count on. I will be home soon." Bertha nodded and turned away from her, saying nothing.

69 | The Sangoma Flies

That night, fires lit up the compounds. Word was spreading fast. Fires burned and people talked.

Who had they seen? What did they know?

Who could the villains be?

In Kalingalinga, the *sangoma* danced. He was beautiful, his slim brown body powdered to an eerie gray with ashes from the fire behind him. The leopard skin tied around his waist shook with the pounding of his feet. The feathers on his head, nodding wildly in the firelight, showed he was son of a senior man. He was in a trance, his body writhing to the drums. He prowled the edge of the sandy stage, hands straight out from his sides, head moving side to side like a cobra about to strike.

He was as beautiful as he was frightening. The women gazed at his lithe body, mouths parted in half grins, and gave their children handfuls of *kwacha* notes to tuck into his belt. The wide-eyed children did as they were bidden, running back as fast as they could to hide in their mothers' skirts.

Malinga whispered to Davison and Asedi. "Albertina told me that the dancer is Kivuli. Redbone is right over there," she said, pointing to the rear edge of the stage. "Davison and I will grab Kivuli as soon as he finishes dancing. Grab Redbone, Asedi. The Federation women will help you. Get ready. It sounds like the drummers are about to finish."

Kivuli jumped forward, fanning the flames of the small fire at the edge of the stage, and grabbed one of the protruding sticks. He arched his back and raised the fiery brand, and as the drumbeats quickened, lowered its flaming end far into his mouth. He held the brand inside his mouth for what seemed like an eternity and then pulled it out and waved it above his head as the crowd cheered.

They gasped in disbelief as he continued to dance, flames shooting above his open mouth. Without warning, he plunged into the crowd, coming straight at Malinga. People screamed and parted in panic, women grabbing their children and running. Malinga stood her ground, although she was bruised from the day before. She flinched when Kivuli blew smoke and ashes into her face. She choked, tears streaming from her eyes. She began coughing uncontrollably and the pain from her ribs was unbearable.

"Get him!" she shouted as she doubled over, and Davison ran, pushing anxious mothers and children aside.

Malinga stumbled toward Asedi and Albertina, who'd subdued Redbone after a brief struggle. Albertina was dusting off her skirts as other Federation members held Redbone down so Malinga could handcuff him. "Take him to your house, Albertina. We'll question him there in a few minutes. Asedi, come with me."

They darted down the alleyway where Davison had disappeared. The darkness surrounded them and Malinga's heart began to pound in fear. Asedi moved in front of her, pointing with her torch. "Look, Mum. Someone has fallen." She crouched at the bottom of a small box hedge lining the alleyway and turned the body over. Davison groaned when they pulled him to his feet.

"Not again, Davison!" Asedi exclaimed. "You are using your head far too much," she scolded.

"Very funny," Davison replied. "I will try to . . ."

"Focus, Davison." Malinga said, interrupting their banter. "Tell us what happened. Focus. Take it slow."

He nodded and took a deep breath. "When I turned down this alleyway a light blinded me. Then something hit me. I think it was a flying stick, still burning from the fire. That is all I remember," he said, rubbing the welt on his forehead.

"Kivuli must have helpers," Malinga said. "Come." With Malinga and Asedi on either side, Davison limped back to Albertina's house and sat on the bench outside.

"Wait here," Malinga told him, ducking inside the door with Asedi on her heels. Redbone sat on the floor with his eyes tightly closed. The women stood around him, their *pangas* ready, but the old man sat quietly, clutching at the sack nestled between his knees.

"What's in your sack, old man?" Malinga asked, pushing it with her toe. He clutched it tighter, staring up at her. Then, without warning, he spat on her feet. Annoyed, she wiped the spit off and raised her voice. "Where's your son, old man?"

"You will soon learn to respect us," he said, holding the bag firmly by its neck.

"Old man, I don't have time to play games with you," Malinga said. "Open your bag and let me see what you have."

He shrugged and raised the bag, tugging open the string at its neck. Hundreds of tiny bones sprayed out at his feet. The women jumped back in horror.

"*Muti*," one of them whispered. "*Muti*," another one cried, edging toward the door.

Malinga was shaken when she spotted a circular bone toward the edge of the pile. She looked at the women plastered in fear against the walls of Albertina's house. "No need to be afraid. These are animal bones," she said, holding them up so the women could see. "The small bones of rats and dogs." She but bent to gather the bones and shove them back in the old man's bag. The women continued to stare at her, doubt written across their faces as she handed the bag to Asedi. "Take these to the lab when we're done here."

Malinga and Albertina pulled Redbone to his feet and pushed him into a chair.

"Old man," Malinga said, learning close, "where is your son?" He stared at her blankly. "Dr. Bleming told me that you and your son are the *muti* killers we have been looking for. Unless you speak and defend yourself, we will take you to jail."

She pointed toward the door. "But first, we have to get you through the crowd out there. They want blood and I may have to let them have it." She glared at the old man. "I think Stewart is right. You and your son are the killers."

The old man screwed his eyes tightly shut and shook his head. "You are wrong," he said. "I have told you. It was the Archbishop. He is dead now." He saw the disgust in her face and laughed. "Yes, be afraid. Your trouble is not over. The doctor will kill again."

Malinga stared at him, eyes widening.

He laughed in her face. "You cannot believe a white man would do this. You think we witch doctors are the savages. Open your eyes and you will see who the savage really is."

Malinga drew back. "You talk nonsense, old man." She turned away from him. "Asedi, take him to the station and lock him up. We'll talk to him again in the morning when he's come to his senses."

Redbone snorted and stuck his hands out so Asedi could cuff him and pull him upright. "You'll see," he muttered as she guided his bent head under Albertina's front door lintel.

Malinga patted Davison's shoulder as she came through the door. "Go with Asedi. Help her with the old man, then go home. Get some ice for your head and get some sleep." He nodded and limped to the car, climbing in after the old man and pulling the door shut. Asedi backed the cruiser up and pulled out quietly.

"Thank you, Albertina," Malinga said as she climbed into her own car. "If your team finds Kivuli, there will be a reward. Tell the others that we are keeping Redbone in jail until Kivuli turns himself in."

She edged her cruiser through the compound's narrow streets and onto Alex Nkata Road, satisfied that they were getting closer. She'd question the old man in the morning and persuade him to talk in something other than riddles. Kivuli's face played across her memory, and she shook her head to clear it. Her eyes stung from the ashes he'd blown into them. She could feel the grime of the fire rubbing against her lids. When she got home, she'd put in drops.

Bertha had fed the children and seen to their baths by the time Malinga arrived. After Malinga cleared her eyes of cinders, she looked in on them. They were both reading quietly in their beds. She tucked Shiko in first, then said goodnight to Katanga, who begged to read a little longer before she went to sleep. Malinga patted her fondly. "Not too long. You've got school tomorrow."

"Mommy?" Malinga turned from the door to look back at her daughter.

"Yes, Katanga?"

"Bertha was crying when she came home. She spoke to someone on her cell phone."

"Could you hear what she was saying?"

"I don't eavesdrop, Mommy. You always tell us how impolite it is."

Malinga patted her head. "You're right, Katanga. I don't know what's bothering her. She seemed to be fine when I saw her at the women's meeting. I'll try to speak with her in the morning. You get some sleep."

Malinga thought about Bertha as she washed her face and brushed her teeth. Maybe the woman was trying to keep too much on her plate, taking care of Stewart and her at the same time. She'd speak to her in the morning. And to Stewart, too. The old witch doctor had implicated him in the murders.

Malinga ran a comb through her hair, took another painkiller, and climbed into bed. No dreams tonight, she hoped. No dreams.

70 | Wilson's Gone

When her cell phone rang well before dawn, Malinga fumbled for the light and looked at the caller ID. It was Wilson. It was 3 a.m. Not a good sign. She sat up in bed, but was immediately doubled over by the pain in her ribs.

"Malinga," a frantic voice said when she answered. "Malinga! We can't find Wilson! Another murder was reported and Wilson went out to investigate. He called us from the scene in Kalingalinga, but when Asedi and I got here, he was gone. The victims are here, but he is not. His car is here, and it was running. The door was open. We found his cell phone on the seat. He was trying to call you a few minutes before we got here."

"Slow down, Davison. Breathe," Malinga said. "Where are you now?"

"We are in Kalingalinga, near the Great East Road, where they sell the columns for buildings. This time, there is not one victim, but two. There is a girl's body next to a full-grown woman."

"Okay, Davison. I'll be right there. I'm sure Wilson is okay. There has to be some explanation."

"Yes, Madam," Davison said woodenly, breathing fast.

"It'll take me about fifteen minutes. In the meantime, secure the crime scene, but turn off the lights on your cruiser. Let's try to alarm as few of the neighbors as possible."

"Yes, Madam. I will do that."

Malinga could hear his breath slowing. "You're a first-class officer, Davison, so act like one. You're in charge until I get there. Call in the medical examiner's team, but tell them to approach without sirens or flashing lights. And call Jacques. Ask someone from the station to pick him up at the Padmozi. No cabs this time. I don't want to lose him." She forced herself to chuckle. "You remember the last time, don't you Davison?"

"Yes, Madam." He laughed. "The white man was taken many places he didn't want to go."

"Yes, Davison, you are right." She managed another laugh. "Stay calm," she said almost as much to herself as Davison. "I'll be there in a few minutes." She closed her phone and groaned. Two. A woman and a girl. Where was Wilson?

Malinga fumbled with the bathroom light and took the lid off the bottle of painkillers, downing two. Two victims this time. She bet it was a mother and her daughter. The public would be outraged once it hit the news. She pulled on her uniform, descended the stairs, flipped on the kitchen light, and knocked loudly on Bertha's door. "Bertha! It's an emergency. Please wake up!" The woman emerged, pulling her bathrobe around her.

Malinga put a hand on her shoulder. "Sorry to wake you up this early. I have to go to work. I didn't want you to be alarmed. I probably won't be home for a long time, so when morning comes, wake the children and see them off to school."

"Yes, Mum. What has happened?"

"Two more women have been killed, an adult and a child. Quite possibly a mother and daughter."

Bertha shook her head, her face twisting in a cry. She put her hands to her head and started to rock. Ah, yes, Malinga thought. Bertha lost her own son not too long ago. She touched Bertha's shoulders and shook her gently. "Bertha, look at me. I know this is frightening, but you must bear up for the sake of the children. Lock the doors behind me and throw all the deadbolts. I will tell Mr. P to be on high alert."

Tears streamed down Bertha's face, but she quieted and nodded. Malinga led her into the kitchen and switched on the light. "I'll put on some tea for us. Drink a little and go back to bed. When you wake up, try not to think about the murders. Get the children off to school and pretend nothing happened. We can't alarm them, so you must not tell them. Don't tell anyone. I'm counting on you."

Bertha nodded, biting her lower lip. Malinga reached for the doorknob. She frowned. "Will you be all right?"

Bertha nodded, managing a small smile. She wondered if she should tell Malinga what she knew, but she'd already turned away. "I have to go now, Bertha, so please drink the tea and get some rest. It will soon be morning." Before Bertha could say anything more, Malinga was gone.

Bertha locked the door behind her. Tears coursed down her cheeks as she searched her pockets for her cell phone. When she punched in his number, it rang but there was no answer.

Where was Kivuli? Had he murdered two more women? Should she warn him Malinga was after him? Did he know that Redbone was in custody? Bertha wrung her hands. She had to warn him. She tried earlier, but he wasn't answering his phone.

Bertha slumped to the floor. What was she thinking? Why warn him? The man was an animal. If he'd killed a mother and her daughter, he'd stop at nothing.

She'd be better off telling Malinga everything. The police had no idea of *muti*'s power, but they would soon feel it. Of that she was sure.

But she was also sure that Kivuli would kill her slowly, with unrelenting cruelty, if she told the police anything she knew. Of that she was very, very sure.

71 | Fashionable Braids

Malinga walked behind the array of pseudo-classic building columns ranged along the roadside, where she found Jacques and the medical examiner's team finishing with the second body. Davison worked to bag the first. The bodies had been photographed, measured, and tagged by the time Malinga arrived. After she talked with the medical examiner, the team moved quickly to clean up the scene.

Like the others, these women had been dumped after they'd been murdered and flayed somewhere else, leaving the police with no evidence once again. The larger woman's intestines spilled from a hole the killer had carelessly nicked in her abdomen while he skinned her, but otherwise, the scene was clean. The medical examiner told her the women had not been strangled, shot or stabbed, and like the others, there was no sign that they had resisted the killer. No marks anywhere on the bodies, no hair or skin under the fingernails.

"At least none we can see with the naked eye," the crime scene specialist said. "Jacques and I will have a closer look when we get back to the station. It is almost impossible to see bruising after the skin has been removed, but we can check for damage to the underlying tissues."

The adult lay on one side of a column, the teenager on the other, lying on their sides to face one another into eternity. This gesture of closeness – this mockery of love -- angered Malinga. Just like the other victims, the two women, young and old, had been flayed. But this time the killer had left the hair on both heads.

The hair triggered a memory, but Malinga's brain couldn't dredge it up. She bent to look in the body bags one more time. There was something disconcerting about their hair but couldn't put her finger on it. She zipped the bags closed again, and rose, shaking her head.

Malinga started when she backed into Stewart. "Doctor! What are you doing here?"

"I was here shortly after you came, but you were so busy, I didn't want to interrupt. Quite a mess you've got on your hands again, Malinga." When Stewart smiled, she could swear he was mocking her. "And so early in the morning," he continued. "My house is just around the corner. Why don't you come for a cup of tea when you're finished here?" She shook her head, remembering the suspicion she and Danise shared, and chided herself for it.

This is ridiculous. Stewart may be a snob, but he's not a killer. He's a distinguished and respected doctor. The painkillers are getting to me.

She forced herself to smile at him as graciously as she could. "Thank you, Stewart, but I can't. I'll be here awhile. I want to talk to the team before they wrap up."

He shrugged and walked off a short distance, turning to watch. Malinga was puzzled. She hadn't asked him to help, but maybe Davison or Asedi had. Davison shook his head when she asked, and said he was sure Asedi hadn't either. "The doctor just appeared," Davison said, shrugging his shoulders.

Malinga nodded. "I guess he was driving by."

"Maybe," Jacques said. "Maybe." He stood and wiped the dirt from his hands onto his trousers. "Let's wrap this up."

"Give me a minute," Malinga said, still nagged by a memory that refused to come into focus. In her mind's eye, she saw the victims' hair again. Copper extensions had been woven into the adult woman's hair, braided back in a complicated arc across her forehead to the left. The girl's hair was woven to the right to mirror the woman's. The copper-colored add-ons were interwoven and swept back through darker braids into beautiful cascades down both women's backs. They had been deliberately draped over the shiny sinews and tendons exposed when the bodies had been skinned. Grotesque beauty, a mockery, a cynical, terrible evil made manifest for all to see.

Malinga gestured to Asedi. "Have you seen these weavings in any shop downtown?" When Asedi shook her head, Malinga drew in a quick breath and nearly gagged when the memory returned full force. She'd seen those elaborate hairdos under construction at Celestin's Palace of Luxurious Beautification just a few days ago.

Malinga gaped at the two bodies, unable to move. She knew them all too well. The smaller bundle was Katanga's friend, Margaret, and the larger was all that remained of her mother, Patricia. The special hairdos Celestin had constructed for their Johannesburg shopping trip looked ludicrous and pathetic now.

Asedi saw Malinga sway and rushed to support her. "What is it, Madam?" she asked gently.

"I know them," Malinga said, choking on her tears. "I've seen these women before. It's their hair, the way it was done. It's so distinctive."

"Yes, Madam," Asedi said. "It is not a common style. It is too complicated. The hair is Brazilian. Very expensive."

"Very," Malinga agreed, "but they had the money. It's Patricia Obono and her daughter, Katanga's friend. They were having their hair done Saturday when Katanga and I were in Celestin's salon in Arcades. They were going to South Africa on holiday tomorrow."

Asedi sighed. "This is very difficult for you, Madam."

Malinga held her deputy's arm so she wouldn't sag to the ground. The soreness in her body had weakened her and she'd had very little sleep, and the painkillers were making her dizzy. "I was meant to recognize them, otherwise he wouldn't have left the hair. The killer is sending me a message again. I'm sure of it, Asedi. First, the body on my back fence, and now a woman I know and my daughter's friend. She's the same age as Katanga."

Asedi held her steady and patted her arm.

"It's too horrible," Malinga said. "I am responsible for their deaths."

Davison supported her other side and took her hand. "Mum," he said, his deep voice stern. "You know that isn't true. Be sensible. If the killer hadn't picked this woman and her daughter, he would have murdered someone else."

"No, no," Malinga mumbled.

"Listen to me, Mum," Davison insisted. "You can't say that he killed these women because of you. I bet there is another tie in, some connection with the hair salon. We'll investigate as soon as they open in the morning."

Malinga struggled to pull herself together. "Maybe it isn't my fault," she said, choking back her tears, "but it's clear the killer is aiming at me. He murdered Giselle after I spoke with her. Now he's murdered two more women I know."

Stewart walked up and stood listening, hands clasped behind his back. "Malinga, come to your senses. Giselle is perfectly all right." When he put his hand on her shoulder, she flinched and drew away. He'd claimed that the body on the fence wasn't Giselle, but she knew he was lying. Why?

"Stay calm, Malinga," he persisted. "Come with me. I'll give you a sedative. The pressure's getting to you."

She shook her head. "I can't do that, Stewart. I have to find this man. I can't shake the feeling that he's coming after me next. He might already have Wilson."

"Malinga," Stewart said. "Calm down. You don't know what you're saying is true. Coincidences often happen." He took her hand. "At least come over for tea. My home is nearby."

She pulled her hand away and shook her head, unsettled by his persistence. "Thank you, Stewart, but right now, I've got to run this investigation and find Wilson. Did you find out how the killer got Giselle's clothing yet? Did Bertha tell you anything?"

"I'm afraid Giselle is still recuperating under heavy sedation. The procedure was extensive. The recovery is typically slow. I probably won't be able to get a sensible answer out of her for another day or two. Bertha said she put Giselle's clothing, hat and glasses on a chair on the veranda. She'd washed the dress and the sash around the brim of the hat, and was waiting for them to dry. They were gone when she returned a few hours later, after she'd cleaned the clinic rooms. That's where the killer got them."

"But why would he take them? It was a risky thing for him to do," Malinga said. "How would he know I would recognize her clothes, that I had seen them just a few hours before? He would have to be following me around. Or know me."

"I don't know, Malinga."

"Have you questioned the neighbors? Did they see anything?"

"Bertha asked them, but no one saw anything. You know how reluctant people are to get involved, especially when it's something like this. They're afraid it will fall on them next, so they suddenly forget everything they know."

Malinga shook her head. "This makes no sense." She gestured hopelessly at the scene in front of them. "Besides the fact that we have two more women dead, we have another potential disaster. Wilson came out to investigate the scene and he's disappeared. Everything but his cell phone is gone. I don't know what to think."

Jacques came up to them, wiping his hands. "Wilson is missing?"

"Yes," Malinga said. "He was the first officer on the scene, but when Davison and Asedi arrived, he was gone. No trace of him. Apparently, he dropped his cell phone in his car."

"Maybe he got a call from the station or his home, an emergency," Jacques offered.

"It's possible, but wouldn't he have used his car?" She opened Wilson's cell phone. "I don't see any calls on this from either place." She turned toward her deputies. "Davison, can you check with the station? See if anyone called out here.

"Asedi, could you start knocking on doors in the compound and see if anyone saw anything?" Malinga motioned her close and dropped her voice. "Do it quietly. We have to keep this from the press as long as we can. Call me if you learn anything at all."

She turned toward Jacques. "I'm heading to the station, Jacques. Can I give you a lift?" He nodded. She raised her voice. "Everyone! When you're finished, come to the station. We need to consolidate what we know." She turned toward Stewart.

There's only one way to know for sure. I have to keep him close to me.

"Doctor, I know you're busy, but could we have your help downtown? I want you to work with Jacques and the forensics group on the new bodies."

He smiled. "Of course, Malinga."

"Thanks, Stewart. It's a great help to have you working on the autopsies." If he could lie, so could she. He was clearly part of this, in too deep. He knew much more than he was telling.

She smiled grimly as she walked toward her car. She knew Jacques could find out what she needed to know.

72 | You Will Know the Killer

She started the engine of her patrol car. "Jacques, I can't thank you enough for your help," Malinga said as she pulled onto the tarmac. "We dragged you out here so early. Let's stop by your hotel so you can freshen up and pick up anything you need. It's still early and I want you to be comfortable."

"Good idea. It won't take me long." He looked at his watch and whistled. "I'm having too much fun in Lusaka, I tell you! We have been so busy, I can't believe I arrived only four days ago." He stretched his long arms and yawned. "Tell me. In Africa, do serial killers usually work so quickly? This one works at a furious pace. You would think they are paying him by the yard. Or the meter."

Malinga wrinkled her forehead. "Meter? I'm not sure I know what you mean."

He chuckled. "The killer is removing so much skin, it is getting to be like . . . How do you say that in English? Dry goods? Yard goods? Something on commercial scale, a commodity, you know?"

She groaned. "What an awful analogy!"

He grinned. "Not really."

She shook her head. "Be serious."

"I am. I've been thinking about these murders. It is very work to remove skin from even a small part of a human body. I've never done it myself, of course, but I have seen it in some autopsies. Skinning an entire human body in one piece is a monumental task. The killer must be precise, orderly. Medically trained. It is not something you do quickly or without practice."

She nodded. "You're right. We've been running around so much that I haven't been able to think." She grimaced. "Too much time with the President, I'm afraid."

Jacques laughed. "I don't suppose he has much stomach for forensics."

Malinga shrugged. "Not so sure of that."

"I don't know about Presidents, but I do know we are looking for a very special man, one who may have a strong interest in forensics."

Malinga glanced over at him and frowned.

"Most serial killers are men," Jacques said. "He's probably African, because most serial killers kill people of the same race as themselves."

"Maybe that's true in developed countries like France, but can we assume it's the same in Zambia? And if he's selling the bodies for profit, he may not follow the typical serial killer's pattern."

"You could be right," Jacques said.

"We can agree that the killer is trained," Malinga said, "perhaps a medical person of some sort, used to handling delicate instruments and complicated procedures."

Jacques nodded. "Right. This killer must have a clean place to work. Human skin is heavy and slippery. It slides around while you are working with it. It's easy to drop it when it's wet. It can tear and stretch, and is easily ruined for commercial purposes."

"Ugh," Malinga said. "What a thought! But I get your point. There has to be a place, a table, a workroom."

"That is right," Jacques said. "Some place where this killer takes the bodies – or the people themselves if they are still alive. We know he drugs them. Also, he probably knows them and they trust him, because they are not resisting him at all. If not a friend, possibly a man who is well known to others generally."

Malinga glanced at him, suddenly thoughtful. "That makes sense." They arrived at the hotel. "While you get freshened up, Jacques, I'm going to get some coffee." She asked the night clerk to call room service and sat in the lobby near the front entrance. She frowned. Her migraine was coming back and the night's work had strained her ribs.

Most likely an African, she thought. A man, a doctor, nurse, or medic. Someone who was targeting her. Someone she knew?

You know him, a voice said. You know him.

She tried to focus, but began to doze and jerked awake when Jacques poured coffee into her cup. "Wake up, Malinga! This is very good coffee. I am so relieved it isn't Nescafe instant!"

Malinga guffawed, nearly spraying herself with coffee. Jacques continued. "When I was a little boy, my grandmother used to get up very early and sit on the balcony. I was always up early, always curious and eager for company. I joined her there, wrapped in a blanket to stay warm. She would give me a little coffee. I was so content to watch the sun rise. But here it is still dark."

Malinga smiled. "In Zambia, the sun rises and sets pretty much the same time all year. It pops into the sky at seven in the morning and disappears in a pouf at seven at night, before you can blink."

He raised his coffee cup as though to toast her. "Thank you for letting me work with you. You are a very smart woman, Malinga, and very kind. It is for these reasons that I have become a little worried about you and what is going on here."

Malinga's eyes widened. "Why would you worry about me?"

"These murders are very personal. This killer doesn't seem to be satisfied just to kill. The way he picks his victims and how they are displayed says that he wants you to notice. More than notice. He wants you to be alarmed, upset, frightened. He wants you to suffer. He is – how do you say in English — in your face with these victims."

She frowned. "He is in in my face, and I am all those things: alarmed, frightened, scared to death. But I can't show it in front of the team."

He nodded. "Yes, I know. You must be very strong."

"Thanks for your encouragement. It helps to talk about how I feel," Malinga said, frowning down at her coffee cup. "Danise also thinks the killer is toying with me. Perhaps both of you are right."

"Don't be too alarmed. A cop who hasn't had this happen is probably not a cop."

"Maybe."

"But this one is more dangerous than most," Jacques said.

"I know, I know. He's a mad man who will stop at nothing. And I'm frightened not just for me, but for my children." Malinga closed her eyes. "He's just murdered his first little girl," she said, her voice choked. She started to cry, but pulled herself up so quickly she felt a sharp twinge in her ribs.

"We're so close to the killer we can't see what's obvious, no matter how much it's pushed in our faces," Jacques said.

"What do you mean?"

"This murderer," Jacques sighed, "is a very evil man, one of the most evil I have ever known. Not only is he carrying out these horrible murders, but he wants to hurt you, too, to unnerve you and make you squirm. He's enjoying your reaction, your terror, your fear."

Her head was down, her mind burdened by his words. She nodded. "You're right. He is."

Jacques cleared his throat. "To do that – to enjoy himself – he has to be able to watch you closely. He has to be able to know that he is having this effect on you. He has to see you suffer or he is not happy. Is that not true?"

Malinga looked up at him, shocked. "Yes," she said. "If he didn't see me suffer, it wouldn't be much fun."

Jacques continued. "You must ask yourself, 'Of the people who are close to me, who would want to do this to me? Who wants to hurt me and why?' When you know the answer to those questions, you will know the killer."

Malinga's eyes widened even further. She pushed her chair back, jumped up, and started to pace.

73 | Public Humiliation is a Terrible Thing

Jacques cleared his throat again. "Malinga," he said, "you can only run from the truth for so long."

She stopped pacing and stared at him.

"I suspect that you already know who it is." When Malinga said nothing, he persisted. "Yes, you know who it is. You've known him for a long time. You've been his friend and you've worked with him."

"Not Wilson?" Malinga gasped. "You don't mean Wilson!"

Jacques shook his head, laughing. "Oh no no no! No one on your regular staff."

"Then who is it?" He said nothing, and she scowled. He was right. She did know who it was. The one person who had met her gaze during the team meeting when she'd spoken of an inside traitor. The man who was lying about Giselle. The man who turned up on the scene before he was called. Stewart. Of course.

It was him. She had to face it. But she wanted to hear someone else say it. She collapsed in her chair, almost knocking her coffee cup off the table. "That only leaves one person, Jacques! But Stewart doesn't fit your description at all."

"He fits most of it."

"He's not African . . ."

"But he thinks of himself that way. He's lived here most of his life."

Malinga leaned toward him. "He's a surgeon, has a medical facility of some kind, although I've never seen what's in it." She sighed. "That would explain a lot of things, Jacques. How, for example, he managed to show up on the scene this morning so soon after it happened, before he was called. How

Giselle's clothes happened to disappear from his compound and end up on my fence. How the killer knew I'd recognize them!" Her eyes widened, and she jumped up. "He has Wilson, Jacques! I know it! Albino skin is so valuable! We've got to do something!"

"You're right, Malinga, but we have to proceed with utmost caution."

She shook her head. "We may be jumping to conclusions. There are a lot of things that are still unexplained. Most importantly, why would he do such a thing?" She shook her head again. "No. I can't believe he could do this. He's an educated man, and he's helped so many Zambians."

"He's killing women who bleach, women who want to be white like him. It's very sick, but it makes absolute sense to me."

"I don't think that's his motive. He's never seen himself as different from or better than us. I think his main motive is money. Remember what Wilson was telling us about the albino killings? I know Stewart's been short on money over the past few years. He cut back on his medical practice after his wife died."

"How did she die?"

"She was injured in a car accident, but not badly. She succumbed during a bungled operation at the local hospital. Her injuries were minor, and the operation should have gone well. There was really no excuse for the result. He was angry and seemed to go a bit off the rails after that. I haven't seen much of him since. We used to be good friends, but he put me off every time I approached him. Said he didn't want my pity. "

She looked at her hands. "I should have tried harder, I suppose, but my new career was on the uplift and my husband and I were getting a divorce. I barely saw my children, and I was hundreds of miles away in Chobe when it happened.

'Tell me what you know about his financial situation."

"He has a small trust fund, but he's bound to have a lot of expenses. Until she died, his elderly mother lived with him. She was a very demanding woman. And he keeps a late model Jaguar."

"Not an especially good car for Lusaka."

"Yes. It needs too many repairs. He's also had some pretty expensive women on his arm since his wife died. He wasn't making any money in medicine, except the pittance we paid him for his forensic work here."

"He can make a lot of money by selling human body parts," Jacques said. "Fast."

Malinga shivered.

"Even good friends can kill. Or turn to it. I had a friend – we were police partners when we first started on the force – who started dealing drugs. Marseilles is famous for it. He started selling drugs from the evidence locker. He used, too. Got in way over his head and ended up dead in a bloody gang battle."

"I'm sorry, Jacques," Malinga said, thinking of Eitone. "I suppose it's easy when the opportunity is right. *Muti* murders have gone on for so long that police look the other way. They're too superstitious, too afraid, too greedy. With the clampdown in Tanzania, there's much more demand here. His house in Kalingalinga has an attached surgery. Very convenient."

Jacques nodded but said nothing.

"It's a horrible thought, but Stewart has motive, means and opportunity, so to speak," she said. Then she shook her head. "Still, I've always seen him as an honorable man. And he's the President's friend."

"He may well be an honorable man, and I'm not saying that you should arrest him," Jacques said. "Just take a closer look at him."

She shook her head again. "I just can't believe it."

Jacques smiled sadly. "The desire for money can do terrible things to people, that much I know. But why would he have a grudge against you? Why would he want to hurt you personally?"

She started to shake her head but stopped when she thought back to Chobe.

"A few years ago, I crossed him on a case he was helping us with. Turns out, I was right and he was wrong. It was an important case. It came to the President's attention. He's Stewart's good friend, but he joked about it in public."

"That might have been enough. Public humiliation is a terrible thing"

Malinga nodded and poured herself more coffee. "He certainly became very bitter after that." She sighed and looked away. "But I don't think it's just for revenge. If that's what he was after, he could be a lot more direct and a lot more effective."

"More effective?" Jacques said. "He's almost pushed you off the police force. He's split your concentration. Along with your husband, he's succeeded in shaking your confidence about your abilities as a professional, a woman, and a mother. A very effective attack, in my book. And he could win, if you don't make an arrest by Friday."

"Humm...." Malinga frowned. "You're putting everything I suspected but didn't want to admit to myself in a new light. Everything," Malinga said, shaking her head. "But it's so hard to believe. He's such a good man. I don't know what to think."

Jacques nodded, sipping his expresso. He was watching the first of the dawn's birds flit through the garden and had a sad smile on his face.

"I know it makes sense," Malinga said. "But we'll need a lot more evidence than we have right now to prove anything."

Jacques nodded. "It's almost the perfect crime. Just like you, not many people would suspect him, and the evidence disappears when he sells it."

Malinga brooded, sipping at the strong, hot liquid. Suddenly, she sat up and her face brightened. "I have an idea that might work. But I need your help."

Jacques nodded. "If it's something I can do without risking my skin," he said, laughing, "I will do it gladly. I know I have quite a lot of it, but it's still very precious to me."

Malinga smiled at him. "Nothing dangerous. I wouldn't ask for that. I just want you to invite him to work with you when you do the autopsies on these women. We film all our autopsies for use by trainees, so we'll just make sure the camera's on."

Jacques nodded. "No problem."

"Don't do anything special. Just chat with him and let him do some of the work if he wants. We'll see if he has any special relationship with these bodies. Let's see if he can't help bragging or showing you what he knows. "

"That shouldn't be a problem. I rarely have a problem playing dumb," the Frenchman said.

Malinga boxed his arm and laughed. "Good. Let's finish our coffee and get to the station." She reached for the bill, but Jacques stopped her and told the waiter to charge it to his room. He reached for the coffee pot again and smiled at her.

"Let me have just one more cup. You still owe me a story about your grandmother. Perhaps, when this is all over, I can cook you a little dinner and you can tell me the story of how Malinga became a policewoman."

"Done," she said, and smiled. "I won't give away all my secrets in one dinner, but it will be nice to do something normal for a change."

Jacques chuckled. "I'm sorry to say it, but it will be some time before anything's normal again in Lusaka."

74 | Sweet Revenge

"Stewart?" Danise shook her head. "I can't believe it. He's done so much for this country!" Then her face darkened. "Now that I think of it, though, three of the victims volunteered at University Teaching Hospital. He must have met them there when he was doing rounds and became friendly with them." She shook her head. "But without a lot more evidence, no one will convict him. He's too popular in Zambia."

"My thoughts exactly," Malinga said. "That's why I asked Jacques to try and draw him out during the autopsy." She looked at her watch. "They finished about an hour ago. He should be here by now."

"Was it fair to put Jacques in that position? Besides, he might be helping Stewart. He might be the mole."

Malinga shook her head. "I trust Jacques. The Inspector recommended him from Interpol Marseilles. He didn't come into the country until well after the murders began and met Stewart for the first time when he came here." She looked at her friend. "It's going to be hard on Katanga when she hears that her friend Margaret was murdered. If Stewart did it, she'll never get over it."

"Yes, that bothers me, too."

Malinga looked down at her hands. "It's heartbreaking. I've always loved Stewart, and Katanga thinks of him as an uncle." She looked up at Danise. "Maybe we can speak to her together."

"Of course we can, but until you release the identity of these victims, we have time. I'll come Friday for dinner, how's that? By then we should have this thing wrapped up and we can celebrate."

"That," Malinga said with a broad smile on her face, "is a terrific idea. After we talk with her, we can have some girl time. Feet up, fireplace roaring, red wine glasses in our hands. Jacques promised to cook."

Danise frowned. "If I make it to Friday." Malinga cocked one eyebrow, and Danise laughed apologetically. "These days I feel a little nervous about being home alone. I'm close to the case and sometimes I wonder if I might be next."

A shiver shot up Malinga's back. "Why would you think that? Have you heard anything?"

"No, but I can read a killer's mind. At least part of it. He doesn't like you, and I'm your friend, which means he doesn't like me. Guilt by association," she said as she slipped out Malinga's office door.

Jacques stuck his head in and looked at Malinga, eyebrows raised. "You look tired."

"Thanks for listening this morning," Malinga said. "I'm going home after this and take a shower and a nap."

"Good. You need a break," Jacques said. "I'll treat you to dinner at the hotel, how's that?"

"You're on. But let's get the case-related stuff out of the way first. Then we won't be talking bodies while we chew on char-grilled steaks. It ruins the flavor." When he grimaced, her grin widened. "And we can pay more attention to the jazz band if we're not talking shop. So let's get it over with now. Sit down and tell me what you have. I've been on pins and needles since you and Stewart went to the morgue."

Jacques shook his head. "It was a disappointment," he said. "Either he's totally innocent or he's a great actor. I couldn't draw him out on anything."

"Nothing?"

"Well, just one thing. But it wasn't very important."

"Try me."

"When we turned the women over, he pointed right at their skin grafts. They weren't easy to see, but he noticed them right away. 'What a waste,' he said, 'that two of these women had skin grafts, then died. Such an expensive waste,' he said, and chuckled to himself."

"That's bizarre."

Jacques shrugged. "It is, but it's not enough to get him thrown in jail. He may just be a damn fine surgeon admiring someone else's work."

"Let me look at the tapes," Danise said. "I may see something you didn't notice."

"By the way, both women had the entirety of their reproductive systems excised," Jacques said.

Malinga shivered. "He's taken other body systems before, so I shouldn't be surprised. I'll ask Asedi to see if there's a pattern." She pushed back from the table and rose. "We'll know for sure when these women were kidnapped as soon as Davison talks with the husband. He's a prominent businessman. We wanted to tell him before the press gets hold of it."

"The man will be inconsolable."

Malinga sighed. "I know. If something like that happened to Katanga or Shiko, I couldn't live with it." She walked to the door. "Right now, I've got to get that shower. Can I give you a lift?"

"No, I think I'll walk out to Levy Mall and try that new coffee shop. I hear they have very presentable cappuccino. Don't worry. I'll be back in time for the staff meeting." He held the door open for her. When she walked through, he frowned. "There was one more thing about Dr. Bleming I didn't mention."

Malinga turned to look at him.

Jacques shrugged. "I don't know if it's important, but what you just said reminded me of how I felt when he and I worked on the other bodies. The butchering was terrible, but he never expressed any concern or sympathy. He seemed accustomed to the carnage."

Malinga frowned. "That is odd. Especially for Stewart, who's such a compassionate man and committed physician."

"He seemed to have no feelings at all," Jacques continued. "I don't know the women either, but I feel very sad when I think how young and beautiful they were and what they might have become."

Malinga nodded. "I know. Now that you mention it, when he did the autopsies on the earlier bodies, it never seemed to bother him. I put it down to the British stiff upper lip."

"That might be part of it," the Frenchmen said. "The English are known for it. But this was different. So emotionless, so clinical. It gave me shivers and the room was not cold. I don't know what it's worth, but I thought I'd mention it."

"Thanks, Jacques. See you later."

The knock on the door was so soft, Malinga barely heard it. Davison entered, fingering the bandage on his head nervously.

"Back so soon!" Malinga said. "How are you doing, Davison?"

"Oh, my head's all right. But my heart is so broken."

She rose and went to him. "Sit down, Davison. Tell me what happened."

"The man was too sad, Madam. He was too too sad. To lose his wife and his daughter both. It made me frightened. I realized this demon could go after my children. We must catch him Madam, as soon as we can."

She patted his shoulder. "Thanks for seeing him. I know it was difficult. Were you able to find out when he'd last seen his wife and daughter?"

"Yes, Madam," Davison said, pulling out his notebook and flipping it open. "The husband was embarrassed to admit it, but he said that he hadn't seen his wife and daughter since Sunday morning. They went off to church and he assumed they'd gone off to visit her mother. Since they were going to South Africa that afternoon, he assumed they went to the airport after saying goodbye to the mother.

"Frankly, Madam, I think this man was too busy with his mistress to care. She answered the door, and I asked her to leave before I told him. I told her to put on some more clothes before she went out the door. She was so frightened of me she almost ran out in what she had on, which was almost nothing."

"It's what? Tuesday afternoon? And he wasn't concerned?"

"He is concerned now, Madam. I mentioned that his wife and daughter might have been killed by rivals trying to get the best of him in the car market. He is a car importer, and he is very concerned now."

She laughed. "Sweet revenge, Davison. Thanks for your work."

She stood. "I've got to go home and check on the children. We'll review everything at the meeting later, so write up your report."

"Good, Madam. The clock is ticking," Davison said. "It is now Tuesday. We don't have much time left before we will no longer be employed."

"Don't worry, Davison," Malinga said. "We'll get him. First, we have to find Wilson. Have you heard anything from him? Does anyone know where he's gone?"

"No one at the station heard from him. Asedi drove to his house to ask his wife if he went home for lunch, pretending that he'd lost his cell phone, but she hadn't seen him either. We're checking the university hospital now. What else should we do?"

"Check with his mother and the private hospitals. Call me the instant you know anything." Malinga frowned as she walked out the office door. So far, all the victims had been women, but what would prevent the killer from picking on a man while they focused on the deaths of two more females? Especially if that man was an albino.

She felt a sudden shiver up her spine. Where is Wilson? If this was an international deal, Wilson was a perfect victim. She tried his number again. No answer. She was really starting to worry.

75 | Safe in Their Beds

Malinga's leaned forward to towel her hair dry. She heard her daughter enter the room and looked up.

"Mommy?"

"What, dear?"

"I heard something at school today."

"What's that?" Malinga flicked the hair back from her face and gave Katanga her full attention.

"I heard that Margaret and her mom — you know, Margaret and Patricia? We saw them at the beauty salon Saturday? – I heard they were killed."

Malinga waited.

"That's what all the kids were saying. No one's seen them today, either of them. Margaret's Mom always drops her off. Everyone thinks they're dead." Katanga's eyes filled and tears rolled down her cheeks. She was trying to be brave but not doing a very good job of it. Malinga patted the bed beside her.

"Come here, Katanga." She put her arm around the girl's shoulders and lifted her chin so she could look into her eyes. "Patricia said that she and Margaret were going to Johannesburg. Remember? In the salon? Maybe they just left early."

"Maybe."

"So cheer up and don't worry. Let's go have some tea, shall we?"

She held out her hand and Katanga took it. "Mummy has to work late tonight, so Bertha will give you and Shiko dinner. Then homework and, if you want, a half hour of telly. But no more, okay?"

The girl nodded, breaking into a big grin. "I love you Mummy. I know you're going to catch this man and make him pay for what he's done. You'll be a hero then!"

"I hope I'm your hero now!" Malinga started down the stairs. "Don't dawdle and bring Shiko with you. Bertha's made some of her famous scones."

Bertha heard her coming and flushed with panic, gripping the phone tight in her hand. "They are all here now," she whispered. "Soon, the mother will leave for work. I will call you then." She snapped the phone shut and turned to smile at Malinga when she entered the kitchen. Shiko and Katanga were a few steps behind her, laughing at a new joke Shiko had learned at school.

"Hello, Madam. Are you going back to work?" Bertha asked.

"Yes, Bertha. I have to. We're working late tonight," Malinga said, feeling a bit guilty about her promise to have dinner with Jacques. "I'll have some tea with Katanga and Shiko first. After tea, they're to finish their homework. They can play out in the garden for a little while if it's still light, but I don't want her outside too long."

"Yes, Madam," Bertha said, forcing herself to smile at Malinga. "That is good. It is too dangerous after dark in Lusaka now."

When Katanga sat down and Shiko popped into the seat next to her, Bertha patted their shoulders gently. "I baked your favorite scones," she told the children. They beamed, reaching for the warm biscuits and butter.

Malinga laughed. "Bertha, these are delicious. I'm so glad you came to work for us."

Bertha nodded, busying herself at the stove.

"I've got to go back to work," Malinga said, ruffling her children's hair. "Thanks for staying, Bertha! I'll be back in time to take you home. It will be late, so you can come in late tomorrow."

"That is very kind of you, Madam," Bertha said, her back turned so Malinga wouldn't see her tears. "Thank you, Madam. Goodnight."

The children didn't hear the knock on the door. The television was turned up and they were laughing at the local comedian who was pretending to be a witch doctor who was having no luck changing chickens into frogs.

Kivuli entered the back door cautiously, and when he saw Bertha in the kitchen alone, he sidled up to her and pushed her against the cabinets.

"Not now," she whispered. "The children are in the next room."

He rolled his eyes and flopped down at the table. She tried to look him in the face, but was too frightened. "You shouldn't be here. I called you to tell you that you can't have the children. You can't have any children, and I will do all I can to stop you."

He smiled lazily. "I can have whatever I want. You above all people should know that."

"I want you to go away and never come near me again." It took all her strength to stand up to him, but she knew she had to do it. "What you and your father are doing is wrong. It is evil. You must stop."

"It's too late, Bertha. You're already in too deep. You can't stop us now, and if you try, I'll tell the police what you've been doing. I'll tell this madam of yours, and won't she be sad to hear it. She thinks you're perfect, but that will soon end." He laughed and stood up, stretched, and walked to the door.

"It's too late for you, Bertha. Too late." He shook his head. "But it is your choice. These children or some others. In the end, it makes no difference." He slammed the door behind him and walked into the night. When Bertha stopped shaking, she slid the bolts closed and went to check on the other doors. Then she sat in the kitchen.

It took her some time to collect herself, but when she did, she felt very proud. She had finally done it. She thought about calling Albertina to tell her that she had seen Kivuli, but decided against it. He was gone, but she had no idea where he would go next, and she was sure that the other women would catch him when he tried to go after their children in the night.

Later, when Katanga was lying in her pink princess bed, surrounded by the stuffed animals Malinga had given her a few months ago for her birthday, he came. Bertha had tucked her in after a very nice bath, and she cuddled deep into the warmth of the duvet. Shiko was already snoring softly in the bed next to her and it made her laugh. Katanga felt very drowsy and content. She could hear Bertha in the kitchen, cleaning up after dinner.

When the man came, Katanga and Shiko were sleeping hard and barely heard him enter. He picked her up in his arms and she felt as if she were dreaming. He was beautiful. He looked just like the fire eater they'd seen at the national show a few days ago. The one who was so brave and strong. The one who ate fire. She sighed and snuggled next to his body.

In her dream, she and Shiko were traveling with the man through the air. Katanga felt herself floating, and then fell gently into the deepest sleep she'd ever known.

76 | Celestin Fingers the Killers

Albertina opened her door a crack and looked out. "Oh, Madam! It is you!"

Malinga smiled. "I was passing through Kalingalinga on my way to the station and stopped to thank you for your help last night. We arrested Redbone, but Kivuli got away. Have you heard anything about him?"

Albertina shook her head. "I'm afraid not, my dear. But come in, come in. We are just sitting down to tea. I am so glad you can join us." The sitting room was jammed with women, about twenty in all, holding chipped teacups and chatting amiably.

Malinga held up her hand and smiled apologetically. "No tea for me, thanks Albertina. I had some with my daughter before I left home. I have to go to work, so I left her with my maid, Bertha. She's from Kalingalinga. Do you know her? She says she is part of your group."

"I do not know her," Albertina said, "but I see her from time to time. I think she helps the old witch doctor you arrested, Redbone."

"I know she knows him, but only slightly," Malinga said. "She still works with Stewart Bleming, and he knows him."

Albertina nodded. "I have seen them together, your Bertha and this witch doctor."

Malinga doubted it, but decided not to pursue it. "Could be. She's only been working for me a little while. She's very good with my children. She seems very conservative, very Christian."

Albertina shrugged. "Maybe so, but she lies with the old man's son, Kivuli, the one you are looking for."

Malinga's eyebrows shot up. "She's staying with Kivuli? Are you sure?" He wasn't the sort of man a woman like Bertha would know, never mind be involved with.

"I think so," Albertina shrugged and smiled. "But I am not really sure. All the women love him and when he is dancing, they send their children to give him money. You saw how he eats fire. He is young, but he is a very powerful man."

Malinga frowned. Had Bertha been as trustworthy as she'd seemed? It was time to make some discrete inquiries about her new maid.

Albertina clapped her hands. "Silence, please. Judith, can you give Malinga the report?"

A short woman stood up. "We are warning women not to move around at night, and to inform us if they see anything unusual. So far there is nothing to report. Except one thing."

Albertina nodded. "Tell Malinga what you noticed about the doctor's compound."

Malinga straightened. "The Doctor? You mean Stewart Bleming?"

"Yes," Judith said. "Since he is your friend, we didn't want to waste your time telling you something you already know." She laughed uncomfortably.

"Please go on," Malinga said.

"Over the last two months," Judith said, "the doctor has changed the entrance to his compound. Where you could see straight up the driveway from the road to the house, now there is a curve and it is not so easy to see the place as you pass by. The fence is now a meter higher than it was, and gives a shock if you touch it. And he has a new gate. He used to welcome everyone from the compound, but now he has a gate and a guard. You must talk to the guard before you go in, even if you have an appointment. He isn't seeing so many patients as before. Perhaps he has become too old, too tired."

Malinga nodded. "I haven't been to Stewart's place in a long time, so I haven't seen the changes for myself," she said. "I will talk with him and see what he says. Perhaps there were more robberies. He used to leave the place very open, but times have changed."

The women clucked appreciatively, nodding their heads. Judith looked relieved. "Thank you, madam. I do not want to say bad things about your friend."

"I want to hear about everything that you notice," Malinga said. "Anything at all. It may not seem important, but it might save lives. Call me immediately if you notice anything else, even little things. Many times, it's the little mistakes that catch bad men, not big ones."

As she ducked out through Albertina's doorway and walked toward her car, she heard a voice calling and turned. It was William. He approached her, pushing his bicycle loaded with firewood. "Madam," he said, "it is very good to see you. We men have heard what the women are doing, and we have decided to help. All the bicycle porters and taxi men are watching. So far, we have seen only one thing, a small thing, but I thought I should tell you about it. Maybe it will help."

"Anything, William," Malinga said, smiling wide to encourage the man. "It is the sum of all our eyes and ears that will catch this crazy man." Her cell phone rang. "Hang on a minute, can you?"

Celestin's voice laughed into the telephone. "Am I catching you at a busy time, Malinga?"

"I'm always busy, Celestin, but I'm happy to speak with you," she said, surprised that the hairdresser had called. They usually spoke only if she or the children had an appointment. But since his salon had been frequented by four of the dead girls, she was glad to have an opportunity to speak with him. "Thanks for calling me. What's up?"

"I have something to show you," the hairdresser said. "I will be here at the salon until late afternoon."

"I'll be there in a few minutes," she said, closing her phone. She turned back to the bicycle man. "Sorry, William. Thanks for waiting."

"This morning," William said, "a local taxi driver was coming from the airport early. He noticed the police stopped by the column seller's place. He said the big white man, the African white man, the albino . . . what do you call him?"

"Wilson?" Malinga asked.

"Yes, that one. He was talking with another white man, a real white man, standing next to his car. That is all he saw. He could not stop. He had a client who was tired and wanted to get to that hotel in Kabalonga. The Ibex, I think it is called."

Malinga frowned. "Thank you, William. That is very helpful." She took a few *kwacha* notes from her pocket and handed it to him. "Buy your children a treat. And keep watching. Call me if anything else comes up."

William smiled broadly. "Thank you, Madam. This money will buy school supplies for my children." He tipped his hat and peddled off, whistling.

Wilson was talking with a white man. Stewart, no doubt. Then he disappeared.

Malinga scowled. It made no sense. Unless . . .

Is Wilson helping the killers? Maybe he's the insider on the prisoners' escape.

As Malinga took the turn for Arcades, she flicked on her wipers. Celestin glanced up when she entered his salon and grinned. He motioned for her to wait, then leaned down and whispered in the ear of the woman he was styling. She laughed and glanced up at Malinga, then smiled at Celestin and nodded when he passed her a magazine.

"Excuse me for a minute, ladies!" he said, coming toward Malinga. "I need to help our beautiful policewoman." He grabbed Malinga's arm and steered her toward the back of the salon. "Come here, my dear," he cooed as he escorted her past the other women. "I have those products you requested in back and I want to be sure I ordered the ones you want."

He winked at Malinga and they ducked behind the curtained arch. "Here," he whispered, pointing to the photo he removed from his appointment book. "Look closely, Malinga. Look at this photograph."

"Where did you get this, Celestin?"

"I noticed it in my client's purse, so I borrowed it from her. Remember how I was telling you that I thought some women were getting skin grafts?"

"I remember."

"This is the man who is doing it in Zambia." He pointed at one of the faces in the photo. "The man on the left, it is him they are talking about."

The photo wasn't old, but it was worn at the edges, as though it had been passed from hand to hand many times. Malinga squinted. When her eyes focused, her jaw dropped. There was no mistake. Stewart Bleming stood on the left, his arm around Giselle. Standing next to him? The Archbishop. Malinga squinted again. He wasn't wearing his collar or robes, but it was him, all right. No doubt about it. Next to him stood Paul, the President's Press Secretary. Behind them to the right stood Redbone and Kivuli.

Malinga took a couple of deep breaths to calm herself. "Thanks, Celestin. I'm in your debt. This is more important than you can possibly imagine. I'll see you get the reward if it leads us to the killer."

He shook his head and waved his hands at her, as though he were warding off evil. "Ah, no, Malinga. Please. No reward! Do not tell anyone where you got this. They will come after me and give me another kind of reward that I don't want. Here. Take it."

"Thanks. Can I keep it?"

"But of course. That is why I borrowed it from my little friend." Celestin grinned. "She will never miss it." He whistled. "This man is giving the women treatments, no mistake. This is the famous Dr. Bleming. Dr. Stewart Bleming."

"Yes, Celestin, you're right," she said, looking at the photo again. "It's him. With other important people. I will use this well. One day, I wil pay you back, be sure of it."

He narrowed his eyes in an expression that wasn't at home on his usually jovial face. "There is only one way you can pay me back. Get them, Malinga. Get them."

She stood on tiptoe to kiss him lightly on the cheek. "I will, Celestin. I will. You can be sure of that. I will pay you back one day."

He bowed over her hand. "Never, never worry about paying me back. Just catch this bastard," he said, nodding at the picture. Then he winked.

"Whoever he may be!"

He grabbed her shoulder as she turned to leave the room and shoved a jar into her hand. "Malinga," he whispered, "Take one of these jars with you. It will look like we have been talking about your skin and not about skinners. I don't want these skin merchants coming after me. I have suffered from enough bad *juju* in my life!"

He laughed as he lifted the curtain and raised his voice. "I am so glad you are happy, Malinga!" he bellowed. "I am so glad this is the one you wanted," he said, winking as he bent over and brushed his lips against her hand. "If you have any trouble applying this, come back in and we will help you."

Malinga looked down at the bottle in her hand.

Mariah's Sturdy Everlasting Skin Bleaching Cream. Results guaranteed.

She laughed in spite of herself.

"I will Celestin, I will. Thanks!"

77 | The Call from Katanga

As she drove toward the station, Malinga puzzled over the photo Celestin had given her. According to Stewart, he and the Archbishop had been friends since boyhood. She knew that Paul was Stewart's brother-in-law. Giselle had adopted Stewart as her 'big brother' when they attended neighboring boarding schools. That explained everyone in the photograph but Redbone and Kivuli.

She shook her head and sighed. Back in the shop, when Celestin had given the photo to her with such an air of secrecy, it had seemed pregnant with meaning, but now, as she tossed the image around in her brain, her excitement waned. The more she thought about it, the more she realized how little it meant. These people knew one another. They were educated, successful people, who'd gone to the same boarding schools and traveled in the upper crust of society. All of them, she was sure, knew the President.

Except Redbone and Kivuli, of course, who had never attended boarding school, gone to an upper-class tea party, or been on first-name basis with Zambia's leader.

Malinga laughed at the thought and laid the photo on the seat beside her. But as hard as she tried to dismiss the image and think of other things, her mind kept coming back to it. She lifted it and looked at it again, but still couldn't decipher any further meaning. It was like a badly tuned instrument in a musical group, or the wrong color in a painting. There was something marring the harmony. Redbone and Kivuli just didn't fit with the happy little group in the photograph, and something about that made her increasingly uneasy for Wilson's safety.

If Stewart was collaborating with Redbone and Kivuli, Wilson was more likely their victim than co-conspirator. Albinos were valuable, hunted, and at risk, even if they'd achieved the rank of Deputy Inspector of Police. Wilson knew what it was like to be hounded every minute of his waking life for what he was. He'd known the suffering that people of his skin color endured every day since his childhood. Images of innocent children with their limbs chopped off trying to learn and get on with their lives must float in many of his dreams. They'd heard nothing from him in almost twelve hours. She didn't even know where to start looking.

But she was sure of one thing.

Wilson would never help a skin merchant. Not in a million years.

So if he wasn't cooperating, his failure to communicate with her was a sure sign he was in danger. She shifted nervously in her seat. There was only one reason the killers would take Wilson: they wanted his skin.

A slow chill of fear crept up her back. She knew there wasn't much time. She had to find where they'd taken him before it was too late.

The team meeting had been going on for more than an hour by the time Malinga arrived. She'd driven as fast as downtown traffic would allow, growing increasingly worried about Wilson's safety. The big man was clever and could take care of himself in most situations, but if the killers had him, all bets were off. She tried to reassure herself that since he'd outwitted the Mailonis and was alive to tell the tale, these killers couldn't hurt him, but they seemed much more sinister than the country bumpkin brothers he'd captured near Mulungushi Dam.

Malinga was comforted by the warmth of Jacques' smile when she entered the conference room. She nodded at him, but her face was deadly serious. "Tell them what we discussed about Stewart, Jacques. Tell them what you suspect. I still haven't heard from Wilson and I think Stewart may have taken him for *muti*. Tell them what you saw, Jacques."

When he was done, Danise sat back. "That's very disturbing. I agree that something's not right about him, but we've trusted him in the past and he's always helped us."

Asedi shook her head. "I hate to think it's him, but he does live in Kalingalinga and all the bodies were dumped near his place."

"Stewart has changed a lot since his wife died," Malinga said. "I just learned that he's also fortified his compound – built up the walls, made the gate impregnable, and added extra security – over the past couple of months. And," Malinga said, pushing the photo Celestin had given her to the middle of the table, "it appears that Stewart has some very interesting connections to people in high places — and low."

The group leaned in to look. Davison whistled.

"Celestin took this from one of his client's handbags," Malinga said, "a client who told him that she's going to Stewart for skin grafts."

"How did the Archbishop play into this?" Davison asked.

Asedi smiled. "I finally found the Archbishop's housekeeper, and she told me that he went to Stewart's parties. He met Ruth and her uncle there."

"And the witch doctors?" Danise asked, raising one eyebrow.

"Stewart told me that Redbone and Kivuli are the murderers," Malinga said. "He claims he doesn't know them, but this photo says otherwise. It looks like they are friends. The witch doctors probably sought Stewart out when they found they couldn't do a proper job with the skins and couldn't find international buyers on their own."

"Maybe the death of Stewart's wife turned him sour," Danise said. "I heard he blamed the teaching hospital for killing her. That's where three of the girls worked before they were killed."

Malinga frowned. "What's the connection to Giselle?"

"The housekeeper said that Giselle was one of the Archbishop's favorite guests," Asedi offered. "When she was in Lusaka, she always visited him for tea."

Asedi smiled. "Maybe the doctor and Archbishop were rivals."

Jacques frowned. "Or accomplices."

Malinga sat back. "Do we have a positive ID on the body on my fence yet?"

"Not yet, Malinga," Jacques said. "I'm hoping we'll have an ID from the dental records later this afternoon."

"That's great to hear. Right now, I'm worried about Wilson. This afternoon, one of my informants told me that his taxi driver friend spotted Wilson talking with a white man, a real white man on his way back from the airport early this morning. I think it was Stewart. He might have kidnapped Wilson. Or . . ." She looked away, reluctant to speak her mind.

Davison hesitated, then blurted out what they were all thinking. "Or Wilson went willingly. He is an accomplice!"

Malinga shook her head. "He would never cooperate with skin merchants." She frowned. "There has to be another explanation."

"One of the neighbors told me she also saw the doctor's car pull up and he appeared to be talking with Wilson," Asedi said. "He said Wilson got in the doctor's car, and they drove away."

"But it makes no sense," Malinga said. "Why would Wilson leave his car running and drive away from the scene of a crime? He should have called us, at least, to tell us what he was doing."

"That's true under normal circumstances," Jacques said. "But not so true if something's going on that isn't above board."

"What do you mean?"

"It's not impossible that Wilson is the doctor's accomplice. This is a lot of work for an older man. Maybe Wilson was helping him."

Malinga frowned. "Wilson would never do a thing like that. He knows only too well what it is to be hunted. "

"Which would make him a perfect hunter," Jacques said sadly.

"It couldn't be him," Danise said. "Wilson was off in Tanzania when the first case . . ." Danise stopped mid-sentence and looked around at them in horror. "Maybe he has some kind of connection to the body snatching circuit in Dar es Salaam."

Malinga's heart froze. "Not Wilson," she said. "Not Wilson! He'd never do anything like that."

"That's what you said about the doctor, Malinga," Jacques said gently. "He may not be collaborating, but then why would he go off with the doctor without telling us what he was doing?"

Malinga grimaced. "I don't know. Maybe he thought he'd get some inside information from Stewart. Maybe he hasn't called us because he can't. Where's Stewart now?"

"He left right after the autopsies to go home and rest," Jacques said. "He said he was seventy-five and not as strong as he used to be, but I don't believe him. He's very strong, much stronger than we think."

Malinga looked at her watch. "Wilson disappeared more than twelve hours ago. His trail is already cold. We . . . "

Her cell phone rang. She didn't recognize the number, but answered in case it was one of her Kalingalinga informants. "Mummy," the girl said in a very tiny voice. "The young witch doctor took Shiko and me to see Uncle Stewart. Wilson's here, too. And Bertha. They want you to come. They are giving us a very big party tonight."

Malinga's heart stopped. The tears began to roll down her cheeks and she could barely control her voice. "Okay, Katanga," she managed to say. "I'll come in a few minutes with Davison and Asedi."

"You must come by yourself. They said not to bring anyone else. No one. This party is just for us." The girl drew in a deep breath. Malinga could hear her voice tremble. "Giselle is here, Mummy. She's bandaged, and I didn't recognize her at first. She can't talk, but she recognized me from The Mint. Remember, Mummy?"

"Yes, I do," Malinga said. The tears were running openly down her face, and she batted at them with her sleeve. "I remember very well."

"Mummy, they say that it's important that you come by yourself. Something may happen if you don't. I have to go now. Please come to Uncle Stewart's for the party."

When Katanga cut the connection, Malinga slammed her phone on the table.

"They've got Katanga and Shiko. After Stewart picked up Wilson, they grabbed my children, along with Bertha. They took them to Stewart's house. Katanga said they are giving a party, and they want me to come. She said I have to come by myself."

"This is monstrous," Jacques exploded. "They took your children! And they've got Wilson! *Merdre!*"

"Okay, everyone! Calm down right now," Danise said. "At least they're all still alive," she added. "Let's be grateful for that!"

78 | Threatening My Cubs

"Oh, my God!" Malinga cried. "Stewart has my children! Bertha let Kivuli take them! Wilson is there, too! To think I left my children in Bertha's care and trusted her because Stewart recommended her! She was giving Stewart information all the time! Now she's helped them take my children! God knows what will happen to them!" Malinga snatched up her phone and headed for the door. "I have to go to them!" she shouted.

Davison rose to block her. "You must wait, Madam. You cannot go by yourself. You cannot do this." When she struggled to break free of his hold, his voice rose. "You cannot. It is too dangerous. They are using the children to bait you. What is it you always tell me to do when I want to run off like you are doing?"

Malinga tried to pull away from him, but he held her tight and made her sit down. She burst into tears.

"What is it you always say, Madam?" Davison urged her gently.

"Make a plan before you go charging off," she answered. Then she laughed. "You're right, Davison."

"Davison is right, Malinga," Danise said, throwing an arm around her friend's shoulders. "Take some time to plan what you'll do. Nothing will happen to the children until you get there. I'm sure this is a trick to lure you to them. Once they are holding you, we can't move against them."

Malinga stood and started pacing. "You're right, both of you. Let's get organized." She wiped the tears from her face. "I must go," she insisted. Her voice broke. "My children. They have my children. Look what they did to the poor girl this morning. What will they do to Katanga? Oh my God! I should never have baited him!"

Jacques came to her and pushed her gently into a chair. "We French have a saying for this," he said. "*Les imbéciles se précipitent.* Fools rush in. We must rescue them, yes, but we also know that this is a very deliberate trap. We must go carefully."

"I have to go, and I have to go alone," Malinga cried. "That's what Katanga said. He wants me. Me and no one else. I have to go now. Who knows what they will do to them if they think I'm not coming?"

"Yes, Malinga, yes," the Frenchman said. "You will go. Very soon. But let us take a moment to make a plan." He cleared his throat as he crouched beside her and took her hands. "Calm yourself, Malinga, or you will be no use to your children or anyone else. This is exactly what they want you to do. Exactly. They want to make you crazy so you cannot think and you make mistakes. If you do not collect yourself, they will kill all three of you and Wilson, too."

Danise dabbed at the tears running down Malinga's cheeks and patted her hand. "Jacques is right, Malinga. You must be well prepared, or you'll be taken along with the kids. They won't hurt them until they have you."

Anger surged through Malinga and she moaned. The sound of her own wild rage brought her to her senses. She sobered and raised her head. "You're right, Danise. Of course. I have to go in there by myself. But that doesn't mean I can't take all of you with me." She smiled and held up her smart phone, its speakers powerful enough to pick up ambient room noise.

"Yes!" Davison clapped his hands together and grinned. "You will keep your phone on and turn the volume up very high. That way we will know what is going on inside. When it is time, we will come in and rescue you. Just like in the movies!"

"I wish you hadn't added that last bit, Davison," Malinga said, smiling at the man." She shifted to face them all. "We have to move carefully. We can't let Stewart get away with this! We need to know who his accomplices are and how they work. If he destroys any evidence or escapes, no one will believe us. We'll be fired, and there will be no one to stop him. No woman in Lusaka will be safe." She took a deep breath. "Let's calculate the odds. Since we have Redbone in custody, the only ones there are Stewart and Bertha. And possibly Wilson," she said, her voice fading.

"And Kivuli," Asedi said. "He may be the most dangerous one of all."

At the mention of the young witch doctor's name, Malinga put her face in her hands. "My children," she moaned. "He's got my children! How can I possibly rescue them if there are four people against me? At least one of them is a psychopath! Maybe more!"

Danise hugged Malinga's sagging shoulders and shook her gently. "Remember what we talked about, Malinga?" She lifted the other woman's chin so she could look into her eyes. "These men are arrogant. They think they are above other people. And because of that, they are blind. You must stay calm so you can see where their weaknesses are."

"Stewart has a weakness, all right," Malinga said thoughtfully. She was beginning to come around, her anger cooling into deliberate thought. "He thinks I'm totally gullible and stupid. He thinks he can manipulate me. Stewart was my trusted doctor and friend, and now he's kidnapped my children, the ones he helped birth. He's holding the two people I love most in the world hostage. The bastard knows how to get to me, that's for sure."

Danise broke through. "He knows your weaknesses better than your strengths, I think. He'll try to presume on your kindness and decency, so you must be prepared."

"That's true. He'll try to play on my sympathies because we're old friends. But two can play that game." Malinga gritted her teeth. "I must awaken his compassion. I'll remind him that he still loves Shiko and Katanga. I can bargain with him to let them go and keep me instead."

"Don't forget that his allies will help him, Malinga," Jacques said, "and they might not feel the same way."

"Kivuli will have no pity, but I might get Bertha on my side if I offer her clemency. She's involved with Kivuli, but he killed her son. She's also a Christian and may feel remorse for what she's doing. I don't know where Wilson stands, but I can't believe he's collaborating. It would violate his deepest moral principles."

"Right now, you can't tell what kind of odds you're facing," Danise said. "Stewart and Kivuli have done appalling things and they won't hesitate to hurt you. Bertha and Wilson may help. You won't know until you're inside."

"That's right. I won't know until I get there." Malinga stood and checked her pistol, tucking it under her coat.

Could I kill him? Could I kill Wilson if I had to? Could I kill Stewart? Absolutely! I'll do whatever I have to do to defend Katanga and Shiko.

Her head suddenly cleared. She lifted her eyes and searched their faces. "I know you'll be listening, so here's what I plan to do. I'll offer Stewart and Kivuli time to escape, so you can intercept them once they leave the compound. I'll tell Bertha that we won't prosecute if she testifies against them, and send her to find you so you can take her into custody, too."

"And Wilson?"

"I'll know what to do when I see him."

She drew herself up. "Are we ready?"

"Absolutely!"

"Let's go get these bastards. They made a big mistake when they threatened this lioness' cubs."

79 | In the Monster's Lair

Malinga accelerated out of the station parking lot, turned on her lights and flashers, and tore through town, siren shrieking. She screeched up to Stewart's gate and laid on the horn. She could think of one thing and one thing only: what would happen to her children if she didn't handle things right. It was a delicate situation, with too many unknowns and too much at stake.

Stewart's guard opened the gate and peered out at her. Once he knew she was alone, he motioned her forward. "Yes, Madam?"

"I'm Malinga Mutende. I'm here for the doctor's party."

"Yes, Madam. Please wait."

The guard fiddled with his radio, spoke with someone, listened intently, then looked down at her. "The doctor says you can come in, but you can't bring your vehicle inside. We have too many visitors." He pointed across the street. "You can park it there."

Malinga grimaced, unwilling to be separated from her only sure means of escape. "But it's raining! I'll get all wet," she protested.

The guard spoke into his radio again, but the reply was muffled. "Sorry, Madam. But the doctor says this is what you must do."

She parked where the guard had pointed. Unfurling her umbrella, she ran across the street, past the guard, and up the steep drive. She paused at the top to catch her breath and look around. Aside from the change in the gate arrangements, Stewart's house looked just like she remembered it.

She'd come running as he knew she would. She stood for a moment, remembering everything they'd said at the station the last time they spoke in person, how cool he'd been and how deceitful. The man was capable of anything. She had to steel herself and not fall prey to him anymore. She drew herself up. "I'm going in now," she said aloud. "Can you hear me?"

"We hear you, Madam. We're ready to help as soon as you need us," Davison responded. She slipped the phone into the vest pocket of her jacket and strode toward the front door.

Here I am. About to enter the monster's lair.

The doctor's head emerged from main door of the house. He looked down from the raised terrace, smiling brightly. "Malinga!" he said, "So glad you made it! Come in! Get out of the rain!"

She squinted, peering up at his face. A face once benign and patrician, lit from below by the lantern he carried, looked old and worn. As he bent his head toward her, his flesh sagged horribly. Ghoulish, yes, but forlorn and weak at the same time.

She swept past him through the front door, "Stewart!" she said, grabbing his arm. "Where's Katanga and Shiko? Why did Bertha bring them here? Stewart, where are my children? Tell me where they are!" She could feel her tears down her cheeks and hated herself for feeling so vulnerable. She braced herself.

I'm at his mercy. But not for long. I'm going to get my children back whatever I have to do.

The anger surging through her strengthened her. "Stewart! Tell me what's going on!"

He patted her hand. "Now, now, my dear. Calm down. You know I mean you no harm. Katanga and Shiko are perfectly safe. They're on the patio. Come with me. Join the party. We'll get you a drink and you'll see." As she followed Stewart through the elegant entranceway, Malinga could hear music playing in the covered garden. Stewart waited for her and took her elbow.

"Remember the dinner parties we used to have, my dear?" he asked as they walked along the corridor. "Remember the patio, the drinks, the garden, people laughing? Remember the wonderful times we had here so many years ago?" She nodded.

"Now there is drumming, dancing, and celebration again." He smiled down at her, his face lit by the swaying lights. "Not so long ago, you used to visit often. You were one of our best friends." He turned to look at her. "We were friends, Malinga, and I want us to be friends again."

Malinga stopped walking and pulled her elbow out of his grasp. "I can't be friends with a man who kidnaps my son and daughter and keeps them against their will," she said.

He laughed heartily. "Don't be ridiculous, Malinga. The children are fine. Why would they be anything but fine? What's this talk of kidnapping? We brought them to our party, and they're with their nanny. You'll see them soon. Come and meet the other guests."

He gestured for her to match his pace in the flickering light. She waited, unable to respond, frozen by the mention of happier days in the middle of this shadowy horror. She rubbed her temples. A headache was setting in and the painkillers were making her dizzy.

Stewart stopped and turned to her again, his brows drawn together. "Malinga, what is wrong? You used to smile and laugh with us. My wife, God rest her soul, so enjoyed entertaining you." He sighed. "What happened, my dear? Why did you stop coming to see us?"

Malinga was struck by how old he looked, how worn, yet somehow infantile and innocent. What had happened to change him? She began to doubt herself, and rubbed at her temples again.

Can he possibly be a monster, the monster, the evil one?

She caught herself. Her suspicions were based on solid fact.

And women talking to you in dreams. Can you be sure?

His voice began purring again, seductive as a cat. "Remember, Malinga? Remember how you brought your children to us? They were so young. They toddled across the lawn, chasing the dogs, trying to find Easter eggs at the picnic." He sighed again. "Of course, since my wife died, I've not been in the mood to give too many parties." He chuckled and turned away. "But now she has come back. You'll see her in the garden and you can pay your respects."

He stopped mid-stride, arrested by a memory, and turned towards her, his eyes narrow. "Do you know that her parents refused to come to her funeral? They said I killed her by bringing her to this country!" He shook his head and laughed bitterly.

"Can you imagine? There is no more wonderful place than Zambia, but they said I killed her by bringing her here."

His face sagged, but he managed a small smile. "They refused to continue her stipend. It made it hard for me to give parties the way we used to. It made it hard, very hard." He shook his head like he was trying to chase his memories away. "That's when people started to pull away from me. Even you, Malinga. Even you. You pulled away, even you, who used to bring your children to visit us."

"I'm sorry, Stewart," Malinga said. "The children got bigger and very busy at school. Then Herbert and I were divorced, and my mother . . ." He wasn't looking at her. He was staring out into space, in a trance.

When he turned to her and grabbed her shoulders, she tried to break away, but he held her in a remarkably strong grip. His face had turned into an ashen, vicious mask. "But that isn't what made me so angry and disappointed with you. I was fine until you embarrassed me, Malinga. You embarrassed me in front of the President, in public, in front of the country that I served. Now the President thinks I'm against him. You took my last important friend from me. Why did you do that, Malinga?"

"Stewart, listen to me. I . . ."

"People can harbor very strange beliefs, I've found. Don't you think that's true, Malinga?" he said, interrupting. "Some people say I am evil. Do you think that's true, Malinga?"

She shook her head, but was too terrified to speak. His eyes were strangely alight. He looked as though he was possessed by a strange internal fire, a fire that was consuming him. A fire fed by rage, anger, and bitterness. A fire fed by isolation and loneliness.

"Stewart?" she said quietly, but he didn't seem to hear.

Instead, he straightened and smiled down at her, releasing his grip on her shoulders. "Let me show you something that you've never seen before," he said, his voice calm once again. "It's what I started doing to pass the time when my wife died." He pulled her toward the entrance of a side gallery and gestured. "Here's my collection," he said, "spare parts, I like to call them. Although they'll never go back into anyone's body." He chuckled.

She hung back, horrified. The room was filled floor to ceiling with glass-fronted display cases. Full, it seemed, of human bodies. The parts, with skin flayed back and muscles gleaming. The same way the girls' bodies had looked when they found them on the sides of Lusaka's roadways.

"Come, Malinga. Look! They really are quite beautiful. See how shiny they are? You can see every detail!"

Malinga shuddered, remembering Davison's claim that "Shiny corpses are a bit okay." She glanced around her nervously. The specimens had been treated the same way as the girls' bodies. What had Stewart done?

His voice had grown dreamy. "It took a lot of practice to get them as good as the ones I first saw in the European shows. I experimented with the plastination techniques developed by the Germans and Chinese. I trained Bertha, and she did many of the treatments after I did the fine knife work."

"Bertha," Malinga echoed stupidly, rubbing her temples again. The headache and dizziness were intensifying. She struggled to clear her brain. Of course. Bertha had brought Katanga and Shiko here. And now the doctor was implicating her in all his crimes.

Malinga remembered Bertha's face at the women's meeting, fervently promising to help Malinga and reassuring her that she had nothing to fear, that the children would be safe. Malinga had believed her and was strengthened by her words. She'd been relieved to have a friend so willing to help her. Now she felt betrayed.

"Bertha helped you?"

"Yes. I never could have accomplished so much without her. I taught her all the techniques, and she's very good, don't you think? She also does excellent work with the bodies, don't you think?"

Malinga nodded, struggling to keep the feelings of outrage and betrayal off her face. Bertha was on the inside. She'd helped these bastards, even though they'd killed her baby. What she'd been thinking!

What would she be willing to do to Shiko and Katanga? What had happened? How had they forced Bertha to help them in this evil work?

80 | Are They Alive?

Before she could regain her composure, Stewart pulled her further into the room and they began walking toward its darkest corner. They passed bodies with organ systems exposed, organ systems without bodies, and bodies sliced into sections, both horizontal and vertical. Stewart prattled on, proud to show her the finer points of his work. He sounded so crazy, she didn't dare interrupt. She looked around furtively, increasingly dismayed by the level of his madness. Are any of these Shiko and Katanga? Are they still alive?

She shook herself, remembering that Stewart said it took days to complete this process – what had he called it? Yes! Plastination – and realized that Shiko and Katanga had been with the doctor for only a few hours. Then she shivered. That was long enough to kill them and possibly to skin them, if not to finish their permanent embalmment.

Stewart was still talking, pointing out various features of the cases as they passed. "These displays show how the body would look if you could see it sliced laterally, or from end to end," Stewart said. "Here is the urinary tract of the adult female and here, side by side, are the reproductive organs of an adult female compared to an adolescent's." His voice grew hushed, and he sounded reverent as he stopped before the next display case.

"Here is my favorite, my *tour de force* so to speak. It took me several tries, but on my third, I reached perfection." Malinga stood mesmerized before a lit glass case in which was suspended the glistening outlines of a human circulatory system. "You can see how fine the work is, exposing vessels as small and delicate as silk strings."

Malinga stared at him. "Three times?" she asked incredulously. Stewart had sacrificed three living, breathing human beings to crate this single display?

"Yes, three times," he confirmed. "It takes a tremendous amount of patience to do this work."

"You killed three people for one display?" Malinga couldn't bring herself to believe what he'd just admitted. "Three people gave their lives?"

He looked at her, disconcerted by her questions, and finally he shrugged. "These displays are important, Malinga. More important than the life of a single individual, especially these people. Even three of them. These people you see here were poor and would never amount to anything. Petty traders, poor women and children struggling to stay alive under the boot of Zambia's merciless administration.

"But while their lives were of no importance, they became very important to science when they died. I think they'd be very happy if they knew that." He chuckled. "They'd be happy to know they are being used to educate future medical students. In fact, it's important that you make sure the University Teaching Hospital gets these displays."

Malinga gaped at him in utter disbelief. "How can you say that? Are you God? Maybe these people were quite happy being who they were, happy to love their children and kiss their babies, and work each day for the future they decided was important for themselves!"

He sighed heavily and lifted her chin in his hand. She tried to free herself, disgusted by his touch, but he held her tightly in his grasp. "Your pity is misplaced, Malinga. I'm a doctor. I've lived with these people and served them. I know what I'm talking about!"

He scowled, and then his face softened. "You'll do that for me, won't you, my dear? See that these get to the university? These are beautiful specimens. The students will learn a great deal from them, and in doing so, will save more lives in the future."

He paused, scowling again. "They will save more lives if they take the time to study these specimens. If they're good students and conscientious. Unlike the ones who killed my wife."

The picture was coming into focus, Malinga thought. All his resentment and anger originated with the death of his wife.

She looked at his face, withdrawn and intense, and knew she had to continue to play along.

"Of course, Stewart," she said in her most earnest voice. "I will do that for you. It would be an honor. Now, should we go to the party? Your guests must be waiting."

Stewart smiled at her cheerfully and released her chin. "You're right, dear, as usual." He took her elbow and began to steer her back among the display cases toward the outside door. "It wasn't so many people. After we harvest what's saleable, I preserve different bits of what remains," he mumbled once they had reached the corridor. He locked the door and tested the handle. "This is the finest collection outside of Germany or China. And I am proud to say that we did it ourselves."

"We?"

"Oh, yes. This is the result of the combined effort of many human beings. Redbone and Kivuli collected the people, Bertha helped prepare them. Most recently, we received the help of two eminent experts from Germany, Victor Von Sorge and his wife, Anita. Victor is the anatomist who taught me all I know about plastination. He creates the Body Works exhibits I showed you on my phone the other day." He motioned her forward, gesturing toward the light at the far end. "Even Wilson . . ."

"Wilson? Wilson Mwiinga?"

"Yes, of course, dear. What other Wilson do we know?"

They rounded the corner to face a wall-size painting of an elephant. The torso of a man was posed in front of it, a torso the size and weight of Wilson. In front of that, two children, skinless and rigid, heads turned back toward to the man behind them. Malinga froze.

They're the same shape and size as my children.

"Who are they, Stewart?" Malinga asked, but Stewart tugged her forward. "Not to worry, Malinga. No one you know. Your precious children and Wilson are waiting for you in the courtyard," he said, smiling brightly, oblivious to the effect the display had had on Malinga. He put a supportive arm around her waist and pulled her by her elbow past the bodies of her loved ones, prattling on.

"You can see more of the exhibits later," he said, "but now, I want you to see the dancers. It's just like the times we had when my wife was still alive." His pace quickened. "You'll see her there, Malinga, watching. Come forward now and see."

Stewart looked eager, more like himself than he had in a long time. He was old and tired, sure, but there was a gleam in his eye, a murderous madness she had never seen before. When they emerged on the veranda bordering the back garden, her eyes teared in the bonfire's bright light. She felt faint and sick, and drew back when she caught sight of the young *sangoma* dancing near the fire.

"Kivuli!" she cried. He was beautiful in the way that all young men are beautiful, but more graceful and beguiling than most. Almost two meters tall, he was lithe and muscular across every inch of his body. He danced around the circle of the fire, his arms flung out and his head thrown back. He was beautiful, but grotesque and aloof at the same time, drawn into himself and his power.

Malinga shivered as she came closer. He was terrifying, his expression inhuman, his face whitened with ashes. Every fiber in her reached for him, every muscle contracted in revulsion. The drummers pounded a relentless beat and he kept up with it. His upper body was naked but for the ashes drawn into striped designs. His lower body was covered with a skin, a leopard skin strapped over a kilt of woven barkcloth.

His face was mask-like, startled, as though he were in a trance. Drugs, Malinga knew. Drugged and dangerous. As her eyes adjusted to the flickering light of the huge bonfire, she noticed that the doctor had gone to the opposite side and was standing over his wife's chair. Malinga's mouth fell open. His wife.

His dead wife.

She was there, smiling up at him, the same woman Stewart had buried six months earlier. Malinga narrowed her eyes and strained to focus in the bonfire's light. She soon realized that the woman didn't move. She was frozen in place like a mummy. Lifelike, yes. But not alive. Stewart had done something to her body to preserve it. But if she was here, whose body had been in the coffin they'd buried at Leopard Hill Cemetery?

Stewart leaned down to whisper in the ear of the woman seated next to his wife. Malinga looked more closely. It was Giselle, yes, Giselle. Giselle with patches of flesh sewn on her face, Giselle with a gauze turban on her head. Giselle, who also looked less than alive. Malinga squinted across the smoky fire, but couldn't tell dead from live in the light.

Insane fear gripped her.

Where are my children? Where is Wilson? Are they alive or has he done this to them, too?

81 | No Sense to a Mother

When Stewart leaned on Giselle's chair and a servant offered her a drink, Malinga could see she was smiling, her lips turned up in what looked like a permanent grimace. Smiling, Malinga thought, at all her good fortune. Stewart had been working hard on her, using the scraps of flesh he'd torn from other women's bodies. The ugly marks and scars of bleaching had disappeared under his knife.

Three other women sat near the fire, fashionable, well-dressed women, their hair and nails beautifully done, laughing and talking despite the bandages on their faces. These must be the women Celestin had mentioned, Malinga thought, the ones receiving skin grafts. Lying gracefully on day beds, sipping drinks and talking, waiting for Stewart's magic to take hold.

She looked up, startled. Wilson was walking toward her, smiling as though he had no concerns in the world. Wilson! He was alive! "Oh my God! Wilson! You're here! You're all right," she exclaimed, speaking loudly so she could be heard through her mobile. "But where are Shiko and Katanga?"

"Look around, Malinga. You'll see them as soon as your eyes adjust. But do it casually so you don't alarm the doctor."

She shielded her eyes against the glare of the fire and scanned beyond the *sangoma* to the right. She felt her blood chill. There were two more captives she hadn't noticed. In a small cage opposite a girl was clinging to the bars, her eyes half-closed and her mouth shaped in a stupid smile. It was Katanga, her daughter, her love, the breath of her life. Katanga! The girl, loose-limbed, was holding herself erect on the doorway of her enclosure, following the movements of the *sangoma* with a rapturous gaze.

"I see Katanga now," Malinga said, bowing her head toward her phone. "She's been drugged, but she's all right."

She felt the outrage seething through her. Her daughter, drugged. Stewart had brought her here and drugged her. But then Malinga realized that it was probably for the best. If Katanga was drugged, then she would remember less. If she lived.

"If Katanga's here, Shiko must be too," she said loudly, looking around her. As she spoke, Katanga lost hold of the bars on her cage and slid slowly to the floor. It was too much for Malinga. "Katanga!" she cried out, and started running toward the girl, but Wilson intercepted her.

"Malinga," he said quietly. "You do her no good by going too close. The less fuss you make, the less likely Stewart will remember she's here. If you let her fall asleep, she'll curl up and become invisible to these monsters. Shiko's there, too, sleeping in the back corner. They'll be safe for the time being."

Malinga shook her head in misery. "Oh, Wilson! He told me you collaborated."

Wilson snorted in disgust. "Collaborated? With that man? I'd just as soon kill him with my bare hands," he said, careful to keep the smile on his face. Stewart was watching them, and Wilson gave him a small wave. "Don't worry, Malinga," Wilson said. "We're going to get out of this. Your children will be all right."

Malinga nodded. Wilson was right. No one would notice the children if they remained unconscious. There was only one problem. While it made all the sense to Malinga the policewoman, it made no sense at all to Malinga the mother.

Wilson forced her to relax slowly back into her chair. "Relax. Trust me. We'll get them out of here."

Malinga's heartbeat faster. Stewart. His dead wife, mummified, keeping him company to eternity. Giselle, happy behind her dark glasses, her signature hat bobbing, her dress lit beautifully by the fire's light. I would trade them all, Malinga thought, to see my children out of that cage.

She panicked again. What if they'd been given too much of the drug? Were they still alive? "Wilson," she called out softly. "Are you sure Shiko and Katanga are all right?"

"I'll walk past by the cage and doublecheck," he said, rising to move around the fire, circling close to the cage. He continued his circle, nodding to Giselle and the doctor. He grabbed a glass of water and brought it to Malinga. "They're fine, Malinga. Katanga and Shiko will get out of here, I promise you."

"I'm wearing a wire, Wilson. The team is listening. They can hear every word I'm saying. They'll come in whenever you're ready."

"Good," Wilson answered, still smiling blithely. "But until we come up with a plan, try to look like you're having a good time. We can't let them know we're plotting something."

"I'm trying to smile, Wilson. Really I am. What are we going to do?"

Kivuli pounded his feet on the sand in time to the drumming. Across the fire, Malinga could see him raise coals from the fire and put them in his mouth. He left them there for a minute, experiencing what Malinga thought must be unbearable pain. But his expression never changed. When the coals started to die and smolder in his mouth, he pulled them out one by one. His eyes were glittering with the same madness as the doctor's, she realized.

The young dancer turned to walk along the perimeter of the fire. When he came near the cage where Katanga and Shiko sat, Malinga held her breath until he passed them and continued around the circle to join the doctor.

"Stay here, Malinga," Wilson said in a low voice. "And don't forget to smile. If we are going to make it out of here, you have to get hold of yourself and stop staring. Smile, will you? That's an order! From your boss!"

"How's this?" Malinga said, forcing a smile that redoubled the pounding of her migraine.

"It's a start. I think I have a plan that will make you really smile," he whispered.

"Let's hear it, Wilson. What's your plan?" she said, loud enough for the phone to pick it up.

"Hang on. Stewart's coming this way. When he's gone back to his other guests, I'll tell you." Wilson turned away and busied himself watching the *sangoma* perform.

"How are you enjoying the party, my dear?" Stewart asked gaily. "Come and sit with my wife." She exchanged looks with Wilson, who nodded slightly. "I'll be back in a minute," she called to him as she stood to follow Stewart across the veranda.

The late Mrs. Bleming sat smiling, her lap full of roses. Malinga recalled how she loved to raise them, but wondered what the woman would have thought had she seen herself now. Malinga raised one hand and gave the dead woman a weak salute.

Stewart sat Malinga down on a garden chair and motioned to one of the servants to fetch her a drink. "Some fruit juice will be just the thing, Malinga." She nodded. After the drive across town and the fright she'd felt earlier when she thought she was viewing her own children's flayed bodies, her adrenalin rush was fading and the pain in her ribs was beginning to distract her.

She looked across at Wilson and shrugged. Then remembered to smile. "Thanks, Stewart." The girl bringing her a drink knelt before her and lifted the glass. It was Bertha, Malinga was sure, although she was wearing skins and rags and a short mask over the top of her face. When the girl spoke, she knew.

"Madam," she said, "please drink this."

"Bertha," Malinga whispered. "Bertha, is that you?"

Bertha looked up at her. Malinga could see the tears in her eyes. "They took away my son, Madam, but they will not harm Katanga and Shiko," she promised in a low voice. "I will help you, but we must take our time. Please drink this."

When Malinga made a sign of refusal, Bertha added, "it is just fruit juice. They put drugs in another one, but I poured that out." When Malinga tried to grab her hand, Bertha shook her head imperceptibly, mouthed the word "no", and moved away.

Wilson, who had rounded the bonfire to sit in the chair next to her, reached over and took Malinga's hand. "Hold on," he said. "Just wait. I know you have no reason to trust her, but I think Bertha's telling the truth." She nodded. Pulling on the drink Bertha had given her, she felt a surge of energy going through her, along with a sense of relief. No drugs.

Stewart approached them, smiling. Kivuli trailed behind him. "Malinga," the doctor said, "we've been talking about what to do with you and your children. I am happy to let you go, but my young *sangoma* friend is not so trusting. He thinks you must be killed." Kivuli was staring at her with coal-black, hate-filled eyes. "He thinks you have caused us too many problems and that you must die," Stewart said.

"He thinks you are cursed. Most people, he says, are afraid of us, but you aren't. You would never give up chasing us, so we decided to let you find us before you caused us any more trouble. Kivuli is annoyed because you are a good policewoman, and because you are a woman and not afraid of him."

Kivuli mumbled something, then sat back, picking his teeth with a small bone he drew from his belt. "This young man has very strong magic," Stewart said, "so strong it frightens me. Normally, I let him do exactly what he wants because I don't dare oppose him.

"The first two murder victims, for example, were his doing. He thought he could butcher the women's bodies as well as anyone, but he found it overwhelming. He couldn't harvest a presentable skin. Even on the second try." Stewart looked over at the young man, who continued to scowl. "Is that not right, Kivuli?"

Kivuli looked away, glowering under his crown of feathers. Even with all the dancing, Malinga noticed, the man had not broken a sweat. He looked inhuman, masked by his powdered white skin, slashes drawn in charcoal across his cheeks and forehead. Malinga knew he was capable of almost any kind of harm, any kind of evil. When he lifted his necklace, pointing the baby's skull toward her, she pulled back. A necklace of bones, she realized, a baby's skull framed in the Atlas bones of more victims than she could count.

"That's Bertha's son's, in case you're wondering," Stewart said. "And those are the vertebrae of other victims, the so-called Atlas bones."

Bertha came up behind Kivuli, knelt and offered him a drink. To Malinga's disgust and puzzlement, she began muttering a song of praise. The young man scowled, but let her continue. He was obviously preening, enjoying her attention and relaxing under her praise. Well, Malinga thought, Danise was right. Every monster has his weakness. She knew, then, that she and Wilson had a chance and smiled. Bertha was gazing at her boldly, sadly, over the young man's shoulder, shaking her head and smiling too.

Oblivious, Stewart was still talking. "I made Kivuli's acquaintance through his father, who's been my neighbor for many years. The old man is actually a very good healer, well versed in the properties of many herbs, but he has a very big problem. He cannot control his son.

"When Kivuli returned from South Africa, he took over his father's life. The old man tried to resist, but he was too weak. When his son decided to enter the body parts trade, Redbone asked me to stop him. I agreed, but after I spoke with Kivuli, I realized that we could work together as partners." Stewart smiled. "Like you and Wilson, Malinga." She tried to smile, and looked at her hands.

Stewart cleared his throat. "So I helped him. We helped each other realize our goals. Our profit is enormous. He has the connections to trade with the South African *sangomas*, and I can sell organs and bodies to museums in Europe and Asia through my new partnership with Victor Von Sorge. We've enjoyed great success for almost three years. Since my wife died," he said, glancing at her body, "we're climbing to new heights."

"Stewart, you have to come to your senses. What you and Kivuli are doing is horrible. There is nothing educational or edifying about it." Malinga said.

He patted her hand, hushing her. "I am sorry that you are visiting me under these circumstances, Malinga. I'll try to make your children as comfortable as I can until I finish my work. Then I'll free you and the children. But I must have Wilson" – Wilson's hand squeezed Malinga's, urging her to stay quiet - "because he is so white. Just one more, one perfect albino, and I will be gone and no longer trouble you."

"Wilson? You want to skin Wilson?"

"Yes," he said coolly. "Victor needs it for one of his shows in Europe. You will help me. Kivuli says that you have harmed us and you must pay your debt. I'm afraid Wilson is the price of your freedom. Kivuli insists. He says it will be your initiation. If you help me skin Wilson, I will let you and your children go."

Her eyes widened in disbelief.

"Stewart, you are asking too much of me. I cannot trade one for the other. I cannot hurt Wilson to save my children. No one can make a choice like that."

He laughed warmly and patted her hand. "I talked Kivuli into letting you live, Malinga, and your children. But now you must help me with Wilson or the deal is off."

82 | No Deal

When she started to shake her head again, Stewart stood up, impatient. "Don't be silly, Malinga. As a mother, you made the decision a long time ago." She glared at him, but he ignored it. "Come. We don't have much time. Our plane for Germany will leave soon."

Malinga thought quickly and swallowed hard. "Fine, Stewart, fine. But can you give Wilson and I a moment to say goodbye? Ask Bertha to bring us something strong, something that will kill our pain. Here, Wilson, sit with me." Stewart nodded and went into the house to find Bertha.

"Fast thinking, Malinga. What do we do now?"

"I thought you said you had a plan, Wilson!"

"I only said that to calm you down."

Malinga started to laugh. "Great, Wilson. Fortunately, I do have a plan. Let me tell you – and everyone else – what it is." She pulled out her cell phone and put it to her ear. "Have you heard everything?" she asked. "Good. Here's what we're going to do. After Bertha delivers our drinks, I'll send her directly to the front gate with Shiko and Katanga. When the guard opens it, come through the house and follow the corridor to the back. If we're not by the pool, we'll be in his consulting rooms." She listened for a moment and turned back to Wilson.

"Until Davison, Asedi, and Jacques come in, we'll play along with Stewart to buy as much time as we can." She glanced up and grabbed his forearm. "Here comes Bertha," Malinga said, smiling at the woman. "Put the drinks down here, my dear." When Bertha leaned closer to put the cocktails on the table, Malinga whispered, "Tell Kivuli you have to put the children to bed. Get them to the front gate as fast as you can. Tell the guard that Stewart said the children should go. When the gate opens wide, the police who are waiting outside will come in, but you take the children and run."

"Yes, Madam. The children will be all right." Bertha circled away from the light and bent to the children's cage.

Kivuli came up and leered at Malinga. "You and the big man have had enough fun. Come with me." Malinga stood, but shook her head. "You must let Bertha take my children for a nap. They are very tired. Then I will help you with Wilson."

Malinga watched Bertha lead her children toward the front of the house. When Kivuli started after them, she held him back. Stewart, who had come up behind them, put his hand on Kivuli's shoulder. "Let the children sleep while she is working," he said. "In the meantime, I'll get Wilson ready for the surgery." Stewart grabbed Malinga's arm and led her down an internal corridor to the rear consulting room. He opened the door and pushed her in. Wilson, strapped to a table, smiled at her. "Be gentle, Malinga."

She let out a moan. "I can't do this, Stewart."

The doctor, who was about to sedate Wilson, laughed lightly. "You must help, Malinga. It's the only way you can save your children."

"I can't, Stewart! I can't do this to Wilson!"

"I think you can, Malinga, and I think you will. I'll give you a few minutes to decide. I don't want to hurry you, but the skinning takes some time and Kivuli and I must be gone within an hour. We've got a plane to catch."

The doctor looked startled when his cell phone rang. "Stewart here," he said when he lifted it to his ear. He listened intently. "You can't mean that. I have everything you asked for! The albino will be finished within the hour and then I'll finish Malinga and her children. The elephant will be at the airport tomorrow evening. I've just got to say the word."

He listened for another moment and turned to Kivuli. "Victor's decided not to wait. He's leaving now. He got a better deal in Central African Republic." He shook his head. "And he was only faking the Parkinson's to get my sympathy."

Kivuli moved closer, standing as though ready to pounce. He stepped toward Malinga, raising his fist. "The German doctor is no matter. We can still sell these ones for a profit in South Africa. There are plenty of others who will want them." He lifted his knife and moved to cut Wilson's throat.

"Don't touch him," Malinga said, pulling her pistol from her bag and holding it to the doctor's head. "If you touch Wilson, I'll kill the doctor."

The young *sangoma* shrugged and continued toward Wilson. Malinga shot once in the air but Kivuli didn't flinch.

Stewart smiled. "You can't do it, Malinga. You were never cut out to be a policewoman."

"You're right, Stewart. I can't do it to you," she said, "but I can kill that man over there." She aimed the pistol at Kivuli and shot him between the eyes.

Tears were streaming down Malinga's face when she turned the gun back at the doctor. "Release Wilson," she ordered. The doctor smiled at her as he let himself quietly out the door.

"Let's get out of here," Malinga said, pulling at Wilson's restraints.

"Whatever you say, Malinga." Wilson rubbed his wrists and looked down at Kivuli's corpse. "Nice shot, Malinga. You were always better than me with a handgun."

83 | Bertha's Own Hell

"My God!" Jacques cried. "I just heard a gunshot. What is going on in there?" He and Davison jumped from the car. "What's going on, Davison?" Asedi came up behind them, pulling on her rain slicker.

"I can't hear anything," Davison shouted. The rainstorm was ruining already weak reception.

Jacques tensed the fingers in his coat pocket, resisting the urge to grab the phone from Davison. "*Merdre*!!" he shouted. "Can't you get that thing to come in? We have to hear what they're saying."

Davison put the phone to his ear again and strained to hear what was going on through the crackling. "I think Wilson and Malinga are . . ."

Asedi leaned past him to point at the house. "Look," she said, "the gates are opening. It looks like Bertha. It is Bertha! With Katanga and Shiko!" she said, leaping forward.

"Run, Katanga, run!" Bertha shouted to the girl. "Take you brother and run." She released their hands and ran back through the gate toward the house. Asedi grabbed the children to her when they reached the bottom of the drive.

"Malinga and Wilson are lost to us! Lost!" Davison cried. "We can't enter the compound until we know she and Wilson are safe."

Asedi elbowed him aside to put the children in the car, then turned back to the other policemen. "We're going in. I've put the children in the car and locked it. They'll be safe until we come back."

"But she hasn't given us word!'

"Maybe she can't! We can't wait any longer, Davison. Let's move!" Asedi said, pulling her gun from its holster and running up the drive ahead of the men. The gate swung open at their approach. Asedi slowed, but the guard was gone.

Behind the back fence, Bicycle William jumped at the sound of the gun. The women with him started to make a racket with their sticks, and the night was soon filled with the barking of the doctor's enormous guard dog.

William pointed to a small hole in the fence. "Throw it through," he said, motioning to the bag of meat held by one of the women. "Throw it through now." Two more fierce dogs joined the melee, and when the woman heaved the bag over the top of the fence, they fell on it, fighting over the generous helping of meat it contained. They were soon lying on the ground, struggling in the last throes of the poison.

William motioned to the women. "Bring the ladder here. We must go quickly. The drumming has stopped and I am afraid for Malinga." Six women rushed to the fence with the heavy ladder, propped it up, and ascended one by one, dropping over the top into the back of the doctor's compound. William motioned to two other men, and they followed the women up the ladder and over the fence.

The group pulled together at the bottom. "Watch out for the guards," William whispered to them. They nodded and disappeared around the corner of the house without a word.

William crept straight to the house, slinking along the veranda and peeking in the windows. He saw nothing in the covered yard but the remains of the party that had been going on a moment ago. Where there had been dancers and guests, there was no one. He moved along the veranda and edged through the main door.

Sneaking down the hall, he was startled by the sight of a human body. "My god!" he called out in spite of himself. It was a woman, but as he looked closer, he realized it was a very dead woman. The doctor's wife glowered up at him, and he stepped hastily back. Dead, but looking like she would come to life any minute and start putting the flowers she held in a vase.

Abashed, he headed toward the center of the house, where he could hear a woman crying. When he opened the door, he saw Bertha, sitting on the floor with Kivuli in her arms.

"Come," he said. "Come with me." She shook her head mutely.

"Where is Malinga? Where are the children?"

She looked up at him, but her eyes didn't focus. "They are safe, they are gone. Leave me here."

William ran back to the main door and whistled softly to his comrades. It was the sound of a nightjar but louder than most. Their prearranged signal. They ran to him.

"William," one said. "We must run. Quickly! The doctor's men have set the petrol tanks in the garage on fire, and the place will blow up soon. Head for the back wall. There is nothing more we can do. Head for the back wall now!"

William ran back to Bertha. "Come, woman!" She didn't seem to hear him, so he ran to her and tugged at her shoulders. "Come, woman! Get up or you will die! They have set the compound on fire!" Her blank face turned back to the figure she was cradling and continued to rock and keen.

William, running for the back wall, was deafened by the first explosion. The second blast tossed him over its top.

At the front of the house, it blew Asedi, Jacques, and Davison to their knees. "Cover your heads!" Jacques shouted as they fell flat to the ground and the air blew up around them.

84 | The Doctor's House Lights Up the Night

As the sounds of the explosions died, Davison raised his head slowly and drew in his breath. "Look!" he shouted to Asedi and Jacques. "It's Malinga! Wilson!" He ran toward the gate to help them.

"Where are the children?" Malinga shouted.

"They are both safe in the car, sleeping on the back seat." Malinga ran for the patrol car just as William and the compound watch members streamed around the corner of the wall.

"You must get back," William shouted to them. "The petrol tanks are on fire. The whole house will explode." But it was too late. The fire took off so fast, Davison backed the car across the street, afraid that flying ashes might catch the vehicle on fire. The flames were spitting out of the gates, consumed in less than a minute. All of the buildings were alight. The flames were white hot.

"They must have put some propellant fuel on this fire," Jacques said. "That would explain how fast it ignited and how hot and high it is burning." Davison moved the car even further away. The blaze was everywhere. "Come on," he said, "we have to warn the people that live nearby so they are not caught in this inferno."

The fire lit the night sky of Kalingalinga in a way no one had ever seen before, as if all the evil in the world was being sucked from the backyards and byways of the poor by a single inferno. The stench was awful. Massive vats of preservatives and barrels of chemicals burst open and caught fire. It was ugly, gristly, frightening, and powerful. No one could escape alive from this blaze, Jacques thought.

And then he started. A man, illuminated by the flames consuming him, whirled through the gate.

"Stewart!" Malinga shouted. "We must help him."

"There is no help for him now," Jacques said, holding her back. "We'll never be able to put out the fire fast enough." They watched as the doctor fell to his knees, his face contorted by pain, watched until his writhing slowed and stopped.

The neighbors gathered as the last of the sparks flew into the air and drifted away. Jacques approached what had been the front gates carefully. He could see the burnt-out roofs of the compound's structures: the house, an intervening garden, the surgery, and a very large garage in the back. More police had arrived and formed a cordon around the doctor's property. Not that there would be anything to loot, Jacques thought. The place was a smoldering ruin.

The neighbors stood in ranks, watching the fire burn. Ma Albertina and her group seemed as stunned and shaken as the rest of the crowd.

Jacques felt the same way. Malinga startled him when she touched his elbow. "Jacques, let's go. I have to get the children to bed. Asedi and Davison will drop you at the hotel. The police will take care of the cleanup."

"But what of the evidence?" he asked.

"There is none," she said, "except for what Wilson and I saw."

"And," Davison said triumphantly, holding up his phone, "what I recorded here."

85 | A Hole in Her Pocket

Malinga pulled Katanga and Shiko close to her heart, one in each arm. They'd needed more sleep since the kidnapping, an after-effect of the drugs Stewart had given them, but otherwise seemed all right. She was glad they'd slept through most of the carnage that last night, and avoided their questions about Bertha, simply telling them that she'd gone away.

Benny was gone too, but Malinga's mother Iris was looking for a dachshund for Shiko. "Not much of a watchdog," Malinga said, laughing, when her mother suggested the idea.

"No watch dog, not even the biggest, can ward off the kind of evil you faced. But a little dog will bring you and the children comfort."

Shiko and Katanga had nodded off to sleep quickly after their baths, but Katanga jerked awake. "Mummy," she cried.

"Yes, Katanga, I'm here."

"I just had a dream. You were in the middle of a fire. All these people were calling to you for help."

"Yes, Katanga, I've seen them, too."

The girl's eyes fluttered closed and Malinga shut her light. Shiko didn't wake after she tucked him into bed. She could hear Danise and Wilson talking in the kitchen as she walked down the stairs.

"Thanks for talking with Katanga about Margaret and her mother, Danise." Malinga said. "She seems to have taken it well."

"No problem."

Jacques popped the champagne cork and they held up their glasses for a toast.

"To the most decorated woman on the Zambian police force!" he said.

"Hip hip hooray!"

Danise raised her glass. "I loved it when the President pinned the medal on you. The Inspector looked so proud!"

Malinga smiled. "He was just relieved that the case was closed before he got back here. He's not a very good detective, you know. He's been in administration for far too long." She shook her head. "It's too bad all the evidence was destroyed by the fire, but it's just as well that Stewart's collection never saw the light of day."

The doorbell rang, and Wilson appeared in the kitchen before Malinga could get up from her chair. She held a glass of champagne out to him. "Thank you, Wilson. For my life. Join us in the toast."

"Thanks, Malinga, but I can't. I promised the kids we'd go see a movie. But I couldn't resist bringing you some more bubbly," he said, handing her a bottle. "Drink it for me."

Jacques poured him a glass. "You have to drink at least one with us. We were just toasting Malinga."

"In that case, let me offer one before I leave," Wilson said. He lifted his glass. "To the bravest woman I've ever known," he said, and drank his glass down in one swallow. "Now I've got to go. The kids are in the car."

He turned to Malinga and hugged her, then held her at arms' length. "By the way, Malinga, can I borrow some money? I know the bonus the President gave you is burning a hole in your pocket!"

About the Author

"Story telling is the best form of advocacy I know."

Author, anthropologist, and activist Susan S. Hunter has lived and worked in Africa since 1989. A Ph.D. medical anthropologist and advocate for the human rights of vulnerable children, Dr. Hunter's extensive publications include three non-fiction books, numerous refereed articles, national and international policy studies and strategy papers for governments, donors, and NGOs. She's worked in 31 countries around the world and visited many more.

Black Death: AIDS in Africa (Palgrave/Macmillan 2003) was ranked as one of the top five AIDS books of all times by the *London Times*. Hunter also holds a Masters of Architecture, and has used it to develop affordable housing programs in Africa.

Books by Susan Hunter

Non-Fiction

Black Death: AIDS in Africa
(Palgrave-MacMillan, 2003)

AIDS in Asia: A Continent in Peril
(Palgrave-MacMillan, 2005)

AIDS in America
(Palgrave-Macmillan, 2006)

Fiction

Malinga Mutende Detective Series

Elephant Murders | Starbuck
(Hudson Run Press, 2015)

Elephant Murders | Justice
(Hudson Run Press, 2015)

Elephant Murders | Memories
(Hudson Run Press, 2015)

Bill Kills: A Wild Game in Botswana
(Hudson Run Press, 2021)

Wilson Mwiinga, Albino Detective Series

Crosses of the Poor: Wilson and the Mailonis
Volume 1 of the companion series featuring Malinga's albino DI
colleague Wilson Mwiinga (Hudson Run Press, 2021)

With Arlin Greene
Tropical Appetites: Fine Cooking and Dining in Tanzania
(Dar es Salaam, 1995)